I0583950

BACKLASH RISING

BACKLASH RISING

THE STAR GUILD SAGA™ BOOK TWO

BRANDON ELLIS

DISRUPTIVE IMAGINATION®

This book is a work of fiction. All of the characters, organizations, and events portrayed in this novel are either products of the author's imagination or are used fictitiously. Sometimes both.

Copyright © 2021 (as revised) Brandon Ellis
Cover Art by Jake @ J Caleb Design
http://jcalebdesign.com / jcalebdesign@gmail.com
Cover copyright © LMBPN Publishing

LMBPN Publishing supports the right to free expression and the value of copyright. The purpose of copyright is to encourage writers and artists to produce the creative works that enrich our culture.

The distribution of this book without permission is a theft of the author's intellectual property. If you would like permission to use material from the book (other than for review purposes), please contact support@lmbpn.com. Thank you for your support of the author's rights.

LMBPN Publishing
PMB 196, 2540 South Maryland Pkwy
Las Vegas, NV 89109

First US edition, May 2020
Version 1.01, February 2021
ebook ISBN: 978-1-64202-939-0
Paperback ISBN: 978-1-64202-940-6

THE BACKLASH RISING TEAM

Thanks to our Beta Team:

Kelly O'Donnell, John Ashmore, Larry Omans, Rachel Beckford

Thanks to our JIT Team:

Peter Manis
Deb Mader
Debi Sateren
Veronica Stephan-Miller
Kerry Mortimer
Diane L. Smith
Paul Westman
Billie Leigh Kellar

If I've missed anyone, please let me know!

Editor
SkyHunter Editing Team

PROLOGUE

Shadows stretched across Starship *Sirona* as the sun descended toward the horizon. On planet Eos, total nightfall never occurred. Strong winds were just as rare.

Sleuth, Captain Diana's right-hand man, felt a vibration coming from his HDC. It told him a motion detector had tripped a few kilometers away. He swiped his finger across the holodisplay to bring up the weather.

He pushed his wide rim glasses up the ridge of his nose and ran his fingers over his balding head. He ran diagnostics and scanned the sensors again. He stiffened, his lips downturned.

Like he thought, calm weather outside. The wind hadn't tripped the wire. Unwelcomed guests did, their ship heading toward *Sirona*.

"Dammit," he said under his breath.

He'd placed detectors in specific locations around the plateau, and he and Diana were the only two who knew of them, for a good reason.

They were preparing for the Monarch, Enlil. The one who masterminded and organized the attack on Starbase Matrona—where most humans lived and worked. Enlil, the man who used humans as slaves, was headed their way. He had used his own, more advanced fleet, to decimate Star Guild, the human star fleet and military consortium.

Sleuth stood back from his desk and scanned Tech Quarters, making sure no one had seen his holoscreen.

He relaxed when no one loomed secretly over his shoulder or sat at a nearby desk, glaring in his direction.

At the moment, a few techs sat on shift, staring into their holomonitors, diligently trying to figure out what had gone wrong with the ship's auxiliary engines and the core reactor.

He could easily see in the eyes of everyone on this ship, they wanted to get this big lug off the ground and into space.

Hank, the overweight, lazy, annoying, unprofessional holocomp technician, was on shift tonight, but Sleuth didn't worry about Hank. The guy paid more attention to food than anything else, and he'd never figure out why the engines didn't fire up and operate.

Sleuth pushed down a grin, shaking his head as he watched Hank and the other techs study the monitors. No matter how hard they worked, Sleuth wouldn't allow this ship to fly.

At least, not yet.

After landing on Eos, where they now sat at the base of a long plateau, Sleuth had hacked into the ship's mainframe, masking the auxiliary engines and the core reactor as being damaged. He and Diana blamed the Anunnaki starfighter attacks, their constant missiles and cannon slugs hammering the ship as the culprit. Attacks Diana and Sleuth helped set up with Enlil before the Anunnaki and human war began.

Sleuth's hack not only tricked the holocomp system, but it had also duped the techs and engineers, and the nearly ten thousand-strong crew.

Sleuth understood his genius with holocomps and holonets, but even he impressed himself with how well he'd dug into the system and veiled his handiwork.

He punched in a command on his HDC, looping still shots on all vidscreens connected to *Sirona's* outside holocams.

He let out a breath, again looking around to see if anyone had been spying on him.

All clear.

The still cams hid any outside events Sleuth and Diana didn't want anyone besides themselves to see, like Enlil's ship coming into view any minute now.

He ran his finger over an icon and tapped, his finger going through the hologram and pulling up the security systems on the ship. "Disable," he whispered. He pressed more buttons, overriding security backup systems. He glanced over his shoulder, clearing his throat. "Gentlemen?"

Hank leaned back in his chair and crossed his arms, his swivel chair dipping back, his hair unkempt, and his beard messy. Bruised shadows surrounded his eyes from his nose's run-in with Chief Petty Officer Alison Johnson's fist not too long ago. He cleared his throat. "Yeah, Sleuth?"

Sleuth calmly nudged his large framed glasses up the ridge of his nose. "It's quiet out there. No Anunnaki detected, so I'm going on a break. Give me thirty minutes."

Hank scrunched up his nose. "I get my thirty minutes next."

"You've already had a half a dozen breaks, Hank. No more."

Hank wiped his nose and shook his head. "Meh, you're no help." He went back to work, dismissing Sleuth with a wave of his hand.

Sleuth walked out of Tech Quarters and headed toward Captain's Quarters, hoping Diana would be there, ready and waiting.

She had slept very little lately. Instead, she paced hallways, going over whatever game plan she and Sleuth came up with on a day-to-day basis. All plans focused on how they could survive this mess, even though Enlil had told them they would.

Sleuth quickened his pace down a corridor, biting his fingernails as he glared at the gray ceiling and then at the black hand railing that lined the wall.

Their survival depended on Enlil, and he always gave ample warning before arrival.

Today, he hadn't. Which meant Enlil was pissed, and when he was pissed, people died.

Captain Diana Johnson walked into her quarters. The door automatically shut behind her with a whoosh.

Much like in the corridors, she paced. This time inside a pitch-black room, the outside ebb armor drawn closed over the windows like the rest of the ship to protect the inhabitants inside. It was all a ruse. The truth was they didn't need protection. Just as Sleuth understood, she knew all too well Enlil wouldn't end her crew, her ship, or her life.

The contract she'd read and signed highlighted that verbiage. She did what Enlil and the contract instructed, even when she continued to sign new contracts full of new orders. She had accomplished all his wishes except his most recent—ending Ali's life—her fake daughter. She couldn't pull the trigger. When she had the chance and finally mustered the courage, she failed. Her daughter and her friend, Daf, had then escaped the confines of the ship.

A tracking device inserted in her daughter years ago had deactivated shortly after she reached Mount Gabriel. Neither Sleuth nor Enlil's people could figure out why.

Which was why Diana paced the hallways for hours, and she continued to pace now, pulling her graying hair, and trying to stop the hundreds of thoughts racing through her mind. Ali had slipped through the cracks, and Enlil wouldn't be happy.

Diana yawned, staring into the darkness that saturated her quarters. She didn't want to turn on the lights and see her traitorous eyes in the mirror. She knew her quarters like the back of her hand, and in the pitch dark, walked to her desk. There she sat, a memory of Ali slowly surfacing like a bubble rising and bursting from a thick, hot tar pit.

It had been the first time they met, the day after the Anunnaki wiped Ali's mind and loaded her with new, false memories, just three days after they kidnapped her from Earth.

They sat inside Diana's home on Starbase Matrona, Sphere One, Officer's District.

Ali hunkered uncomfortably on a chair at Diana's dining room table and rubbed her eyes. "Mom, I have a headache, and I've been vomiting all morning." She lifted her head, squinting. "Why am I at your house? Did I get drunk last night and stumble here? I did, didn't I."

Diana never had a child. She didn't know what to say or do, so she rushed to Ali's side and rubbed her back. She wondered if that's what a loving, attentive mother did. A nearly absent mother raised Diana, so she figured doing the opposite of her own mom sufficed.

She didn't want to piss off Enlil either, who threw his little experiment—Ali—into her lap. He told Diana to lead the young woman to military life to see what might happen.

"She's of mixed blood," he said. "I found her and want to test her. I like games, and this might be a good one for us to experiment with."

Diana shook her head at the recollection. She rested her elbows on her desk, slumping her chin in her palms. *Why did I align with Enlil?* She'd pondered this for countless hours on countless occasions, and always came up with the same conclusion. Enlil forced her to comply. He never came out and said what he more or less insinuated, "I'll spare your life and your crew's life if you betray your race for me."

She ran the mixed-blood thing over in her mind. *Why were mixed-bloods so important?* She never got the answer from Enlil, though she once asked if there were more on Starbase Matrona or in Star Guild. He just gave a nod.

At the time she asked, they were in a secret underground room on Starbase Matrona, in a meeting suite to speak about the plan. It was a place only privileged Anunnaki gathered, like Enlil and the Prime Directors, unbeknownst to humans. They had ushered her into the club for her undying loyalty to the Monarch, the only human to ever enter.

Enlil stared into Diana's eyes as if telling her never to ask that question again. "Very, very few mixed-bloods," he said. "And like the contract and the plan, this is between you and me."

Diana stood at her desk, thinking of turning on the lights to see her quarters, her potted plants, her beautiful paintings on her walls. She shook her head and sat back down and leaned against her backrest.

She stared at the blackness, recalling the first time she met Ali.

Ali stood from the dining table, her legs wobbly. Diana held on to her to help her balance.

"Thank Guild dad isn't alive," said Ali. "He'd probably beat me over the head with a frying pan for drinking so much. You know, mad for being left out."

Diana had never married, but apparently Enlil gave Ali memories of a father, Diana's now fake and dead husband. "He would have been proud of you, dear." She didn't know what else to say. Did widowed wives say such things to their children?

Ali shot her a look. "He hated me with every cell in his body. You know that." She furrowed her brow. "What are you talking about?"

Diana remembered backing away, her hands up, apologizing.

She sighed, coming back to the present, wishing that day never happened, and that Ali, the bullheaded, independent nuisance had never entered her life. "Lights on."

The quarters illuminated, and she glanced at the panel beside the door. "Door, lock and unlock on my command only." A beep confirmed her order.

She leaned forward and pulled a key from her pocket. A glimmer of light reflected off the key as she slid it into a desk drawer's keyhole. She turned it and pulled the drawer open.

Inside rested a single item—a holopad full of Robert Rose's art, put together by the artist himself. It was Diana's most prized possession. Not because of the beauty held within it, but because of what she believed acted as its purpose.

She supposed Robert knew the reasons he drew and painted these images. She'd crap her pants if she learned anyone else had caught on, too.

She placed the holopad on her desk and turned it on. A hologram of a book floated above the holodisplay. She flipped the pages by swiping her finger over each holographic page, stopping when she saw a gorgeous blue planet.

She slid open another desk drawer and grabbed a magnifying glass. She placed it over the upper portion of the planet, and in tiny letters, Robert had etched the word Earth. To the naked eye, the word looked like part of the landscape.

She'd never visited Earth, but in her conversations with Enlil, that's where her race originated. It was where Ali had come from—the most recent human taken from that planet.

Turning the page, she paused. Starbase Matrona. An image of the starbase's construction came to the forefront with massive assembly ships surrounding it, and a large golden planet in the background, planet Eos. "Building the starbase probably took years," she said to herself.

Robert Rose's paintings took a life of their own and were breathtaking. Hence, why the man became the most famous artist in the history of Matrona. Too bad he hid in secret.

She turned the pages until she came to a painting rendering a plateau with a vast ridge. An erupting star hovered at the base, looking like a tiny supernova.

She pressed her thumb against her teeth. How can a star explode on a planet? Is it even a star?

Experts had interpreted all of Robert's art, but never decoded the author's mind or his prophetic style. They spoke about his exquisite brush strokes, his perfect symmetry, his ability to capture a feeling. They didn't see his futurist eye, or his ability to forecast potential future events. The experts more or less discounted his foretellings.

None of them saw what she had always seen, a pattern to every piece of Robert's work. He painted the past and painted possibilities of future outcomes, a history book combined with prophecy.

She flipped the page, then quickly flipped back. She couldn't help it. No matter how many times she told herself that was just a piece of art, she thought the painting with the supernova depicted a future event on planet Eos.

And the ridge?

She tapped her teeth again and shook her head. "It has to be the plateau's ridge I've parked Starship *Sirona* next to." She bit her lower lip and scratched her chin. She paused, staring at the image. She huffed. "The exploding star has to be *Sirona*."

A Robert Rose prediction.

But it couldn't be *Sirona*. She'd signed a contract with Enlil. Her ship, her people, and most importantly, herself, would be safe.

She turned to the previous page and squished her eyebrows together. This image baffled her the most, always holding her attention longer than any other Rose painting.

"A knight holding a sword." Diana lightly brushed her fingers over the knight's face. "A Space Templar." She traced the sword with her finger, noting the purple haze around the blade's edge.

She leaned in with the magnifying glass. Robert had written Sol in the purple haze, again too small for the naked eye to notice.

A brisk rap on her door gave her a start.

She placed the holopad in her drawer and locked it. She slid the key into her pocket. "Yes?"

"It's Sleuth."

She turned on her desk's holoscreen, and waved her hand over an application, bringing up the holocams outside her quarters.

Sleuth paced back and forth, much like she had fifteen minutes ago. He pinched the back of his neck, his head down. Diana didn't need to be a photon scientist to figure out something bothered him.

She stood. "Open."

Sleuth stopped pacing and stared blankly through the doorway. His large glasses were close to the end of his nose. He peered above the frames and kept his chin low.

Diana crossed her arms. "You look like you just saw a ghost."

"Ali left with Daf. " He shook his head and put his arms out. "Maybe twenty-five or thirty hours ago?" He pushed his hands in his pockets.

Diana stepped toward the door. "I know. We already went over this."

"Throw Wrench in the brig, Captain."

Diana shook her head. "I've interrogated him. He thought he was carrying out my orders. He was aloof to it all. I've told him another major screw up, and he's demoted."

For as long as Diana captained this ship, Wrench stood by her side through thick and thin. Loyalty was his backbone, his integrity absolute, not only for her but for every crew member on the ship. She overlooked his mistake because no other person made her feel loved and accepted like Wrench.

Sleuth massaged his temples, his face reddening. "I'm sorry, Captain, but it's time."

She eyed him, knowing exactly what he meant. Her face went pale. She hated meetings with Enlil. "They're here? Why didn't Enlil message me?"

"They're almost here, and I don't have the faintest clue why they are arriving without contact first." He fidgeted with his badge attached above his shirt pocket. "Maybe because you didn't finish the deal."

She didn't kill Ali. A "to-do" high on Enlil's wish list and Diana failed. An order that had come shortly after Enlil tracked Ali to Starship *Sirona*.

Enlil probably figured it would be a simple job, and quick. Even though Diana despised Ali, the idea of pulling the trigger on Ali spun circles in her stomach faster than a pulsar. It made her nauseous thinking about it. She didn't know why. Maybe fake daughters, let alone real daughters, did this to a mother? Somehow through the years, Diana had developed a kind of love for Ali. Diana couldn't figure out why Enlil wanted Ali dead so badly, but questioning the Monarch never sat well.

She eyed Sleuth. "Wait outside my office. I need a moment."

The office door closed, and Diana pulled the key from her pocket. She rounded her desk and unlocked the drawer again.

She plopped the holopad filled with Robert Rose's book down and paged through until she came to the supernova. She stared at it for several minutes and let out an uneasy breath.

She flipped the page to a painting of a palace next to a lake, a place she knew little about. She wondered if that would change this very evening.

Enlil had promised to show her Eos Two someday, a habitable area on the other side of the planet. Whether it be an award for her participation in throwing her race under a hover-train or where he'd execute her if she broke or failed the contract she had signed, either way, she'd see it.

She eyed the page more closely. Near the middle of the lake sat two small islands with tall buildings on them. The structures rose high into the air, like spikes thrusting upward from the islands' crust. A city stood around the lake with nice-sized trees, grasses, and a rolling hill landscape like nothing Diana had witnessed on this side of Eos.

She put the holopad back in its place and locked the drawer. She patted her captain's uniform, unholstered her gun, and placed it on her desk. New orders came through yesterday, and anyone near Enlil with a gun faced execution.

Perspiration formed on her upper lip and she bit her cheek. "Why is he coming?" It didn't matter. He was on his way, regardless, but whether for a meeting or to kill her, she'd at least see Eos Two.

ALI

Eos—Mount Gabriel

Ali let out a heavy breath. She walked down the path to a city inside Mount Gabriel, a city that had been under her nose the entire time she mined on Eos. She couldn't make this up even if she wanted to.

She took a step forward and kicked away a pebble. Her hand slid across the damp rock on the side of the walkway beneath a glowing lantern attached to the wall.

She glanced at her father, who walked by her side. Her insides contracted as she held down a smile. She was doing her best not to look like a fool in front of Star Guild's Fleet Admiral, Shae Lutz, her dad.

This is insane, she thought.

She'd just been on the adventure of her life, dodging starfighters while in a mining mech, making it to Starship *Sirona*, only to escape her fake mother, Captain Diana Johnson, and finally arriving here, inside the mountain. Furthering the insanity, she skipped the portal hop to her homeworld, Earth, only to see Shae in the mountainous cavern staring back at her.

Ali and Shae followed a hobbling Daf and a strange but kind

Anunnaki fellow named Chan-Ru. Several mumbling small men from a race known as the Bawn lined the front of the pack, leading the way. They traveled down a spiraling path, heading for Dirn Garum, the city in the mountain.

Ali shook her head and looked at what she clasped in her hand, almost rolling her eyes and laughing. Again, she couldn't make this up. Her fingers wrapped around a sword's hilt, a sword named Sol, Sword of Light.

A bloodline flowed through her and her father, allowing only them to wield the sword. Mixed blood didn't make much sense. She was part human and part Anunnaki? If so, she didn't stand ten or twelve feet tall and twice as wide as a human like the Anunnaki, so she figured the amount of Anunnaki blood in her was minuscule.

Shae rested his arm around Ali's shoulders. "How are you doing?"

"Good." Ali inhaled a gob of breath. Damp air carried through the deep mountain tunnel, the temperature cooler the farther they followed the descending trail. "I'm a little nervous." She looked down, her voice soft. "I can't stop thinking about getting back to *Sirona*." She had people to save.

S, the woman she met on a Tech Quarter's HDC, Holographic Display Console, explained to Ali that a weapon of mass destruction was on its way to blow *Sirona* to Guild and back, and she had two days to get these Bawn people to help her.

If they could save *Sirona's* people, she and her dad could then enter the sarcophagus in a cave off the upper mountain tunnel. They'd then jump into the portal and see the woman Ali wanted to see for so long, her real mom, Helen.

She swallowed hard. She could tell that getting these Bawn people to join her mission to save *Sirona* would be a hard sell.

"They apparently have advanced technology," said Ali. She glanced at Shae. "I wonder if the Bawn has ships and military vehicles."

"What makes you think they can help us?" Shae dipped his head in the other direction. "My starjumper sits just outside. We can get in there, head to *Sirona*, and warn them."

Ali shook her head. "Captain Diana Johnson isn't on our side. She tried to kill me."

Shae's eyebrows raised. "She tried to—" He cut himself off. His fingers curled into a fist, his teeth gritted. "Does she know about the weapon you mentioned heading their way?"

"I think she does."

"But you're not sure."

Ali shook her head. "No."

Shae halted, motioning with a flick of his head. "Then we get into my starjumper and do what I said. We warn them."

It's not that easy, thought Ali. There had to be a reason S wanted Ali to get the Bawn on her side. Perhaps they could help aid her in fighting Diana and whoever else stood at her fake mother's side while Ali notified the starship's crew they were in danger.

Ali stopped and prompted Shae to do the same. "What you say makes more sense than what I'm about to say. It's just that I have this strange feeling that I must somehow get the Bawn to help me. I think you'll have to trust me on this." She squeezed Sol's hilt, and the sword's plasma flame lit up around the edges. She relaxed and the plasma blaze died down. She continued forward.

Shae walked with her. His expression tightened. "Are you sure?"

"I am."

"The moment I see Diana, I'm throwing her in the brig. I don't give a rat's butt if it's not standard protocol."

"Good." Ali glanced ahead. "Chan?"

Chan-Ru walked in front of her, strolling too close to the path's edge for Ali's liking. Nothing but a black, infinite abyss dropped past the edge.

"Yes, Ali?"

"I mentioned S to you before, but you've never heard of this person?"

Chan folded his hands into his robe sleeves, crossing his arms over his stomach. "I can't say I have. Is this person meaningful to you?"

"I don't know." Deep down and on a soul level, this person felt meaningful, but she didn't want to give it away, especially since she didn't know Chan from Adam. She frowned. Adam? Probably an expression she learned during her life on Earth.

Chan glanced over his shoulder. "Is there anything you can tell me about this S?"

Ali shrugged. Giving him a little information wouldn't hurt. "S told me to come to Mount Gabriel and that my destiny awaited here. She said these people would help me."

Chan continued to walk, Daf hobbling by his side. "That's quite a statement. It sounds like this S person pointed you in the right direction. Now that you know you and your father are both Chosen Ones, that has to be a great feeling."

A great feeling? For Ali, not in the slightest.

Daf limped as she walked, her hand pressed against the rock wall to help keep her upright. "I was there. We communicated over an HDC, and she told Ali a lot of stuff that made little sense to me."

Ali eyed the back of Chan's head, noting he reached ten feet tall or more and was twice her width. She imagined S stood the same height since S shared the same race. "I'm not seeking anybody. I just want the truth. I want to know if I'm in the right place and if these people will help me."

Chan nodded as if in understanding. "These people are a stubborn lot, but they will help...eventually." He stopped and raised his arm, pointing. "Here we are."

Ali shifted her eyes, and her mouth gaped open. She looked at Shae and then Daf. "Do you see what I'm seeing?"

Daf stopped and gasped. "Oh, my word."

Shae let out a laugh. "Who would have thought, and all the way down here?"

In front of them stood an enormous, ornate door, with animals etched into the steel, and landscape all around. Artistic and gorgeous, a sun crested above a mountain, rays beaming down upon animals in a lake, some creatures ferocious, and some calm. A dragon flew to the left of the mountain, and a winged horse hovered to the mountain's right.

Thun, the nicest of the Bawn, bowed in front of Daf, Shae, and Ali.

He extended his arm. "The door to Dirn Garum, my home, my heart. I hope you feel as welcome as I always have."

Harak, Thun's brother—one Ali dubbed a pissy soul—elbowed Thun out of the way. His thick beard shook as he laughed, his bushy brows lifting when he rolled his eyes.

He spat on the ground and grabbed his family jewels. "Surface dwellers. Let's see how welcome you'll be, shall we?" He glared at Ali, and then the door, and back at Ali. "You like the door art, eh?" He spat again. "You don't know what that is, do you? Of course not. You and," he motioned toward Daf and Shae, "they know nothing."

"I beg to differ, brother." Thun pushed his brother out of the way, grunting loudly. "These surface dwellers come from the same planet we originate."

Daf shot Ali a look. "What are they saying?"

Ali ignored her, remembering Daf couldn't understand anything the Bawn said, though somehow Ali and Shae could. She didn't want to miss anything jabbering out of their mouths, not now, not ever. Everything might be important.

Thun lifted his hands, his voice echoing through the cavern. "Burakin."

The door creaked loudly and slowly opened, moving by wheels on a metal track mounted to the rock wall.

Light spilled outward, and Ali put her forearm in front of her face to shield it. She slowly dropped her arm by her side. "What the…"

Her eyes widened, and her jaw nearly hit her chest.

2

KODA

Starbase Matrona

"This is a little creepy," said Devon. He glanced at a gigantic clock hanging at the far end of the station. "It's before supper, and on this station, it's usually a madhouse at this time."

Sphere Nine's Prime Overseer Koda Lutz and I.T. Specialist Devon Gray stood in Sphere Six's hovertrain station.

After nearly dying by the hands of Payson, the rogue commander for Prime Director Zim Noki's guard, and after Naveya, an undercover Space Templar stationed on Starbase Matrona, saved their butts, a quiet station didn't seem all that bad to Koda.

They were heading to Zim's office in Sphere Eight to hack as much information from Zim's holocomp as they could to keep Starbase Matrona and its people safe and informed. Devon could hack into anything, the best asset Koda could ask for in a time like this.

Koda shifted on his feet and surveyed the station, his insides wanting to leap out of him and run. The last time he showed himself in public, gunfire nearly killed him.

He barely escaped after jumping from Savanna Levens' office with papers in his hand titled, *The Kill-off*. Devon accompanied him, leaping two stories to the ground by his side. He couldn't be luckier than the young man with him.

A snap by his ear brought him to the present. "Koda, you all right?" Devon waved his hand in Koda's face.

Koda eased Devon's hand away. "Just lost in thought, buddy."

He made his way to a ticket booth. A loud sound echoed in the station, and Devon jumped back.

Koda rubbed his back. "Easy there, man." Koda's heart raced as well, and his eyes darted around the room, looking for Payson or anyone else with a gun. A hoverstation attendant had merely dropped a holopad.

Devon touched his forehead, wiping perspiration away. "I don't know what's gotten into me. I keep thinking I'll be shot."

Koda nodded. He knew the feeling all too well. He reached the ticket booth and rested his hands on the counter. "Two tickets to Sphere Eight, please."

The hovertrain approached, its engines sending out a hum, and growing louder the closer it came. It moved quickly above a long rail, slowing when it reached the platform Koda and Devon stood upon. A few hovercars passed before the train stopped.

"Get on the last car so we can keep our eyes on the passengers," said Koda. "Just in case."

They hurried to the last car and stepped into the car's cabin. Koda found a seat in the back and Devon scooted next to him, clearing his throat. "Only a few passengers. You have nothing to worry about, Koda."

"Next station, Sphere Eight," said an automated voice through an intercom. "Closing doors now."

The doors hissed shut, and the hovertrain shuddered. It lifted into the air, and slowly moved forward, gaining speed meter by meter. Traveling from Sphere to Sphere usually took twenty minutes to an hour, sometimes longer, depending on the stops. During a non-stop ride, hovertrains reached speeds up to three-hundred miles per hour. Koda had purchased a non-stop ride.

Like this hovertrain, trains wound through Spheres on a magnetic track three stories high, nearly hugging the windows that lined Starbase Matrona. It gave the occupants an incredible view of their place in the Eos system. At least, that's how it used to be. Today, and every day since the starbase had jumped into a new sector, a green planet blazed in full glory, its glow like an aura highlighting space around it.

Devon leaned into Koda, catching a glimpse at the planet in the distance. "Look at that thing. I wonder if it holds an atmosphere."

Koda nudged him away to give more room. "We won't be in this sector of space for long, I don't think. So, don't get too attached."

"Wouldn't you like to explore it, though?"

"Not at the moment. I have a starbase and its people to save."

Devon nodded.

"Have you ever been in a craft?" asked Koda.

Devon shook his head. "I've never been off Starbase Matrona. You?"

"Oh, yes." Memories of Star Guild Academy, its tough training, becoming a starfighter jock, and the recent surprise attack that took a chunk of the human population, slumped his shoulders forward. "I was a starfighter pilot once. If I hadn't gotten into politics, I would still be in Star Guild and most likely space debris with my friends after the surprise attack."

"I guess you got lucky."

"I got injured." He grasped his arm. "Wrestling injury in the Star Guild Academy Games. I was winning when it happened."

Devon ran his hand through his black, curly hair. "They sent you to the Suficell Pods for recovery, right? You could have still been in Star Guild."

Koda nodded. "That's true, and I recovered quickly in the Suficell Pods, but I went after another calling—politics. I did so to help the people on Starbase Matrona. Now here I am, doing just that."

"And you became the best politician in the governance's history."

Koda laughed. "It had only been two weeks after I won the election when the attack happened." He pondered for a moment. "Maybe I would have been the best." A goal he still secretly strove toward.

He stared through the window, imagining a plaque awarded to him in front of a crowd of people. The plaque was inscribed: "For saving your race. You are the people's politician." That was why he was headed for Zim's office, to dig up more truths for the citizens of Matrona, to give the people what they deserved. Freedom. Maybe he could move his people as far from their controllers as possible. As the days ticked by, Koda learned more and more about the slavery thrust upon his race. It slowly burned his insides.

The hovertrain stopped, and Koda stretched his arms, yawning. "Let's go."

They stepped off the hovertrain and saw the top of Sphere Eight's capital building through the station's windows. They took the elevator to the lower level and headed out the lobby doors.

"I can't believe how quiet it is, especially in the capital. Especially for the capital," Devon said.

They strolled on a sidewalk lined with grass, flowers, and a tree here and there. Reaching the capital building, they walked up the steps and to a glass door.

Devon looked inside. "The capital building is a ghost town. It's vacant."

The lights were off and the front desk empty. Devon pushed the door open and entered, the sound of a jingling bell peacefully echoing in the room.

"Hello?" called Koda. "Anyone here?"

There was no answer.

He took a step forward. "I guess we just go on in?" It felt weird walking into the Prime Director's office with no one telling him he couldn't.

Passing the reception desk and past vines and flowers growing from pots around the lobby, they walked down a hallway and to Zim's office.

The door was ajar, and the office tidy. Koda eyed stacks of filing cabinets that lined one side of the room, and shelves with books that looked like no one ever touched them butted up against the cabinets. A couch, long and wide, was on the other side of Zim's desk and hugged the wall. On Zim's desk sat a glass of mead along with a half-full bottle.

Koda walked in and moved the bottle and glass to the side. He gestured for Devon to take a seat at Zim's desk. "All yours. Do your specialty."

"This isn't my specialty." Devon sat, wiggling his fingers, ready to perform. "I'm just good at it for some reason."

Koda leaned the top of his hip against the tall desk. "Not your specialty? Then what the Guild is? I don't know anybody who can decode all of this stuff like you."

Devon turned on Zim's HDC. "You haven't met my friends. I'm in a network of dozens of people who could decode twice as fast as me and figure out a heck of a lot more."

"Where are they?"

Shrugging, Devon pressed some buttons on the holographic keypad. "Knowing my friends? They're probably hacking everyone's bank accounts right about now."

Koda raised his brows. He didn't like the thought of hackers getting into his bank account, let alone other people's. He pushed the image away, the sour taste in his mouth remaining. It didn't matter. He needed Devon to help him find the truth, and what they'd uncover he'd present all over the vid channels.

Koda would be the savior. They'd make statues of him, honor him for thousands of years, if not longer. He'd set a precedent, never hide the truth from the people. Koda shook away the thought. "If this isn't your specialty, then what is?"

"You wouldn't believe me if I told you, so I keep it under wraps." Devon typed in some commands on the keypad. He swiped his finger on the holoscreen, pulling up a handful of icons.

"Interesting. I would have pegged you for a genius on the holocomps."

Devon shook his head and swiped the screen again and tapped an icon. He pressed more commands, typed in a password, and leaned back, interlocking his fingers behind his head. The screen changed to streaming lines of data. He put his feet up on the table.

Devon's mouth gaped open, and he dropped his feet off the table a moment later. "What the Guild? No." His fingers raced over the keypad. "The algorithm is all off, or worse yet, someone or something is changing it."

Koda peered into the holoscreen. "How can you tell?"

Their job, at least in Koda's mind, was to dig up more information, especially about Destination "N", something they'd found on past encryption breaks. Koda needed to know what Destination "N" meant, the location, and what occurred there. He wanted no more trouble on the way, but here one presented itself immediately.

Devon cupped his mouth, letting out a quick breath. "Do you see how fast the data is streaming?"

"What do you do about it?"

"I hack into the main network and see exactly where this stream is going. From that point, the algorithm won't be erratic at the receiver, so it will be easy to stop." He paused. "But where the hell is it going, and to what receiver?"

Devon linked into the network and typed in several codes Koda didn't understand. The screen changed to a box, and **LOCATION** blinked underneath.

Devon pointed at the screen. "There. It's going to that box."

"Where is that box?"

"It's not a box in actuality. The box represents the receiver. It's there that we will get the information, whatever information that's stored there." He continued typing, his shoulders dropping the more he went from screen to screen. "Wait," said Devon. "Like I suspected, the receiver isn't located on Matrona." He pinched his lower lip. "It's on Eos Two?"

Eos Two was something else they read in the material Devon hacked. They didn't know the exact locale, yet they knew it acted as a waypoint for Starhawk Transports that carried mined ebb.

The bell jingled in the lobby.

Koda held up his hand for Devon not to speak, his stomach sinking and his spine tingling. Someone entered the building.

Koda cautiously walked to Zim's door and peered into the hallway. He almost gasped but held his breath. He ducked around the office door and lowered into a crouch.

A guard wearing odd military fatigues that camouflaged to the colors nearby, stood in the lobby, rifle in hand, observing the vines and flowers that climbed the walls. The man leaned against a wall, his fatigues changing to white, matching the wall's shade.

An assassin? One of Payson's men?

The guard pressed on a silver shoulder band, similar to the comm devices Star Guild wore. "I've arrived at the capital building." He tapped on a different device connected to his ear and listened to a response. He shook his head. "No. It seems I'm alone. No one's touched this place since the last time we cleared this office."

Koda crawled away from the door, scanning Zim's office. Bookshelves, the desk, cabinets, a bar, a couch, they didn't have a place to hide. He hurried to Zim's desk where Devon stood like a statue, and although Devon had black skin, Koda could somehow see Devon turning pale.

"Thank you," came the guard's voice. He slowly walked down the hall, his boots creaking the floor. "We tracked them coming this way, but I don't think they are here."

Koda scanned the room again. He had no choice, and it screamed "ridiculous" to him, but only one hiding spot presented itself. Koda motioned for Devon to get behind the couch.

Devon complied and Koda followed suit, pulling the couch away from the wall, cringing and hoping for no sound. They crawled behind it to hide. Koda thanked his lucky stars they had barely made a peep.

The boot steps neared and halted at the doorway. "No one is in Zim's office," said the Guard, walking into the room. He sat at Zim's desk, his voice rising. "Zim's holoscreen is on and someone—a programmer—had to have been here only five minutes ago. The HDC is warm, too."

The guy paused. "Yes. That's what I think. And there is a Program Decode on the screen." The guy started pressing on the holokeypad. "They did most of the job." A longer pause. "I don't think so. Unless…"

Koda took short, quiet breaths, not moving a millimeter. Devon did the same, pressing against him and the couch.

The guard stopped typing. "I know exactly who wrote this program."

Koda squeezed his eyes shut. He got Devon into this situation, and he likely just got himself and the young man killed. He wanted to yell, to do anything to magically throw this guy out of the building, down the street, and into a garbage bin.

"I'm sure it's him," said the Guard. "Yes, Devon Gray."

Devon's eyes widened, and he swallowed hard. How the Guild would this guy know Devon was the originator of that program?

"It doesn't matter," said the guard. "I know Devon created this program, though he didn't need to. It's still effective, but again, rather elementary. In fact…" the chair swiveled and Koda could hear the guard standing, then walking in their direction. "…how are you doing, fellas?"

A chill went down Koda's back, and he felt his hair stand on end. He eyed Devon and gave him a nod as he slowly raised his hands. Devon did the same.

The guard leaned over the sofa, pointing his rifle at Koda. "Both of you step out from behind the couch."

3

ALI

Eos—Mount Gabriel

Pickaxes clanged in the distance, rushing water roared in the background, and hundreds of voices reverberated off building walls. Ali's mouth remained open.

Immaculate structures like newly created medieval architecture filled the underground city. Edinburgh, Scotland came to mind. Her head jerked back. Where the heck did Edinburgh, Scotland exist? Memories hit her like a flash, and she stiffened. When she lived on Earth, she'd visited Edinburgh when she traveled to Scotland. This place reminded her of Edinburgh's orderly Georgian terraces.

She stood in a cavern inside a mountain, staring through a door's opening at Dirn Garum, the Bawn's home. The city was lit up by pale white lamps on short city poles mounted to rock walls and the sides of buildings.

A path led through the doorway and down several glowing stone steps, ending in a gigantic public square.

Bawns busied themselves, all wearing similar green, wool-like clothing, the men with long hair and beards, their eyebrows bushy. The women had mostly golden hair, long and curly, and wore dresses much like the men. The square bustled with Bawns, bartering and selling food at market stands.

Daf nudged Ali in the ribs with her elbow. "Are you seeing what I'm seeing?"

Ali, speechless, bobbed her head up and down.

"It's majestic," Shae said in a hushed voice.

At the center of the square stood a fountain, shooting water in an arc from one end of the water display to the other. Ali glanced near the top of the great ceiling and her jaw dropped more. Up above, a giant wooden wheel spun by the flow of a waterfall that spilled onto it, the water cascading into a river below before streaming away from the middle of the city.

This time Ali poked Daf's ribs and pointed at a ten-story tall golden statue. It hugged a far wall. Its face was like that of a Bawn, wearing a helmet. Body armor went from its torso down to its hips.

The pickaxes stopped picking, the people stopped talking, and silence fell on the square. The Bawns stood wild-eyed, glaring at them.

Harak nudged Ali, Shae, and Daf forward, grunting.

Daf limped, and Ali held onto her arm, making sure she didn't fall down the steps and break her neck. Shae walked beside Ali, his chest out, his chin high, acting the part of an admiral.

Daf pushed her dark hair from her eyes. "They are looking at us like we're monsters."

"To them," said Ali. "Perhaps we are."

"Be calm and cordial," said Shae.

Taking a step down, holding Daf at her waist and letting Daf use her as a crutch, they took step after step down the wide stairway toward the city. Whispers filled the square, and Ali noticed a few eyes fall on Sol, the sword in Ali's hand. The few whispers turned into more.

A grunt echoed behind them, and Harak and a few other Bawns who led them to this underground city, pushed past Ali, bumping her hard. She wanted to kick Harak in the rear but refrained. "Watch it."

She glanced over her shoulder at Thun, who ran his hand through his hair, his brows nearly touching the crown of his head. "I'm worried my father won't accept you. I'm worried he'll look past the fact that you wield the Sword of Light, something he shouldn't turn a blind eye to."

Daf took a step down, doing her best to match strides with Ali, though hobbling along. "What did he say, Ali?"

"His father might not accept us."

Daf's lips turned down. "Wonderful."

"He's a leader, and so am I," said Shae. "We'll see eye to eye. I'll make sure of it."

Ali eyed the area for any possible quick escape, just in case the Bawns decided to jump them. She wouldn't put anything past anyone anymore, especially after the Anunnaki attack. Who knew when another race would strike again?

She quickly calmed, feeling Sol's hilt in her hand. She took a step off of the stairs and into the square, confidence surging through her, nearly boiling her veins. She took a hefty breath and filled her lungs, invigorating herself. The sword vibrated with energy. Guild, it coursed with power. Raw power. An electric sensation pulsed up her spine, and she went rigid, her lips tingling and her toes curling.

A light flashed from Sol, brightening all around. She squeezed her fingers tightly around the hilt, and an electric-purple plasma flame radiated from the sword's blade. She felt like squeezing harder and sending a plasma bolt into the air.

That would be taking it a bit too far.

"Sol," yelled a Bawn, his voice booming across the city. He walked forward in a hurry, his blue robe flowing behind him. The small man walked with authority, parting the crowd as he approached. He pointed an axe at Ali. "You can't be the Ones."

He then softened and lowered his axe to his side. His shoulders drooped. "But you are." He went to his knees and bowed, pressing his forehead against the cobblestone. "I am king, and we all hail to the bloodline. We hail to Berronar the Truesilver, the revered mother, the mother goddess, matron of home and hearth, mother of safety, truth, and security."

27

He paused and glanced at Ali, his eyes glistening. "Thank Berronar you've all arrived. Finally, after all these years." He stood. "We have a lot to discuss and a crackin' ton to do."

Chan stepped down the stairs, his long strides taking two at a time. He made his way to the blue-robed man, towering over him. He bent down to one knee, and rested his hand on the man's shoulder, flicking a look over his shoulder at Ali and Shae. "This is Bilrak, father of Thun and Harak, and also the sworn guardian and king of his people. Bilrak, this is Shae, leader of his people." He motioned at Ali. "And this is Ali, a great leader herself. They both stand before you as the Chosen Ones. They carry the blood inside of them, the blood you've been waiting for." Chan tipped his head toward Daf. "Bilrak, we'd appreciate it if you could tend to the black-haired woman. Give her leg a bit of herb, life force, and healing?"

Bilrak nodded and turned to Ali. "And you, the red-headed fair lady..." he shifted his eyes to Shae, "...and you, leader of your people, I see you are both tired. Before we begin our journey, please sleep. But, Shae, you and I must first talk...alone."

Ali raised her brows. "Journey?" Hopefully, he meant helping Starship *Sirona* off this planet, though she highly doubted it, since they'd not yet discussed the ship. She felt the sword again, its strength bleeding into her. An energy rush flowing into every cell of her body.

Bilrak's expression hardened. "We'll talk about our journey later."

Ali dipped her head. "All right." She didn't like this Chosen One nonsense. Just play the part, she told herself. But how could she play the part? The entire idea blared "absurd" to her and would get in the way. Thun, and now probably everyone in Dirn Garum, believed her and her father to be some magical gift.

She'd go with it, as long as they helped her with *Sirona* like S said they would. She hated being fake, but she feigned a smile anyway. "Well, whoever this Berronar is, I owe her a drink. In fact, I'll get her the best damn mead I can find."

Bilrak shot her a look and drew back stiffly, holding a hand up in protest. "You will do no such thing. Berronar is our goddess, not yours, young woman." He threw his arms toward the tall, cavernous ceiling. "We will get Berronar the mead."

An eruption of cheers and laughter filled the square.

Daf whispered in Ali's ear. "What the hell did you just say to them?"

Before Ali could answer, women approached Daf, gesturing for her to come with them.

Daf gave Ali a look. "What do they want?"

Ali tipped her head toward the woman. "They want to help your leg. Chan instructed them to heal it."

"I'm not leaving your side. You've got the sword. I don't. They respect the sword. There is no way they respect me."

"Here." She handed Daf the sword. Maybe Ali could get out of this Chosen One infliction abruptly cast upon her.

Daf touched it and, screaming, dropped the sword to the ground. It clattered, and the little women stepped back, their hands coming to their faces.

Daf shook her hand. "It zapped me."

A woman stepped toward Ali. "Young lady, only the Chosen Ones can wield this sword."

Ali nodded and picked up the sword. "Daf, I suggest you let them heal you."

Daf snorted. "Yeah, right. It can heal on its own."

"They mean business. I wouldn't go against their goodwill here."

"Fine."

Ali watched as the women helped Daf limp to a mushroom-top building nearby. They walked in and shut the door. Someone's yelp took Ali's attention away.

Bilrak stood in front of her, shaking his hand, his lips curled downward. "Your sword has a bite to it." He gathered himself. "I'm sorry. I just had to touch it. Sol is a legend. I've never seen it away from its guardian statue. When Sol glowed moments ago, it was brilliant."

"Can I have my water and rest now like you promised?"

"I didn't promise water."

"You're kidding me, right?"

Maybe they rationed water here. She eyed the waterfall and the small river flowing through the city. From the looks of things, they had plenty.

Shae stepped forward. "Sir, give her water. I'd give you the same courtesies were you in the same position as us."

Bilrak grunted, standing still and not budging.

Chan clapped and rubbed his hands together. "Right, well, I'll give her water from my supply. After all, Bilrak, water freely gives itself to you. Wouldn't you think it'd freely give itself to all?"

Bilrak snorted, then turned and walked away. "Show her to a bed. Shae, follow me. We have much to discuss."

Ali grimaced. "My Guild, that guy is a grump."

Shae stepped toward Bilrak after gently squeezing Ali's forearm. "I'll see you soon."

"Be careful."

"Will do."

Ali watched as her dad made his way to Bilrak's side. They walked toward an immense palace-like structure, its white casing and golden roof shining.

"It's their personality," said Chan.

Ali turned to face the Anunnaki. "What?"

"The Bawn are usually grumpy, but I find it strangely charming. You get used to it after a while." Chan stretched his arm outward, motioning down a cobblestone road off the main street. "Shall we go to my dome? You can sleep there, and I'll wander the streets until you wake."

"Sure." Ali needed some shut-eye. Her eyelids were becoming heavy even though the sword seemed to give her a bit of energy.

They made their way down several roads, past metallic statues, and to a large, circular stone dome.

"My home away from home, as the Bawns say."

Ali walked into Chan's dome, ducking under the short archway. She flopped onto a bed, too tired to investigate the dome and its windows, furniture, kitchen, faucet, and more.

She scrunched up a pillow at the head of the bed, patting it to make it fluffy. "Good night, Chan."

"Good night." He walked out of the dome, closing the door behind him.

She stretched her body and laid her head on the pillow. She closed her eyes, smacking her lips. "I need this sleep so badly." Her hands and legs twitched as a vision flashed in her mind. A Knights Templar statue, the very statue that held the sword that Ali rested on the bed by her side. She attempted to open her eyes, but her eyelids felt like five-ton weights.

"Alison," said the Templar, his body again now flesh, the statue's stone shed from his body. He bowed. "You and your father are the Chosen Ones, that is true, but let your father go, let him experience his way, his truth, his journey. Let him go, Alison. Let him go."

Ali's eyelids shot open, and she stared at the dome ceiling, her breaths coming fast from the sudden vision, her stomach fluttering with nerves. Her heart pained, and she rested her palm on her chest. "Let him go?"

What did that mean? Was he going to die? Did Bilrak take him to the slaughter? Were they going to throw him out of the city?

She closed her eyes, wanting to talk with the Space Templar, wanting to ask dozens of questions that entered her mind.

Blackness filled her vision. "Space Templar, where are you?"

"Let him go, Ali. They will not allow him to remain in the city. Let him go."

She squeezed her eyelids, doing her best to focus. "He's leaving? Why? Please tell me. Please."

No response.

"Tell me."

Silence.

She let out a big gush of air and bolted to a sitting position. She pushed out of bed and stood, adrenaline giving her a blast of energy. "Dad, you're staying with me." He's not thinking of leaving me, is he? She shook her head. No way he'd do something like that. They'd just reunited.

She straightened her lips and tightened her jaw muscles. If Bilrak had plans other than to welcome her father into this grand city, then she'd find the king, and stop whatever those plans may be.

She grasped Sol and rushed toward the door. She wouldn't let Bilrak or anyone harm one hair on her father's head or force him to leave.

Not now. Not ever.

4

SHAE

Eos—Mount Gabriel

Bilrak crossed his arms, leaning back as he walked into his large palace. "Welcome."

Fancy stone chairs with intricate patterns sat in the foyer, the floor some type of glossy, smooth dark rock. Stairs on both sides of the foyer led up to a large landing. Beneath the landing, and on either side of the entryway, it split into several hallways, leading to places too dark for Shae to see.

"Have a seat." Bilrak gestured toward the middle of the room at two short chairs with a round table in between them. A lantern on the table glowed brightly, the rest of the room lit by lanterns attached to the white, bare walls.

Shae took a seat and a male Bawn servant with a long silver beard, pale skin, and a dark green dress-like robe, waddled from a hallway with two steaming mugs in his hands.

He placed the mugs on the table and walked out of the large room in a hurry, keeping his eyes off both men.

Bilrak sat and motioned to the drink closest to Shae. "Root tea. Drink. It revitalizes the soul."

Shae took a sip, his nose wrinkling on its own. It was bitter, yet it felt good going down, the liquid tingling inside his mouth.

He let out a satisfied, "Ah," and dipped his head. "Thank you." He folded his hands in his lap, straightening in his posture. "Now, what is this about?"

Bilrak snapped his fingers, his face like stone, his eyes penetrating Shae's soul.

The same servant rushed back in the room with a large book in his hands and dropped it on the table. A cloud of dust parted upward from the book, and Bilrak leaned forward, blowing more dust off the book's cover.

Shae leaned forward, studying the large item.

Worn by age, framed by wood, the middle of the cover bore a picture of a man in armor, perhaps a Bawn. The figure held a bright sword edged in purple.

That must be Sol, thought Shae.

Bilrak inched forward, licking his finger, and flipped through the book. He read several passages, his lips moving, though no words escaped his mouth.

He turned the page, then paused and grunted. His finger moved down several lines. "Yes, right here." He tapped his finger on the page. "Yes, yes. This was what I was looking for." He looked up. "I used to read this every day, so I have a lot of what's written here locked away in storage." He patted his head. "But as I age, my memory locks more into the storage without letting it out."

Shae leaned in further, his brows furrowed. "What exactly does it say?"

Bilrak closed the book, and shifted in his seat, resting on the chair's backrest. He stroked his beard, again staring deeply into Shae's eyes. "I'm afraid you have to leave."

Shae cocked his head to the side. "Excuse me?" He shook his head. "Leave to where, exactly?"

He'd just met his daughter after twenty years of feeling an emptiness he couldn't pinpoint, and now for the first time he could remember, he felt whole again. He wanted more than anything to speak with her, enjoy her company, and get to know her more.

Leaving was out of the question. At least, not yet. He planned on helping her with her mission to help *Sirona*, not duck out of here the first chance he got.

"It speaks of two Chosen Ones in this prophecy book." Bilrak laid his hand on the cover. "This book is known as the *Bawn Seer* and has never steered us wrong."

Shae crossed his arms and sat straighter. "Go on." None of this sounded promising, and he held down the anger that wanted to rise.

"Yes, yes." The Bawn King bobbed his head up and down, then took a long, hefty drink. He set the mug down and belched, patting his stomach. "Drink more."

Shae would rather not, but to appease the man, he took another sip, swallowing the strong concoction. "Like I said, you need to give me more information. I will not leave for the sake of leaving." In fact, he wouldn't leave at all, not without Ali. Perhaps the guy didn't like another strong leader in his presence. Maybe it made the king feel less superior.

If that was the case, then Shae would give him more leeway, would stay a few paces back. But ending his and his daughter's reunion was not happening. Shae had his sidearms holstered around his waist and would stand up to anyone trying to break his new, growing bond with his daughter.

"You run a group called Star Guild, according to the prophecy book. Is that correct?"

Shae nodded. "It says Star Guild?"

Bilrak leaned back more, sizing Shae up and down. "Don't question the *Bawn Seer*." He continued. "One Chosen would choose Sol, the other Chosen would not. The one without the sword belongs to Star Guild, the one with the sword belongs with us. You, my friend, are a strong leader, and according to the great book, now stronger after reuniting with the one with the sword. Your daughter, correct?"

"Yes."

"Your Star Guild." He snorted. "It's such a silly name, but your

Guild won't survive long without your leadership. You're a missing piece in their puzzle right now."

Shae pushed out his lips, his gut falling to his knees. He didn't like the sound of Star Guild not surviving. It tore at his insides, and he shifted in his seat and cleared his throat. "You're sure this book is accurate?"

"You're questioning the great book?" Bilrak shook his head. "The great Goddess spoke through our scribes long ago, scribes without names, for they don't take credit for the goddess's work." He straightened his lips. "No one questions the Goddess." He shook his head and let out a huff. "Your starbase, one the book calls Matrona, hovers near a green planet at this very moment?"

Shae swallowed hard. How the hell would a book know something like that? "Yes."

Bilrak threw his hands out. "So, it is not wrong. You must go."

Shae closed his eyes, his gut suddenly sparkling with nerves, not wanting to leave Ali. "I'm sorry, but if I leave, so does my daughter."

Bilrak shook his head. "No, that will not happen."

Shae stood, his hand on his holster, his nostrils flaring. "How would you like me to take one of your sons?"

Bilrak gazed at Shae's hand that rested on his gun. He stood quickly, the chair tipping and falling, crashing on the floor. "You plan on killing one of my sons?"

Shae relaxed his hand, letting it fall by his side. "Of course not." He stood, eyeing the small man. "But I tell you now, I'm not leaving until Ali leaves."

Bilrak took a step forward, shoving the table into Shae's knee. "What kind of leader would leave his people to the dogs?" He stepped back, shaking his head and picking up his chair. "Star Guild doesn't deserve you. Your daughter doesn't deserve a coward father, either."

The man had a point. It pained Shae to no end that Star Guild needed him.

"One more thing," said Bilrak. "Who is Helen?"

Shae froze, a hitch in his breath. "What do you mean?"

"The Seer Book mentions a Helen. She is your wife, isn't she?"

Shae nodded. "I can see it in your eyes, and your breathing is quickening." He looked away, rubbing his knees as if he were getting antsy and bored with this meeting. "She will die if you do not go back to Star Guild."

Shae stepped back, almost involuntarily. "How...would you know any of this?"

"Do not question the *Bawn Seer*."

Shae crossed his arms, glaring down at the man. "Tell me how you would know any of this."

"Do not—"

Shae put his hand up. "Yes. Do not question the *Bawn Seer*. But you don't know how this book is so accurate, do you?"

The king looked away. "No."

Shae sat, his insides turning, having a hard time with the information presented to him. That Star Guild may be in trouble, and his wife, Helen, may perish. "I can't take Ali, no matter how much I ask, can I?"

Bilrak rested his index finger on the book. "She is ours until she fulfills her own prophecy." Bilrak looked away as if hiding something.

"There is more to it, isn't there?"

"There's a reason my son, Harak, has a distaste for outsiders." His eyes lowered. He quickly raised his chin, perhaps catching himself showing weakness. "But we are Bawn. We are strong, no matter what comes."

"What's coming?"

"With the sword bearer's arrival, two changes occur. We leave the mountain for good, never to return, and a death in the family."

Shae sucked in, not liking the death part, fearing for his daughter. "Who dies?"

"Someone of royalty. Harak believes it's one of my own, either him or Thun."

"Why doesn't he think it's you or the queen?"

"He believes his mother and father are gods and nothing can kill us. He's wrong, but there isn't any changing his mind. We do not dwell on that. What comes, comes. What happens, happens. We are strong and do not fear death. But you must go, please. Leave before I force you out."

Shae wiped his hand across his forehead, wishing he could wipe away this conversation and the reality of it all. "So, I have to leave and rejoin Star Guild." He exhaled sharply. "And I can't take my daughter." He bit his cheek, nodding. "I guess I'm between a rock and a hard place."

Bilrak grinned. "As are all leaders." He grunted again. "The great book, the *Bawn Seer*, is demanding you take your place back on the Star Guild throne."

Shae dipped his head. His job description called for saving humanity above all else. An oath, a life mission. "How quickly do I have to leave?"

Bilrak stood. "Now. There will be no compromise. We stick to the prophecies. If you don't leave on your own free will, like I said, we kick you out." He extended his arms out wide. "There are more of us than there are of you. We won't hesitate to hurry your exit."

The front door flew open, and there stood a heaving Ali, Sol in hand, purple flames sparking off the sword's edges.

Shae stood.

Bilrak went for his belt, pulling out an axe, holding it up at his ear, ready to heave it at the intruder.

Shae put his hand up. "Stop." He walked to Ali and stood in front of her, his back to Bilrak. "Are you all right?"

Ali loosened her grip on Sol, her eyes drifting from Bilrak to Shae, the sword's purple flames dying down. She lowered her head. "I-I had this..." She looked down, her eyes to the floor, her voice soft. "I have to say goodbye to you, don't I? I have to let you go." She bit her bottom lip, her chin quivering. "But I just found you. We just met again after..." She sniffed. "...Dad. Please stay."

Shae wrapped her in a hug. "I'm sorry, Ali. If this was a perfect world, I'd have my life with you and Helen, always. But right now, I have to join Star Guild, and it's immediate."

"But we just—"

Shae pushed away, grasping her shoulders and crouching slightly to see eye to eye with her. "We'll be together again soon. Do you understand? We just have some kinks to work out, then you and I will not only reunite, but we'll reunite with your mother as well."

Ali cringed and took a long step back. Her eyes shifted to Bilrak, the sword sparking up again. It diminished in strength as she lessened her hold. She looked up at the ceiling and let out a big sigh. "Okay, but let me escort you out."

Shae forced a smile. "I'd like nothing more."

5

DIANA

Eos

Diana glanced out of the transport ship's window.

She didn't know the Anunnaki ship's exact class type, though it seemed a more advanced Star Guild Starjumper design. The designers for this ship made large seats for the Anunnaki, a race twice a human's width and height. The rest of the craft screamed bigger as well, made for giants.

"I assume you're still pleased with our agreement?" said Enlil.

Diana looked at the man across the aisle. Strong arms and broad shoulders, a long beard covered his cheeks and chin, matching his flowing red hair. He wore a black coat with yellow trim that draped to his knees and coordinating black pants.

"I'm still pleased with the contract," she replied.

A portion of the agreement within the contract guaranteed, and gifted, Starship *Sirona*, Captain Diana Johnson, and her nearly ten-thousand-member crew a habitable moon in another system. All in exchange for disabling her race's weapon's array, scrambling her race's radar when the Anunnaki first attacked, and making it as difficult as humanly possible for Star Guild to defend themselves against Enlil's rookie fleet.

"And you're fine with the agreement we had with *Sirona?*" he said.

Said contract stated that Enlil would use *Sirona* for a short time as a shooting target for his rookie pilots and novice infantry. Nothing more, nothing less. Once training ceased, Enlil would allow Diana to turn *Sirona's* engines back on and fly to the promised moon.

She bit her tongue. The agreement had taken a lot longer than she originally estimated. "I'm fine," she lied.

Enlil slammed his fist against his seat's armrest, wincing in obvious pain. "You didn't kill Chief Petty Officer Alison Johnson." He bared his teeth. "Why?"

Diana's hair stood on end, her eyes widening. "I don't know. I tried, but she had help. She knew what I was about to do." She swallowed, her nerves trying to rise.

He peered into her eyes. "Are you nervous?" Enlil swept his hands through the air, wincing again. Clearly, he was fighting against an acute injury. "Everything went as planned." He glared at her. "Except for one tiny little thing." He patted his chest. "That little thing almost killed me."

Diana's eyebrows rose. "Ali almost killed you?"

"Yes, but that's for a different time and a different place because I'm not pleased with you. You've become a splinter in my skin because she's become a splinter in my skin. Ending her miserable life was the last task I gave you before handing you riches beyond belief, Diana."

"When do we get those riches?"

The riches referred to the moon he promised. Houses, breathable oxygen, great temperatures, infrastructures such as roads, government buildings, skyscrapers, and much more. She'd be the first leader there, the one who kept her race alive, and they'd start anew. Her people would revere her, laud her as a queen, the heroine.

He didn't respond.

She raised her voice. "Is the moon ready?"

Enlil rubbed his chin, exhaling softly, almost as if he didn't want to talk about the gifts he promised to give her and her crew, who knew nothing about the treasures he'd promised, and that Diana signed off to receive. Without their knowledge, Diana sold her crew out to the highest bidder. "It's ready," he said. "But you're not going there yet. I still have plans for you."

Diana's lips pressed together in a slight grimace. She loosened them, not wanting to irritate the Monarch, especially without weapons at her side.

He leaned toward her, resting his elbow on the chair's armrest. "You don't trust me, do you?"

She thought she could trust him, but the more she came to know the man, the more that trust slowly withered.

"I trust you," she lied again.

He sat straight, looking away. "I haven't destroyed your ship, as we had agreed upon several months back." He placed his hands together like a prayer, resting his chin on his fingertips. "Me keeping you alive should warrant at least some trust, shouldn't it?"

She dipped her head. "Like I said, I trust you."

He looked off. "You're holding something from me." Enlil faced her, wincing in pain. Whatever Ali did to him had definitely created a heap of agony for the giant. "What are you pushing down that you aren't telling me?" He puffed out his lower lip, his eyes narrowed. "I don't like it when someone holds back."

Diana glared out of the window, watching a blade of yellow grass growing through a crack in a long, thin ebb rock. The grass blew in the breeze. She eyed an Eos Two lake in the distance, something her eyes had never witnessed before. She wanted to see the mountains flowing with trees, and the cities filled with tall buildings. She figured they'd need to travel further east.

She continued to stare at the grass. "Many of my friends died during the initial attack. Your race killed hundreds of thousands of my people. I didn't know there would be so many fatalities."

She could hear Enlil shift in his seat. "This saddens you?"

Diana turned. "Imagine your race being annihilated right before your eyes and you were a major player in the conspiracy. That is what I am. I'm a traitor. I helped attempt to kill my race, even though I wasn't expecting a kill count so high. So, yes, this saddens me."

It didn't just sadden her. It ripped her heart apart, and every day the ache grew stronger. It burned a hole in her soul. She signed up to help this Monarch, but the devastation went above and beyond what she ever imagined.

Enlil frowned. "My race dying before my eyes wouldn't sadden me. It would anger me, but no, I wouldn't be sad." He put his finger up as if about to give her an important lesson. "Your people and my people are different emotional Beings. I don't feel sadness for anything my race does or doesn't do. Most times, fire erupts in my belly when I deal with my race, especially with my family." He cupped his hands and placed them over his stomach, leaning back and looking at the cockpit. "I have tried to kill my brother many times. I dislike him more than anyone will ever know. My father sends a rage through me when I think of him." He laughed. "But that's how I am, and I've observed that many in my race are similar." He brought both hands to his heart. "Our agreement is right here in my heart." His brows drew downward. "Please don't disrespect me by thinking me a liar."

"I don't think you're a liar. I was just not ready for what—"

Enlil slammed his fist on his armrest again. "You would have stopped my plans if you knew them fully, so I couldn't risk telling you the entire truth, Diana."

Diana shrank in her chair, feigning calm, though her heart sped faster than a starfighter evading a missile. She looked out the window a second time, not able to look him in the eyes. "I would have gone with your plans, regardless. I value the prize you'll give my crew and me."

He rested a heavy hand on her forearm. "I don't think you would have gone through with my plans. Diana, don't think of me as a bad man because I can see in your eyes that you do. I do for my people what you would do for yours. Only the circumstances are different. Our intellect is far superior to even the most genius of your race. We created you so you'd be inferior to us, but intelligent enough to perform the tasks we wanted. Even if you could have stopped the attack, we would have outwitted you no matter how many left turns we had to take."

A drudge, a cross between a medium-sized dog and squirrel, ran across the ebb terrain and disappeared under the craft they sat in. She wished she could disappear like the drudge. "So, when can I leave this planet with my crew?" If she could get to the moon and give her crew a peaceful place to live for the rest of their lives, she'd at least have given something to humanity.

He stroked his chin. "Trust me." He held out five fingers. "Five days starting tomorrow. Until then, we will leave you alone." He paused, a small grin growing on his lips. "However, I think there are a few more training sessions with our infantry, so Starship *Sirona* might feel more bumps and shakes, but nothing too harmful."

Diana nodded. *Sirona* could take a beating, and unless they were sending massive cannons her way, the starship's armor would hold. "And the moon?"

Enlil squeezed his eyes shut as if her relentless moon question scraped him like a rat scraping to get out of a cage. He massaged his temples. "I do not want to repeat anything I've already said."

"I know. I just want to know, is it beautiful?" She eyed Eos's landscape. "Or, like Eos?"

"Yes, it's much more habitable than this planet but smaller. It's a moon, mind you, but the temperature is fair, and the resources are plentiful. You should have no trouble creating a happy life there."

"I wonder what my crew will say when we get there."

Enlil swatted at the air. "Please, little lady. You saved them. You gave them continued life, and in that, you've allowed the human population to prolong its gene pool. If they find out you set up your people, kill the disgruntled ones, and let those who remain alive honor you. Be fierce and lay down the law if they show no gratitude."

The drudge ran out from under the craft and in full view. "I would also like—"

Enlil cleared his throat, cutting her off. "You humans want a lot, don't you?" He didn't wait for a reply and flicked his gaze upward. "I will not go any further with this meeting." He eyed the cockpit, his focus on the Anunnaki pilot. "Our meeting is over. Please take the nice captain home."

The pilot nodded and started the ship's engines. The craft vibrated and lifted into the air.

Diana gazed forward, looking at Enlil out of the corner of her eye. He held a fist, resting it on his armrest. She wanted to point a gun at him and pull the trigger, blowing his brains against the side windows and wall for making her do horrible acts. Had he really made her, or was she a willing victim?

She wanted to start her life over and be a good human. Right now, misery clouded her soul. She had done the worst—helped Enlil kill hundreds of thousands of her race, maybe more.

The starjumper turned one-hundred and eighty degrees. Its boosters initiated and her body drew into the seat, gravity pushing against her as the ship flew toward Starship *Sirona*.

"And, Diana," said Enlil. "A group landed here recently. If you happen upon them, kill them. Every. Single. One."

Diana touched the base of her neck. He needed to explain more. "What group?"

"They'll introduce themselves as the Space Templars."

6

EDEN

Starship Sirona, Eos

Eden followed a balding man who wore overly large bifocals, his name Sleuth. They walked down a Starship *Sirona* corridor toward Captain Diana Johnson's quarters. Eden didn't trust Sleuth, and sure as hell didn't trust Diana, a traitor to her own race. Eden's stomach tightened when the image of Diana came to mind.

A few nights prior, as Eden and her Space Templar friends approached Starship *Sirona*, they caught sight of Diana leaving and entering an Anunnaki ship. Eden and the Templars waited a day before arriving at Starship *Sirona*. The crew invited them inside, and they'd been here ever since.

Eden huffed as they walked down the corridor, Sleuth stomping with every step he took. Maybe a walking defect, but she doubted it. It reminded her of her mom, the way she'd lead Eden as a child to a biosphere park, practically stomping her feet like a spoiled child as they'd go. "I do this for you, and I do that for you. Can't you give me some time to myself?" Eden didn't know how much more time she needed to give her mom. She barely spent five minutes a day with her. The woman was usually injecting a nasty substance in her arm with one of her many boyfriends. She'd daze off and lean back in bed minutes later.

Sleuth turned down another corridor, his weasel-like eyes narrowed as if wanting to spill a secret he'd been hiding, though enjoying the idea that he knew something Eden didn't.

"Our second meeting." He shook his head. "I thought one was enough."

The moment after Eden, Skye, and Nyx entered the ship, Skye wanted a meeting to point out the traitor—Captain Diana Johnson. The meeting lasted less than a minute, Diana coming up with an excuse to rush everyone out of her quarters.

"There is a discovery in the engine rooms I need to attend to right away," she had said.

That occurred yesterday, and last night Eden and the Space Templar crew slept in the launch bay, awaiting their own sleeping quarters to be cleaned and ready. Of all things, and what the Star Guild and Starbase Matrona myths told everyone, you don't mess with the Space Templars. She imagined Diana shook in her bones, knowing she couldn't do much about the Templars on her ship.

"Eden." Skye approached her before this day's meeting and shuffled her to a corner in the bay next to a parked Thunderbird starfighter. "Let me handle this. We have a change in tactic, a change in energy."

Eden scrunched her nose. "A change in energy?"

"A subtle feeling that outing Diana wouldn't be the best approach. To worm our way to the person calling the shots, we need Diana to show us this person's exact location."

"You mean an Anunnaki. The real ones calling the shots."

"Yes, and the Anunnaki leader, Enlil. He moves from place to place. He's near impossible to pin to a location. If we can get a way in without him knowing, then we can stop him with less of a fight. We defeat the head of the chain, the rest of the chain crumbles apart."

Eden nodded, though she didn't approve. She wanted Diana in the brig, and now.

Continuing down the hall, Nyx, Skye and Jantu walked behind her.

They rounded a corner, and Eden instinctively rested her hand on her holstered pistol. A corridor light flickered as their boots thumped softly behind her.

Sleuth stopped in front of the Captain's Quarters. The door opened, and there sat Diana, diligently going over documents on her holomonitor. Diana turned it off quickly and stood. "Welcome." She forced a smile and waved for everyone to enter.

Eden's hand fell off of her gun and to her side, her mouth going slack as she stepped inside, her friends in tow.

Paintings in the dozens, all beautiful, all Robert Rose, were hanging on the walls. Plants in pots mounted on the walls, green with gorgeous flowers, grew toward grow-lights.

Diana remained standing behind her desk, her hands behind her back. Sleuth stood off from her, holding a holopad in his hands.

Skye made his way toward Diana's desk and stopped in front of it, his hands behind his back. "You have a great eye for art, Captain." He glanced around the room, his lips upturning. "I'm very impressed."

"Thank you, sir..." She extended her hand as if not remembering Skye's name.

Skye took her hand in his and slightly bowed, obviously sensing her confusion. "My name is Skye. I'm the Grand Master of the Space Templars."

Diana stiffened for a moment, and Eden brought her hand back to her pistol.

Diana took her hand from Skye's. "You're the Grand Master?"

"I am."

Diana looked at Sleuth. He dipped his head and typed something into his holopad.

"I apologize for the last meeting. Things slithered their way to my attention. Now, about that traitor." Her voice lowered. She flicked her head, and several *Sirona* Guards stepped through the doorway from another room attached to Diana's quarters.

Skye rubbed his chin, his lips curling downward. "What's this?"

Eden noticed Nyx and Jantu eyeing the handful of new men in the room. Nyx and Jantu brought their hands quickly to their holsters.

"Just in case, Grand Master. I don't know you too well, and I don't know what to expect." Diana touched her chest. "It's for the captain's safety."

Skye dipped his head, his calmness nearly taking over the room. "Call me Skye. No need for formalities."

"And this traitor?" asked Diana, her lips flat. "You know who it is?"

"Not exactly," said Skye. "You have a traitor in your midst, and if you want our help, we can discover who this person is and root him or her out."

Diana tipped her head to the side, one eyebrow raised. "How do you know of this traitor?"

Eden's insides burned. She gripped her fingers around her gun's grip. "We watched a craft pick this person up two nights ago. The craft hovered just above this starship." Her nostrils flared. She hated knowing the word traitor was practically tattooed on Diana's forehead, and yet, she couldn't do a thing about it. All because Skye wanted to play it cool and figure out how to get to the top brass. "What do you know?"

Diana gave Sleuth another look. He gave her a nod.

Diana pursed her lips. "We suspected a traitor, but this is our investigation, and we did not invite the Space Templars. I don't need any more screw-ups."

The guards stood behind her, their hands on their rifles, still as a statue.

Eden took a step forward. "Why?"

Skye shook his head. "Eden, they have it handled."

Eden raised her chin, keeping her focus on Diana. "Why, Captain? You have the most advanced warriors in the galaxy here to assist you, and you turn them down?"

Diana crossed her arms, her lips pursed. "Since when does a major question a captain?"

"Since a major became a captain herself. I'm a captain in the Space Templar fleet." She pushed her chest out, her breaths shallow. She wanted to throw Diana on the ground and cuff her. Eden stood taller.

"And I'm a person of the human race. I have every right to uncover the truth for my race, and I don't care if you have—"

A hand rested on Eden's shoulder, interrupting her. Skye's voice came gently. "Eden, we're guests on this ship, and we'll act like good guests."

Eden shrugged his hand off and glared at Diana.

Diana sat, dropping her hands underneath her desk.

Eden pulled out her pistol and aimed it at Diana's chest. "Slowly put your hands on your desk."

The guards stepped forward, their rifles drawn. "Don't do that, Miss," said a guard.

Diana gave Eden a blank look, shifting her eyes to Skye. "Is this how your Space Templars captains act, Grand Master?" She scrunched her brows. "I'm lifting my arms. Stay your weapons." She slowly raised her hands, showing empty palms.

"I assure you it's not." Skye pulled Eden closer to him, his voice hushed and sharp. "Put that gun away."

Eden holstered her pistol, her face reddening. She let out an exhale and cupped her shaking hands in front of her, setting her gaze more deeply on Diana.

Skye smiled and bowed. "My apologies."

Diana sighed. "I understand. I have insubordinates as well."

Eden blinked. Her throat was tight. "I'm sorry, Captain. I don't know what came over me. I guess...the war and all."

Diana's shoulder's lowered, and she waved the guard off. They stood down.

"Sleuth, do we have their rooms ready?" asked Diana.

"Yes, Captain," Sleuth replied.

Diana clasped her hands and rested them on her desk. "Show them to their rooms. Unless you want to shoot me over something else that is bothering you, Eden?"

Eden shook her head. "A misunderstanding. My apologies."

"Sure," said Diana. "Grand Master, do you have any other members of your Space Templars who would like to end my life? I mean, tell me now, so I know who to avoid."

Skye put his hands together at his chest, touching his forehead against his fingertips. "I assure you we don't." His face firmed. "Unless you give us a reason. If I were you, I wouldn't give us any reason."

He turned, his robe whipping around. The door opened, and he paced out of the room, Jantu and Nyx behind him.

Nyx kissed her fingertips and slapped her fingers on the wall before exiting. "To remember me by."

Sleuth breezed by Eden, his face buried in his holopad. "Are you coming?"

"Yes." Eden dipped her head at Diana. "Good day, Captain."

Diana leaned back in her chair, folding her arms. "I'm allowing you all on this ship. I'm giving you one day of rest and relaxation. Day two, you all leave. Do you understand?"

"We're here to help you." Eden motioned to the armored slat over the window, remembering what Skye had seen while piloting an Aven, a Space Templar starfighter, on a trip toward the east. "Not far off is a weapon, and it appears large enough to heavily damage this ship. It's heading your way. The traitor probably knows about the weapon already, so be aware of any tricks that may arise. Once we rest, we'll stop the weapon at the pass." She stared deeply into Diana's eyes, wanting to call her out as the traitor here and now. "I'm sure the traitor wouldn't want that weapon stopped, but we do, and we will stop it."

Diana sat up, her eyes widening. "A weapon?"

"You don't know?"

Diana bolted out of her chair, her brows v'd. "Of course not. If I did, I'd have my starfighters scrambling now."

"Well, scramble them," said Eden.

Diana turned in her chair, eyeing the window. "How far away?"

"Roughly two days, maybe longer. I haven't seen it, but our sensors indicate it's moving slowly."

Diana went rigid, her lower lip twitching. "That bastard."

"Who?"

Diana pushed her chair out of the way and walked toward the open door. "We have to get this ship off the ground and starfighters scrambled. I have no time to talk." She pointed a finger through the doorway. "Out."

Eden dipped her head. "Yes, Captain."

She marched down the hallway, moving quickly to catch up with Skye. She turned a corner, and saw him leaning against a wall, smoldering and waiting for her. His face flushed red, his eyes nearly shooting lasers, something she'd never seen from him before.

He calmed the closer she approached. "I'm sorry, Eden, but we need to strip you of your rank. Nyx will hold your position from this point forward."

7

ZIM

Starbase Matrona

Prime Director Zim Noki rested his behind on a chair in an empty Sphere Eight Prime Overseer office, staring at a holoscreen. The office sat in a nearby skyscraper, his capital building close-by. Sabra informed him that his capital building office crawled with potential danger, ending her sentence, saying, "It's the last place I want you."

Right now, he wanted nothing more than to send Enlil a message. But what exactly would he say?

He grumbled and wrung his hands together. Changing his fate riddled his mind. He wanted to live, to let Enlil know Sabra forced him to out Enlil and coerced him to state the truth about Fleet Admiral Shae Lutz's innocence.

A traitor was a traitor, though.

Maybe Enlil would have mercy on him, knowing Enlil's sister, Sabra, betrayed him as well.

He put his fingertips on the holokeypad, typing with ferocity and purpose, his eyes glued to the words. He had to expose Sabra, and let Enlil know about her plans. If he found his way back to Enlil's good grace, he could live.

A knock on the door and Zim jerked back. His pulse rose, and he pressed transmit, sending the unfinished communication to Enlil. He shut off the HDC and spun around, moving out of his seat. He plopped his butt on top of the desk and placed his foot on the chair's seat. "Come in, Sabra."

The door opened and the ten-foot-tall woman walked in, her beauty on full display. She held herself strong, her long strides athletically graceful. He marveled at her incredible looks, her red, flowing hair, yet wanted to spit on her face for what she'd done to him.

He'd changed, yes, and become sympathetic to the little Earthlings for a short time. He understood their plight, and that slavery clamped hard on their souls, a cruelty like none other. However, he wouldn't have felt that way if she hadn't placed a gold, sparkling helmet over his head—the Crown of Accountability. It made him sympathize with the little nitwits, the dumbed-down humans.

The Crown of Accountability's effect had worn off. Snapping out of a compassionate, understanding state proved easy, especially when he realized that he'd sealed his fate by taking orders from this woman.

Sabra touched the HDC. "It's warm."

Zim nodded. "It sure is." He grinned, then walked to the office bar, a place he regularly visited in his own office. "Want some mead?"

"You know I don't touch that stuff." She sighed, sliding her hand across the top of his desk. "And here I thought you'd changed."

He opened a bottle. "I did for a moment. You signed my death sentence, Sabra. I am trying to unsign it if you catch my drift."

"I let you in here, in this Prime Overseer's office to test you. You didn't pass the test." She looked off and out a window. "My other brother, the one who seeks the light in all things, Enki, has plans for you. He sees something in you that could benefit all intelligent life in the galaxy. You have a way with people and convince others to see your truth. Once you see the real truth—that life encompasses all of us and that we are all truly one—I think the Space Templars will embrace you with open arms."

Zim chugged down a few gulps and waved his hand in the air, dismissing her reply. He burped, then took another gulp. "The truth of the matter is that you killed me. Enlil will do anything in his power to knock me down so I never get up again. I wish to rectify that and change his mind."

"What else were you doing on the HDC, Zim?" She cocked an eyebrow.

"I searched the vid channels, and yes, watched myself spill my guts to the population." He wanted to gut himself. He looked like a pansy.

She studied him. "Was I right?"

He took another chug of mead. "Right about what?" He wiped his mouth.

"I told you the humans would applaud you for telling the truth."

He shrugged. They applauded him, which felt well and great, but none of that mattered. Getting things right with Enlil mattered.

After Zim won the Prime Director election over twenty-years ago, Enlil promised Zim treasures beyond anything he could imagine once this human cycle ended, and here Sabra stood, delaying the human's destiny and the inevitable kill-off.

He folded his arms over his chest, his hand grasped around the bottle of mead. "Now, Sabra, tell me this one thing. How long do you think it will take for these humans to change their minds and turn on me? I give it a week, maybe two."

"They won't. They celebrate you. Are you paying attention or asleep at the helm, Prime Director?"

"How in the Guild would I know? You've kept me under wraps and away from them—"

"To keep you safe from Enlil."

He slammed the bottle on the bar, shattering it, the broken neck of the bottle in his hand as mead splattered on the floor, his shirt, and pants. "That's what I'm saying. You've killed me. He'll have my head any day now."

Sabra shifted her eyes from Zim to the mead dripping off the bar. "Have a little faith. You're not dead right now, are you? And I won't allow it." She brought her gorgeous eyes down on him. "If you weren't with me, then you're right, Enlil would already have your head."

Zim went to the desk and sat in the chair, his fingers forming a steeple. "Not anymore." He grinned. "I sent him a message and told him everything."

She smiled back, dipping her head. "I told my techs to intercept anything you attempted to send to Enlil. Once you sent your message, I imagine they received it immediately and deleted it from the holonet. Enlil won't ever see the beautiful words you wrote."

Zim's lips dropped, and he slumped, his excitement snuffed out. He wanted to show her up.

Sabra walked backward, butting up against a wall, keeping eye contact. "Plus, Enlil already has hit men looking for you. Or, I should say, your hitmen."

Zim straightened in his posture and tapped his chest with his index finger. "My hitmen?"

She nodded. "Yes, Payson and his crew. They posed as your secret guard, but they'd always been Enlil's guard. He brainwashed those poor souls, and when, or if, he needed them, he'd make them strike and strike quickly. He had them under his control, whether those elite soldiers knew it or not." She tapped her finger on her elbow. "He programmed their DNA if you remember. He owns their minds."

Zim shook his head. "No, those are my guys. I control them." He dropped his shoulders, realizing his folly, and his naïveté. He didn't control them in the slightest.

"So, you're dead if you leave my protection," said Sabra. "I'm the only chance you have. Enlil has played this game many times and has more Plan B's than you could shake your finger at."

Zim looked away, breathing heavily through his nose. "Now what? If Enlil sent Payson after me," he stood, anger rising from his belly, "that means I have little time. I'm a dead man walking."

"Your chance of staying alive is minimal, yes, but that's if you're not with me like I keep telling you. But if you die, it's no big deal. It's an easy transition. It's not something you need to fear."

"Okay, Miss Righteous One. Take me to your leader."

She walked to the door. "My leader, Enki, is on planet Aurora. It's packed with Space Templars, so don't let them get on your nerves when you get there. They are good people here to help and serve the galaxy."

Her wrist band beeped, and a voice blared through. "Payson and his men are on their way. Leave the facility now."

Zim threw his hands in the air, his eyebrows rising. "Great."

She extended her hand. "Follow me and I'll get you off this star-base, but we have to go now."

8

SHAE

Shae and Ali stood outside Bilrak's palace, the door closed, the grumpy King still inside, most likely drinking the root tea Shae never finished.

"I don't like saying it, but I have to go, Ali." Shae pursed his lips, hating the taste of the words coming out of his mouth.

Ali nodded. "Then you need to go." She looked away, shaking her head. "How will I see you again? How can we reunite?"

Shae eyed Chan, who approached with several Bawns by his side, including the blond, Thun.

Chan bowed. "News travels fast in a small city like this one." He folded his hands in his sleeves. "I apologize your visit was a short one, but before you leave, we need to deactivate your tracking chips. Once outside the mountain, you'll be easily trackable again."

"I need a holopad or something. Once you save *Sirona*," Shae looked at Ali, "you need to rendezvous with Starbase Matrona, and I need to give you the new coordinates."

Chan tapped his head. "I have an incredible memory." He turned toward a large mushroom topped building, the walls made of stone, the roof bronze colored. "Follow me."

They did, and reaching the mushroom-shaped structure, Thun pushed open the door. Ali ducked inside under the archway, Sol in hand. Shae came next, followed by Chan and several Bawns.

Shae's jaw dropped, and he slowly spun around the room. "Holy Guild."

Rock-like holocomps, holographic monitors, and holokeypads lined the walls. Data streamed across the screens.

"They will deactivate your chips now," said Chan.

Ali eyed one of the holocomps. "I can't believe this has been under our noses the entire time I've mined on this planet."

"Put your arms to your side."

Shae and Ali did as instructed. A small man holding a flashing wand connected by a long cord to a holocomp held a scowl on his wrinkled, beard-covered face. He waved the wand up and down Shae. A flash of light came from the wand and lit up the room. "Done," said the Bawn. "Next." He walked to Ali, waving the wand up and down her body until another bright flash engulfed the room. "Okay, you're done. Get out."

Shae frowned as the man shuffled everyone out of the small building like he was brushing out unwanted dirt.

"It can't be that easy," said Shae.

The door slammed, and they stood outside. Ali stared at the door, expressionless. "That's it? We're not bugged anymore?"

Chan bowed. "You're now free to travel without risk or care of being tracked." He turned to Shae, again tapping on his own noggin. "I'll take the coordinates, please."

Shae walked up the mountain's long inner spiral pathway toward the tunnel's exit, loneliness coming over him as the wholeness he felt while in Ali's presence slowly diminished. She had watched him leave until the shadows darkened Shae as he walked up the curving trail. Before leaving, he mentioned to her why Harak disliked the one who wielded Sol, hence Ali, and any outsider. Harak believed someone in his family would soon die after the Chosen One arrived.

She shrugged it off. "It's just a belief."

"Be careful."

"Don't worry about me."

Easy for her to say.

"Bye, Dad," he heard her shout shortly after he walked away from her. "I love you."

He waved. "I love you, too."

Ten minutes later, the crunching pebbles underfoot pounded his ears. He slapped his hands together, talking out loud to himself. "Don't start feeling sorry for yourself. She's alive and well, and you'll see her shortly."

He made his way through the tunnel and eventually stepped outside. He eyed his Starjumper, thankfully untouched. He took a deep whiff of air, filling his lungs with fresh oxygen. They could have lived on this planet the entire time Matrona orbited Eos.

He cringed at the lies drilled into his and everyone's mind. The overly intense gravity. A lie. No oxygen. Another lie. The unbearable heat, and no mention of gold and crystals in the ebb terrain, and humans the only Beings in the galaxy. Lie. Lie. Lie. The list could go on for kilometers.

A triangular-shaped starfighter rumbled across the sky, interrupting his steaming thoughts. The craft dipped a wing, and quickly faded into a small dot in the distance.

Shae gulped and ran for his craft. He didn't know if the dipped wing meant the pilot saw his Starjumper, or he noticed Shae and was giving him a heads-up that a strafing run would come in Shae's direction soon. He doubted the latter.

He raced across the ebb field, jumping over small jutted rocks, and rounding large boulders. He eyed the sky, noting the ship didn't turn around. He blew out his cheeks. Either the son of a bitch enjoyed playing with Shae's nerves, or Shae stood a lucky man. Again, he doubted the latter.

He placed his hand on the cabin's exterior control panel. A beep and the side door flipped upward. He hurried inside, hearing a rumbling sound fill the sky and shaking the earth. The starfighter indeed turned and was coming in for another pass. He rushed into the cockpit and glared at the sky through the window. A dot in the sky grew in size with another dot accompanying it. They moved fast, turning from dots to miniature starfighters, soon to be larger and sending cannon fire.

He slapped a button on the flight console to close the cabin door. It clicked and hissed. Airtight. He plopped onto the pilot's seat and activated engines. The Starjumper purred, and Shae flicked on belly thrusters, lifting the craft off the ground. He pulled up radar, now noting three starfighters in the vicinity.

Crap.

He tilted his Starjumper toward the heavens and the long wispy clouds in patches across the early blue sky. He moved the throttle forward, engaging aft boosters. He sank back into his chair as the gravity pressed against him.

The Starjumper blasted like a rocket, moving at incredible speed toward the upper atmosphere. A beep sounded. The radar showed the starfighters headed his way. He stiffened, readying himself for some fast, quick maneuvering.

He gulped hard and patted his flight console. The ship was shaking the higher he flew. "Just get me into space, baby. I'll take care of the rest."

Another loud warning reverberated off the walls. A moment later, several alarms filled the cockpit. He eyed the radar. Missiles had launched heading his way.

He blasted through the upper atmosphere and banked hard as he broke through the exosphere, his heart pumping quickly.

The alarms stopped, the missiles having reached their measured limits.

He thought of his daughter as he punched in Starbase Matrona's coordinates on his nav panel. Another beep sounded in the cockpit, and then another blared on the holomonitor's radar read. Four starfighters inbound, and probably more on the way. They closed in on Shae's small Starjumper.

Tracer fire let loose, red, fiery streaks gaining on him. He pulled the control stick to his right, easily avoiding the slugs. More warnings echoed in the cockpit. He glanced at his radar, counting eight missiles inbound.

Shae pressed on the Negative Matter Jump Drives, NMJ Drives for short. "See you later," he called out, wiping the sweat off his brow.

Everything in front of him stretched long and wide, and silence filled the cockpit, a popping sound accompanying static erupted in his ears. The stars changed into streaks of lights, and his eyes blurred before everything stopped as if time stood still. Another pop and the streaks disappeared. He sat staring at Starbase Matrona, her silver shine catching his eyes.

He pressed on the commlink. "Starbase Matrona, this is Fleet Admiral Shae Lutz. Open bay doors, I'm heading in for a landing."

"Affirmative Fleet Admiral. Sphere One bay doors opening. You're clear for landing."

Shae smiled, thinking about his daughter, happy they'd be together soon. First, according to Bilrak's prophecies, he had a starbase and her people to save. "See you soon, Ali."

He steered his craft toward Sphere One, his thoughts turning to Payson. If that bastard still lived, he'd soon be Shae's number one target.

9

ALI

Dirn Garum, Eos

A loud horn blasted, and Ali jumped to a standing position, her eyes blurry from tears, and her stomach sick from watching her dad leave.

Moments ago, the doors to Dirn Garum closed, and she'd made her way down the stairs to the public square. She walked to the tallest man in the vicinity, Chan. Before leaving, her dad gave Star Guild's current location to him.

She touched Chan's robe, pulling on his sleeve. "You remember the coordinates?"

"Yes, and have no fear, I'll remember them always."

Another horn bellowed, shaking the ground. She covered her ears. "What's all the racket about?" The horn ceased, and the city illuminated. She glanced around. Light bounced off walls, flooding the entire area. Little men and women, thick and stalk-y, slowly gathered in the town square, eyeing the cavern's ceiling.

Someone jabbed Ali's hip. She looked down to see Thun standing near her, his long beard moving upward with his smile. He rested a pickaxe over his shoulder, his fingers wrapped around the handle's throat. "I'm sure you haven't forgotten me already." He pounded his chest with his other hand, his face strong and fierce. "Thun, son of King Bilrak, brother of Harak, first in line as king."

"Yeah, yeah." Ali yawned, shaking off her exhaustion and depressed state. "What's going on?"

"Look up." Thun pointed, and Ali followed his finger.

Light streamed from the corner of the monstrous cavern, beaming brightly. Another horn echoed off the rocks and walls. Ali held her hands over her ears.

Thun tugged on Ali's pant leg. "Watch."

The light transformed into a thin laser-like ray, shooting straight into an enormous golden bowl on top of a building a few blocks down the way. The bowl reflected the light back, slowly turning the light into a blueish-white color that flooded the upper rock walls. The crowd broke into a cheer, then bowed, going silent. The light continued to spread throughout the cavern. Minutes later, the Bawns dispersed, heading back to their mingling.

Ali glanced down at Thun, then up at Chan. "Again, what's going on?"

"That's how we get our energy to power the lights in the city. At this time, the rising sun delivers important light," said Thun. He perked up, clearly excited to tell her the process. "We direct that light with mirrors throughout a tunnel system we created in the upper portion of the mountain." He pointed at the beaming light. "A Bawn operates our last mirror. He positions the mirror exactly where it needs to be to send the light into the golden bowl."

Ali crossed her arms. "Neat, I guess?"

Thun continued as if not hearing Ali. "Blue selenium fills the bowl which collects the power and streams it down to our capacitor building that the bowl sits atop. It stores energy and shares energy to the accompanying buildings." He gave a pleased look. "It's amazing, actually."

Ali eyed the capacitor building. "Are—"

He wiggled her pant leg. "No, no. Don't interrupt. I'm not done." He stroked his long beard. "We've attached copper coils to each building, where it also collects and spreads the energy to the next building, acting much like a partnership. This illuminates our lights. Since we are not surface dwellers, this energy system gives us all the nutrients from the sun that we need."

This guy spoke a mouthful. She thought for a moment. "Wait, so you have tunnel systems throughout the mountain?"

Thun grunted. "Not much, but yes."

She tapped her front teeth, thinking more. With several tunnel systems, they could probably find a safe tunnel to exit and get to Starship *Sirona*. "Do you have warriors among you?"

Thun gave her an odd look. "We're all warriors." He swept his arm out in front of him, indicating the people all around. "Can't you tell?"

She nodded. She couldn't tell, but she didn't want to insult him. She needed to get the ball rolling, to get the Bawn to do what S said they'd do, help her and her people.

"You mentioned you wanted to fight these Anunnaki. In fact, you want to kill them."

Thun folded his arms. "I'll dig their graves for them, and you can shove their dead bodies inside."

No, thank you. She swallowed her thoughts. "Then we start today. Let's get a band of your greatest warriors together and head to a specific location where I know these Anunnaki will be."

She didn't tell him they'd be going to *Sirona* instead, a minor detail.

Thun shifted and his brows drew low. He paused for several seconds in deep thought. "You're ready to fight?"

"No, but I must. Will your warriors do what I tell them to do?"

Thun looked her up and down. "You show them the sword, and they'll do what you ask." He waved her to follow him, a gleam in his eyes. "I'm pleased you're ready because I have something important for you this way." He turned and headed for a mushroom-shaped cottage.

"Where are we going?"

"We have fashioned you a baldric for your sword. During battle, you'll have a place to pull your sword from, and a place for your sword to rest."

Oh, Guild. She wanted to get to *Sirona*, get everyone off this planet, and get to her dad. She didn't want anything fashioned for her and didn't want any reason to owe these people anything.

Thun flicked his hand. "Come, come."

They walked around the mushroom building and headed toward a large boulder sitting between two structures.

"Where's Daf?" asked Ali.

Thun grunted.

"And that means?"

"It means I don't know."

"Okay, where did Chan Ru go?"

Thun grunted, continuing to walk toward the large boulder.

"I guess that means you don't know."

Thun ignored her.

Reaching the boulder, Thun pressed a button on the rock. He stood straight, waiting and humming a tune.

Ali felt a hand on her back. "I'm right here, Ali."

She turned to see Chan.

He touched a hand to his heart and bowed. "I'll accompany you to your fitting if you allow me." He handed her a mug. "Drink up. It gives you energy."

Ali took the mug and drank, a thick liquid like milk washing down her gullet. It tasted sweet, though she couldn't pinpoint any resemblances that touched her palate from past beverages before. In seconds, she felt alive and energized. She opened her eyes wider. "Thank you."

"You're welcome."

She put the mug on the ground and gestured at the rock, scrunching her face. "Is this the fitting room?"

Thun kicked the boulder. "You sun dweller piece of pebble-crap." He pressed the button again.

Chan cracked a smile. "A Bawn's patience is nothing to be envious about. Making a Bawn wait is worse than cutting their throats."

The boulder clicked, and a door-shaped portion of the boulder moved inward, rumbling rock against rock. The rock-door slid to the side, opening into what looked to be an elevator.

Ali took a step back. "What the..."

"Come," said Thun. "No questions."

No questions? A door practically formed out of nowhere in a giant rock. To top it off, an elevator. She shook her head and kept her mouth shut, stepping inside, accompanied by Thun and Chan.

The elevator shook, then descended, opening moments later. Before her was a brightly lit, immense facility about the size and shape of a mech warehouse.

Bawns moved about, busying themselves behind rock-like desks similar to stations on a starship's bridge. They pressed buttons, barked orders, and swiped across holographic displays.

She caught her breath and tipped her head to the side, squinting. The rock desks projected holoscreens, much like an HDC in Star Guild and Starbase Matrona.

"Follow me." Thun motioned for them to exit the elevator.

Ali walked toward the Bawns' stations. "How the Guild did all of this get down here?" She gestured toward the elevator, now behind her. "And the elevator?"

Chan walked by her side, stroking his chin. "The Space Templars built everything below Dirn Garum eons ago. This used to be one of their strongholds in this region of the galaxy. After the Anunnaki's failed experiment with the Bawns as their slaves—the Anunnaki simply couldn't control them—the Bawns who survived a genocide type of event escaped to this mountain. The Space Templars were long gone by then, leaving this facility to the Bawn. But the Space Templars didn't create Dirn Garum, the city above this facility. The Bawn did. The good news is Enlil doesn't know what goes on in Dirn Garum, at least not to our knowledge. He doesn't patrol this area much, either."

Ali pursed her lips. "Enlil doesn't know what's going on down here?"

Chan nodded. "We suspect he doesn't."

Ali fixed Chan with a stare. "Well, of—" Ali cut herself off, her eyes transfixed on a brilliant radiating purple glow coming from a thick slab of ebb that acted as a wall at the back of the facility.

Ali leaned closer to Chan as they walked toward the stations. She whispered, doing her best not to bother the busy workers. "What are they doing?"

"It's their workstations. They monitor the outside, plus they keep Dirn Garum operating efficiently. You know, controlling the flow of water canals, watching for any intruders outside the mountain, managing the electricity, and many more things."

Thun grunted, slamming down his pickaxe. "We're here."

Ali eyed the smooth and perfectly chiseled ebb wall. It reminded her of Earth's Pyramid of Giza and the Queen's chamber, a chamber lined with perfectly smooth, granite blocks.

Ali went rigid when something wrapped around her waist. She threw her hands out, hitting against something hard and bendy. A heavy object fell, and she instinctively caught it, feeling a thick, coarse, and strong material against her fingers.

Harak glared at her, wiping his hands. "Pay attention. That's your baldric. Wear it well and often."

Ali flinched. Harak was now standing next to his brother.

He rolled his eyes, shaking his head, his lips in a frown. "I was trying to put that on you, sun worshiper." He stalked off toward the large ebb wall.

Thun clasped his hands together. "Ali, you now owe him your life."

Ali slapped her chest. She didn't owe that guy anything. "Why?"

"He made you the baldric. It's fit for a king."

Chan lightly touched Ali's back. "Or a queen."

Ali held the baldric in her hands, the well-made item fashioned to fit around her waist and torso.

Thun marched toward his brother. "I have another surprise for you, Ali."

"Now what?" asked Ali, walking after Thun.

Thun picked up his pace. "To our ships and vehicles."

Ali halted. "Huh?"

Chan walked with them, nodding. "They are quite advanced engineers, masons, and carpenters but as impatient as they are with each other, they are just as impatient with what you're about to see."

They reached the ebb wall. Harak stood with his arms crossed, the always disappointed wrinkles on his face. He turned and faced the wall, lifting his arms. "Awake." The ebb slab split in two. One side opened to the right and the other to the left with light spilling through the opening.

Ali gasped loudly. "Whoa." Her hand came to her mouth. In front of her sat an orb-like craft as big as a starship class vessel. The orbed-shaped front attached to a long, egg-shaped second and third portion. Gigantic landing sleds connected to each section of the craft, and boosters and rockets went from the midsection to the aft.

"That ship's gorgeous," said Ali.

It glistened and glimmered, pulsing a translucent silver glow.

"That large craft," Chan told her, "is Starship *Tranquil*." He turned to her, dipping his head, Harak and Thun doing the same. "Welcome to your new ship, Captain."

10

KODA

Starbase Matrona

Devon and Koda rose slowly, arms up in surrender.

A man stood before them with a rifle pointed at Koda's chest. "S sends her regards, sirs."

Koda gave the guy a blank look. His heartbeat rose, waiting for bullets to slam into him. He flicked a glance at Devon, who stood as still as a building, his eyes focused on the gun.

The soldier lowered his weapon, his neck bending forward. "You don't have a clue who S is, do you?"

"S?" asked Koda, hands still up.

"Are you serious?" The guy swept his eyes around the room, almost as if looking for a hidden holocam recording them. "I thought by now Devon would have found her name hidden amongst the junk data. Zim had recently been communicating with Enlil, telling him S was a traitor to his race." He lifted a single eyebrow. "No recollection?" He continued to stare. "Nothing?" He slumped, his face slack. "All right, it's okay. Just know that she's on your side, boys." He looked off, saying under his breath, "I thought this would be more exciting." The man shouldered his rifle. "I think you can put your hands down now, fellas. I'm not going to shoot you."

Devon let his arms fall to his sides. Koda lowered his arms a second later.

"Who is S?" asked Koda.

The guard cocked his head. "Sabra." His shoulders rose, the rifle moving upward. "Does that ring a bell?"

Koda and Devon shook their heads.

The man let out a loud sigh, wiping his hand over his mouth. "Sabra is Enlil's sister, and I know you've figured out who Enlil is, right?"

Koda nodded, his mind spinning. For one, the soldier standing before him wore military fatigues that seemed to camouflage into any color the guy stood beside, the colors melding into the surrounding textures. It was a strange tech. Two, what group did this man belong to?

Koda glared at an insignia on the man's jacket breast, a geometrically shaped ensign three circles intertwined, creating a three-leafed looking design.

The guy placed his palms on his hips. "Okay, Enlil is the bad guy. He's a leader of a race, the Anunnaki, who attacked you. Though a leader only in this sector...well, and some other sectors. They—"

Devon interrupted him. "We know. I hacked into the mainframe and found that information." He scratched his temple. "I think we were about to find more information, and then, you know."

"Then I screwed it all up." The soldier winked. "I know. I walked in and scared the living daylights out of you two." He extended his hand toward the holoscreen. "I'd like you to come see my handiwork. It's all here for you." He smacked his hands together. "You're welcome for doing your job, boys."

Koda walked out from behind the couch and around the desk, Devon following.

On the holoscreen streamed paragraphs and paragraphs of junk data translating the stream into reading material underneath. The stream spewed out flight information, the comings and goings of Starjumpers, Starhawk Transports, and other cargo crafts from Starbase Matrona to Eos Two. Reading further, jump point coordinates in the Adarta System and coordinates outside the Adarta System flowed on the screen. Destination "N" blinked in bold next to one of the coordinates.

Devon pointed at the screen. "What is Destination "N"?"

The guard frowned. "To tell you that would take hours, and to answer your subsequent questions would take longer. I don't have that time. I apologize for being vague, but I have a race to save."

Koda dipped his head. "My race?"

"Our race. The human race."

Koda blinked several times, trying to put two and two together. "Thank you for helping Devon and me, but why are you helping us two specifically?" Maybe this guy knew Payson and worked for him.

The guard smiled, shaking his head. "I'm a Space Templar, my friend. They've trained me in the subtle art of the Sight, part of the Templar path, and I can see by your aura you don't trust me." He motioned to the screen. "Just know that this is a gift offering to you so you can trust people wearing fatigues similar to mine. We won't harm you. We are here to protect you, just as you are attempting to protect your citizens. You're on a hunt for the truth, and that truth will set your people free."

The man's shoulder band beeped, and a woman's voice blared through, "We located Payson. Naveya is close by and on his tail."

The guard tapped the band. "I'll be right there." He took a step toward the door and halted. "I'd stay if I could, but there are some cunning men on the loose."

He ran out of the room and down the hallway, bellowing, "My name's CJ. Welcome to my life, gentlemen." The bell jingled as the lobby door opened and shut.

Devon showed his palms. "Uh, what just happened?"

Koda rubbed the back of his neck. "Yeah, I don't know. You don't see that every day."

"Did a woman say Payson?"

Koda screwed up his face, his brows furrowing. "Yes."

Devon looked around absentmindedly at the screen. He hurried to the seat as if seeing something important. "Right here." He wiggled his finger in front of a translated paragraph. "There are several Starhawk Transports coming and going as we speak. But why? Our miners aren't mining ebb at the moment, plus we aren't near Eos to gather any remaining ebb storages either." He scrolled down and stopped. "Yeah, right here. It says a short repair stop before they depart to those coordinates." Devon ran his finger under the coordinates and punched his fingers on the holokeypad. A star map materialized in front of them. "Whoa. They're going outside of the Adarta System to a planet on a wide orbit in a system called the Solar System. A planet named Nibiru? Maybe that's Destination "N"? The planet has its own system attached to it, too." He shook his head as if in disbelief. "That's strange."

"Yes, that must be Destination 'N'." Koda leaned in and swiped his finger over the screen, bringing up the previously translated stream. "Look at that. Some Starhawks are departing soon." He made a dash to Zim's office door and toward the lobby. "Let's go."

Devon didn't move, continuing to read the information on the screen. "Look at this. Zim has moved all the barrels of batrachotoxin to Sphere One. You don't think Payson is heading that way, do you?"

Koda hesitated. "The toxin hasn't been sent out of the airlocks yet?"

"It's in the airlocks, but not yet released."

Koda bit his fingernail. "Damn. If Payson seizes the toxin, then what?" He paced, thinking. "The airlocks connect to the air ducts. Could he get the toxin into the air ducts?" He pinched his upper lip. "I mean, who knows what will happen if he lets the toxin loose through those air channels. How many people would it effect?" Koda wrung his hands together, his heart picking up speed as panic raised the hair on his skin. "We have to go to Sphere One. There, we'll find the toxin and send it out of the airlocks, and then investigate the Starhawks."

Devon rubbed the ridge of his nose.

Koda halted his own pacing. "Are you having second thoughts?"

"I just want to rest. I have a family. You know, my mom, dad, and my sister. Maybe I should see them and tell them I'm alive. Or, I could stay here in Zim's office and hack for hours and hours, grabbing more information for us. Other than Shae, don't you have a family?"

"No, just Shae. My mom and dad died a while back." Koda stood in front of the doorway. "And now I got you as family." He winked. "I need your help, Devon."

Devon dropped his head in his hands, rubbing his face. "Oh, Guild. I guess you're right. We have to do this, don't we?"

Koda motioned for Devon to follow him down the hall. "Yes, it's a must. After we let the toxin out of the airlocks, then like I said before, we'll look at the Starhawk Transports. It's just another lead to what Destination "N" is, and if it's indeed the planet Nibiru it may lead us down another rabbit hole that will help us discover more about the Anunnaki and what else they have in store for us."

Koda paused and stopped in the hallway. What was he doing? This was his mission, and he was dragging the poor kid along. He had no right, especially if Devon wanted to see his family.

Koda turned and placed his hands on Devon's shoulders. "I'm so sorry. You're not going anywhere except to your family. I can do this on my own."

Devon dropped his chin and stared at his feet, nodding his head. "Yeah, but..." He lifted his chin and his lips slowly perked into a smile, a gleam in his eyes. "I won't have a family if we don't open the airlocks and suck the batrachotoxin into space. And I won't have a family if we don't detach and free ourselves from the Anunnaki race. They are a pain in all of our asses, Koda. You're right, you probably need my help." Devon flexed his skinny arm, grinning.

Koda snorted. "You think that will convince me to take you along?"

Devon shook his head. "Yeah, I know. I need to work out."

"Yep." Koda took a step toward the exit and put his hand on the door handle. The handle shook, and heat radiated from it. Everything slowed, and he looked out of the glass window. A loud concussion pushed him backward and into the air. Broken glass flew, sticking into his body and littering the floor and walls.

A blast of fire erupted in front of him and he smacked into Devon, sending them both to the floor.

ALI

Dirn Garum, Eos

Daf gave Ali a blank stare. "You're pulling my leg, right?" Daf looked at the green leaf wrapped around her shin and ankle. "Actually, don't pull my leg."

Ali stood over Daf. "I'm telling you the truth."

Daf lay on a small bed in an earthen hut, her leg raised on top of a few pillows. "How could these Bawns get a ship like that?"

Ali couldn't believe it either, and wouldn't have if she hadn't seen it for herself. "They want me to lead a crew of Bawns to take out the Anunnaki. I told them it had to be right away, and they liked that idea." She unsheathed her sword and held it up. "This thing may get me into more trouble than I can handle." Purple plasma flames rose an inch off the blade's edges.

"You're ready to fight now?"

Ali pursed her lips, her eyes narrowing. "We have little choice. We have to save *Sirona* right away." She stared at the flames dancing off the sword, her voice lowering. "I'll make them think we'll attack the giants, but I'll deviate from that plan and get our asses to *Sirona*. It ain't going to be easy, but maybe we can convince *Sirona*'s crew to board. We'll then head to my father's coordinates."

"Starship *Tranquil?*"

"Yeah, that's what the Bawns call the ship, the one I'll be captaining."

"And you thought of this plan that quickly?"

Ali sheathed Sol. "It's the only plan that would work, the only way I can save our people."

Daf pointed to the sword sheathed in Ali's new baldric. "You're telling me you need that sword to start the starship?"

Ali nodded. "Yes. That's what they say. It activates the ship. I don't know why or how, but I have little time to question." She glanced at Daf's leg. "How's your leg?"

Daf's nose curled. "It was gross. They put a strange mixture of green plants and smeared it all over my leg. It smelled like chicken crap mixed with mint. Made me gag a few times."

"Does it feel better?"

"Yeah, mostly. I can walk better, but I'm letting it rest for the moment as they ordered." Daf took a long breath. "So, when are we going to get that ship running so we can get our people to safety?"

Ali shrugged. "I don't know, but it has to be soon. S was correct about the people in the mountain, which means she was probably correct about that large weapon heading *Sirona's* way. So, again, we need to get going right away." Ali huffed and bent down, rubbing the ground with her thumb. She tapped on it a couple times with her knuckles as if knocking on a door. "How stupid are we, Daf?"

Daf crinkled her brow. "What?"

Ali eyed the ground, her palm now touching it. "Sorry, change of topic, but there are plants on Eos, not much, but some, and plants give off oxygen, and yet we still went with the story that there isn't an ounce of oxygen here."

Daf turned her head and stared at the ceiling. "Next topic, please."

"Why?"

"Because when you get on a subject you're angry about, you freak out. You go on a tirade, and it's hard to pull you out of it."

"We've been lied to."

"Yes, I understand, and I'm pissed about it too, but there's nothing we can do about it. Bring it up to the governance if we all survive this. Until then, can we just figure out how to get everyone off this planet? Heck, get everyone on *Sirona* to safety before they get blown to the sun and back."

Ali gave Daf a stony expression. "The Bawns will mutiny once they figure out we're not going after the Anunnaki, won't they?"

Daf shifted in her bed. "Then we don't take them."

"What?"

Daf gave Ali a mischievous look. "Don't take them with us."

"We have to take them."

"Why does it matter? They have a great place to live. It's peaceful here. It's gorgeous. They have everything they need."

Ali cringed. "The Bawn won't like this one bit." She thought for a moment, letting the idea percolate in her mind. She slowly gave a wry grin. "Are you ready then? We'll head to *Sirona* and save our friends."

"What about Diana?" asked Daf.

Ali's shoulders dropped. She almost forgot about her. Another liar that clouded Ali's life the moment she arrived on Starbase Matrona. Diana probably set *Sirona* up, keeping it grounded on Eos for her own evil reasons. If she had, then Diana would do everything in her power to keep those people on board.

Ali needed a quick in and out; land, evacuate, take off. With thousands of people onboard *Sirona*, this would be harder than she could imagine. She frowned. Could she actually pull this off? "Do you think we can get a hold of Wrench and tell him to get everyone ready? Or tell him to cuff Diana to her desk so she can't stop the evacuation?"

Daf lifted an eyebrow. "Since the Bawns have a ship, they probably have a way to communicate with *Sirona* from said ship."

Ali cocked her head to the side. "You're right." Ali tapped her fingers in deep thought.

Daf fell silent.

After a few moments, they looked at each other.

Ali grinned.

Daf grinned back. "Are you thinking what I'm thinking?"

"It'll be the easiest way around all of this, except Diana."

"Are you seriously thinking what I'm thinking?"

"I thought so." Ali couldn't help but smile. "We take Starship *Tranquil* now without the Bawns, communicate with Wrench, and see if we can get him to stall Diana somehow, perhaps figure out a way to throw her in the brig, then we can do this. Hell, we know he's buddies with officers in the *Sirona* Guard. Maybe he can convince them Diana isn't on their side."

"Well, that's not exactly what I was thinking, but we must leave now. Like right now. We'll take this *Tranquil* craft and figure out things more easily when we're away from the mountain, away from the Bawn. But like I said, we leave this moment."

Ali nodded. "Yes."

Daf sat up. "We don't have a choice, really. *Sirona* doesn't have much time."

Ali stood. "For the sake of *Sirona*."

Daf pushed into a standing position, keeping more weight on one leg than the other. "When the Bawn find out we took the craft, they'll crap their pants."

Ali shrugged off the comment. "You ready?"

Daf nodded, a smile hanging on her lips. "Ready."

1 2

ALI

Dirn Garum, Eos

Ali helped Daf around the mushroom top structure, her hand against the building's hard exterior surface.

"I told you not to help me," whispered Daf, her eyes nearly burning a hole in Ali's forehead.

Ali glanced at Daf's leg and let go of her arm. "If you don't want help, then stop hobbling. It looks like you'll topple over any minute."

Ali looked around the corner of the building. Bawns amassed at the town square, trading foods and supplies with one another. Ali eyeballed Daf, thumbing over her shoulder. "That way." Ali raced to the next building, Daf limping quickly behind her.

Dirn Garum's public square and all the surrounding streets leading through small little neighborhoods and eateries were busy with small people, but none in Ali's vicinity or on her path to the boulder.

Good.

Ali pointed to the massive boulder that sat between two buildings. "We're almost there."

"Got it."

Ali tiptoed to the stone, hoping the workers in the facility down below milled around up top, taking a break and mingling with their friends. It was late, and she figured their shifts must be over. If a few Bawn remained at their stations below, she had the sword, and they seemed to obey Sol and would probably let Ali and Daf observe Starship *Tranquil*.

Maybe.

Ali pressed the button on the wall.

"What are we waiting for?" asked Daf.

"An elevator."

Daf's head slightly jerked back. "An elevator?"

"I just told you they had a starship and other vehicles, and an elevator is what's impressing you?"

A portion of the boulder moved inward, leaving the door frame exposed. The door slid to the side, rock crunching against rock. Ali turned, hoping no one heard. She put her finger up for Daf to be quiet.

No one seemed to notice.

Ali stepped inside, motioning for Daf to join her. "We're heading down."

She pressed the only button inside.

Daf leaned against the back wall, her arms folded, watching the door close. The door shut, and she gasped. "Did you see that?"

Ali glared at the closed door, her shoulders drooping. "What?"

The elevator descended.

Daf looked down, blinking as if trying to remember. She shook her head. "I'm probably seeing things. I thought I saw someone walking between a building, heading our way."

The door opened.

In front of them sat the rock stations, all empty. She remembered how Harak had opened the long slab door.

She hurried out of the elevator with Daf in tow. Ali grasped Sol's hilt, just in case someone jumped her. Boots in the distance sliding across rock carried to Ali's ears. She froze, holding a hand up, and Daf halted.

"Did you hear that?" Ali whispered.

"Sure did."

"Which direction?" Ali glanced around.

Daf pointed at the ebb slate that reached from one end of the structure to the other. "I think it came from over there."

"Perhaps a drudge," said Ali. Those creatures probably liked it underground here. Regardless, Ali's eyes darted around, her senses on high alert. She didn't want anyone catching her snooping. What would they think? They'd probably accuse her of wanting to steal the starship. She'd deny it, but they'd be right.

"Let's go," Ali whispered. "But keep it down."

They walked quietly to the ebb slab wall, planting their feet in front of it.

"Are you ready to see it, Daf?"

Daf put a hand on Ali's shoulder, steadying herself on her good leg. "I'm not only ready to see it, but I'm also ready to get our friends off of Starship *Sirona* and back home." Excitement practically oozed out of her.

Ali nodded. "Me too." She sheathed her sword and raised her hands. "Awake." The door rumbled, then cracked open.

Moments later, the rock fully opened, and Daf's eyes widened. "Holy mother of ebb."

"Yeah, isn't she a beauty?"

Before them sat Starship *Tranquil*, its orb-like body glistening. It glowed silver and dimmed a gold, then shined in gold, and dulled to silver, only to brighten to a silver sheen an instant later.

"I can't believe it. It's immaculate." Daf stepped forward. "What type of ship or what class is that?"

"I don't know exactly, but Chan called it a starship. To me, it's a little smaller, but who knows how the creators of this vessel labeled their ship class types." Ali quickened her pace, hurrying toward the ship. "But we can figure it out once we get on board and—"

"Halt," boomed a voice, its inflection reverberating off the walls.

Ali and Daf stopped dead in their tracks, Ali's spine tingling and her gut clenching. She squeezed her eyes shut, opening them a second later, hunching in her posture. "For Guild sakes."

They turned, and Harak stood near a corner of the mammoth

room. He held an axe and pounded the handle's knob on the slated ground. "What are you doing here?"

Daf jostled Ali's arm. "What did he say?"

"He wants to know what we're doing here."

"Oh, fabulous. Just tell them you were showing me the ship."

Ali put her hand up. "Yeah, yeah. I got this."

Harak tilted the toe of the axe toward the ship, and then the butt of the axe toward Ali. Footsteps and movement echoed in the building. From behind the ship's landing sleds stepped several Bawns, some carrying small swords, and others hammers or pickaxes. More footsteps and Ali flicked a glance over her shoulder. Another set of Bawns, all smirking, ambled toward her.

Ali lifted her sword, its blade gleaming brightly. She squeezed the handle, and a flame encircled the sword from the top of the hilt to the tip of the blade. "I'm the Chosen One."

The Bawns hesitated, pausing for a moment, then continued advancing toward her. This Chosen One nonsense didn't help much.

Ali placed one hand on her hip. "What do you want, Harak?"

Harak raised his axe. "Hold." The Bawns stopped. He lowered his axe, his eyes narrowing. "What are you doing here? You came here to steal *Tranquil*, did ya'?"

"Are you serious?" Ali acted shocked. "I wanted to show Daf the ship. She didn't believe it existed." She curled her lips into a feigned smile. "I won the bet."

Harak shifted his eyes from Ali to Daf. "Is what she says true?"

Daf shrugged. "He's talking to me. What the Guild is he saying?" She elbowed Ali in the arm a few times. "What's he saying?"

"She can't speak Bawn, Harak." Ali went into a defensive crouch. "You're taking this prophecy a little too far. I'll bet my left toe no one in your family will die because of my arrival."

Harak looked a bit surprised Ali knew about the prophecy. He shook it off and scowled. "I don't want to wait and find out."

"What were you going to do, try to kill me?" said Ali.

Harak chuckled, his shoulders bouncing up and down. The rest of the Bawns followed suit. "Did you say try? No. I would not try. I will kill you. Plus, it's against Bawn law to use this craft without the king or the king's heirs onboard."

"Fine, then we'll leave." Ali went to turn, then stopped, and faced Harak, a fire igniting in her belly. "The next time you try to kill me, you'll have this sword down your throat." She eyed more Bawns. "All of you." She flattened her lips. "Do you understand?"

Harak nodded to his cohorts, grunting loudly. "Kill them," yelled Harak, going into a run, his long hair trailing in his wake.

Daf put her hands up, her fingers curled into fists. Ali brought the sword in front of her. As they neared, Ali went into a lower crouch, and a force she didn't understand took hold of her like a tornado forming in the clouds. The sword vibrated, and tingling went through her body, up to her crown and down to her toes. She let out a ferocious yell, squeezing her hands around Sol's hilt. "Daf, get on the floor."

When Daf hesitated, she twisted and threw a kick at the back of Daf's knees, sending her friend tumbling to her side. Ali squeezed the hilt harder and raised the sword above her head, squaring her body in front of Harak, who approached quickly, readying to put his axe in her chest.

A blast of purple fire blew from Sol, sending flames out and upward. Gasps filled the room, and the Bawns fell back, skidding to a halt, some landing on their rears. Their weapons flung from their hands, including Harak's.

Ali brought down her sword with rage boiling inside her. She pointed the sword at Harak, who lay awkwardly on the floor. He twisted, scrambling for his axe. She squeezed her hilt yet again and plasma shot from the blade's tip, singeing the floor next to Harak. Chunks of rock spewed everywhere, pelting Harak and several other Bawns.

Harak stood and retreated, patting himself down, clearly wondering if a bolt hit him. He grimaced when his hand touched his face. "You sun worshiper." Blood bubbled from his now-exposed charred skin, part of his beard and hair burned off.

Ali continued to point Sol in Harak's direction. "Now leave and let me be with my friend here."

Harak slowly shook his head. "It's forbidden to enter Starship *Tranquil* by word of the king and the laws binding that word."

"Don't throw that crap my way. You're here to kill me because you think you'll die because of me."

He hissed at her like a snake warding off a trespasser. He threw his hands out wide and waved for his men to follow him toward *Tranquil*. "Everyone guard the ship." He crossed his arms and dipped his head at Ali. "I honor the sword's power, but I do not honor the sword's wielder."

"That's apparent." Ali eyed the men standing in line. "Tell me, Harak, where is King Bilrak? If you are really worried about me stealing the ship, shouldn't you have brought the one who lays down the law?"

Harak ignored her. "We don't fear you, sun lover."

Daf pushed to a standing position. "All right, we should go."

Ali eased her grip around the hilt, the flame dissipating. She dipped her head at the Bawns. "I didn't intend to harm any of you." She turned and walked away, heading toward the elevator.

"Ali," came Harak. "Know this isn't over. There will be a time you do not have that sword with you. When that time comes, I'll end you."

Ali stiffened, doing everything in her power not to turn and throw the sword into Harak's stomach.

"Remember." Harak's voice rose higher. "You will die by my hands, and by my hands only. I will then place Sol back in its place where it belongs."

KODA

Starbase Matrona

Koda picked a shard of glass out of his forearm, wincing, his ears ringing from the concussion blast. "Are you all right?"

Devon stood, wiping dust and bits of concrete off of himself, his eyes on the burning structure across from the capitol building. "What happened?"

Koda plucked another piece of glass from his palm. He dropped it on the floor and wagged his head back and forth. "I don't know." He tugged his ear. The ringing persisted.

Payson walked from the torched building, covered with weapons. He had a rifle on his back, pistols on each hip, and his teeth were clenched on a dagger. He dragged a bulky man who wore fatigues similar to CJ's. Payson pulled out his gun and held the muzzle to the soldier's temple, the man's face covered in soot, his eyes closed, unconscious. Payson pulled the trigger.

Koda gasped and looked away. "It's Payson," he said, backing up, his boots crunching on broken glass. "How did he get to Sphere Eight so fast?"

"You got me."

Koda's heart beat hard, the back of his spine growing cold.

"There's no way we can get to the hoverstation and to Sphere One right now." Or ever, if Payson caught a glimpse of them.

Devon sidestepped a thin pile of glass and moved toward the back of the capitol building. "What do we do?"

Payson shifted his attention to Koda as if he'd sensed someone. He grinned and relaxed his fingers from the soldier's shirt, the dead man sliding down Payson's leg and rolling onto his back.

Payson spoke into a comm device on his shoulder and walked onto the street, making his way toward Koda, and pulling the dagger out of his smiling mouth. "Your uncle is dead," he shouted. "You're next."

Koda froze, his heart sinking to his knees. My uncle is dead? He shook his head, backpedaling toward Zim's office in the back. How could that be? Shae left the star system to go to his daughter on planet Eos. No way he died.

"Payson lies, Koda." Devon shook his head, taking cautious steps. "Don't believe him."

Koda dipped his head. "Yeah, I know." A strange sensation pulled at his gut. Maybe Payson was telling the truth this time. He flexed his abdomen, constricting the feeling, pushing away any thoughts that Fleet Admiral Shae Lutz kicked the bucket.

Payson stepped onto the sidewalk leading to the capitol building.

Koda flicked a glance over his shoulder at Devon. "Zim has to have a weapon somewhere."

Devon picked up his pace, turning and running into Zim's office.

Koda stood his ground, swallowing down an electric jolt his mind sent to his arms and legs, telling his body to run, to hide, to live for another day, but he couldn't. Running out of the door meant running through Payson. He needed to buy Devon some time to find a weapon if Zim had even stashed one.

He moved behind a wall, Payson now out of view. He crept next to the desk in the lobby and lowered into a crouch, facing the hallway, his body hidden.

Bells jingled and broken glass crunched under a boot, then another crunch carried across the office. Payson had entered.

Koda's heart raced, thinking up a plan, and when only one plan made sense, he squeezed his eyes shut, not wanting to go through with it. He had to keep Devon safe or buy him time to escape. He figured that when Payson walked down the hallway and passed the desk Koda hid behind, he'd jump him and wrestle the guy to the ground.

You better find a weapon by then, Devon.

"Yo, Koday! Yo, Koday-poo," said an amused Payson. "I can smell your fear. Don't hide. Come out, and I'll be nice and end your life quickly. It's the least I can do for a well-meaning politician."

Koda's chest tightened. Who was he kidding? He couldn't fend off Payson, an elite soldier who could probably take Koda down with his pinky.

Payson walked onward, the floor creaking under the weight of his body. The *phtah* sound of a gun echoed loudly. Koda ducked more in a start, and Payson grunted. Koda shifted and turned, looking behind him. Devon stood in Zim's doorway with a gun extended, a thin waft of smoke trailing upward from the muzzle.

Devon's mouth gaped open, his eyes focused on Payson, not that Koda could see the soldier, but from Devon's look, Koda knew who he stared at. Devon ducked inside Zim's office, undoubtedly crapping his pants in fear.

Another grunt from Payson and more crunching. "You got me. I wasn't paying attention." He laughed. "Don't worry, guys. It's not bad. Just a little blood."

Koda slowly peeked around the desk, noticing Payson grabbing his side, blood dripping from his hand. He took a wobbly step toward the exit, cringing, his face reddening. He twisted around and Koda lurched back behind the desk, hoping Payson didn't see him.

"That was a lucky shot, kid." Payson clapped his hands. "Stay here, okay? I'll get patched up and come back."

Stay, my ass, thought Koda. He glanced around the desk again. Payson limped out of the building and meandered across the street, the bullet in his side having an obvious effect on his leg.

Koda hurried to Devon and curled around the door frame. Devon stood against a wall, the gun in his hand, his breaths shaky.

"Is he gone?"

Koda nodded. "You saved us, buddy."

"He's coming back, and probably with his friends."

Koda put his palms out. "Not if we get out of here right now."

Devon nodded in quick succession. "I second that."

Moments later, they burst out of the building, their arms and legs pumping fast.

Koda pointed ahead. "Hoverstation. Let's get to Sphere One."

14

KODA

Starbase Matrona

Koda glanced behind him, the eerie sensation of Payson sticking a dagger in his back creeping up and down his spine.

He leaned against a hoverstation ticket counter, and after three attempts, the woman behind the counter gave up. His card didn't work.

The woman set the card on the reader a fourth time, waiting. "You look familiar." She glanced at the reader. "Two people to Sphere One, right?"

Koda took a glance behind him again and rapped his knuckles on the counter. "Yes, two, please." Devon stood by his side.

Besides a few lonely travelers, the hoverstation sat empty. Koda would easily glimpse the rabid killers—Payson and his crew—if they entered the building.

"Okay." The woman cleared her throat, sighing loudly. "I'm sorry. It's denied again."

Koda wanted to pound his fist into the counter but refrained like a good politician. He gritted his teeth, as beads of sweat formed on his forehead. "Try again."

The woman shook her head, her posture wilting as she stared at her holomonitor. "It won't work, sir. Sphere One is the military sector. Are you sure you have access?"

Koda pulled at his hair. "Yes."

She paused, tilting her head. "Why do you look so familiar?"

Koda shrugged. "I don't know." He tapped his finger on the counter, wanting to get this card working. "I know that Sphere One is the military sector, but that shouldn't restrict my access."

Devon rested his hand on Koda's back. "She's already tried it several—"

Koda put his finger up. "We're getting to Sphere One."

The woman handed Koda his card. "Denied."

A clang vibrated through the hoverstation, and a hum echoed off the walls. Koda spun around on full alert, his adrenaline spiking. A hovertrain stopped at a platform on the upper deck. He shook his head at his overly sensitive nerves. *Payson screwed me up.* Koda turned and crossed his arms over his chest. "Patch me through to your manager..." he took a quick glance at her name tag, "Sarah."

She gently bit her finger. "I know you from somewhere." She leaned on the counter. "You're an action vid star, right?"

Koda rolled his eyes. "How I wish, but no, I'm part of the governance, and I should have easy access to Sphere One without trouble. Now, your manager, please."

Sarah slowly nodded, though she didn't do as asked. "Well, maybe they are restricting access to everyone but military personnel today. You know, with all the chaos going on around the starbase."

Devon stepped forward. "How? The military doesn't have authorization over a Prime Overseer. The only person who has authority over an Overseer in the governance is Prime Director Zim Noki, and he publicly made an apology—"

Sarah backed away. "You're a Prime—"

"But," Koda interrupted Devon. "It doesn't mean Zim's being sincere. He's a known liar and may pull the covers over our eyes again like that Space Templar CJ guy said. He sent that Enlil fella a message, and that doesn't seem upstanding to me." He looked at the holostation's entrance across the station. "Zim may have restricted any access from people with Lutz in their name."

Sarah clutched her hands over her heart. "You're Koda Lutz, right? I have the biggest—" she cut herself off, blushing.

Koda walked around the counter, ignoring the star-struck crush in Sarah's eyes. He pressed a holobutton on the screen. He brought up a commlink to Sphere One, doing his best to get to someone in charge.

Sarah's hand rested gently on his upper back. "Excuse me, Prime Overseer. You don't—"

"This is an emergency." Koda didn't have time to argue. If Payson found him, he'd be good and dead, along with the two standing with him.

A young woman answered the com, her brown hair in a ponytail, her brown eyes staring back at Koda. "Star Guild Aviation and Flight Training, how can I help you?"

Koda stood tall. "My name is Koda Lutz, Prime Overseer to Sphere Nine. I need access to Sphere One, and now."

"Koda Lutz?" She bit her lower lip, eyeing a holomonitor near her and out of Koda's view. "Yes, here you are. I'm sorry, sir, but you're denied access."

Koda folded his arms across his chest. "Who denied me access?"

"Prime Director Zim Noki. He's cut off a few politicians and high military leaders."

"Well, get me access. This is an emergency."

The woman shifted in her seat. "I'm sorry, sir. I can't." The screen blipped off, going dark.

Koda's jaw dropped. He smacked the side of the HDC. "You piece of Guild."

"Don't," yelled Sarah, pulling Koda's arm away from the holocomp. "This isn't your property."

"Zim," said Devon. "That piece of Orion's snot."

Koda lowered his brows. "Yep, can't trust the big guy. Who knows what plan he concocted with blaring my uncle's innocence all over the vid channels?"

Devon nodded. "We can get back to Zim's office and change the orders. We'll get you access."

Koda's stomach felt as if about to rip apart. "With Payson on the loose and Zim screwing us over behind our backs, we have to get to Sphere One and stop the toxin from being released. We don't have time, nor is it safe to go back to Zim's office. Payson's most likely tearing it apart now, looking for us." Koda paused, slowing his pulse, and taking a deep breath, reverted to politician mode. He turned and faced Sarah.

"Toxin?" said Sarah, pulling back. "What do you mean?"

He grinned and shook his head, not wanting to rile the young lady. "It's just an expression we military and politicians use with each other. I assure you, there is no toxin on the starbase."

Koda put on the best, good-looking shine he could muster, standing straight, confident, bold. "Sarah, I see you work hard, and you want to help us out, but as you know, the card reader won't let you. I know you can manually print a ticket for us with a special family code that they give each employee. So, I want to make a deal with you..."

15

ZIM

Starbase Matrona

Sabra stood over Zim, a gun in hand. "Get up and keep going."

A blast shook the hallway and small pieces of ebb dust fell, slapping against the floor next to where Zim crouched.

Zim rubbed his chest. "How did they find us?"

"It's Payson. He can find anyone." Sabra grabbed him by the shirtsleeve and pulled. "Fear is the only thing standing between you and staying alive. If you want to live, stand up and follow me."

"All your friends are dead."

"Our guards are not dead, just a little discombobulated at the moment. Have faith. They are some of our elite Space Templars. They've seen and dealt with worse."

"They've taken on worse? Who?" To Zim, the only worse thing than Payson was Enlil, the Monarch.

Sabra waved her comment away. "Never mind."

Zim looked left and right. The hallway seemed to close in on him by the second, the way his insides felt. A bang echoed in the hall. Zim lurched to the side in a start, his shoulder hitting the wall. He covered his head with his hands. "I can't get up." He lay frozen on the floor in terror.

Sabra kicked him in the leg. "You must."

Zim grimaced, rubbing at his thigh and finally standing. "Why are you keeping me alive?"

She pushed him forward. "I told you. We have plans for you. So, move."

They rushed through a hallway in a building's basement in Sphere Eight, trying to get to Sphere One where they could take off and leave the starbase. Above them, blasts from Sabra's Space Templar Knights and the *ratatatat* of rapid gunfire pierced the air. The fight between the Templars and Payson's crew had carried on for more than ten minutes already, much too long for Zim's taste.

Zim grunted, hurrying down the hall and toward a door. "It doesn't make sense. They found us. Do you have a snitch on your team?"

"No, so stop your bellyaching." Sabra pushed him again. "My care, and my mission, is for your safe transport to planet Aurora where Enki awaits."

Zim's heart burned as anger rose in him. Sabra spoke nonsense. "How do you suggest we get there, woman? We can't even get out of this building, let alone to the docks."

"Yes, to the docks in Sphere One."

"Enlil will find us and hang us both."

Sabra laughed. "I'll make sure he hangs before us. Now, let's get going."

They reached the door as the building shuddered again. Sabra turned the handle. "Locked." She reared back and kicked it open. It flew off its hinges, and an underground hovercar parking garage was now before them. A concussion went off, and a car went flying in the air, spinning and landing on its hood. Fire licked from the passenger window, sending thick, black smoke toward the ceiling.

Zim fell to his knees. "Just...let's hide."

"My mission is to take you to Enki, and I'm not diverting." She grabbed his shirt and pulled him through the doorway and behind a pillar in the parking garage. Several clacks of gunfire reverberated off the walls, and chunks of ebb broke from the pillar, falling next to them.

Sabra shoved Zim further behind the pillar. "You move, you die."

She leaned her back against the ebb, her breaths heaving in and out. She clenched her jaw and lifted the plasma blaster in her hand. She counted under her breath, or maybe she was praying, Zim couldn't tell. She peeked around the corner, taking count. Zim did as well. They ducked back around.

One Space Templar lay dead next to a vehicle, a few of Payson's men dead nearby. Four of Payson's men hid behind pillars and hovercars.

"Did you see them?" she asked.

"Yeah, four."

She shook her head. "From the trajectory of the bullets in this pillar, there is a fifth over there." She nodded her head toward the east parking entrance.

"Yes, we go back inside, then."

She shook her head again. "No. I have an escape vehicle ready in here."

Zim squeezed his fingers into a fist, his knuckles going white. "If we go out there in the open, we're dead."

"No, you'll be dead." She closed her eyes, her lips moving, but no words came out. She opened them as if she had just calculated the perfect plan. Her eyes set, and her muscles tightened like a warrior ready to pounce. "Stay here and I'll be back."

Zim took a quick peek around the pillar. "What? Where are you going?" He quickly pulled his head back.

Several whir sounds from her plasma gun blared through the garage, followed by grunts and a few gasps. Someone gurgled as if choking on their own blood. He stole another glance.

Sabra crouched in front of a hovercar, her gun in hand. Three dead enemies were lying across from her on the floor, blood pooling on the concrete around them.

A guy leaped out from behind a nearby car, firing. She moved quickly as if calculating the enemy's actions. She jumped on the car's hood. His bullets sparked across the asphalt, and she littered him with several plasma bolts. His arms and legs flailed as he went into the air, landing lifelessly on his back.

"That's four," she shouted. "I know there's a fifth." She hopped off the car and whipped her head around to Zim, her face contorted in terror. She reached her hand out, yelling, "No." She pointed her weapon at Zim and fired.

Zim's heart skipped a beat, and he fell to the ground, getting as low as possible and slipping under her shots.

"Get behind the pillar," she yelled.

A sharp sensation grabbed at Zim's side and then another at his back. His legs spasmed as if out of his control, and he let out an involuntary scream. He flipped on his back as more agony tore through his body.

Cold metal touched between his eyes, and one of Payson's soldiers stood over him, blood seeping out of his neck. Zim turned his head, his eyes blurry, his vision doubled.

Sabra hurried his way, her eyes set on the man standing over Zim. She pulled the trigger again and again.

Payson's soldier took a step back and lost his grip on his gun, letting it fall to the ground, and bounce against Zim's leg. Sabra reached Zim and placed one more shot into Payson's soldier. Blood splattered, and he fell through the doorway into the basement she and Zim had come from.

Sabra fell to her knees, her hand coming down on Zim's chest, grasping his shirt. "You stupid, stupid man. Get up."

Zim shook his head, blood oozing out of his mouth and down his chin. He coughed and cringed as a pain swelled in his stomach. "I... can't...move."

"No, no." She shook her head, her eyes wide. "We'll get you patched up."

Zim's energy dimmed, and he gazed out at the parking garage. "I'm good...as dead." He spat out blood.

"Not on my watch." She bent down, picked him up, and threw him over her shoulders.

"Why do you need me?" begged Zim, wanting to die. The pain consumed him and the blood oozed from his body, making him weaker. He wouldn't live, no matter what medical magic Sabra and the Space Templars attempted.

"I won't fail my brother," she said, moving toward a hover vehicle. "You are our chance, Zim. Enki needs you for information, to set up Enlil, to prove once and for all to our father that Enlil needs to be cut from all money, from all military, and all ties to the family."

Zim tried to laugh. "Good luck...with...that."

His body bobbed up and down as Sabra walked, his limbs going numb.

"On Planet Aurora," Sabra told him, "they'd tap your brain, gathering memories from you. We'd send your memories to the Nibiru council where my father presides as king. It would be proof, and my father would have to act so his people and his council don't look down upon him. My father knows what's going on, but he hides it from the council. Enlil would finally be cut off from future business, from future dealings."

Zim grinned. "Dumb plan. Your...father knows...and will...always turn a blind...eye."

"You're not hearing what I'm saying. He wouldn't be able to anymore." Sabra opened the door to a large vehicle. She shoved Zim in the back seat where he lay motionless, his vision fading. He stared at the car's ceiling, wanting to go to sleep.

Sabra sat in the front and reached back, slapping his face. "Stay with me."

"Yeah." He slowly closed his eyes and let out a breath, wanting to go to sleep forever.

Another slap, this time harder. "Don't do that."

His eyes opened wide, his heart somehow beating faster.

She touched her wrist band. "Status report."

"Just a moment," a woman said over the wrist band. "Payson and his team have left the building."

"How many down?"

"One of our Templars, and seven of his elite."

"Make it twelve. I took out five down here. How many does that leave Payson?"

"Fourteen."

Sabra glanced around the parking lot. "Where is Naveya?"

"We don't know. She had the antidote. She couldn't get it to her target, Devon, so she left it with us. We're getting it coded into the Suficell Pods, just in case."

"Do we have eyes on Payson?" She started the hover vehicle, and Zim felt it lift off the ground. He turned his head toward her and reached out, mumbling something he couldn't understand himself.

She looked back at him as the woman on her wrist band comm replied, "No, ma'am. We think he's heading for Sphere One."

"The toxin." Sabra gently slapped Zim a few more times. "You never let it out of the airlocks, did you?"

Zim forced a grin, though his face did its best not to cooperate, his muscles numb, and his body weak. "I tricked...you."

Sabra palmed her forehead. "I missed a step." She sighed and tapped her wrist band. "Operator."

"Yes."

"Payson knows the toxin's location. Zim never ejected the toxin into space. Set everyone's new path to Sphere One. We cut him off. Out." Sabra pressed the accelerator, heading up a ramp and out of the parking lot, the streets empty of cars. Zim vibrated on the back seat, his vision narrowing as his eyelids became heavy. She turned a hard right, bringing the car to a stop at the side of the road.

The hovercar descended, and Zim watched her open the window and speak with someone in Space Templar fatigues. "Medic, I need immediate help. Get in and work on Zim."

A woman jumped in the passenger seat with a box in her hands. Her hair was disheveled, and her face covered in soot. She pulled out an injection gun and pressed it against Zim's shoulder. A shock went down his arm and spread across his chest and stomach.

"That will stop the bleeding," said the medic.

Sabra gave a nod, then sped off toward the hovercar tunnels that connected each Sphere. She glanced in her rear-view mirror, her eyes focusing on Zim. "You'll be fine." She lifted her gaze, looking beyond him and out the back window. She smiled. "We have several Space Templars in hover vehicles following us. Good." She winked at Zim. "We'll get Payson soon enough and get you healed."

Zim let out a soft laugh, the best he could force out. He knew he wouldn't live, and he didn't want to. He failed his Monarch on so many levels. "I'm...dying," he muttered.

The medic nodded, pressing something else he couldn't see against his chest. "He's lost too much blood. We're losing him."

Sabra slowed her vehicle and lowered her head. "We can't save him? Not at all?"

The medic shook her head. "I'm afraid not."

"I...told you." Zim stiffened and his body went cold. He closed his eyes, unable to keep them open no matter how hard he tried. He lifted his hand, and it fell just as his life left his body, his lungs pushing out his final breath.

16

KODA

Starbase Matrona

The hovertrain switched tracks, moving from the hovertrack leading to Sphere Nine to Sphere One.

Devon snorted. "I can't believe you asked her on a date for family passes."

Devon and Koda sat on the last seats in the back car. Other than them, the car was empty.

Koda smiled. "Let alone granting us access to a restricted Sphere." He leaned back, clasping his hands behind his neck. "I have my ways."

"It's that easy?"

"Sometimes." He glanced out of the window, seeing dozens of skyscrapers whizz by in a blur, something he remembered fondly as a child.

His father, Shae's brother, captained a vessel for the Star Guild fleet before his mysterious death. Koda was four years old when his father passed. Shortly after, Koda's mother became a hovertrain conductor. Many times, he sat on his mother's lap in the hovertrain driver's seat, watching the world go by, wondering where his dad went and why he left him. Shae then took over as the father, and did the best he could, visiting Koda often, playing with him, buying him toys, and roughing him up like a father did to toughen their sons.

He rested his head against the cold window, his mind shifting to the dangers at hand. He was running from Payson and his men while trying to uncover truths. The more crap he found on the Anunnaki, the easier it would be to free his people from those bastard's chains, but opening the airlocks and releasing the toxin into the cosmos came first. Perhaps a simple task. Quick, even.

He let out a sigh. In these times, simple never occurred. Only an hour ago, he thought Payson would end his life. He glanced at Devon, who settled his head in his hands, bouncing his knee up and down.

Koda put his hand on Devon's knee and gave it a friendly squeeze. "We can do this."

Devon's posture stiffened. "When we get to Sphere One, then what? We investigate the Starhawk Transports?"

"Exactly, but after we check the airlocks first. When we find the toxin barrels, we release the barrels into space. That's priority one."

"Then what? We just search for information?"

"We'll hang around Sphere One and dig for whatever we can find. Maybe we'll find the location of Destination "N" or other crap the Anunnaki don't want us to see." Koda didn't know what he was looking for, per se, but maybe an empty Starhawk would grant him more information when he snuck inside and pulled up the data on the monitors.

He gulped down apprehension. What if pilots, perchance Anunnaki, occupied the Starhawks?

Devon rubbed his hands on his pants, his breathing shaky and his movements interrupting Koda's thoughts.

"Something on your mind that you're not telling me?" asked Koda.

Devon leaned forward. "I should have realized. I'm sorry, Koda. We need to get off the train at the next Sphere Nine stop."

"Why would we do that?"

"Payson and his team."

"We're on a hovertrain. We'll get there before him."

Devon shook his head. "I don't think we can stop him and his gang no matter what we do or what we find."

"If you need to get off at the next stop, I understand."

"It's not that, really. It's…" he let out an exasperated breath. "Your uncle should have killed Payson while they were in their cells."

Koda shot Devon a look. "Yeah, I know, but killing prisoners is against Star Guild law, and as the head of Star Guild, my uncle couldn't and wouldn't end their lives."

"It would have been smart to make an exception." Devon curled forward more, his forehead against his fist. He squeezed his eyes shut, agitated.

Koda put his arm around Devon's shoulders, calming his friend. "We're fine. Are you worried about the toxin?"

Devon abruptly sat tall. "I painted it."

Koda gazed blankly at Devon, wondering what drug someone slipped into his drink.

"Painted it?"

"Sometimes I paint things that come true, and I painted the poison unleashed on all of us. Many dead, more dying, and it felt like all of Matrona fell ill."

"I'm not following. You painted something?"

"Remember when I told you I had another skill besides hacking holocomputers?"

Koda nodded.

"Well, that's my skill. You asked me what I'm good at—my specialty —and that's it."

"Again, I'm not following. What's your skill?"

Devon looked left and right as if searching for someone hiding in the car. When he didn't see anyone, he leaned his head back against the wall. "I'm Robert Rose."

Koda hesitated for a moment, then chuckled. "You ought to be a politician. You're good at keeping a straight face."

"I'm not lying. I'm serious. Well, actually, I'm Robert, and another person is Rose. Rose taught me how to find my talent and how to follow my intuition. When I combine the two—talent and intuition—I'm fantastic. I predict things in my paintings."

Koda put his hands up for Devon to stop. "Whoa. Slow down. You're talking nonsense—"

"No, I'm not. I'm Robert, and Rose is...well, I told you who she is a while ago. I can prove I'm the painter, though."

Koda leaned away and gave Devon an odd look. "Yeah, I'd like to see that." The attack, Payson almost killing them in the capitol building, and the chaos happening all around rattled Koda's brain. Many artists claimed the Robert Rose name and were proved liars soon after. Devon had lost his mind.

"There." Devon pointed at a pad and paper attached to a wall next to a hovertrain door. He walked to the door and swiped the items off the wall. He plopped down on the seat. "What do you want me to draw?" Devon held the pen's tip over the paper.

"I don't know." Koda didn't care. He wanted this nonsense to stop.

"What's your favorite Robert Rose?"

Koda rolled his eyes. "Uh, Star Fire, I guess."

"Star Fire? That's one I blazed with color. I don't have paints with me, just this pen."

Oh, brother. "Then I guess you can't draw it."

"Without color is fine." Devon drew a torus-shaped nebula. "This is a butterfly nebula. Don't ask me how I know, 'cause I wouldn't be able to answer that." His strokes flowed quickly, nearly flawless. "I see it like I'm staring right at it in space. To me, it's like two nebulae crashing into each other." He drew faster. "I see it on the page before I finish. It's almost like I'm tracing, really." Moving the pen over the paper, he composed a ship flying toward the nebula. Then another ship, and another.

Finishing, he let his hand fall to the side and picked up the paper. He held it in front of Koda. "Those are Space Templar starships. They are more cylindrical and aren't as big as ours. Here, just like the Star Fire painting you liked, I portrayed the ships coming to save us." He pulled the paper into his lap and shaded in the nebula.

Koda caught his breath. "Okay, stop." He eyed Devon and then the paper. "What the Guild?"

The resemblance was uncanny. Devon had drawn an exact copy of Star Fire.

Devon lifted the pen slightly off the paper. "I know. It's poor quality, but I can't make it fiery like I did in the original."

"Put that pen and paper away. Don't let anyone see it." Koda looked around. Robert Rose had a certain style, one that nobody could duplicate correctly, or so the art critics said for years. Many artists made attempts, and every time the experts caught the lie.

Koda blinked rapidly, not believing what he just witnessed. He slapped his face gently, running his hands over his eyes and slowly down to his chin. "You're Guild'n kidding me, right?" He took another glimpse at the drawing. "You're him? Who...how..." Koda shook his head back and forth like a wet dog. "This is insane. You're only a kid. What the—"

"I'm not that much younger than you. I'm not a kid."

"Well, you look like a kid, and you're what, eight years younger than me? You're a kid in my book." He threw his hands up. "How can I be sitting next to the most talked about artist in all of Matrona? You're Matrona's biggest mystery."

He looked Devon up and down. Maybe Devon lied, maybe not, but who knew. Weirder things happened, like the Anunnaki invasion or finding out he'd grown up and lived his entire life as a slave in a slave race.

"I'm a mystery because I keep it that way. Again, I'm Robert and someone else is Rose. Rose said they would hunt and kill me for what I put in my art. It's all about truth. Many people resonate with my paintings, but Zim would have me killed."

"Who is Rose?"

"I can't say."

"Why?"

Devon's expression softened. "She won't let me. I'm not even supposed to say who I am."

"Your paintings talk about the future. How is that possible? If your paintings warn us about future events, why is it you don't know what's happening now? I mean, you didn't know we were a slave race until you figured it out via hacking into Zim's database."

Devon tapped the pen against his lips. "How do I answer that?" He looked off. "What you say is true. I didn't know what was really happening to us until I hacked Zim's holocomp. When I'd paint, all I'd get were these weird visions, and then I'd paint them. It's that simple. The media talked about it before on the news channels, though they didn't get it right. They didn't understand my paintings, other than they thought they were unique and original."

"A month ago, maybe longer, I can't remember, you painted the next line of Overseers, including me. I thought that was a hoax or a damn good guess."

"Not a hoax, but I figured that's what people would say. I did my best. I had someone put that painting in the Sphere Six museum, cover it up in a white tarp, and unveil it the moment the elections ended. People thought I had painted it after I knew who won and switched the paintings, but how could I paint something like that so quickly?"

Koda shifted in his seat. "I'm in your painting. That was weird."

"I painted you because you'll be the best politician this starbase has ever had."

Koda leaned back, crossing his arms, his lips turning up. His ego liked the idea, though he doubted Devon. "Well, cool. What else did you predict?"

Devon bit on the end of the pen, looking away as he remembered his predictions. "I painted Comet Vega coming so close to Matrona and Eos, and I made a good depiction of everyone's panicked reactions." He gave a short laugh. "I created that painting to let people know they'd be fine, the comet would miss us." He shook his head. "But before Vega passed, the media played it out like it would hit us and everyone would perish."

Koda tapped his head, pulling up another prediction. "There's the kidnapped woman one. You painted exactly where the kidnappers hid her, and that's where the authorities found her alive."

"There's more," said Devon. "Such as a recent one where people die from a toxin released all over Matrona."

"Is there any way we can change that prophecy?"

Devon shrugged.

Sphere One's stations came into view. Koda stood, not remembering passing Sphere Nine's last hovertrain stop. Regardless, he hoped his need to be a good politician and uncover the truth wouldn't get Devon killed.

Devon walked toward the car's exit as the hovertrain slowed. "Almost time to get off."

Koda looked at his hands. "Maybe we'll stop the toxin."

Devon shook his head. "It's a big hope, but I'm rarely wrong."

The train stopped, and the doors opened. Koda took a step onto the platform, impatient to get to the airlocks. "But you have been wrong, and that's what we can hope for."

17

SHAE

Starbase Matrona

Shae sat in his parked Starjumper, the ship still warm from landing in Sphere One's bay only moments ago.

"Where am I meeting you?" he asked Louise over the commlink.

"We're in pursuit of Payson and have just entered Sphere Eight, soon to be in Sphere Nine where we think he's heading."

"Good." Shae leaned into the mic. "Do you have my gear?"

"Yes, Marine helmet and rifle. We don't have your fatigues."

Shae glanced at his jumper suit, his sidearms at his hip. "That's fine. I'm heading out. Exact location?"

"Head to Sphere Nine, Cornell Park. We'll be there soon."

"Got it." He turned off the comm and stepped out of the Starjumper. He stopped and bent over, his hands on his knees. He shook his head as a memory jostled loose from the back of his mind.

He was standing in front of his wife. She wore a beautiful white gown and headdress, tears welling in her eyes. He smiled gently and sweetly. "I do."

"You may kiss the bride," said a minister.

He leaned forward, pressing his lips against hers. They were soft, young, and they tasted like a fragrant rose. He slowly pulled away and stared into her eyes, mouthing, "I love you." She wiped a tear and spoke the same words back.

Shae lurched away, wrapping his fingers on a handhold on the exterior of the craft. He kept his balance and looked around. His eyes swept over Sphere One's docking bay, feeling Helen's touch still on his lips, her hands lightly pressing against his face, the love he felt for her opening wide in his heart.

He shook his head, blinking several times to bring himself back to his senses. "I better get going. No time for memories." Regardless, he smiled, feeling Helen's presence over him like a soft pillow he could snuggle with for the rest of his life.

He ran toward Sphere One's hovertrain station. He'd take a private train and tell the conductor to take the train as fast as it could go. He'd reach Sphere Nine in no time.

He gave a wave and a nod to the train conductor, and hopped onto Sphere Nine's hoverstation platform, exiting the hovertrain. His boots echoed across the lobby as he ran toward the exit, the hoverstation like a ghost town. Across the street he spotted Louise, her blonde hair in a bun and dressed in Brigantia Guard gray and blue mesh Marine fatigues.

He rushed to her, his breath coming fast. Louise eyed him, nodding. Manning stood by her side, his gun pointing outward, his eye peering through the scope, looking for Payson and his men.

Several Guards littered the area, moving slowly, some crouching behind benches, statues, and large cement trash cans that were scattered throughout the park. Others waited behind large trees, or lines of bushes, ready to pick off Payson if he showed himself.

Shae reached Louise and gave Manning a nod. "What's the status?"

Louise flicked her head to the side. A soldier hurried to Shae, a combat helmet in hand, along with a rifle. Shae shoved the helmet over his head and shouldered the weapon.

"Chronometer, sir," said the soldier, handing him a wrist band.

Shae nodded. "Thank you." He slipped it over his wrist and tightened it.

Louise glared through binoculars, surveying the area. "We've not seen Payson, but we have Brigantia, Taranis, and Matrona Guards in every Sphere searching for the lousy piece of ebb-trash. We've—" She thrust her finger to her ear, listening intently to someone speaking. She nodded. "Admiral, I think you should hear this."

"What channel?" asked Shae.

"The ISA, channel zero-one-one."

"All right." Shae tapped on his helmet, and his visor lowered. "Comm channels," he said. A holographic image of a radio dial appeared, highlighting his face green. "Channel zero-one-one." The dial adjusted, and the visor rose. He rested his hand on his rifle and crouched next to a wide lamp post at the park's edge, a tree's branches casting a shadow over him. "This is Fleet Admiral Shae Lutz. Who do I have on the comm?"

"Blythe Parker, Internal Security, ISA agent."

"Great. What do you have for me?"

"I have Payson and his men on a holovid. They bypassed a security system and broke into a grocery complex on the Sphere Nine and Sphere One junction. They are eating mushrooms from the fresh food section."

Shae's eyebrows squished together. Did he just hear that correctly? "They're eating...mushrooms?"

"Yes, and Payson seems injured. He's limping. Someone is stitching his side, and it looks like one of his men performed minor surgery on him, but I can't confirm that."

"Interesting." Maybe someone shot Payson, but it wouldn't surprise him if these elite warriors healed incredibly fast.

Shae glanced over his shoulder. Dozens of Brigantia guards were behind him, scanning the area, taking slow steps, some passing him by, all looking for Payson. Apparently, this woman from ISA had found the bastard.

"And, sir," said the agent, "they don't seem to know or care that you're on the way."

"Understood." That didn't surprise Shae. Payson and his elite soldiers didn't seem to have a care in the world if they lived or died.

Shae rubbed his eyes and yawned. He needed sleep, probably like the rest of the surrounding soldiers. He took a few steps forward and crouched next to a stone statue of old Prime Director, Vlamus Shims, someone he never met. The eight-foot Prime Director ruled Starbase Matrona years before the Anunnaki stole Shae from Earth. He eyed the street sign across the way. "Blythe, are you still with me?"

"Yes, sir," came the woman. "I'm here until the operation is over."

"We're near Columbia Street. Where's Payson's exact location?"

"Sphere One Junction Grocery, 117 Exeter Way."

"How far is that from here?"

"Exactly nine blocks south, sir."

"Patch that into my chronometer."

"Done."

Shae tapped on his wristband, and a holographic image of a map pulled up. He noted the streets, the back alleys, and faster routes to the store. Grabbing all the information he needed and storing it in the back of his brain, he deactivated the map. He motioned to his men, pointing to the south. With his rifle forward, he moved quickly through the park, his men and women picking up speed and spreading out around him.

He switched comm channels to Louise. "Louise, did you hear Payson's location?"

"Affirmative," she said. "I've already sent the information to the Marines in the other Spheres. They're on their way."

They moved quickly through Sphere Nine. Passing through the tunnel into Sphere One, he noticed the military station that granted access in and out of this Military Sphere smoldering and in shreds. A few guards lay on their stomachs or sides, smoke streaming off of them, dead. Bullet holes dotted the military station and charred steel hung from the structure, burnt to hell.

They hurried quickly past the station and out of the tunnel to a building marked Military Complex for Starfighter Design, Aerospace

Corp. He leaned his back against its ebb wall. The lamp mounted on the building near him was flickering.

The ISA agent clicked on the line. "Incoming, sir."

Shae dove, yelling, "Down, down." His shoulder hit the ebb floor first, and he rolled, keeping his rifle off the ground. He looked up to see everyone hitting the ground, some rolling away, others lying face down, covering their heads.

He waited.

There was nothing. No explosion. No bullets. Only silence.

Louise lay face down across from him, her hands out, mouthing, "What the Guild?"

Shae touched his earpiece. "What did you see, agent?"

"Eight hovercars en route to your location."

Shae rolled his eyes. Maybe the sleep got to this woman too. "Next time say that. Incoming is a Guild damn bomb thrown our way, gunfire, or any other projectile. You got me looking like a fool in front of my men and women."

"My apologies, sir. They're almost to your location."

Shae wanted to squeeze the ISA's agent's throat. "Copy."

A humming sound of approaching hover vehicles echoed in the distance. He tapped his ear. "Are these friendlies?"

"The cars are unmarked."

Great.

Shae stood and raced across the street to a thick, concrete garbage can on a sidewalk. "Everyone find cover. We have unknowns in hovercars heading our way."

His troops spread out, crouching behind trees, lampposts, and smaller buildings lining the street, their guns aimed at the incoming vehicles.

"Shae," said Louise, approaching his position, "got word that the Matrona Guard are on their way, and the rest of the Taranis and Brigantia Guard are coming." She went to her stomach, one eye looking through her rifle scope.

"Good." Shae eyed the hover vehicles. They slowed as they came closer.

"Sir," said the ISA agent. "Payson is back on the move."

"Where is he headed?"

"Looks like he's headed your way. He may have detected you."

"ETA?"

"Ten minutes at most, sir."

"Copy." He glared at Louise. "Did you get all of that?"

Louise held her position, her eyes trained on the vehicles. "Affirmative."

The hovercars stopped and descended at the far side of another park across from Shae. He and his team advanced forward, taking cover behind hovercars parked on the side of the street, some troops moving to shrubs and trees on the park's edge, one crouching alongside the park's sign, Menlow Park.

Shae eyed the potential targets, now only a stone's throw away. Some were four-seaters, and others hovervans, and all were black with tinted windows. The lead car's back door opened. A man wearing fatigues that seemed to meld into the surrounding environment stepped out, his hands up. "We mean you no harm. We are the Space Templars, here to stop Payson." He kept his hands up as he waited for a response.

"Manning, bring Team Ten with you, and follow me," ordered Louise. She slowly rose from her position, her weapon pointed at the man. He cautiously approached, moving toward the middle of the park. Louise slowed. "Keep your hands up."

Shae crept closer, finding another ebb statue of an old Prime Director as cover. He wanted to kick it over for principle's sake. He aimed his rifle at the vehicles just in case someone got a little fancy.

"Yes, ma'am," said the man, making his way to her. "My name is CJ."

"Get on the ground, face down, CJ," Louise instructed.

CJ got on one knee, then the other, and laid on his stomach and chest. Louise patted him down. "Slowly roll to your back, hands still in the air." He did. Louise patted him more. "Who else is in the vehicles?"

"Sabra and the Space Templars."

"Executive Officer Louise Stripe of Starship Brigantia," said a woman emerging from one of the hovercars, her hands up. "Greetings, my friends. My name is Sabra." She stood behind her car, her shoulders and head just above the roof, her arms still in the air.

Shae's eyes went wide, and he imagined the rest of the squad's eyes did as well. The woman was a giant. She wore a white outfit, tight like a jumpsuit. She smiled, her face calm, and her features were gorgeous like a beautiful flower inviting Shae to take a sniff.

"May I walk your way safely?" Sabra asked.

Louise stood, her foot on CJ's chest, her rifle pointed at the guy's head. "You may, but any wrong move, and you'll have fifty bullets in you before you can blink."

"Understood." Sabra moved around the car. She carried herself like a queen, her strides nimble and fluid, almost taking Shae's breath away. She stopped several meters from Louise and gave her a nod. "I'm Sabra of the Space Templars. We're here to help you." She eyed the entire squad, landing on Shae last, and dipped her head his way. Sabra continued, "Payson is closing in on this location. We have parked our hovercars in between you and his approaching team to act as a shield from his fire."

Louise flicked a glance at Shae. He nodded, something deep down telling him to trust this woman. He didn't know what overcame him, perchance the glow that came off of her, or the fact that good exuded from her like aroma from a freshly baked pie.

Shae lifted his chin high. "Place your men and women where you need them. We'll take up positions and wait."

Sabra put her hands together in a prayer position and bowed. "Thank you for trusting us. We'll take action now."

The doors to the vehicles opened, and Space Templars poured out. They wore fatigues like Shae had never seen, changing colors into whatever they were near. They held weapons thicker and shorter than Shae's and raced toward buildings on each side of the park.

Shae's jaw dropped when they climbed the walls, their gloves suctioning to the buildings like spiders. Their clothes turned dark gray, mirroring the walls as they climbed. Some made it halfway up, where they clung to the walls, waiting, their guns aimed at the ground while their other hand on the building seemed to glue them in place. Others scaled higher, crawling onto the top of the buildings, and taking up positions.

Sabra walked to Louise and stood next to her. Shae hurried their way as he searched for any sign of Payson coming down one of the many streets.

"Can I get up?" said a man's voice.

Shae glanced down. Louise's foot remained planted like a tree on CJ's chest. She stepped back.

"Thank you." CJ stood and bowed, then ran across the street at incredible speed. Reaching the building, he scrambled to the top in a matter of minutes.

Sabra folded her hands in front of her. "Payson will be here soon. Understand that he and his team have a highly developed intuition factor, something we Space Templars call the Sight. They already know we're here, and since they haven't changed their course, we can assume they intend to fight."

"Good," replied Louise. "I owe him a bullet to his head."

Sabra bowed again. "Perhaps you do." She smiled. "Until then." She turned and ran toward the building CJ scaled and climbed up and over the top edge.

"Shae, I've never read about Space Templars climbing like that. Never in any fairy tales or myths."

"As long as they're on our side, they can flap their arms and fly for all I care."

"Ditto." Louise touched her comm device on her shoulder, sliding her finger across it to broadcast to all Marines. "Everyone listen up. We have Payson on his way, and he means to fight. Make sure your shots are true. Find cover and shoot to kill."

"The Matrona Guard will most likely arrive behind Payson." Shae backed up toward a tree. "We'll surround him. I don't think he'll be able to get out of this one."

Louise frowned as she moved behind a statue. "Don't be so sure."

"We have two men heading toward the airlocks. Potential danger, maybe players in Payson's crew," said the ISA agent over Shae's com.

Shae jerked back, almost forgetting about her. "Could they be civilians?"

"I don't know. One looks familiar, but the other one doesn't. My guess is they're from Payson's crew. No one else would be up at this hour, and they look alert. They seem to be looking for something."

Shae eyed a dozen Marines and called them over. "Head to the airlocks, we have possible targets and—"

The ISA agent interrupted. "They are opening an airlock room now."

Shit. "Which airlock room?"

"Eighteen."

Shae pointed to the Marines he chose. "Go now. Airlock eighteen. I'm going with you."

Louise nodded. "Admiral, stay in communication."

"You bet."

Shae and his team raced down the block opposite the coming fight. A shot rang across the Sphere, then another. Shae and his team rounded a building as another shot pierced the air behind them.

Payson's team had arrived.

18

ALI

Dirn Garum, Eos

Thun and Chan stood by Ali's side in front of Starship *Tranquil*, the same place she nearly died hours ago.

Chan cupped his hands in front of him. "I heard you had some difficulty the last time you were here?" He turned his attention toward her. "Is that why it was hard for us to convince you to come?"

After the incident with Harak, Ali and Daf made their way up top to Dirn Garum, and into Daf's hut. There, Ali hid out with Sol by her side, waiting for Harak to locate them and attack. He never came. Thun and Chan arrived instead, pleading for Ali to take her first steps inside *Tranquil*. "You're one of the Chosen Ones," Chan said. "You're supposed to lead these people."

But Harak wanted to kill her, and probably for good reason since he believed the Chosen One would set in motion Thun's or his death.

Ali glared at Thun. "My dad mentioned that Harak believes either you or he will die because of me."

Thun straightened his lips, his demeanor more serious than usual. "Yes, my father showed your father the book of prophecies, the *Bawn Seer*. Harak has read it, just as I. He thinks you're the outsider, the sun lover that will carry out either my death or his.

Truthfully, he couldn't care less if I died, but one of us dying isn't exactly what the book says. It speaks about a death in royalty, and that can be any one of the royal line. This includes cousins, their husbands and wives, their children, brothers, or sisters. It could mean a metaphorical death, too. Once we free ourselves from this mountain, will we continue to rule as we did before? Most likely not."

"Then why does he think the death means either you or him?"

"He doesn't agree with the metaphor and doesn't consider cousins direct royalty. Me, our father, our mother, and he are direct. To him, the gods and goddess protect our mother and father above all else. But the book of prophecy isn't clear what royalty means."

"Well, then I think your brother needs a new head screwed on. He's deciding without proof. That jerk tried to kill Daf and me. If it wasn't for Sol," she held up her sword, "we'd be dead."

Thun gave a hearty laugh. "But you defended yourself. Regardless of how much Harak dislikes you, he now respects you a little more. Those who evade death with bravery are revered here. Harak, despite his actions and belief that he's correct about the prophecy, no doubt places you a notch higher than he did a few hours ago." He clapped. "Congratulations."

Ali rolled her eyes. If she didn't have Sol, she would be in the grave, which seemed to go over Thun's big head. She sheathed Sol. "All you Bawns want to do is fight, to make you feel better about yourselves. To top it off, you want war with the Anunnaki." She gritted her teeth. "Do you know how stupid and crazy that idea is?"

Thun grunted, his face reddening. "Do not call my race stupid." His eyes dropped to Sol, and his expression softened. "It's our destiny, our birthright to let the Anunnaki know that they can't best the Bawns. Karma will pay them back three-fold."

Ali let out a sigh, shaking her head. She couldn't wait any longer. A weapon of mass destruction was headed toward her friends on *Sirona*, even if she had to take the damn Bawn along with her.

She took several steps toward *Tranquil*. The ship hummed and a platform descended from under the bridge. She waved for her companions to follow. "Let's go." If they insisted on joining her, then she didn't want them to hold her up.

The platform raised shortly after they stepped onto it. Chan placed his hands in his robe sleeves. "What do you think?"

Ali glanced up as the platform continued to ascend. The bridge's ceiling brightened with an inner glow. "I think it's a ship."

Reaching the bridge, the platform stopped, clicking in place. Ali's eyes about bulged out of her skull. The bridge radiated with an immaculate soft shine. With a vidscreen circling half the area, and stations spread throughout, it looked very advanced. Unlike Star Guild's bridges, this one had space. The captain and XO seats looked comfortable, and the nav station was long and wide with buttons blinking and monitors streaming data.

A chime sounded, and the walls abruptly hummed. A deeper light glowed from the ceiling, penetrating the bridge. A vibration went up Ali's body and calmness took over, along with a thought saying *welcome*.

She paused and pursed her lips. Where did that thought come from? She walked to the captain's chair and plopped down onto it. Perhaps she needed to give this captain idea a shot. It felt right. She had led a team before, albeit just a team of misfit ebb miners, but she led, nonetheless. She couldn't wait any longer. She had to get this ship off the ground and to *Sirona*.

She rubbed the armrest. "When do we get this thing off the ground?"

Thun grunted. "This is where you will see why Sol and your bloodline are so important."

Ali instinctively moved her hand to Sol's hilt and felt the gentle energy it gave off and the confidence it brewed through every cell in her body. She sat more upright.

Thun rested his hand on a round knob on Ali's chair. A hiss and the floor between the captain's chair and the XO chair opened up. A stone emerged and rose.

Ali leaned away. "What's that?"

Thun motioned toward it, a grin creeping on his face, his dirty beard and thick eyebrows moving. "It's for Sol. Please insert the sword."

She stood and took a few paces forward, seeing an opening the size of the sword's shaft at the stone's apex. "You want me to place my sword in there?"

Chan nodded, and Thun grunted again.

A part of her didn't want to let go of Sol, her protector. Other than Harak and his gang, the Bawns seemed to respect it and respect her because of it. She didn't want to take the chance of losing such a vital item. "Are you sure? I think it's good by my side."

Thun shook his head. "It's how you activate Starship *Tranquil*."

Chan patted the stone. "It's safe. Trust me."

"All right." Ali unsheathed her sword and slowly slid it into the stone.

The ship vibrated, and the bridge's walls and ceiling grew brighter. The vidscreen blinked on, displaying the cavern, along with hundreds of military vehicles dotting the area.

Thun let out a happy yelp as if he'd been waiting for this moment his entire life. He clapped his hands together, letting his axe fall to the floor. "You did it, Ali." His expression shifted, his face becoming stern as if he'd caught himself showing too much joy. He looked away, wiping a tear from his eye with his thick sleeve.

"Now what?" asked Ali.

They looked at her blankly.

Ali puffed out her lower lip. "That's it? It's ready to fly?"

Thun and Chan glanced at one another. They both shrugged.

Ali lifted her hands in the air. "You're looking at me like I should know something."

Chan brought a fist to his lip and cleared his throat. He took another look at Thun then shifted his focus to Ali. "We are wondering if you hear anything."

Ali looked around, listening for something. She didn't hear anything except the slight purr from the engines. "The engines are quiet."

Thun rested his palm on the stone. "That's not what I'm looking for. Now, what do you hear?"

Ali lifted her shoulders and dropped them. "I don't know. You two breathing? How about you clue me in?"

"Just listen. I mean, really listen," said Chan.

Ali wanted to get this ride into the air and get to *Sirona*. Screw this listening crap. She shook her head. "I hear nothing peculiar."

Thun's shoulders slumped. "According to our legend and the *Bawn Seer*, the one who wields Sol and is of the royal bloodline can hear Starship *Tranquil* speak."

Ali leaned her head back, her mouth open. "That's what I was listening for? A ship talking?" Bawns obviously don't take many rides on ships. Ships don't talk.

Unless...

Ali took a seat in the captain's chair. "Does this ship have artificial intelligence?"

"In a way, yes. This ship is a biological entity, and only three exist in the entire galaxy. *Tranquil* has a brain and controls the ship like we control our bodies," explained Chan. "It's part of the Space Templar technology, and Space Templar lore suggests these ships speak, though telepathically. Until now, I never questioned the idea."

A brain on a ship? A ship as a biological entity? Pure fairy tale, just like magic wands and dragons in mythological stories. Her two new friends needed to understand the difference between make-believe and reality.

Thun slapped Chan's lower leg. "Let's inspect the rest of the ship. Then we can try to fly this thing."

Ali held down a smile. "Yes, let's get this off the ground and into the air." The sooner they flew, the better. "How do we get this vessel out of here?"

Thun walked toward the bridge's exit, which led to a corridor. "According to legend, once this ship lifts off the ground, the rock walls inside this cavern open, then close once *Tranquil* disembarks from the mountain."

Ali tightened her lips. "I don't know about trusting these legends." Then again, they got this craft in the cavern somehow.

"Our legends say the bloodline can lift Sol from the statue," mentioned Thun. "You did just that. Hence, our legend was correct. This legend will be correct, too."

Tell them all to leave, said a voice.

Ali jerked in her seat, the back of her head hitting the soft padding. She rubbed the back of her neck. "What was that?"

Chan took a step toward her, his eyes wrinkled in worry. "What was what?"

Thun stood straighter and marched toward Ali. "You heard *Tranquil*, didn't you?" He licked his lips, bobbing his head up and down.

Tell them to leave, Ali.

Ali glanced at the sword, then lifted her eyes to Chan. "You must go. Take Thun with you."

Thun widened his stance and rested his axe on his shoulder. "No."

Chan crouched slightly and placed his hand on Thun's back. "She is the Sol carrier. We do as she bids."

Thun pushed Chan's hand away. "I'm not a fan of my brother, Harak, but I suspect he is correct when he said Ali was here last night to steal the ship. I can sense her goodwill, but this ship doesn't leave without us Bawns onboard."

Get them to leave. You must be alone and out of distraction's way.

Ali dismissed his argument, although true. "Guys, you got to go."

Thun shook his head, creasing his brows. "She will take *Tranquil* to free her friends on the other starship and leave us here."

Chan dipped his head. "According to your legends, the Chosen One is also the captain of this ship. In that case, this is her ship."

Thun's face hardened. He paced back and forth, his axe in his hands. He halted. "Fine." He pounded his palm on his axe's handle. "I'll leave you on the ship if you promise not to fly *Tranquil* out of Mount Gabriel unless my men and women are on board."

Let them leave, Ali, came the voice again, soft and hypnotic.

Ali leaned forward, pushing a strand of hair behind her ear. "Guys, I don't even know how to fly this, so getting out of here is the least of my concerns. My first concern is the voice I hear in my head."

Chan folded his hands inside his sleeves again. "So, you hear it."

Thun wiggled his finger at Ali while looking at Chan. "She's not lying. I can tell she's not lying. The prophecies and legends continue to astound me." He walked forward, halting in front of her. He placed his hands on his knees and looked up into her eyes. "What's the voice saying?

"Like I said before, it's saying for you two to leave the starship."

Thun slowly stood, pushing air between his teeth. "I don't understand. The lore says that we are part of the Chosen One's team, her crew. So why are we being told to leave?"

Chan went to his knees, getting on the Bawn's level. "Right now, we're in Ali's way. Perhaps we need to leave her alone for *Tranquil* to train her. Let's give her space." Chan stood and bowed, his hands in prayer position at his chest. He walked toward the platform that brought them onto the bridge. He motioned for Thun to follow.

Thun lowered his head, his chin practically touching his chest, and walked reluctantly to the platform. Thun stood firm as the platform clicked loudly and descended. They disappeared from view, and minutes later, the platform returned empty, locking in place.

You are of the bloodline, came *Tranquil's* voice. *But not of the temperament to fly me...yet.*

Ali dropped her hands in her lap. "The temperament?" I have to get this thing into the air now.

I'm not a thing, I'm Tranquil. Thank you.

Ali gasped, her muscles tightening. "I see. So, you can hear my thoughts just like I can hear yours?"

Yes.

"So, why can't I fly you then?"

In order for you to operate me to your potential, you must learn that being right or wrong isn't the basis of life.

That made no sense. Why would the ship bring something like that up? "And your meaning?"

You are challenged in life with the urge to always be right, which you are...often, and that's because you have an aptitude for acute observation and an intellect for analyzing things quickly.

If someone has a differing opinion or a different way of doing things, it doesn't mean they are wrong. They simply do it differently and in their own way. In this subtle way, you are inclined to taking the Bawns away from their destiny because it doesn't benefit your current belief structure—that Starship Sirona won't survive if the Bawns come along with you.

It's best to take other's greatest assets and use them for the benefit of all, rather than looking at their faults. You can use the Bawn's assets in order to successfully fulfill your wish to save your people. Do you follow?

"How do you know this about me?"

I have an expansive consciousness. I see beyond what borders me, and I send my consciousness through the soil, the roots, and into the air. I've been watching you mine on Eos for a long time. That's why you have always come near me and have been drawn to Mount Gabriel, my home. I've been calling you, watching you, and I'm the reason you felt that pull.

"Look, I just want to get my people to safety and get home to Earth with my dad. It's simple, really."

You will. In time. But you need to be a good, worthy leader. You are of the bloodline, yes. You are chosen, yes. Your willingness is lacking.

"It chose me. I didn't choose it."

Leaders don't choose to be victims and live in victimhood, which is what you're doing at the moment. Change that. Realize that you are responsible for everything you do in life, including being a Chosen One.

"Uh...right." Ali couldn't believe the ship was lecturing her.

To be a good leader, you want those around you to follow you through the worst situations, no matter what. Not because they are called by destiny to do so, but because they love you beyond their own mortal life. The best leaders are those whose crew will do anything to protect her, and in that sense, she will do everything in her power to protect her crew.

Ali thought for a moment. Her mother, Helen, and her father, Shae, came to mind. She remembered, as a little girl, her dad telling her how good she bucked hay. "You know, I couldn't do this without you," he said. "You're my big, strong girl." He rubbed her back, making her feel warm and wanted. A tear came to her eye. She wanted nothing more than to be with her real family again, together.

Thank you for your vulnerability. It's now time to lift off.

Ali snapped back to the present. "Excuse me?"

The large craft lifted into the air.

"What are you doing?"

We are going for a test run. You not only need a lesson in being a worthy captain, but you also need a lesson in piloting me.

"No, I can't. I made a promise to Thun I wouldn't leave the cave."

Did you make a promise, or did Thun throw a demand your way without you agreeing to said demand?

Ali thought for a moment, then bobbed her head up and down. It was true. Thun forced the promise, and she never responded to it.

The starship shuddered, turning. A portion of the mountain opened like an elevator door. Bright light streamed in, and *Tranquil* pitched back a few degrees. Horns blared throughout the cavern.

"Look, if you want me to be a good leader, you better not leave. The Bawns will be pissed."

Let them be pissed. We have little time left to save your friends. We're heading to the Anunnaki's stronghold, the best place to learn to pilot me.

"What?" Ali stood, violently shaking her head. "Are you crazy?"

Tranquil's engines revved louder, the ship vibrating. Ali pushed back into her seat as the ship blasted forward and slipped through the opening in the mountain.

19

EDEN

Starship Sirona, Eos

Eden walked with Skye down a Starship *Sirona* corridor, her mind turning a million loops, twisting around as if nothing made sense anymore. He gave her the position of captain on Starship *Swift* and now took it away?

"Right here," she said, her lips numb, her eyes vacant. She stopped and stood in front of door thirty-six. Sleuth had given her this room as her sleeping quarters, mentioning it when he quickly passed her down the corridor.

"I gave you the position of captain because you're of the bloodline. I failed to see that you would so easily allow emotions to take control of you, rather than balancing reason and emotion." He dipped his head, bowing slightly to her. "I had to take the position away and give it to Nyx. She is more qualified and up to the task."

A memory of Diana placing her hands under her desk came to mind. Eden was certain Diana had gone for a gun but had obviously been mistaken. "I can't stand knowing she is a traitor and I'm not allowed to do anything about it."

"I'm not seeking to out her right now. I'm seeking to gain her trust, to turn her in our favor, and for her to help us locate Enlil's location."

"My apologies."

He folded his arms over his chest and leaned against the wall. "Why did you overact?"

"I was certain she was going for a weapon."

"Remember, we have Nyx and Jantu with us, plus myself. We're Space Templar-trained and skilled with the Sight. If she had pulled out a gun intending to use it, Nyx, Jantu, and I would have put a plasma bolt in each person in the room before they could blink an eye. When I give you an order, you take that order to heart. Do you understand?"

She nodded, biting her cheek. Memories of Admiral Shae Lutz chiding her for making a rookie mistake came to mind. She hitched her breath, remembering Shae pressing his finger into her chest. "You do that again, and you're off the ship. Hell, you're out of Star Guild. I had hopes for you, Lieutenant." She'd pulled a maneuver in flight training, going against a direct order from a superior. Topping it off, she talked back, claiming she'd been right. She didn't make that mistake twice.

Until today.

She eyed Skye, her stomach in her throat. "Understood." Her style was off the cuff, quick and reactive, flying her into combat and into torpedoes. It worked, but her tendencies tied themselves around her emotions, her heart reaching out to those who couldn't protect themselves. Right now, she knew more than ever that her style didn't match captain material. Admirals and captains wore higher ranking devices for a specific reason; their minds were trained to keep war as orderly as possible, to keep themselves alive in order to keep humanity alive and to understand a situation before it arose.

"This reminds me." Skye placed his hand on her shoulder. A warmth came from his palm, calming her. "I still believe in you. I think in time you will be a great leader. But I've forgotten one major aspect, something you felt for a while, and no doubt been wanting."

Eden cocked her head to the side. "What's that?"

"Training, not only to be an incredible captain but advanced in the

Sight." He turned and walked down the corridor and rounded a corner. "I'll be back soon."

She let out an exasperated breath and leaned against the door, dropping her chin to her chest. "Son of a Guild." She'd screwed up royally. She shook her head and turned, opening the door into her room. "Home sweet home, I guess."

It didn't feel like Starship *Brigantia*, her real home, but close enough, almost mirroring the sleeping quarters she slept in on her old ship. One full-sized bed, a locker and a closet. Nothing more. Bathrooms and showers were probably someplace down the corridor like her old ship.

She touched the bed's cover, feeling the rough, ebb fabric. "Cheap ebb-spun fiber. Yep, back to military life." She sat on her bed and touched her pendant, a silver Space Templar symbol of two knights on one horse wrapped in a crystal overlay.

Her mind churned over the events in Diana's quarters. Why had she reacted like that and not kept her cool? Never having encountered a traitor before, she didn't realize how much it would anger her. Just the thought of Diana burned her gut.

She turned the pendant, twisting it, then letting it dangle from her neck and twist back around on its own. She grabbed a pillow, fluffed it up, and laid her head on it, staring at the ceiling, the crystal warming her chest.

There was a knock on her door, and Eden sat up. She crossed her legs. "Who is it?"

"It's Captain Diana Johnson. Can I have a quick word?"

Eden quietly moved to the control panel next to the door and punched in a lock code. She pressed several more buttons, bringing up a holodisplay connected to a holocam outside her door. There stood the captain, her hands behind her back, looking as if she hid a gun.

"Captain, I apologize for my blow up. I've been stressed. I'll find you after I take a nap and calm down."

Diana squared her shoulders to the door, her back straight, her chest out. "Major Eden Gaines, this is an order. Open your door and let me in. We have important information to discuss."

"I'm sorry, but I can't. It's—"

Diana's voice boomed through the panel's com. "You are still under Star Guild law, and by Guild, you will obey that law or find yourself in the brig."

Eden put her hands over her face. She couldn't use her captain card anymore. Diana wouldn't buy it, anyway.

"Ma'am, I'm under a different law now. I'm in the Space Templar ranks, and I take orders from the Grand Master, Skye Vortek."

"Look, I won't harm you. I want to know more about the weapon you saw."

"I didn't see the weapon. That was Skye Vortek. Talk to him."

"When he's around, I'll question him. In the meantime, I still have some other questions for you."

"I can answer them from behind this door."

Diana flared her nostrils, keeping her hands behind her back. "Sleuth, come here, now."

Sleuth came into view, his head in his holopad. "Yes, Captain?"

Diana stared at the door, not moving a millimeter. "Sleuth, use my captain codes on your holopad and override this door. Eden has it locked, and I want it unlocked."

"Just a moment." Sleuth tapped away on his holopad, then pointed it at the control panel next to Eden's door.

Eden looked around for cover.

The bed. She didn't have another option in these tight quarters. She unholstered her gun and walked backward, pointing her weapon at the door. Several footsteps pounded from down the corridor, coming closer.

The door beeped and opened. Eden went to a knee, her gun extended. She narrowed her eyes. Diana was not there. In her place stood several *Sirona* Guard, leveling their rifles at her.

"Eden," came Diana's voice from around the doorway, "surrender your weapon. You're being moved to the brig."

Eden clenched her jaw, crouching lower, her gun's muzzle pointed at a *Sirona* Guard's forehead. "I already told you, Captain. I'm under a different law now. So, my answer is hell no."

20

ALI

Dirn Garum, Eos

Starship *Tranquil* flew toward a white, wispy cloud, the sun's rays glistening through the cloud's openings. "Pull up rear cams," ordered Ali. The vidscreen split and a view of Mount Gabriel appeared on the display. The sliver in the mountain they had flown through had closed.

Ali massaged her temples and blew out a gush of air. The Bawns had probably thrown a conniption fit when they saw her fly out of the mountain. "Oh, well." They'd live, but she might not, as *Tranquil* zipped toward the Anunnaki's stronghold.

Great.

She wanted to save her friends on Starship *Sirona*, not come face to face with the very Beings that wanted to kill her. Her stomach fluttered, recalling Enlil's face glaring at her the many times she'd run into the piece of Guild. Their last run in involved her shooting the bastard several times, and him escaping, a trail of blood behind him.

Tranquil punched through the cloud cover. Ali studied the controls at the captain's chair. It held a commlink console, a holographic display icon, and several more buttons to help her navigate through a holographic screen, though she didn't know why as the ship navigated itself.

I'm not like any starship you've ever encountered.

Ali set her hand on the armrests. "That's for damn sure. I've never been in a talking ship, let alone one that can launch itself."

I can also land myself. That's not something you need to worry about. You also need not worry about navigation, steering this craft, or weapons. All is in my hands.

Ali eyed several stations lining the wall, and a large desk with a holographic schematic of the ship lifted above of it. "Then what are the stations for?"

In case I lose consciousness, the mission operation console steers and accelerates me wherever you wish to go. My stations can act as my eyes, my heart, and my organs, or in your terms, my biological scanners and my biological engines. If I lose consciousness, you have a way to operate every aspect of me.

"If you lose consciousness?"

In the past, I've experienced direct impacts that have impaired my systems, which in your terms would indicate that I blacked out.

"I see. And does that happen often?"

Thrice. Slipping through a cloud, *Tranquil* veered left in a long, wide turn.

Ali pointed off in the distance. "Is that the canyon where *Sirona* is located?"

Yes. Shall we inspect?

"And pick them up? Yes." She pushed down a grin, not wanting to show her excitement, let alone her relief. Maybe they could evacuate *Sirona*...somehow.

Tranquil picked up speed, descending.

Ali flattened her lips. "Do you even need me? Or any crew?"

Yes. I'm not all-seeing, even though I see a lot. We'll help each other. Your aptitudes with piloting and observation are beneficial to our partnership.

Ali's eyebrows rose. "How do you possibly know my aptitudes?"

I scanned you upon entering my bridge and was pleased. You make quick decisions and stand by them. Most of your decisions are correct, though many are bone-headed and brash. Something inside you wants to help others, and something else inside of you wants to put on the appearance that you don't care that much about humans. This is beneficial because it counteracts arrogance. This makes you believable, even if people don't agree with you. This also makes you trustworthy, a quality all captains and admirals must have.

Tranquil went into a steeper dive and Ali sank into the seat, her body feeling three-hundred pounds heavier. *Tranquil* slowed and went into a hover.

Sirona is three-hundred and ninety-six point two meters below.

"Holocams, please."

The vidscreen split again and Starship *Sirona* came into view, though like *Tranquil* said, hundreds of meters below.

Sirona was massive. Large boosters were attached to each side, its rectangular body coming to a point at the ship's bow, and cannons jut out from every nook and cranny of its exterior.

"Zoom in."

Tranquil complied.

Sirona 's armor looked torched, full of black scorch marks from enemy fire, accompanied with blown-out chunks and pockmarks scattered across the exterior.

"They were working on the engines before I left. Is there a way to check the progress?"

Tranquil zeroed in on the mid-section, where the main power generators, core, and engines were located. A blue glow highlighted the area with red intermixed.

"What does the blue mean?"

That the engines are fully operational and deactivated. From my sensors, they don't appear damaged, and there are no recent repairs to report.

Ali grimaced. "No, re-scan. That can't be. It has damage. That's why they haven't rocketed out of here yet."

Nothing is wrong with the Starship Sirona 's flying abilities, and the last severe damage report indicates nothing major for the last two years.

Ali shook her head, leaning forward. "That makes no sense. They could have lifted off this planet the moment I walked onto the starship?"

Tranquil leveled out and hovered several dozen meters above *Sirona*. *Correct,* said *Tranquil*.

Ali tipped her head to the side. "Correct?"

They could have flown off this planet, yes.

Ali bounced her knee up and down, doing her best not to kick something. This didn't surprise her, but fueled her belly, nonetheless. She figured her mother—no, not her mother—Captain Diana Johnson played for the other team. She shifted in her seat. "Please check if there's damage that's not allowing this ship to move."

A brief pause. *Fuel cells are online, full. There aren't any issues with recharge sockets, the coolant pumps, the energy core lines, the compressors, the sensory arrays—*

Ali jerked her hand through her red hair, squeezing her hand into a fist. "Okay, stop."

Diana was a traitor, and that bitch deserved to die a horrendous death. Almost ten thousand souls crewed Starship *Sirona,* and here sat Diana, gambling with their lives. They could leave planetside any minute and have been able to for weeks. It made little sense unless Diana had a death wish herself.

Ali shook her head. Her ex-mom didn't have a death wish, more like an agenda, but what exactly was it? Ali stood and slowly walked toward the screen, her brow wrinkled.

I detect seven Anunnaki starfighters lifting off three kilometers southeast of us. They are fast approaching our locale.

"How fast?"

Strap in now. Twenty-four Missiles launched.

"Ours?"

Theirs.

"Crap."

Ali turned to jump in her seat, but her legs went into the air and she landed hard on her back. Grunting, she slid across the floor, bumping into the base of the captain's chair.

The ship trembled, and Ali pulled herself onto the chair. She sat, blowing her hair out of her face. "How many hit us?" Restraining straps automatically wrapped around Ali and sucked into the back of the chair, belting her in.

Tranquil flew forward, twisting the ship on its side. *I shot down all but two missiles. I'm taking evasive actions. Be my eyes. I'll draw them far away from Starship* Sirona. *Tranquil* pitched to the right.

"Show me."

The vidscreen went to rear cams, and tracer fire zipped by in thin, red lines. Seven Anunnaki starfighters flew in pursuit, closing the distance.

Tranquil lurched to the left and shuddered. Ali gripped the armrests tighter. For a starship, *Tranquil* flew incredibly well, almost nimbly. "Did *Sirona* monitor our presence?"

No.

"How could they have possibly missed us and the starfighters?"

They turned their security systems and HDC monitors off. A loop feed is present. *Tranquil* banked left then dipped. *Permission to fire?*

"Per—" Ali threw her hands in the air. "Yes, permission to fire. Fire, fire."

The vidscreen expanded and a string of bluish-purple bolts expelled from rear cannons. Several bolts impacted a starfighter, slicing through its wing, and sending it into a downward spiral. A fireball rose from the ground and debris flew across the ebb-desert.

"What kind of weapon was that?"

Plasma bolts.

"Plasma bolts? What exactly are—"

Tranquil arched high, blasting more plasma bolts through its rear cannons. A fiery explosion lit up the sky, and burning entrails dropped toward the ground, black smoke trailing from them.

Ali wanted to get back to something else *Tranquil* mentioned. "A loop feed? You mean to tell me that Diana hijacked the system?"

Yes.

"But why would Diana sabotage Starship *Sirona*?"

You're not doing well being my eyes.

"You don't need my eyes. You're doing better without—"

The ship shook. *What were you saying?*

"Are we hit?"

Yes, and to answer your next question, we're not damaged. I've already repaired myself.

A loud beep and two dozen dots filled the screen, slowly getting bigger at every passing second. "Twenty-four starfighters incoming? Evade, evade."

I'm much bigger than them. Put them all together, and they're still a fraction of my size. So, no, I won't need to evade. Plus, I'm taking their attention away from the real danger.

Ali scanned the sky, her lips pursed. "Danger?"

A starfighter erupted, then another, the flying enemy formation scattering erratically.

Swift *has entered the fray.*

"Who?"

Swift *is the same starship class as me. We're family. We're twice as dangerous together.*

"Show me."

A small box formed on the upper left of the screen and an orbed ship exactly like *Tranquil* filled the box. *That's* Swift. *Less talk. Be my eyes.*

"On it." She scanned the heavens, pointing at a cluster of lights coming their way. "On your ten."

Aye. Bolts lit the sky, slicing through the starfighter's exteriors like a knife through butter. A handful of starfighters plummeted to the red and black rock below, rocks and dust poofing into the air on impact.

Ali, for future reference, you need not point to danger. Your thoughts are connected to mine. Focus on an incoming starfighter and I'll get to it as soon as possible. Do you understand?

She nodded, her eyes widening. "Are the starfighters retreating?"

Yes, that was Swift's *goal and mine. We're two sisters communicating with each other, and we don't wish to take lives if we don't have to. No one has the right to invade the space and life of another, especially if it is to end that Being's life. Yet, you always have the right to defend yourself. That is Universal Law. We were defending ourselves.*

Ali slowly leaned forward, glaring at towering skyscrapers with needle-like roofs in the distance. She eyed the mountain range around it. Small trees and green foliage dotted the mountain like a painting. Eos wasn't supposed to have ample vegetation.

"Am I seeing that correctly?"

She peered longer, making out palaces, dome structures, and tall landing platforms. An entire civilization lived there. She swallowed hard when she saw large lakes. "Water above ground?"

This is Eos Two, named by the Anunnaki of Nibiru, who created this city. Your people have been persuaded to keep away from this part of Eos.

Ali threw her hands to her face. "I should have known." She leaned back and sighed. "There really isn't a radiation zone, is there?"

You've been lied to and more so than you realize.

"Yes, that seems to be the theme lately."

It's time to return to Dirn Garum, Ali. Are you prepared for your welcome when they see you?

"They'll think I stole you."

You'll be fine. Just tell the truth when you return and say that I was the one who took you out on your first spin.

"Can't you tell them that?"

They won't be able to hear my words. None are Space Templar-trained or of the bloodline.

"Of course."

Tranquil spun around and sped for Dirn Garum, keeping low and hugging the red terrain, the trees becoming sparser the farther they flew away from Eos Two.

"They better not kill me."

They'll do no such thing. You are of the bloodline. Plus, some of them will be your permanent crew.

Ali sat forward in a start. "Excuse me?"

Mount Gabriel came into view, its tip touching the white clouds.

Ali, pay attention. This is important. You're my captain now, and the captain for every future crew member of this ship. You're here with me to explore the galaxy and right its wrongs.

"Do I get a choice in the matter?"

There's always a choice. You can take me or leave me. Another will come

147

along. Another will fulfill his or her life mission. But I think I know your choice.

Ali didn't reply, knowing her choice as well; to use this ship to get her friends off of this planet. "Wait, wait. We need to turn around and destroy that massive weapon heading *Sirona's* way."

I scanned the area. We have time. The weapon is on a slower course than when it originally started. Someone has interrupted its navigation and driving systems.

S jumped into Ali's mind. The Anunnaki most likely worked his or her magic, messing with the weapon.

The slit in the mountain opened as they drew nearer. *Tranquil's* bow thrusters hummed loudly, slowing the ship down. Ali shifted uncomfortably in the seat.

Are you prepared?

"What do you think?" Ali grimaced.

You'll be fine.

"Easy for you to say. They won't yell at you."

No, they won't.

Entering the mountain's belly, the opening rumbled to a close behind *Tranquil*. The ship shook when it touched down, and Ali's nerves felt like they spun erratically through every facet of her body.

She stood and walked toward the viewscreen. A hoard of Bawn warriors gawked at the ship, their long axes resting on their shoulders, their hands clasped around the axes' handles.

This didn't look good.

21

EDEN

Starship Sirona, Eos

Eden crouched lower, her gun hand shaking, the *Sirona* Guards pointing their rifles at her. Calm, Eden, she told herself. Adrenaline coursed through her veins. She took a deep breath, and her hand steadied. "Diana, tell them to stand down." Eden slipped her finger through the trigger guard, her muzzle aimed at a guard's nose. "This is a plasma weapon and your men don't have a chance."

True or not, perhaps different technology, unknown to anyone in Star Guild, would put some hesitation in the guards' minds. Several clicks sounded from the corridor, and a few of the guards flinched, glancing to their right.

"Do you want to die, mortal?" Nyx's voice echoed off the walls in Eden's sleeping quarters.

"Tell them to stand down," yelled Eden. "You don't want blood on your hands, Diana...*Sirona* blood."

"I'd do as she says," came Skye's voice.

A pause and Eden steadied her aim.

"Stand down," said Diana. The guards lowered their weapons.

"And back away," ordered Nyx.

Eden stood and moved toward the doorway. The guards moved

aside, slowly backing down the corridor. Eden leveled her gun, tracking the middle *Sirona* soldier. Entering the corridor, she found Diana and Sleuth.

Diana's hands hung by her side, empty. She didn't have a weapon like Eden thought. Perhaps she actually had come to talk, and not to kill, but better safe than shot.

Jantu walked past Eden, his blue fur brushing her arm. He held a long rifle, his face calm. How the hell did that guy do that? In the middle of stress and potential combat, he kept it cool and compassionate even.

"Do we have a problem, Diana?" asked Skye.

Diana nodded. "That's a bad question, sir. You ever see weapons drawn when there's not a problem? The answer is yes. Major Eden Gaines pulled a gun on a superior officer. She's going to the brig. There she'll answer many of my questions."

"Under what Space Templar law do we allow Star Guild military to apprehend our own officers?" spat Skye.

Diana cleared her throat. "She's not a Space Templar, and if I considered her part of your...gang...she's on my ship. On my ship, Star Guild laws apply."

Skye shifted his eyes to each of his small crew. "Put your weapons down."

Eden lowered her weapon to her side. Jantu and Nyx did as well. A light in the corridor flickered just above Sleuth. His eyes focused on Eden, a scowl across his face.

Skye continued. "I'll tell you what. If I promise no more incidents on your boat, will you let this one slip?"

Diana cocked her head to the side. "Slip? No." She bit her lower lip, thinking for a moment. "All right. A warning, but that is all and never again." She eyed her men. "Let's go." They marched down the corridor, Diana in tow. She flicked a look over her shoulder. "Do not point another weapon at my crew or me. If I see it again, I'll throw your entire team in the brig." She disappeared around a corner.

Skye's hand gently fell on Eden's shoulder. "May I have a word?"

Eden dipped her head. "Yes."

He looked at Nyx and Jantu. "We need to be alone. Guard the door." Skye led Eden into her sleeping quarters. The door shut behind them. "One word of advice, if you don't mind me giving it?"

She stiffened, wondering what else she'd done wrong. "I defended myself." She pointed at the door. "They came here with their weapons drawn. I had no choice but to draw my own." She patted her holstered pistol.

He folded his arms, tapping one finger on an elbow. "I understand. I need you to understand that I'm on your side and always have been from the moment we met. If they took you to the brig, we'd bust you out." He motioned toward the door. "You saw how quickly we responded to a threat to your life? We are watching."

Eden's muscles relaxed. "What do you mean you're watching?"

"Your crystal."

She touched her pendant. It radiated warmth. "You monitor me through this?"

He shook his head. "It's monitored through mine, Nyx, and Jantu's wristband." He showed her the gold band he wore and tapped on it. A line shot from it and a holographic schematic of the ship fizzled outward, displaying above his wristband. The entire ship, however, didn't come in view. Only areas she traversed on this craft displayed on the blueprint. "If your crystal senses stress beyond normal, it lets us know."

She wrapped her fingers around her pendant. "This thing senses me?"

"Yes, but don't let that get to you. All it does is report when you're in danger. Nothing more. We don't have a holocam inside of it if that's what you're thinking." He folded his arms across his chest. "But that's not why I want to talk with you alone."

"What is it, then?"

Skye sat on her bed, his eyes bright. "It's time to train. It's time for you to learn the Sight."

"Now?"

"Yes. Until you learn the Sight well, Nyx remains the lead. Watch her. See how she does things. When she feels you're ready, she'll give you the position back."

"The captain position?"

"Yes."

Eden snorted. "What makes you think she'll ever give me the position? She dislikes me like a fish to dry land."

"She will. I assure you. She has honor. She has brains. It doesn't matter if she dislikes you, she'll see with her own eyes when you're fully qualified."

"Why can't you promote me when the time comes?"

"It's an agreement between Nyx and me." He looked off, shrugging. "Let's just say she's not done with her training either. Observing and noticing when you're ready is an assignment I've given her, because like you, she has a lot to learn. Plus, the last thing she wants is to be a captain. She leads squads, not fleets. It's just not her style." Skye sat cross-legged on her bed. "Copy me and close your eyes."

"Now?"

"Now. Your training with the Sight begins at this very moment."

Eden stood motionless. "I just about got blasted by the *Sirona* Guard, and you want me to train this minute?"

"There's no better time than here and now."

"Wow." Eden shook her body, her arms flailing back and forth to get the sensations out of her central nervous system. Only minutes ago, men pointed deadly weapons her way. She took a deep breath and exhaled, then sat on the bed across from Skye. She crossed her legs and closed her eyes.

"Clear your mind," he said.

Eden scrunched up her nose. "Easy for you to say."

"Focus on your breathing. In through your nose, out through your nose. Hold for two seconds before exhaling, expanding that count at each breath until you reach twenty seconds before each exhale."

Eden slowly shook her head. "All right." She took a deep breath, then held, breathing out two seconds later.

After ten minutes of deep breathing, Skye spoke, "Open your eyes."

Eden jerked back, her mind focused on the breathing, her body now relaxed. She opened her eyes and blinked several times. "Everything is brighter, clearer."

"Good. Now, focus on your pillow, and ask to partner with it."

She furrowed her brow. "Partner with it?"

"Yes, it's an ask and answer partnership. You ask, and you feel the object's answer. Watch." He took a deep breath through his nose, and the pillow lifted off of bed, floating. With a dip of his head, it slowly lowered, resting gently back in its place.

Eden's mouth gaped, and she put her hands up. "What? How?"

"Energy makes up all of life. By Universal Law, we're allowed to partner this energy. When you feel the confirmation, the energy is subtle, yes, you and what you're partnering with will...partner. When partnering with the pillow, I felt the confirmation right here," he touched his heart, "and the more you practice the Sight, the faster and easier it is to partner, and the quicker you feel the link."

"You lifted the pillow off my bed."

"A bend in physics, yes. A lightening of the energy around the pillow, lifting it up, and setting it down."

"So, you partnered with the energy around the pillow, too?"

"Yes, simultaneously, but I needed confirmation from the pillow and the energy around the pillow to allow me to lift it, and back down again."

"Again, how?"

He tapped his head. "With imagination. I imagined it lifting. It's like robotics. You can place a chip behind your ear, a chip that's connected to a robot. You can imagine the robot moving its arm, and the chip senses that brain impulse and tells the robot to move its arm. It's almost instant, but with the Sight, and all the wonderful things the Sight can do, it's not almost instant, it is instant."

Eden bit her bottom lip, doing her best to understand.

Skye brought his hands together at his chest and dipped his head. "Close your eyes and continue. By the end of the day, you'll lift that pillow. Then we move on to the next step."

She closed her eyes, and breathed through her nose, held her breath for several seconds, and exhaled. After several minutes, she opened her eyes and stared at the pillow. She silently asked if she could partner with it. Her heart felt the connection, like a ship docking with an airlock. She imagined a glow of energy surrounding the pillow and asked to partner with the glow. Her heart warmed, and she pictured the pillow lifting off the bed.

Her eyes widened as the pillow shifted. She pulled in another breath. Energy, emotion, and anything she could muster flowed from her gut, and out like a geyser ready to explode as she exhaled. Her abdomen contracted, and the pillow jumped off the bed, landing on the floor.

Skye clapped his hand and grasped her wrists. His lips curled into a smile. "I've never seen someone pick up the Sight so quickly."

"It jumped off the bed. How did I do that?" She looked at his hands. He sat at the foot of the bed and far from the pillow. He couldn't have kicked or pushed it off of the bed, especially without her noticing.

"You partnered. That's the first step. Next, you'll learn to control the pillow and the surrounding energy." He touched her chest, the energy coming from him practically calming her to sleep. "Now, close your eyes and begin. This time, you'll attempt to lift the pillow from the floor to the bed."

2 2

ALI

Dirn Garum, Eos

A torch's flicker cast shadows from the cell bars, striping Ali's face.

She cracked her knuckles and leaned against the cold ebb-rock wall, then slid to the ground. She shook her head. "These Bawns will be the end of me."

She'd placed herself in a bad predicament. When she first arrived in Dirn Garum, she was a hero. Now, locked up in a cell, surrounded by ebb bars, she had been downgraded to a prisoner. Harak threw her behind bars while King Bilrak, Thun, and Chan had seemingly disappeared, but to where? Harak no doubt locked her up without his father's knowledge.

"That bastard tricked me." She leaned forward and touched a bar, pulling hard on it to test its strength. She sighed. "Impossible."

Bawns were master ebb craftsmen and craftswomen. They built statues, homes, streets, and most likely cell bars that withstood earthquakes of the worst sort, let alone her attempts at breaking or bending them.

She felt the baldric's fabric and touched the hilt of her sword sheathed to her side. Maybe Sol's blade could make a dent in the bars, or more. She curled her fingers around the hilt, then relaxed. Just in case, she didn't want to break the sword. She let her arm flop by her side.

Hours ago, she landed *Tranquil* with a hoard of Bawn warriors waiting. They informed her King Bilrak needed a word with her immediately. She followed them, thinking it was a strange path they'd taken her on. She passed an open jail cell, then they shoved her inside, the door swinging shut before she could react.

They locked it, and Harak walked down the tunnel a moment later. "Since I can't kill you with Sol by your side, you can starve to death in here."

"What are you doing? Does your father know you did this? Or Thun and Chan?"

"Don't worry about them," he said, his voice echoing down the tunnel as he walked away.

Ali huffed and leaned against a wall. How the hell did Harak constantly convince several Bawns to join his side? First, he had a gang try and help him end her life. Now a group of warriors had done Harak's bidding and threw her in a cell. What the hell did he tell them? His race branded her the Chosen One. Upholding the prophecy apparently didn't matter to some.

She banged on the cell bars for the umpteenth time. "Help. Anyone." She sat down, wanting to be free of this mountain, and of this sword. She tossed Sol to the ground, the metal clanging as it settled on the rocky floor.

Guild, she wanted to be free of it all. Not just this prison, but everything that felt like a prison. On Earth, she remembered many times as an archaeologist that she wanted freedom from the female stigma. Men didn't consider females smart or resilient enough to lead an expedition. That's all she ever wanted to do, lead an excursion, uncover ancient artifacts, decode them, and share her findings with the world. Finally, when she led one, it threw her into this world— Starbase Matrona, Star Guild, and Eos. A world of slaves. She couldn't get around it. Lack of freedom filled every nook and cranny of her life, no matter which planet she lived on.

During her last weeks on Earth, near the time of her expedition, her mom begged her not to go. "Ali, I lost your dad when the military asked him to leave us. I can't let you go. Something doesn't feel right, just like it didn't feel right when your dad left."

They stood at the University of Michigan's main entrance where Ali taught, the spring flowers beginning to open on the trees, and a slight breeze swirling in the air. Ali held a suitcase, packed and ready.

"Mom, it's the Joint Chiefs of Staff. You don't turn down orders from them. Plus, I can make history. I'll be the first woman in the United States to lead an archaeology expedition, especially one of this magnitude."

Helen lowered her gaze, her large-brimmed hat hiding her facial features. "I know you want to do this and badly, and it's your dream, but please wait until the war is over."

The United States hadn't entered the war, dubbed World War Two, but the Nazi's were fully involved. Their experts and soldiers scoured the ancient lands, finding relics and artifacts of immense proportions. Rumors floated that Nazi expedition parties followed foreign digs, and had killed foreign expedition teams, running off with their prizes.

She understood her mother's fear. "I'll have a small troop with me, plus some professional archaeologists. I'm in good hands."

Helen glanced up, her eyebrows curled in worry. "I hope so." She held out a note. "I'm giving you this to see you off."

Ali opened the small, folded paper. "I love you" had been written in her mother's pen. And "I believe in you."

That had occurred years ago, and as Ali sat in the prison cell, she buried her face in her hands. "She knew like a mother does. She knew I was heading into trouble." She shook her head. Even though Ali didn't listen, her mother still believed in her.

She picked up a rock from the ground and rubbed it between her palms. She pushed to a standing position and jumped up and down, performing jumping jacks, something her father taught her. Commotion came from the corridor and she halted, her eyes on the torch flame dancing on the wall across from her cell.

Footsteps and garbled words echoed down the hall. Someone, or several people, came closer. She stepped back as the footsteps grew louder, and the muffled words turned into Daf's coherent demands. "Get your hands off of me." Long, wide shadows approached. Daf and two small men. The shadows shortened until Daf and two Bawns appeared. "I said, let me go." Daf pulled away from them, thrashing her feet. They pushed her, and she fell on her rear.

Ali reached for her sword as a Bawn thrust and turned his key in the keyhole, unlocking the cell. Ali flexed her fingers around Sol, a flame blazing around the edges.

The Bawn kicked the bars hard, smashing the cell door into Ali. She stumbled back. They threw Daf in and slammed the door shut. A click, and the door locked. The Bawn pulled the key out of the keyhole and laughed down the tunnel, vanishing from view.

"Daf?" said Ali, rushing to her aid. "What's going on?"

Daf kicked her in the thigh. "Get away." Her hair was strung chaotically over her face as she crawled backward. She blew strands out of her face and jumped to her feet, her hands up in fists. "I'm not scared of you guys. I—" She dropped her guard when she saw Ali. She slumped to the ground, letting her hands fall lazily into her lap, and hung her head. "Thank Guild it's you. I'm exhausted."

"What did you do?"

"What do you mean, what did I do?" She put her arms out wide, smacking the bars and the wall. "Ow, son of a—" She wiggled her hands. "I did nothing. They grabbed me and told me to come with them. I'm assuming you had something to do with it?"

"Harak has everything to do with it. Did you see Chan or Thun? Maybe even King Bilrak?"

"No, no, and no."

"They want us to starve in here."

"Bilrak won't allow that." Daf eyeballed the bars. "I don't think."

"He won't, me being the Chosen One and all, but we need to let him know we're down here. Did anyone see you?"

"No, because they said that Bilrak wanted to see me and led me here. As you saw, they threw me in here with you like I was some measly dog."

Ali palmed her forehead. "What are we going to do?"

"Where have you been? In here this whole time?"

"I took Starship *Tranquil* for a ride, then I got tossed in here."

"You took *Tranquil* out? You're kidding me."

"No."

"You took the starship on a joy ride without me?"

"Her name is Starship *Tranquil*, and no, I didn't take it for a joy ride. She took me."

"Uh-huh." Daf rolled her eyes. "So, you're telling me that the starship can navigate itself?" She lifted a brow.

"Yes, it sounds weird, but the ship is a sentient Being. It can fly on its own, and it can chat with me. It can even shoot enemies out of the sky—"

"Okay, stop. You shot enemies out of the sky?"

"I didn't shoot anything. Starship *Tranquil* shot the Anunnaki." Ali realized how odd it sounded. Daf probably thought the Bawns had drugged Ali before locking her up.

Daf pushed her hair out of her face. "It's hard to believe." She pulled back and leaned against the damp wall. "Did you see *Sirona*?"

"Yes, and she's in one piece."

Daf let out a breath of fresh air, her body relaxing. "Good. And the weapon that's supposed to kill *Sirona*?"

"No. *Tranquil* said it's approaching slow and won't reach *Sirona* for days. I think S screwed with its navigation systems."

Daf blankly stared at her. "You're not telling me that to just make me feel better, are you?"

"Hell no. Since when do I care if you feel any better?"

"True. So, what's our plan now? Can that sword break through these bars?"

"I don't know," said Ali. "I'm not going to try."

Daf rubbed her brow as if warding off a headache. "Of course not. The usual Ali, making things difficult for herself, and in the process, making it difficult for everyone else."

Ali flared her nostrils. "Sol is all I have down here, and these bars are Bawn-built. I don't want to risk breaking the sword."

"So, we just starve."

"If push comes to shove, I'll try. We wait until Chan or Thun figures out that we're gone. They'll find us." She hoped.

"If they're alive."

"You think Harak had them killed?"

"Who knows?"

Ali tapped the ground with her fingers, thinking. "You know what?"

"What?" Daf's voice cracked.

Ali tilted her head to the side. That better not be tears falling from Daf's eyes. Ali's stomach fluttered. She didn't know how to deal with crying. "Are you all right?"

Daf wiped her eyes with her forearm. "I'm fine."

Ali gave her a poignant stare. "Really? 'Cause you don't sound like it."

Daf covered her mouth, holding in a cry.

"Daf."

"Leave me alone. I'll stop soon."

"Come here." She patted the ground next to her.

Daf shook her head.

"It's an order."

Daf sat up, her eyes welled in tears, her hand over her lips. She slid over to Ali and sat leaning on the wall next to her. "My family, my mom, dad, brother, and sister. I just don't know if they're safe, or even alive."

Ali patted Daf's arm, then wrapped her arm around Daf's shoulders. She pulled her in close. "There, there."

Daf stiffened and started laughing. The longer Daf laughed, the harder it seemed for her to stop.

Ali let go of Daf's shoulders. "What's so funny?"

"You." She put her arm around Ali, making a pouty face. "There, there?" She cracked up. "That's the best you got?"

Ali went rigid. What did Daf want her to say or do?

Daf patted Ali's shoulder. "For what it's worth, thank you."

Footsteps reverberated off the walls. Ali stood and raised her sword. A figure in a robe, hands in his sleeves with arms crossed, stopped in front of the cell. A Bawn stood by his side.

"Chan?" said Ali.

Chan bowed. "My apologies for my late arrival. Harak tricked us, for lack of a better word."

"Get us out of here," said Daf.

"We're working on it. Harak hid the keys." Chan motioned his head toward Thun.

Thun nodded, looking at his feet, clearly embarrassed. "I'm sorry about my brother. My dad's giving him a tongue lashing right now."

Ali furrowed her brow. "Where were you guys? Where was your dad?"

"Harak had one of his followers sound the blow horn. A sound I've not heard my entire life. It meant we were under attack."

"I thought you monitored outside comings and goings?" Ali remembered someone mentioning the Bawns had that capability.

"The man who blew the horn was on monitoring duty. It was planned and well-executed. We gathered our warriors and headed through the tunnels, ready to slay some Anunnaki scum." Thun looked up and rested an axe over his shoulder. "Why did you take Starship *Tranquil*, Ali? I trusted you, and my father knew I trusted you. They have shamed me on your account. My brother, however, couldn't be happier that you disappointed us." His face reddened, and he held up a fist. "You have abashed me in front of my family. You—"

"I didn't steal *Tranquil* or take her anywhere. She took me for a test run, so I could get used to her. That's all. And I protested...a little. We didn't stop at Starship *Sirona* to pick up my friends, so—"

"Are you looking for the keys?" Daf interrupted.

"Yes. We'll find the keys." Thun rubbed the back of his neck, scrunching up his nose. "Ali, we don't have thievery down here. Negligence, on the other hand, we have some of that." He glanced at Ali. "You're the Chosen One. I thought you'd follow our rules, that you'd understand."

"That ship took me for a ride. I didn't control her. Do you want me to continue to repeat myself until I'm blue in the face?"

Thun crossed his arms. "No. I can see in your eyes you're telling the truth, and I'll let my father know." He held up his finger. "But give me time. I'm enjoying my brother being told a thing or two."

Chan gently nudged Thun. "Let's get to finding those keys."

Thun nodded. "Ali, the next time we return, I promise you we'll get you out of this cell." He turned and walked away, shaking his head. "I can't believe my brother thought he'd get away with this." He paused and turned. "One more thing. Our tunnelers completed the tunnel to Eos Two. We're directly under the palace where we believe the Anunnaki headquarters are located."

Ali stared at Thun, waiting for an explanation. None came. "Good news, I guess? What for?"

"Our first wave commences in two days. That's when we strike. You'll join the first wave by air in Starship *Tranquil*."

Two days? That wouldn't do. By then, the weapon S warned about would reach *Sirona*, even if *Tranquil* said the weapon moved slowly. Something else itched Ali's mind. "The Anunnaki will detect you coming, especially if you tunneled so closely."

Thun shook his head. "We believe that it's the Anunnaki's weak point. Their technology isn't set underground. They'll never know what hit them."

"Are you sure?" asked Ali.

"If we're wrong, we attack anyway. We've waited a long time for you to arrive, and for this war to begin. The Goddess has our backs, that we know. She'll protect us like always."

"Then tell Bilrak we have to go sooner," said Ali.

Thun smiled. "The sooner we get to the Anunnaki, the better. I'll see what I can do." He raised a fist, grunting. "I like your fighting spirit. No patience like the Bawn."

Ali held up a fist, grunting as well. She faked a grin. "How are you going to get the military vehicles parked around *Tranquil* through the tunnel you created?"

Thun tilted his head like a dog observing a stupid human trick. "We don't use vehicles. We have legs to walk and run. We have arms to wield our weapons. That's all we need."

"I don't think that's wise."

Chan stepped toward the cells. "I've talked to them a dozen times over this very situation. They are bullheaded. They won't change their minds."

"Because we fight like men." Thun continued to hold his fist in the air.

Ali sighed. "Then it is what it is."

Chan bowed to Ali. "That's what I end up saying." He swung his arm out wide, motioning to Thun. "Did you assemble the team?"

Thun awkwardly bowed. "Yes? I think?"

"A team?" said Ali.

Chan intertwined his fingers together at his waist. "We imagined you'd agree to help the Bawns fight, so I had Thun gather a crew for you."

Thun dipped his head toward Ali. "The starship will be under your command, of course."

Ali dipped her head in return, swallowing down her misgivings. She didn't want to fight, but refusing while in the cell might not be the best tactic. She could head to the weapon S spoke about first and blast it to Guild and back. She'd then rain plasma fire down on Eos Two.

"We'll be back." Chan left with Thun.

Daf turned to Ali. "So, we'll blow some shit up?" She thrust her hands on her hips. She obviously didn't like the idea.

"Guild, I hope not, other than the weapon heading for *Sirona*." Ali brought her eyes to Daf's. "These Bawns don't understand destruction and terror like we witnessed." The memory of her fellow mech worker, Hendricks, came to mind, his mech ripped to shreds by an enemy starfighter. Hendricks had died in flames. It made her nauseous. She put her hands on her knees and bent over, shaking her head. "I don't want to see it anymore, Daf."

"I guess we don't have a choice."

"You know what? We have a choice." Ali stood straight, her chin high. "We're focusing on saving *Sirona*." Her mind was set. "We take out that weapon and detour to *Sirona*'s coordinates, evacuate her, then leave the planet."

23

KODA

Starbase Matrona

Slipping by a Starhawk Transport, Devon and Koda made their way to the airlocks.

Devon rubbed his eyes and yawned. "I could fall asleep right here and right now."

Koda gave him an odd look. "How?" Koda was wide awake, stress buzzing through his insides.

Devon shrugged. "I've probably had less sleep than you."

Koda doubted it. "Slap your face, man."

Devon rubbed the skin beside his ears. "That's a better way to keep you awake." He shook his head like a wet dog and jumped up and down, then ran in place. "That's another way. Anyway, do you think when this is all over, we can get back to normal life?"

"Guild, you must be tired. Nothing will ever be the same. After this is all over, the corrupt governance will fall along with all the politicians. I'll make sure of it." He gave Devon a friendly jab to his shoulder. "Let's go and save the masses. Then gather some valuable information for them."

The more he uncovered, the more he realized how much the governance kept hidden. Although new to the political game, Koda figured most of the political figures on the starbase had concealed countless lies for years.

He wanted to put a rope around their necks and pull, but that would be uncivilized. They deserved it for the incivility his fellow members in the governance provided the people for who knew how long. The governance, other than Prime Director Zim Noki, may not know about the Anunnaki, but all the politician's middle names began with "bought" and ended in "and paid for." They'd passed evil bills under the people's noses for centuries.

Koda's blood boiled, and he clenched his jaw, staring off in a daze at a wall lined with doors that led to the airlock hangars. He imagined slamming prison doors on the likes of Sphere Three's Prime Overseer Jeffrey Dolms, or Sphere Seven's Prime Overseer Laura Cran. Hell, every Overseer, every Prime Administrator, and every Prime Executive.

"You said let's go. So, let's go," said Devon.

"Right."

They rounded a starfighter and ducked under a Starjumper's wing, creeping below the craft's underbelly. Koda looked left and right to make sure no one was around, particularly Payson and his gang. They hurried under the next Starhawk Transport, crouching next to its port landing sled.

"If nothing will be the same, then maybe you could be the next Prime Director?" suggested Devon.

Koda shook his head. "Let's not think of that right now."

"What? You'd be a great leader."

"Perhaps, but after this whole shit-show, I may never lead anyone ever again." Who knew what the governance would look like when, or if, everything settled down?

Koda glanced around. Huge tinted ebb windows encircled the Sphere, much like the rest of the starbase. Unlike the rest of the starbase, the windows ended where the airlock rooms began. Door upon door lined the walls, and behind those doors housed small cargo hangars for dangerous chemicals and weapons, or something as mundane as garbage.

When the airtight doors inside the hangars opened, the materials inside the hangars was sucked into space. When ships attached to the airlocks, they sent or received people and shipments through the pressure vessels, usually taking the shipments down to the Eos warehouses.

"Now what?" said Devon.

"We look through the window of each door for containers that look like they're holding toxins." He moved out from under the ship. "Go." He bolted toward the first door, Devon behind him. Reaching it, he peeked through the window at the giant hangar inside, seeing damaged ship parts and metal scraps. No barrels.

"Next," said Devon. "This may take forever."

Koda looked down the long line of doors. This would take a while. "We don't have forever." He pointed at the last door. It seemed like it was a kilometer away. "I'll start down there, and you start here."

"Good idea."

Koda patted Devon's back and jogged to the far door where the airlock rooms ended, and the windows began.

"This one is empty," yelled Devon.

Koda gave him a thumbs up and peeked through another door's window. Empty cannon shells, broken down rifles, and other weapons were strewn about. He moved to the next room and caught his breath. He squinted his eyes, making sure they didn't deceive him. He waved his hand. "I think I found what we're looking for." On the other side of the door sat hundreds of black barrels.

Devon ran toward Koda, his footsteps pounding loudly.

Koda held up his access card. "Let's hope this works." It hadn't worked at the hoverstation, but maybe Zim limited his access to hovertrains arriving at Sphere One only, not to Sphere One's airlocks.

Devon looked through the door's window. "There's gotta be a hundred or more barrels in there."

"Maybe more." Koda held the card in front of the door's control panel. "Cross your fingers." There was a beep and the door unlocked, then opened. Koda let out a gush of air. He nodded and pointed to several barrels in the corner. "Check those but don't open them, and I'll check the ones on the other side of the room."

They entered the large hangar, and the door shut behind them. "Check the tags, the markings, the whatever. See if anything says baktotoxin."

"Batrachotoxin," corrected Devon.

"Yeah, what you said." Koda rushed toward a group of twenty barrels, maybe more, all lined neatly next to each other.

"Here's some," said Devon, his fingers on a long tag attached to a barrel. "This one's labeled batrachotoxin, so are the rest in this corner."

Koda fumbled with a tag and flipped it over. "Batrachotoxin," he said, under his breath. He clapped his hands together. "Looks like Zim had them ushered in here but didn't open the airlocks."

"Okay," said Devon "Let's get out of here and open this airlock. The barrels will suck into space."

Koda hurried toward the door. Once the door was shut, opening the airlock through the control panel remained the easiest task. A knock pounded against the door's window. Koda halted, his pulse quickening. Men stood at the door.

A static sound crackled through the room as the comm turned on, followed by a man's booming voice. "Stay where you are and put your hands on your head. Do not move. I repeat, do not move."

Koda put his hands on his head, eyeing the men, not able to tell exactly who stood out there.

"Do you have your access card with you?" whispered Devon.

"Right here. If those are Payson's men, they can't get in."

"Are you sure?"

Koda wanted to shrug, but don't move reverberated through his mind. "Truthfully, I don't know."

"Crap."

"Exactly."

The male's voice came over the comm again. "Get on the ground and stare at the floor."

They lay face down, the ebb floor cold against Koda's body. A horrible thought entered his mind, and he squeezed his eyes shut. "Devon, if this is Payson and his team, we have to do something..." He didn't want to say it.

"Like what?"

Koda kept his eyes closed tightly. His desire to become the greatest politician ever to grace the governance screeched to a bitter end. His next actions would never see the light of day, never don a holovid recording, and never meet the eyes of Matrona's population. But, for the good of his people, he must do the unthinkable.

"We manually open the airlock and let the toxin out." His voice cracked. He had single-handedly steered Devon to his death.

Devon let out a long breath. "Dammit." He slowly nodded. "Yeah, we don't have any other option. Are we sure it's Payson's men?"

"They'd be inside by now if it were the Matrona Guard or any other Star Guild Marines. So, yes, I'm sure this is Payson and his assholes." Koda's face went pale, not believing his next question. "Do you know how to manually open an airlock?"

"Yes."

The airlock was attached to the wall across the room, space-side. A lever mounted next to the airlock allowed manual openings. Warnings painted on the walls and above the airlock, read in big letters, DO NOT MANUALLY OPEN IF VESSEL NOT ATTACHED TO AIRLOCK. They only used the manual lever when all else failed. And today, Koda had no other choice. But regardless, he'd never opened one and didn't know how.

"How do you open it?" asked Koda.

"It's easy," said Devon. "You just push the lever down, and the airlock's door spins open."

"I'll stand and block their view, okay?"

"No." Devon's voice echoed through the room. "Guild, no."

"One..."

"Listen, there has to be a better way."

It was now or never. They couldn't wait it out. If Payson broke in and released the toxin through the air channels, he didn't want to think about the death toll.

"Two...and you better run your ass over there the moment I stand, got it?"

"Shit, Koda. I don't know."

"Do it." He knew they'd both be dead, but if Devon's prophecies were real, they had no other option.

"Okay, okay." Devon moaned. "Start the count over."

A hiss and the door to the room opened. Boots marched in, and a hand grabbed Koda by the back of the shirt and pulled him up. Someone spun him around and forced him against the wall, a gun to his temple. "Do. Not. Move."

Koda's eyes went wide, and he looked the man up and down. "Oh, my Guild." He let out a sigh of relief. "You're not Payson or his crew."

"No," said the man, the smell of coffee wafting off of his breath, and veins popping out of his neck. "You better not be one of his men either, or I plug a hole into your pretty face."

Koda smiled. Brigantia guardsmen, and from the sounds of it, a handful of them stood in the room. Another Guard enjoyed a similar conversation with Devon.

"I'm Prime Overseer Koda Lutz. I was just in the infirmary with you guys." He wanted to point to his face, but moving his arms probably wouldn't be the smartest move at the moment. "Do you recognize me?"

The guard spat on the floor. "No, and I don't care. They can confirm who you are later."

"I have my ID Card on me." Koda went for his pocket, chiding himself a second later.

The guard slammed him into the wall. "What part of 'don't move' don't you understand?" He twisted Koda around and pulled Koda's arms behind his back. Steel wrapped around his wrists, clicking shut. The Brigantia guard nudged him toward the doorway and out of the hangar. The rest of the soldiers and Devon, handcuffed as well, followed.

The door shut, and they were pushed toward the docking bay. Koda pulled back. "Listen—"

His head whipped forward as a guy's palm whacked him across the back of his head. "Shut up and keep moving. We'll identify you later, but right now, you're one of Payson's men."

"I am not." Koda dug his boots into the floor. "No, you will not identify us later. Identify me now and get me back into that airlock. The toxin needs to be—" A heavy boot sank into his back, sending him forward. He stumbled but maintained balance and stayed on his feet.

"Shut your mouth."

Koda turned, his eyes tightening. "Your very survival depends on getting that toxin off of the starbase. Open that hangar's airlock."

The guard flattened his lips and widened his stance. He glared at Koda for what seemed to be several minutes. He slowly pulled the comm device on his shoulder closer to his mouth. "Fleet Admiral Shae Lutz, do you copy?"

"I'm on my way," replied Shae.

"I've captured the trespassers. One claims to be—"

"That's my uncle," yelled Koda. A fist crashed into Koda's face, and he dropped to the ground, his chin aching.

"Fleet Admiral, where would you like us to put these two captives?"

"Somewhere enclosed. I'll be there any minute."

Devon took a step forward, his hands cuffed behind him. "Tell him you have Prime Overseer Koda Lutz. They are related."

The guards looked at each other. The lead man pointed to a Starhawk Transport. "In there." He grabbed Koda's shoulder and lifted him off the ground, escorting him toward the ship.

Koda leaned back, doing his best to fight against the guard's strength. "No, listen. Open the damn airlock and—"

"You won't shut up, and I don't have time for this." The guard wrapped his arms around Koda, giving him a bear hug. He picked him up off his feet and carried him to the Starhawk. "Open the side panel door."

A guard stepped in and slammed his palm into the side door panel. The Starhawk's door opened. They threw Koda in, and then Devon. The door shut, and the cabin light dimmed.

Koda moaned, wanting to rub his face. "That smarts."

Devon scooted back against a wall. "We almost changed the prophecy. Almost." He eyed the floor, shaking his head, his eyes drooping.

Koda looked around. They were in the ship's cargo hold. "Almost? We'll get that toxin out. Wait for my uncle. He'll be here any minute." He looked into the cockpit at a heavily tinted window that blocked anyone from seeing inside while allowing the pilot to see outside fairly easily. He'd never been inside one of these, and for all he knew, not a single human alive had been in one of these transport ships either. This one was unlocked, or the guard somehow hit the right codes with his palm, deactivating the locked door and opening the ship up. "Does the pilot and co-pilot seat look abnormally large to you?"

Devon shook his head. "Not large, huge."

He threw Devon a look, and from Devon's pinched expression, they both knew Anunnaki piloted these craft.

Koda went to stand. "We've got to get out of here."

The Starhawk rocked back as an explosion blasted near the ship's nose. A handful of ebb chunks cracked from the flooring and ricocheted off the cockpit window.

Koda rested his shoulder against the bulkhead. "I'm not getting the best feeling right now."

The door opened, and there stood Shae, smoke twirling into the air beside him. His eyes widened. "Koda?"

Another blast lifted Shae off his feet and threw him inside the Starhawk. Ebb flooring cracked upward, sending dozens of pieces spitting into the Starhawk's cabin, riddling the walls.

Koda ducked low, turning away from the concussion blast, his forehead against the floor. A moment later, his uncle tumbled into him, sending Koda hard against the wall.

24

SHAE

Starbase Matrona

Shae pushed himself up and faced the open door. Payson and his men, at least a few, ran down the street. They headed to the docking bay, guns in hand. Either the rest of Payson's team had died, or they'd stayed behind to fight the Space Templars. Shae bet the latter.

Brigantia guard fired their rifles, and Payson's men dove behind a gray and black ebb constructed building. Trees and shrubs next to the sidewalk and building shook, bullets slicing through leaves and bark. Sparks bounced off the building, the *ratatatat* echoing inside the Starhawk's cabin.

Shae hurried to his nephew and helped him up. "What are you doing here?" Shae put his hand on his helmet, not waiting for Koda's response, and patched through to a nearby guard. "I need you to uncuff these men you placed in the Starhawk Transport."

"I'm on my way," replied a Marine.

Another explosion rocked the area, and more dust kicked into the air, clouding the view outside the ship cabin's open doorway. A guard entered, waving his hand in front of him, clearing the dust cloud out of the way and coughing. He tossed the keys at Shae, and turned, He held down his rifle's trigger, blasting through the cloud at Payson's men.

"Go, go," yelled Shae. "Get to the airlocks and find the toxin."

"I know where the toxin is," said Koda, turning his back to Shae.

Shae uncuffed him and threw the cuffs on the cabin floor. "Then show the guards the way." He unholstered one of his sidearms and handed it to Koda.

"On my way." Koda rushed out of the ship, firing toward Payson's soldiers.

Shae grabbed Devon's arm and spun him around. "Turn around." He fumbled with the keys and dropped them on the floor. "Dammit." He bent down, picking them up and fit the key in the keyhole. Just as he went to turn the key, the co-pilot's door swung open in a hurry. Devon moved toward the back of the cabin in a start, and the key fell to the floor again. Shae turned, eyeing the cockpit.

An Anunnaki taller and more robust than Prime Director Zim Noki, fell over the co-pilot seat in a hurry, her breath coming fast. She landed hard on her shoulder, then somersaulted onto her back. She sprang to her feet and flung herself at the cockpit door, slapping a button and shutting it quickly. The cabin door hissed and closed, clicking in place.

"Oh my, oh my, oh my," cried the woman, plopping on the pilot chair. She flicked a few levers and pressed several buttons on the cockpit ceiling. The holomonitors activated and a vidscreen appeared on the cockpit window, brightening the tint. The cockpit and cabin dimmed to a darker blue hue.

She turned on the commlink. "Control HQ Eos Two, this is Kalista. I'm experiencing heavy fire. I need the launch bay doors open." She eyed to her right. "A battle rages, I repeat, a battle is raging. I need to get out of here as—" Her voice cut off as the launch bay doors opened, displaying several launch tubes before her. "I'm leaving Starbase Matrona right now, soon to land on Eos Two. Thank you, Enlil, if you're listening." She pressed several more buttons, and the engines roared, the Starhawk shaking.

Shae pulled out his other sidearm and aimed it at the back of the woman's head. He tightened his lips. "Open the cabin door, now."

She gasped and slowly raised her hands. "Who are you?"

"Doesn't matter. Let us off of the ship and I won't pull this trigger." Shae's heart pumped quickly, his stomach churning in many directions he didn't want. If the toxin indeed resided in an airlock, he needed to get it into space. He didn't want to visit Eos Two.

The craft lurched and shuddered violently. Another concussion blast hit nearby. Shae lost his balance and fell on his back, Devon doing the same and slamming hard into Shae. The gun was flung from Shae's hand and slid across the floor, knocking into a wall. Shae grimaced and pushed Devon off of him. He dove for his gun.

A *phtah* echoed in the ship and a bullet cracked Shae's gun barrel in half. Another loud crack split the air, and a sharp bite went deep into Shae's shoulder. He grunted and brought his hand to his shoulder, feeling warm blood from a fresh wound. He rolled onto his back, his eyes wide, to see if a bullet had sunk into Devon too.

Devon lay on his side, frozen, obviously not knowing what to do, his hands cuffed.

"Devon, are you hit?"

"No."

"You move another muscle, you die." The large Anunnaki woman stared at Shae, her lips downturned. She held a gun. "I'm not a killer. I don't want to kill you." She sat down in a huff, and held onto the control stick, pressing holographic buttons on the flight console.

Shae went to stand, to run at her, to stop her from taking off. The Starhawk rose violently, and he fell yet again, yelping loudly when his wounded shoulder hit the floor. He clutched his bloodied arm and winced in pain.

"Fleet Admiral, you've been shot!" Devon crawled toward Shae, looking like a fish out of water with his hands behind his back.

The Starhawk pitched. Devon and Shae slid toward the stern, moving deeper into the cargo hold.

"This is Kalista," said the woman, leaning into the commlink. "Heading into the launch tubes, preparing for takeoff."

Shae shook his head. "No, no. Let us off. We have—"

She turned, her gun pointed at Shae, her voice sharp. "Don't talk." She turned and steered the Starhawk into the launch tube, pressing another button on the holodisplay. She jostled her control stick and pushed on the throttle, slowing the ship down and stopping it in the middle of the tube. The cockpit and cabin changed to an amber glow from the launch tube's lights beaming inside the craft.

"Close rear launch tube door," said Kalista. "Thank you. Open forward launch tube." The forward launch tube door opened, the cosmos like a black abyss set before them, ready to swallow them.

"Please, don't," pleaded Shae, his arm going numb. "I need to get to my people."

She kept her eyes toward the stars. "This ship and me aren't prepared to fight. Hold on. We're blasting out of here."

Shit.

Shae tapped his helmet, bringing up his com. "Louise, status, please."

Heavy breathing came on the other end. "Manning and I, and several of our Brigantia Guard, are heading your way. The Space Templars are having their way with Payson's men, but Payson and a few of his soldiers slipped through. They're on their way to the airlocks."

"Yes, they attacked us from behind. Get to the airlocks fast. We need you there. Keep Koda safe."

"Where are you?" said Louise.

The Starhawk launched out of the tube and Shae felt the rush, the high blood pressure, and instant weight increase grab his body, pressing him against a back wall. When they exited the gravity field, his body lightened and his commlink went to static. He pressed his hand against the side of his helmet, whispering, "Louise, do you read? Louise?"

No reply.

His shoulder's drooped. The last thing he needed was to leave the starbase and his soldiers behind. Shae glanced at Devon and raised his brows. "You all right?"

Devon nodded. "We need to stop that bleeding."

Shae leaned his head back, taking a deep breath. He had to think of a way out of this.

"Setting course now," spoke Kalista. "Things have gone awfully wrong. Is it safe to land on Eos Two?"

"It's safe," a voice replied. "However, we're re-routing you."

Kalista gave a curt nod. "Coordinates?"

"Zero-zero-one," responded the voice.

"Zero-zero-one?" She thought for a moment. "Nibiru?"

"Yes, and we see two heat signatures on your craft. Two humans. I repeat, two humans are in your craft. Eliminate them. They pose an immediate threat to classified operations."

Shae flexed his good hand and pressed his fist against the floor, helping himself to a standing position. Although she bested him in weight, height, and strength, he wouldn't allow her to end his and Devon's life without a fight.

Kalista flicked off the com, sighing. She bounced the back of her head against the pilot seat's headrest as if shooting Devon and Shae ruined her already horrible day. "Activate autopilot," she said as she stood. She turned and faced Shae, her fingers wrapped around her gun's grip.

Shae remained silent, gritting his teeth. He could run at her, but she'd pull the trigger. Perhaps if she took a few steps closer, he could do something, anything, but he knew she had the advantage, had the easy kill shot.

She slowly walked toward Shae, then motioned with her gun toward the stern. "Back up."

Shae shook his head. "No."

She turned her weapon on Devon. "Do you want to watch your friend die?"

He looked at Devon, who gave Shae a nod, his arms tucked into his sides, making himself smaller. "I'll go first. Don't worry about me. I'm okay."

Shae faced Kalista and stepped in front of her aim to make sure her bullet hit him, not Devon. Not that it really mattered. She'd take

Devon out next. Perhaps he didn't want to witness another person on his watch die, he didn't know, but the young man should live a lot longer. That he knew for sure.

Shae thought of Ali and briefly squeezed his eyes shut, sending her a silent apology. They had been together, and although short, it had been the best day of his life. He wanted to be with her, to see his wife, and to reunite his family back together again, but sometimes fate had other plans.

"I said, back up." Kalista lurched forward, her gun extended. "Now."

Shae slowly moved toward the stern, focusing on her trigger finger. She held fast, keeping her finger outside the trigger guard and not through it. She walked toward a bench attached to a cabin's side wall. She bent down and reached under the bench, unclasping something, keeping her eyes on Shae, her other hand holding the gun.

She pulled out a large toolbox, and still keeping her attention on Shae, she opened it. Reaching in, she lifted a giant snip cutter, similar to something Shae had seen in the biosphere, usually used to cut large branches. Kalista eyed the tool, then eyed them. She frowned and walked toward Shae.

He swallowed hard. Was she going to cut them up first, or after she blasted them with her gun?

25

KODA

Starbase Matrona

Koda followed a few guards, running low. Another blast sent chunks of flooring into the air, and the Brigantia guards dove to the ground, Koda diving with them.

"This way," called a guard, pulling Koda to his feet and shoving him under a starfighter belly and behind a landing sled.

"Where's my uncle?"

Tracer fire glanced at the ship and the ebb floor. The guards, a handful in all, took positions around the starfighter, their weapons drawn and ready.

"Who?" asked a guard, his chest heaving in and out, his face covered in black. He steadied his weapon on the landing sled Koda hid behind, eyeing his scope.

"I mean, Admiral Shae Lutz." He looked around. "And my friend, Devon."

More gunfire carried across the distance. Koda instinctively ducked. The guards returned fire. Then silence filled the docking bay as all maintained aim but held their fingers off the triggers.

The guard next to Koda shrugged. "I'm sure they're safe. I've heard no updates otherwise." The guard brought his hand to his ear, nodding. "XO Stripe has Payson's men pinned down. We're on their twelve, she and her team on their six." The guy brought his hand to his ear again, his eyes almost bulging out of his sockets. "How?"

Koda noticed the rest of the surrounding guards now eyeing the airlocks.

"What's the status?" asked Koda, his voice low, nerves tingling in his hands and feet. He didn't like the guy's expression. Did he get word that his uncle died?

"I don't understand how, but an ISA agent just informed the XO that Payson and a few of his men got inside an airlock. They locked it down, preparing to release the toxin. The ISA agent has eyes on Payson now." He spat on the ground. "Shit."

More gunfire went off from the opposite direction of the airlocks. Payson probably used a few of his troops as a diversion while he slipped by them.

"It makes no sense how they could have gotten past us." He grabbed the back of Koda's shirt and pulled him out from under the starfighter. "We need you and your weapon. Come with us."

They rushed past the launch bay and entered the large hall where the airlocks were located. The Brigantia Guards went to a knee, some finding cover, all focusing their weapons on the row of doors.

The guard next to Koda held his hand over his ear. He nodded and eyed Koda. "XO Stripe dealt with Payson's soldiers. She's on her way to us now."

Tracer fire whizzed over Koda's head in a continuous stream. He went to the floor, quickly crawling toward the closest craft in the launch bay. He turned and placed himself behind another landing sled. The man who had been next to him only moments ago lay on the ground, blood pooling around his head, dead. Koda's heart dropped. "Oh, no." A few other guards near the airlocks were face down, not moving.

Another bullet whizzed by. Koda backtracked and found another craft for cover. He held his gun tightly, his hand shaking, remembering his Star Guild academy training. None of the simulations he went through felt like the real thing, a bone-chilling nightmare. "Concentrate, Koda," he told himself, his body tense. He checked his gun and flicked the safety off, then pointed it toward the airlocks. He swallowed. He had to stop Payson, but how? If he took a step toward them, he'd end up dead like the guards.

Louise's voice carried across the launch bay, and for a moment, Koda relaxed. He quickly shook his head. With Payson in the airlock hangar housing the toxin, okay didn't exist.

Boot steps pounded, coming in his direction. He shifted his aim, eyeing the smoke swirling and fogging the street entrance into the docking bay. He lowered his gun when Louise and several guards emerged and headed toward Koda.

Koda kept low and raised his hand. "Louise, Prime Overseer Koda Lutz here."

She paused for an instant, her eyes surveying the dock. She nodded when she made eye contact and motioned for the Marines to follow her. She rushed to Koda's side. "What do you have for me?" Manning and a few Guards took positions in front of Koda, their rifles aimed toward the airlock hangars.

"Several Brigantia Guards were shot, I think killed. There might be two or three others alive, but I'm not sure."

"Where's Shae?"

"I don't know, but he wasn't with the Guards or me. Maybe heading back to Sphere Nine?"

"Probably toward the Space Templars. They have the situation handled, so he'll be safe there."

"Contact him. Find his location."

Louise pushed a strand of hair off of her sticky, perspiring forehead. "His comm malfunctioned. I can't get a hold of him." She stood. "Stay here."

Koda shook his head. He knew which airlock hangar held the toxin. "No, I'm coming. I'll lead you to the right hangar."

"Just tell us the airlock number," she said.

Koda thought for a moment. "I don't know the number."

"Dammit, Koda." She let out a puff of air and hurried forward. "Let's go."

Manning and his men dashed behind a wall that jutted out in front of the line of hangars. Louise and Koda rushed to the wall across from the airlocks and used another jutting wall as cover. Koda eyed several limp bodies on the ground. The Guards he'd taken cover with earlier lay deceased, their blood splattered on the floor. Payson and his men were nowhere in sight and were presumably in the airlock.

"Which airlock?" asked Louise.

Koda pointed, his finger extending toward a door, though he couldn't see the actual number. "That one."

"Manning," said Louse, "take the lead. I'm behind you." She turned, grabbing Koda's shirt and scrunching the cloth between her fingers. "Get back to your uncle in Sphere Nine. Got it?"

Koda put his hands up. "Got it."

"Good."

She let go and spun on her heels, running after her men. They reached the airlock in no time and kept their distance from the thick ebb wall.

Koda went to turn, then hesitated, watching Louise take out her ID Card. She said something to Manning and the rest of the Marines, and they went into position, ready to sweep the area or send in massive gunfire. Which, Koda didn't know. Louise dipped her head at Manning, and he nodded back. She swiped the card, and Manning's muscles flexed. Then he paused, easing up.

The door didn't open. She said something else to her team and swiped again. Nothing. Manning ripped his ID Card from his belt and handed it to Louise. She swiped. The door remained closed.

Louise clenched her fists, baring her teeth. Koda grimaced. Unless Payson had somehow deactivated the control panel, Koda's ID would work. He ran forward and reached Louise, resting his back against the wall.

She shot him a look. "Off the wall. Get to your uncle. That's an order."

He moved away from the wall, remembering his Star Guild training. Never stand against a wall before or when clearing a room, just in case interior blasts tore apart said wall.

He held up his ID Card. "I used this last time, and it opened the door."

Louise raised her eyebrows.

He wanted to look through the door's window, but refrained, not wanting a bullet through his head. "Are you sure Payson and his crew are in this one?"

"Yes, we peeked through the window and eyed Payson and three of his soldiers. They're opening the air channels. They have a duffle bag and are using a long, thin hose with a device of some sort. That's all we got."

Koda nodded, impressed they'd seen so much with a quick look through the window.

Louise continued. "My guess is they'll go from one barrel to the next, sucking the toxin up through the hose and blowing it through the air ducts. Who knows if the strategy will work, but if it does…"

"They're wearing gas masks, too," said Manning. "They came prepared."

"Let me see," said Koda.

"Quick-like," replied Louise.

Koda took a quick look, his eyes resting on several men all wearing masks, pushing containers toward an air duct attached to the wall. A man glanced at Koda and lifted his weapon. Koda ducked back around. A knot formed in his throat. He tried swallowing it down. His job to keep the people on Starbase Matrona safe had failed on all fronts. He should have opened the airlock when the chance presented itself earlier.

Louise held up his ID Card. "I can't get through to the Internal Security Agency for some Guild damn reason, so we can't override the system and open the airlock. Our next best bet is that we open this door up and send some bullets through their throats."

Guards stacked to the side of the door, several positioning themselves low. Koda held his gun up, standing on the other side of the door near Manning and Louise.

"On my mark, open fire but aim high, chest level. We don't want to hit any of those barrels, though if we did, it would contain the exposure to that room." She glared into her soldier's eyes. "We sweep the room when the exchange stops. If it doesn't stop, Manning will crawl in a meter, me two meters, and pick them off. Your gunfire should keep them busy." She held up Koda's ID Card. "Are you ready?"

They all nodded.

"On my mark," said Louse. "Three...two...one...*now.*"

She swiped the card, and the door opened.

26

DIANA

Starship Sirona, Eos

Diana pulled her hair back in a bun. Her door buzzed. She leaned forward and swiped across her desk's HDC's holomonitor, pulling up the corridor cams outside her quarters. It was Sleuth. She let out a sigh. "Come in." She pressed another button, and the door slid open.

Sleuth walked in his hands behind his back. "Don't let these new people scare you out of the agreement we made with Enlil. They're here to distract us. Like you've said many times, we stay on course."

"Are you saying they know?"

Sleuth took a seat in a chair at the head of her desk. "I think Eden knows we're in cahoots with whom they claim is the enemy, but I'm sure the rest of those idiot Space Templars don't agree with her assessment."

"My gut's telling me to trust them."

"Trust them?"

"Yes, Eden and those Space Templar fools. They told me a weapon is heading our way. Enlil never informed us of any such weapon. The contract only involved his people's fleet, their rookie starfighter pilots, training on our starship. It included his rookie infantry as well. Never, and I repeat, never, did he mention a weapon coming our way."

Sleuth choked and covered his mouth. "You're serious? You're trusting them? What are you thinking? You don't want to blow this with Enlil. This is more than just your life, Diana. If we don't follow through, all lives on this ship are lost."

Diana paused and cocked her head to the side. "Are you hard of hearing? I said a massive weapon is heading our way."

Sleuth shrugged. "The Space Templars will say anything to get this ship into the air and out of the system. We stand firm and keep our people on this ship safe."

Diana almost laughed. Sleuth couldn't care less about the people onboard *Sirona*. "I think Skye can be helpful for us. He can get us someplace safe and secure. We won't need Enlil to do that for us. Not anymore."

Sleuth's face reddened. "Enlil offers riches and our own moon to live on during the next human cycle, a cycle we'd miss, and gladly. That moon is plush. It's beautiful and suitable for humans."

"Have you seen this moon? Do you even know where it's located? Have you ever stepped foot on it?"

Sleuth waved a dismissive hand. "You know I haven't, but that's not the point. I can't—"

"We can do this on our own. You know, leave Eos and find Star Guild and Starbase Matrona or have the Space Templars take us to a safe planet nearby. The only thing stopping us is…you and me."

Sleuth's nostrils flared, and he stiffened as if rooting himself to the seat. "Are you crazy? It's too late. We stand to be stoned to death if we got this ship up and running."

"You're just as blind as you are hard of hearing. Listen, if we tell everyone on the ship that engineering has fixed…everything…then why the Guild wouldn't they believe us, let alone me, their captain?"

"When the engineers claim they didn't have any hand in repairs, then what?" He huffed. "Let's kickoff, or kill these newcomers, especially that freak-show, Eden."

Killing them would make things much easier for Diana. It would remove an enormous weight off of her shoulders. She could continue on with Enlil's plan.

She remembered the look on Eden's face when Eden told her about the weapon. The woman told the truth, and since she hadn't lied, that meant Enlil hadn't been upfront with Diana again. She cleared her throat. "No."

"No? Enlil will find us and kill us if we disobey his orders. Are you suicidal?"

Suicidal, thought Diana. You have no idea.

"Okay, at least hold off on that thought for a while. It may have to come to that, but I need to clear up one important thing." She shifted in her seat. About a year ago, Enlil explained the human cycle to her and the Kill-Offs at the end of each. To get some information from Sleuth, she needed to fudge a bit. "I'm confused about the cycle. Enlil spoke of it as if I had full knowledge, but I don't. Yet you seem to know more than me. He sent you something?"

"He has. After this current genocide succeeds, this current human cycle ends. That we know. The Anunnaki will then nab thousands of humans on Earth and bring them to Enlil's labs. Apparently, he needs live subjects. He'll begin a new batch of humans, using fresh DNA, and begin birthing humans for a new cycle. As they grow, Enlil's technicians will mold batches of humans into powerful, working machines to gather as much ebb as possible for the Anunnaki. To us, it won't matter. We'll be safe on the moon like he promised."

Diana ran her hands down her face, rubbing as much stress off as she could. She studied Sleuth's eyes, his confidence nearly blowing her away. She realized that Enlil had lied and had done so from the first moment they met. Enlil never told her about the labs, about fresh DNA, or about kidnapping thousands of humans. The Monarch held a lot from her. She wouldn't be surprised if he didn't tell the truth about this so-called moon. Now, she doubted it even existed. And keeping *Sirona* and *Sirona*'s crew alive? Probably fiction.

For the first time, she saw the truth. She didn't control any of this, not in the slightest. Sleuth called the shots and had manipulated the shit out of her. She believed she received the orders from Enlil, then passed them on to Sleuth. That was not the case. Sleuth knew her inside and out, having been her right-hand man since first captaining this ship years ago. Sleuth knew the orders before Diana did and helped steer Diana where Enlil wanted her to go. If second thoughts ravaged her mind, he had a way to stop them.

An image of Sleuth holding a document he claimed he hacked from Fleet Admiral Shae Lutz's holocomp came to mind. He'd presented it to her a year ago, maybe longer and told her Shae had sent the document to every captain in the Star Guild fleet, explaining his dislike for Captain Diana Johnson and her many mistakes, none of which he had the guts to say in front of her. "She won't ever be Fleet Admiral material, and I'm monitoring further improper actions in hopes of finding a better reason to demote her."

It bit her insides to no end. Captain Boyd Reynolds and Caption Patricia Hannig had denied ever receiving the document. They didn't deny it to save her feelings. They denied it because they'd never received it, the entire document having been created and manifested by Sleuth. That sly piece of Orion's broken belt. Sleuth had shown her myriad similar documents, all of which she now knew he cropped up on his own holocomp. The documents gave her impetus to join Enlil when the big guy appeared because screw those who would slight her like she thought Shae had done.

She shook her head, her eyes set on Sleuth. Through him, Enlil controlled Diana. Sleuth probably knew more than he was spitting out. Every vein in her body about burst at the thought.

"You little—" She reached over her desk and snagged Sleuth by the collar, pulling the skinny prick onto her desk, nose to nose. She bared her teeth, seething. "New batch of humans? What more do you know? You know about the weapon, don't you?"

Sleuth grabbed her hand, trying to force Diana to release her strong grip. "I...I don't know, Diana. Nothing. Please let me go. I know only what you know."

She squeezed his collar tighter. "I'm not letting go until you give me all the information you're withholding from me." She pointed to an armor-covered window in her quarters. "Enlil's fleet attempted genocide on our people and we cooperated. You, me, and Captain

Stan Jenkins." She stood, thrusting her free hand against his neck, wrapping her fingers around his blotchy skin and squeezing.

He tried to pull back unsuccessfully. The veins in his forehead were bulging, and his face was turning scarlet. She pursed her lips and let out a growl, pushing him away like a rag doll. He landed on his rear, sucking in much-needed air.

She plopped in her seat and rested her forehead on the edge of her desk. "I almost killed our entire race, all because of lies. Now Enlil's weapon heads toward *Sirona*."

Sleuth picked himself up. He backed away from her and toward the doorway. "You warned our race. That could have been a huge problem."

"I did what?"

"Starship *Sirona* was the first to fire when the Anunnaki's fleet showed."

"That wasn't me. That was our weapon's operation specialist."

"The Anunnaki weren't on any of our fleet's radar. I made sure of that. Yet, our weapons specialist knew where they were and fired upon them? The only person who would have been aware of such a threat was you and that buzz-brain Jenkins on Starship *Taranis*. I sure as hell didn't order those first shots and I know Jenkins didn't."

Diana sat straighter. "There wasn't supposed to be an attack, Sleuth. At least, not to that magnitude. Enlil informed me it would be a quick in and out exercise for his green fleet—his novice pilots." She pounded her fist on the desk. "Yet nearly half the population perished. All because we wanted riches and a new place to live—planet-side. How stupid could we be?" She paused, another truth forming in her. "Holy Guild. You knew he would send his entire fleet, didn't you? You knew he'd try to wipe out all of humanity."

Sleuth blinked rapidly. "Are you going to tell me you're not on this mission anymore?" He pointed to his chest. "It's just me and Enlil now?"

Diana dropped her head in defeat, the weight of the galaxy too much. "You know what? I'm done. We're activating *Sirona*'s engines and getting off Eos. We'll join the rest of Star Guild fleet at the rendezvous point…if they're still there."

Sleuth sidestepped slowly and butted up against the wall beside the door. "You're killing me, Diana. You really are."

Diana's voice dropped low. "Tell the crew to get ready. We leave at," she glanced at her watch, "fourteen-hundred hours."

"In four hours?" Sleuth shook his head, pushing his glasses up the ridge of his nose. "I'm sorry. I can't do that."

"You'll do as I ask, or I'll reprimand you."

Sleuth smirked. "You reprimand me, and this all comes out to the crew." He reached into his pocket, pulling out a small, round device. "All of our dialogue has been going to Enlil for months. He's listening now. If you—"

"Who the Guild are you working for? Me or them?" She knew the answer before she asked, but it came out anyway.

He took in a deep breath. "Let me start again. If you reprimand me, Enlil will see that *Sirona*'s crew hears every word coming from your snaked tongue. Or he blows the entire ship to Guild and back. *Sirona* stays here until further orders." He grimaced, rubbing his heart as if pained by Diana's sudden change. "You disappoint me. I don't know about you, but I want to live. Perhaps some of our crew want to live as well."

"Sit down, Sleuth."

Sleuth spat on the floor. "Your orders mean nothing." He turned and swiped the control panel next to the door. The door slid open and he walked down the corridor. The door shut.

Diana looked at the door. She rested her head in her hands and spoke to herself. "What did I do?" She wept. After a few moments, she lifted her head and stared at her wet palms. "I'm a monster. How could I have considered aligning with Enlil? All because I had an imaginary gripe with the fleet admiral and the captains?" She slid her hand under her desk and pressed a button. The desk drawer opened. She reached in and took out her pistol and placed it against her temple. She squeezed her eyes shut, her finger twitching on the trigger. She pulled the trigger. An empty click sounded.

Rearing back, she threw the gun against the ebb door. "I can't even get that right." She'd have to deal with the shit she created like everyone else.

27

EDEN

Starship Sirona, Eos

Eden yawned and stretched her arms wide. She was on top of her bed, the sheets still tucked in. She abruptly bolted upright, her eyes bright. She eyed the bed and then her pillow. Did she dream it? She shook her head. Last night, she'd practiced the Sight with Skye, and eventually lifted the pillow off the ground and onto her bed. It took great effort and drained her to near blackout.

She moved to the edge of her bed. "How was any of that possible?"

Something inside her stirred, and she jumped to a standing position. She touched her stomach just above her belly button. It felt warm. "What's going on?"

She turned and pointed her hand at the pillow. Her emotions swirled inside her, everything from the love she had for the man she considered her father, Fleet Admiral Shae Lutz, to the rage she felt knowing Diana walked around a traitor.

More images appeared: her first kiss, and the longing for the boy, the uplifting sensation when he told her he was the one. The sadness that took hold when he kissed another girl a week later. Then another image slowly turned into a movie. Eden watched as her mother stomped down the hall, pushing fifteen-year-old Eden along, screaming at her, "I told you to get my medication."

Eden had refused. The medication had become an addiction, a drug, and at that young age, Eden finally understood why her mom turned into an abusive monster.

She shoved Eden out of the house. Eden's heart plummeted, the love for her mom thrown in her face as if it didn't matter. Her mom locked the door. "Don't come back until you have my meds."

Eden never returned and never saw her mother again. That day tossed love and confusion into a tangled spider's web.

She snapped out of her thoughts and let out a breath that came from deep in her belly, almost like dragon's fire. A sense of connection came from the pillow, and the surrounding energy clicked inside her as if she pressed an on switch. Then a sweet, peaceful sensation engulfed her like a ladybug landing on her finger in the biosphere.

"Lift." She raised her hand, and the pillow moved upward. Her hand shook and her body perspired. Her knees wobbled and she fell to the floor, and the pillow plummeted to the bed. She sat on the floor, panting like an overworked dog, sweat dripping down her face.

She took a deep breath, and thoughts of Shae entered her mind. During a Starfighter combat training exercise, he told her how impressive her quick thinking had been. Her fast reflexes gave her Starship *Brigantia's* top score. She smiled when his face came to mind, his lips holding down the grin he wanted to give. As Admiral, he couldn't show favorites. Yet, she knew his favorite was her.

She quickly gained strength at the thought and pushed off the ground, wiping the sweat off of her brow. She stood tall, a smile growing on her face. Never in her life did she imagine conjuring anything like the Sight or manipulating physics in such a way.

Two days ago, she would have thought it impossible. The impossible became reality, and she rushed to the door, wanting to run to Skye for more training. If she could pick up lifting a pillow so quickly, what else could she do with the Sight? Could she shoot electric bolts out of her hands? She snorted at the crazy thought.

The door opened, and she squinted her eyes, a strange buzzing sound entering her ears. A thought entered her mind, and the buzzing stopped. Did she feel a shift in energy on the ship? The thought centered on the big glasses-wearing, short and balding man.

"Sleuth," she said. "There's a shift in him. He's more dangerous." She shook her head, pushing the idea and sensation away. Diana ran the ship. He didn't.

Energy slammed into her heart, and an intuitive sensation rang through her body. "They split? Sleuth no longer works for her?" She rolled her eyes. Her mind and body were playing tricks on her.

She rounded a corridor, looking for Skye. The smell of fresh bread wafted to her nose, and she stopped in stride, glancing to her right. Her stomach growled, and she patted it. "All right, we dine, then we find Skye." She walked toward the cafeteria. The door slid open.

Utensils scraped plates brimming with food, and people occupied rows and rows of tables. Her eyes halted on a man to her right.

Overweight, his hair unkempt, he held a fork over his plate of food. There were bruises around his eyes and a bandage over the ridge of his nose as if he'd lost a recent fistfight. He stared at Eden like she wore a crown and a princess gown. He stabbed food and shoveled the fork into his mouth, chomping. He kept his eyes on her and motioned her over.

Eden wrinkled her brow and made her way to him. She sensed something important and stopped at the head of the table.

"You're Major Eden Gaines, right? The one I saw on the vidscreen replays ramming your starfighter into the torpedoes?" He shook his head. "I heard you were on *Sirona*, but how the Guild did you survive?"

"All I can say is the Space Templars helped to keep me alive. The mechanics of it and their technology to do something like that is still way over my head." Why did Eden feel he had significant information for her?

He grabbed a sandwich from his plate and took a tremendous bite, taking half the sandwich in his mouth. He flicked his finger at someone, calling him over, his mouth full.

Eden glanced at his food. Corn, mashed potatoes, gravy, and you name it, all in a huge clump on his plate. She frowned. "Why do you have such large portions?" She glanced around the room, studying several other plates. "You're all eating like kings and queens."

He picked up his plate and scooped sloppy corn into his mouth. "I'm Hank." He glanced over Eden's shoulder. "And that's Doctor William."

"Great, but really, how do you have so much food?" It made little sense. They should ration their food, not shove food in their mouths like fat pigs.

"You're Eden, correct?" came a strong, male voice.

She turned to see a handsome man with brown hair, hazel eyes, and a doctor's gown on. He stood behind her, his hand extended for a handshake. She shook his hand as he leaned forward, whispering, "I'm Doctor William Simmons, and we need your help."

Eden nodded, understanding they probably had questions or fears, but she didn't have time to deal with them. She had bigger fish to fry.

She continued to look around. No way this ship could have this much food without a supply chain of foodstuffs nearby. "I'm sorry, but I have to go." If she could figure out exactly where the food came from, she may find a clue to Enlil's location.

William gently grabbed her shoulder. "I'm a doctor, and Hank over there is a top tech. We have a serious concern that you can help us with."

Eden eyed one, then the other. "Tech, you say? And I assume you have access to Tech Quarters?"

Hank nodded, chewing loudly. "Yep."

Eden grinned. "Then why don't we help each other."

Hank planted both hands on the bench and pushed himself into a standing position. He eyeballed William. "Should we talk to her now?"

Eden motioned for them to follow her. "Let's talk on our way to Tech Quarters."

The cafeteria door opened, and they walked down the corridor, Hank's heavy footsteps pounding behind her. "And how can we help you, Major Gaines?"

"We need to find where you're getting your food supply."

"What do you mean?" said Hank. "We get them from the cooks who get them from the kitchen and supplies."

Eden flicked a glance over her shoulder at Hank. "Unless you refueled with extra food reserves the day of the attack, you should be out of food by now."

"We're on rations," said Hank, throwing his thumb to the side. "Tech Quarters right here." Hank walked inside, Eden and William in tow. Hank collapsed in a chair in front of a holocomp, his head in his hands as if he were catching his breath.

William patted his back. "When we get done with all of this crap, my friend, you're seeing me, and I'm getting you healthy and in shape."

Hank snorted. "Good luck."

Eden rested her hands on her hips. "Was today by chance not a ration day?"

William shook his head. "No, today was a ration day, just like every day."

Eden pursed her lips. "Then we definitely need to know where your food is coming from because those weren't rations." She touched the holoscreen at Hank's desk, her finger going through the holographic display. "Pull up storables and supplies." She faced Hank and William. "If you consider those rations, then someone is supplying you with food outside of Starship *Sirona,* and I want to know who."

Hank swiped his finger over the screen. "We also get food from the Warehouse next door."

"You don't get that kind of food from a warehouse, and if you did, you wouldn't have that much of it. A warehouse supplies food for a hundred people who work in that specific warehouse. You have ten thousand people on Starship *Sirona,* maybe a little less. The food from a warehouse would last you half a day if that."

William dipped his head toward another workstation far across the room in a corner where a bald man wore a headset, talking to someone, his back to them. "Sleuth would probably know."

Her heart burned at the name, and she took a step back. "Best we keep this between us."

Hank shot William a cold look. "I told you, man. I don't trust that swine, and she clearly doesn't either."

Eden narrowed her eyes. "Stay away from Sleuth."

"We want to show you something," explained William.

Eden blew out spent air. She wanted to look for the food supply route, not whatever these two wanted to show her.

"Just, humor us." Hank pulled up an outside view of the ship. The vid glitched for a millisecond. "A vid loop, and we know who placed it." He eyed Sleuth.

Eden watched the screen. "Is the loop going on now?"

"Yes. There are several loops for different times of the day. What we're seeing isn't what's occurring outside." Hank leaned on his armrest. "I have night shift, and I like to hack into Sleuth's HDC through my holocomp when he goes on breaks. I was doing it so he could eventually find out. I enjoy pissing him off." Hank pressed a few holographic buttons. "I accidentally stumbled on the loop. He's into some real bad shit."

William ran his hands through the back of his hair. "Hank is confident Sleuth works for the other team, you know, those who attacked us."

Eden pinched her lower lip. "I surmised the same."

"Why else would he secure a loop? What's his angle?" asked Hank.

Eden didn't know. Diana and Sleuth benefited somehow by helping the Anunnaki.

William tapped Hank's shoulder. "Show her the other vid."

Hank looked at Eden. "The most important vid. Here, pay close attention." Hank typed in several strings of code and an image popped up, then blipped off.

"What was that?" That didn't show Eden anything.

"I'll pause it right where I need to." Hank typed in a string of code again, but this time a little different. "Watch." He turned on the vid, and just like taking a snapshot, the vid paused.

Eden leaned forward. "What am I looking at? The inside of a ship?" She looked at Sleuth. The guy was still talking on the comm and hadn't noticed her.

"I took this from Sleuth's HDC when I hacked him a day ago. It's a little fuzzy. The bald bastard was sloppy. Out of all that he erased and covered up, he screwed up on this one. Look." Hank outlined an image on the screen with his finger. "You can barely see it, but here you have a human and someone that looks like a giant. But, when I do this..." he pressed a few buttons and the still vid brightened, "...you see Captain Diana Johnson and some big-ass guy sitting in the seat across from her."

Eden gasped. "How did Sleuth get that recording?"

"Whether or not Diana knew it, Sleuth placed a bug on her, a small video device," said Hank. "He erased or vid-blocked most of the recording but left a smidgen for my hacking skills to find." He cracked his knuckles.

"Who's that big guy with her?"

"One of the bad guys, I think. Maybe the one in charge, but who knows?" replied Hank.

"Can you triangulate the location where that vid was taken?" asked Eden.

Hank wiped his hands together. "I already did."

"Excellent. Write the location on a piece of paper and hand it to me." She eyed Sleuth, his back still to them. "I'll get on this right away." Perhaps she didn't need to find the food supply, and this was all she needed.

"Also," continued Hank. "We've heard a rumor that a weapon of some type is heading our way."

Eden tilted her head. Who would let out the rumor? She held back a grin. Perhaps Skye or one of the Space Templars started it. Deep down, and perhaps because of the Sight, she figured that's exactly what happened. "And?"

"Sleuth is keeping that under wraps. I don't know what he's thinking, because if the rumor proves correct and this weapon can blast us off the face of Eos, why would Sleuth and Diana allow it? They'd die, too."

"I mentioned it to Diana. She didn't know that it existed," said Eden.

William jerked back. "You know about the weapon, too?"

Eden nodded. "Yes, and regarding Diana, she was genuinely surprised, and if I'm not mistaken, a little pissed."

"Well, here it is." A vid appeared on the screen, showing a massive cannon atop a thick, hovering platform. "As you can see, it's moving slowly. Sometimes it stops, and we see giants wearing jumpsuits and helmets get out of the damn thing and repair it."

"Good." Eden flattened her lips. "How long will it take to get to us?"

Hank let out a gush of air, thinking. "I don't know. Maybe thirty-six to forty-eight hours?"

"I'll need those coordinates."

Hank nodded, pulling out a piece of paper and jotting down coordinates. He handed her the paper. She folded it and slipped it up her sleeve. Eden had the location or a location near where the suspected leader conducted his operations, along with the weapon's coordinates.

"Thank you." She went to turn and find Skye. She needed to get Skye into the air and destroy that weapon. In the meantime, she and the rest of the Space Templars could head toward the other coordinates, and hopefully take out the enemy's base of operations.

Hank clasped his hands together. "Wait, one more thing." He moved to another application on the screen. "I found this on Sleuth's HDC." A schematic of the engine room came into view. "Everything is in the blue, meaning, ready to go." He bit his lower lip, his cheeks flushing red. "I accessed *Sirona's* engines from Sleuth's HDC to see how well repairs were going. As you can see from the date, engines have been fully online since we..." he made air quotes, "...crashed landed. All the HDC's in Tech Quarters show we are in the red and engines aren't fully repaired. We've been a fully functioning starship the entire time we've been on Eos."

Eden nodded, a better plan hatching in her mind. "Leak this information to the entire starship as fast as you can. We need everyone in the know. Since I by chance have the enemy's coordinates, I'll let Skye know we can arrest Diana and Sleuth. We then take this ship off this planet. We could get this done quickly if we act now."

William and Hank looked at each other knowingly. Hank shrugged. "No, no arrest. If you do, maybe they'll have some way to communicate with the jerks who attacked us, and all hell would break loose. The only thing William and I can think to do is...well...kill them. We know Diana has the *Sirona* Guards wrapped around her fingers, so they won't pull the trigger on her or Sleuth. You and your Space Templar friends are more than capable."

28

KODA

Starbase Matrona

Koda stiffened as two Brigantia Guard sent gunfire into the hangar. One guard was on one knee, the other standing, and they held their weapons toward the doorway, their bodies out of Payson's view. The other guards stacked behind them, waiting their turn.

Payson and his men returned fire, sparks flying off the edge of the door frame and the wall across the way. Then Payson's teams' gunshots ceased. The Brigantia Guard filed in, their rifle's sweeping the area. More gun blasts and a guard flew against the wall. He slumped to his rear, his head tipped to the side, lifeless.

Manning army crawled inside, Louise following him, and positioning themselves on the far side of Payson and his crew's location. They both opened fire. A cloud of white dust erupted, and the Guards fell into coughing fits while continuing to fire, moving deeper inside the room.

Louise coughed, looking away. "Payson is sending bullets into some barrels."

Koda watched as white dust misted outside of the hangar, spilling into the large hallway where he stood.

"Close the door, Koda. Close the door," yelled Louise. "We have to contain this shit."

Koda fumbled with his belt, searching for the ID Card. "You still have my card."

Through the white haze, he could see Louise's outline and the orange bursts exiting her rifle's muzzle. She turned to the side and tossed the ID Card Koda's way. It ricocheted off the door frame, bouncing inside the hangar. Koda held his breath and rushed inside, sliding to his knees. He patted the floor, the white dust stinging his eyes.

The *ratatatat* and bangs of gunfire died down, with a few shots cracking here and there. Someone grabbed Koda and threw him to the ground. He involuntarily inhaled a moment later and convulsed in coughs, wheezing. There were a few beeping sounds and the door closed. The dust cloud slowly settled, and Koda glanced up at four men in black gas masks staring down at him. One pointed a gun at him.

A blast of bullets came from across the room, and one of Payson's men jerked back and forth blood splattering. He dropped to the floor. A Payson soldier in a black mask turned and opened fire, sending the culprit sliding across the floor, his legs twitching a death dance. He looked down at Koda. "You made me take out some of our containers. I don't like that." He sounded like the leader, most likely Payson.

Koda turned and saw Manning and Louise. His heart dropped when he saw both of them dead, blood soaking Manning's back and blood dripping from Louise's lips. Payson took a step forward, pressing his gun's muzzle against Koda's temple. He turned, facing his two remaining team members. "Finish what we started."

Koda gazed at the contraption Payson's men had put together. A long hose connected to a barrel's small, round opening. A machine attached to the middle of the hose, the end of the hose laying on the ground beside the barrel. A ladder leaned against the wall, its upper rungs near an air duct. A man ran to the hose and climbed the ladder. He slid the end of the hose inside the air duct just as a shot blared in the room. The man on the ladder lurched, his head whipping back, and fell lifeless to the floor, thudding loudly when he hit. The hose dropped, landing on top of him.

"You," yelled Payson, his eyes resting on someone else in the room. "You're absolutely annoying." He shifted his weapon from Koda's temple and pointed it at Louise, who held a rifle now aimed at Payson. Koda, realizing he still held his gun, brought up his weapon, aimed at Payson, and pulled the trigger. Payson moved quickly and jumped away, bringing his gun back just as Koda's bullet slammed into it, kicking it out of Payson's hand.

Louise took a shot a moment later, missing wide as Payson ducked out of the way. The way this guy moved was uncanny as if he was predicting each shot. Koda's shot had been incredibly lucky.

Koda coughed, figuring he didn't have much time before the batrachotoxin took effect and eventually took his life. This one's for my people, he thought, narrowing his eyes and focusing on the manual airlock lever. He scrambled to his feet. Louise crawled toward Payson and threw herself at him. Blood streaked down her chin.

Koda ran toward the airlock. A gun went off, and a sharp sting grabbed his upper back, his left arm instantly going numb. He was steps away from the ladder and another gunshot rang out. A stabbing sensation plunged into his lower back and shoved him forward. He stumbled face-first to the floor, hitting the side of his head on the wall. Dazed, he looked up to see the manual lever in reach. Koda coughed, his lungs feeling like glass as the toxin settled deeper. Nausea rose to his throat, and vomit full of blood sputtered out of his mouth.

He pushed up, his muscles shaking, his eyelids wanting to shut, his insides melting away.

"Where do you think you're going?" Payson's muffled voice echoed in the large room. Another bullet sunk into Koda, entering his middle back and out his chest, blood spraying against the round airlock. Koda let out a gush of air, most likely his last. He lifted his weary arm and pulled down on the lever. As he fell to the floor, the lever moved down with him.

Koda's lips upturned, though barely, his muscles too weak to show his satisfaction, his win for his people. Koda clutched his chest, the pain overwhelming. Bye, Matrona.

There was a click, and the airlock spun open. Another click and the secondary airlock door slid upward, exposing space. Wind overtook the hangar, and a loud whoosh filled the room, sounding like a heavy waterfall. Koda's body was sucked out of the airlock and he spun in the frozen black expanse, his vision dotted by stars billions of kilometers away. As he spun, Starbase Matrona came into view, and the airlock pushed out hundreds of black barrels, twirling rapidly in his direction.

His eyes and body swelled. His vision lessening, his last sight was of Payson coming in his direction. The guy's mask had ripped off, and his mouth was open as if stunned at the turn of events. Louise and Manning, both dead, spilled out of the hangar and into the dark void. They saved thousands, maybe more from a terrible toxic death.

More men exited the airlock, twirling away from Starbase Matrona.

A strange thought came to Koda. War is empty. His body slipped deeper into the cosmos. We saved our people. Perhaps Devon had been right. Koda's reign as Sphere Nine's Prime Overseer had proved short, but he may have been one of the best politicians Starbase Matrona had ever seen.

He forced a smile as blackness overtook him, the pull of space slipping him further away from his home. He never felt so close to his people, so at peace, and so alive when death came.

2 9

SHAE

Starhawk Transport, Unknown

Shae puffed up his cheeks, then blew out. He put his hand up, ready to defend himself and Devon against the giant woman. He fought against the pain from the bullet wound. "I may be smaller than you, but you lay one hand on us, you get bloody in the process."

Kalista held the snip cutters. "Your talk is cheap, old man."

Devon stared at the cutters. "Please, ma'am. We don't want to harm you."

"Listen..." She tilted her head at Devon, lifting one eyebrow as if silently asking for his name.

"I'm Devon."

"Devon," she continued, "turn around, and I'm snipping your cuffs. I won't kill you two." Her eyebrows rose, her eyes innocent. She holstered her gun. "I don't kill. Just not my thing unless I have to."

Shae studied Kalista, looking into her eyes and studying her physiology. He didn't know the Anunnaki's facial tells, except for Prime Director Zim Noki's, but if Zim's physiology was a marker for their race, this woman was telling the truth. Kalista lowered the cutters and walked behind Devon.

Devon squeezed his eyes shut. "Don't dismember me."

Kalista rolled her eyes.

"Devon," said Shae, taking a seat on the cabin bench attached to the wall, blood dripping down his arm. "Stop overreacting. She won't harm you."

There was a snap and Devon flinched, then another snap. The sound of chains jingled against the floor. "Look at your hands," said Kalista, moving toward the toolbox she pulled out from under the bench. She tossed the cutters in the box and slammed it shut, wiping her hands together. "You're still in one piece."

Devon brought his hands in front of him, the cuffs were still around his wrists, but the chains connecting his cuffs were gone. He sighed in relief. "Thank you."

Shae leaned against the wall, rubbing his forehead. "Look, Kalista…" he lifted his head from the wall, the ache in his shoulder from the gunshot wound growing. "…I need you to turn this ship around and head back to Starbase Matrona. My people are in need, and I'm their Fleet Admiral."

Her mouth gaped open. "You're Shae Lutz?" She stood still, resting her hands on her hips. "I'm impressed. From what I've heard through past genocide cycles, you're the only one who ever successfully stood up to my race. I'm in the presence of a hero."

"Hero?" Shae shook his head. "No, but I understand you're an Anunnaki and love your race. I'm a human, I love mine. I can't let them die. Please, I implore you to—"

"I don't love my race. I don't approve what they do to you, but I also have a job to do, gold and crystal to deliver, and a family to feed. I can't deviate from my course. I apologize, but when all is said and done, you can come with me on my trip back to Starbase Matrona."

Shae grasped the edge of the bench with his good hand, flexing his fingers around it, his knuckles going white. "How long will that take?"

"Four, maybe five days at most."

Shae exhaled sharply, standing. "I can't do that. I'm sorry. Turn this ship around."

"I'm not a killer." She walked to the co-pilot seat and pressed her palm on the back of it. A drawer opened at the chair's base. She reached down and picked up a large gun, then holstered it on the other side of her hip. "But as a non-killer, I can make some exceptions."

"Wait, hold on. Maybe we don't need to return right away." Devon grabbed his ears as if listening to headphones and sat next to Shae on the bench. His lips moved as if silently speaking to someone. He smiled and shifted on the bench, facing Shae. "I can hear Naveya again."

"What?" said Shae. He knew Naveya, though he had only met her once. She showed him her Space Templar pendant, identical to the one Shae wore. "Excuse me? Did I hear you right? You say you can hear her?"

Devon tapped his head. "Yeah, yeah." His face slowly turned into a frown. "Sorry, Koda knows what I'm talking about, but I haven't discussed it with you, so you're a bit out of the loop." He cleared his throat. "Naveya and I are connected in a way I can't really explain, but I can feel and hear her sometimes."

"In your head?" Kalista chimed in, her face twisted in confusion. "You humans are very odd."

Devon dipped his head. "Very odd, especially—" he paused, his grin widening. "Holy Guild." He stood, throwing a fist in the air. "We don't need the antidote. The Star Guild Marines sucked the toxin out of the airlocks."

"You're not lying to me, are you? You're not trying to make me feel better, or lighten the air?" Shae studied Devon. The kid's eyes didn't dilate, they didn't move to his left. He wasn't making it up.

"No, Admiral, I'm telling the truth." He glanced out of the cockpit window. "But still—" Devon held up a finger, listening more. "Oh, my. Payson went out the airlock with the barrels of toxin, and the Space Templars took care of the rest of Payson's team." He wiggled his ear with his finger. "There's more. I can't quite make out what she's saying now." He huffed, dropping his arms to his side. "I lost the connection."

Shae plopped on the bench, his shoulder throbbing. He cringed. "I hope you're right."

Kalista stepped back, pulling out a needle gun from her toolbox.

She took a step toward Shae and quickly jabbed the needle into him and pulled it out.

He lurched away in a start. "Son of a Guild."

She threw the needle gun in the toolbox. "That will dissolve the bullet and seal the wound. The serum is also packed with an anti-pain med, so you won't feel much in that shoulder for a few days. After which, I'll inject you again until it's completely healed and pain-free." She held up a thumb. "Got it?"

Shae rolled his shoulder back and forth. "Warn me next time you do that." The pain had already diminished. "Nonetheless, thank you."

His thoughts quickly turned to what Devon said before Kalista jabbed him with a needle. Devon could talk to Naveya? Maybe the kid was schizophrenic and heard things. If he was telling the truth, then holy crap, life had brightened right before him. Shae needed to see it himself, to believe it. He needed to get back to Matrona.

"Please." Shae cupped his hands in front of him. "Kalista, I need to get back to my people. I can't wait a week." Especially if he wanted to see his daughter. Heck, since his starbase could potentially be good and saved, he could grab the Brigantia and Taranis fleet and head to Eos. There, he'd be able to help Ali.

Kalista touched both holstered pistols. "I'm going to Nibiru. I'll hide you in the cabin until my cargo," she pointed at a wall at the ship's stern, "behind that door, is off the ship. Then, I'll find a reason to get you back to Starbase Matrona. My guess is that since you made a wreck of things there, we won't be returning for mining minerals soon."

Shae wanted to set her straight, tell her he and his people had freed his race, and if it wrecked Anunnaki plans, then so be it. They'd live, and so would Matrona and Star Guild.

A beep sounded from the cockpit flight console. Shae twisted his posture, looking at the cockpit. A voice blared, "Kali, this...be Y'taul."

Kalista's eyes narrowed, and she walked hastily to her pilot seat, punching several buttons on her holographic display as she sat down. She turned and pointed to the back left corner of the cabin. "You two.

Slink back there as best you can. Whatever you do, do not stand or move to the right. He'll see you if you do."

Shae bit his tongue, not used to being ordered around. Devon hurried to the corner and plopped on his rear, leaning his back against the cargo bay door. Shae sat next to him.

Kalista pressed another button. "Y'taul?" She acted surprised. "What are you doing in this sector and so close to Starbase Matrona? Enlil would have your neck if he knew you were upsetting his galactic rules and procedures."

"We...intercept call from Eos Two to...you. I...how do you say?" He paused, most likely trying to figure out the right words. "You are going to Nibiru, yes?"

"I am. Why?" Her voice rose, becoming defensive.

"So, you must have gold. Only reason you go. We detect it on your ship."

Kalista hesitated. "I do."

Shae shifted uncomfortably, his butt on the floor, his knees tucked into his chest. He pulled his knees as tightly into himself as he could. Not a position an old man, let alone a Fleet Admiral, usually held.

Devon whispered. "Are you okay, Admiral?"

Shae nodded, pressing his finger to his lips.

Kalista pressed a few more buttons. She stood, moaning, and walked in Shae and Devon's direction. Stopping beside them, Kalista kept her eyes forward, doing her best to ignore her two unwelcome guests. She pressed some numbers on the console above their heads and the cargo bay door clicked and began opening. Shae and Devon scooted forward, and Shae looked behind him, at the cargo now in full view.

Devon gasped, and Shae gently elbowed him, saying in a low hush, "Keep your mouth shut, young man." Devon nodded, but Shae couldn't blame the kid. Clear barrels of white gold filled the cargo bay, the gold glistening in powder form, bits of crystal sprinkled inside.

Kalista sighed, glancing back toward her seat. "Yes, Y'taul. I have a large load. It's heated and cooled to the white powder etherium form."

The cargo door closed. She twirled around and headed back to the pilot seat.

"Prepare...board us, Kali."

She shook her head. "I'm Kalista for the millionth time. Stop calling me Kali. All of this gold is accounted for. Trust me. I can't give you any. But thanks for trying."

"You never give, Kali. We always pay," said Y'taul.

"Are you hard of hearing? I said it's in the white powder form. That's not something you take from the Nibiru king."

"How much do you have?"

Kalista's shoulders dropped. "I don't know. Maybe three thousand troy ounces?"

"We buy five hundred troy ounce."

"Why are you bringing your ship in closer, Y'taul? I haven't agreed to any such deal." She pounded her fist against her armrest.

Out of the side window, Shae and Devon watched as a large ship slowly approached. It could easily hold one of these Starhawk Transports in its belly, and probably a handful more. It was longer than it was wide and about the size of a frigate in the Star Guild fleet. Its belly hung low as if it were pregnant.

"You cooperate, no? We buy. If no cooperate, we take," said Y'taul.

Kalista wilted. "And if I report this incident to Nibiru authority?"

"You report...we report. We will show them vids of our past dealings. Okay?"

Kalista tightened her mouth. "Okay, pull me in."

"Already done so, Kali. We tractoring you now."

"We look forward to seeing you, Y'taul. And my name is Kalista."

"We?" asked Y'taul.

Kalista leaned against her armrest, shifting in her seat, then leaned back. She placed her hands behind her head as if resting from a hard day's work. She waved her hands toward the front, making sure Devon and Shae saw her movements. "Boys, come up here and show yourselves."

What was she doing? thought Shae, both Devon and him giving each other a look.

"Guys," blared Kalista. "Now, please."

Shae shook Devon's shoulder. "Let's do as the woman says." Maybe they did things a bit differently in the extraterrestrial world, or maybe humans scared Y'taul's race. Shae didn't know, but proceeded forward, Devon behind him. He approached the cockpit, and in front of him and on the small vidscreen, stood a humanoid—Y'taul. He had scruffy long, blond hair, and steely blue eyes, and was wearing a ragged silver robe with a tight-fitting collar.

Y'taul stepped back. "What is meaning of this? Humans?"

"You caught me at a bad moment, Y'taul. They were in here hiding when I took off."

Y'taul crossed his arms. "How much you sell them for?"

Shae pulled back, instinctively yanking Devon back with him, protecting the kid. "We aren't for sale."

"Not up to you." Y'taul pointed at Kalista. "Up to her."

Kalista put her hands in the air. "Up to me?" She gestured to her flight mates. "I don't seem to have much of a choice with you today, Y'taul. So, I'd say it's not up to me at all."

"Okay, we will come to agreement." Y'taul's image blinked out.

Devon curled his lips in displeasure. "What?"

Shae glanced at his broken gun laying in the cabin. "Like I said, we're not for sale."

Kalista sank deeper into her chair, crossing her arms. She stared out into space as the craft was pulled to the side, moving closer and closer to Y'taul's ship. "It's how life is in this part of the galaxy. Deal with it."

30

DIANA

Starship Sirona, Eos

Diana sat at her desk, the skin between her eyes creased, thinking hard. Earlier, she contemplated scrambling starfighters to locate and attack the weapon Eden claimed headed toward *Sirona*. She backed out of the idea when Sleuth threatened her, taking Enlil's side over hers. She weighed stripping Sleuth of his electronics and throwing him in the brig, but thought somehow Enlil would know, and his inside man wouldn't be so inside anymore. Enlil would no doubt bring down a hell storm on her with heavier weapons or speed up that weapon heading her way now.

"I have to attack the weapon or bypass attacking the weapon altogether." And get the hell off this planet with the rest of her crew intact. A weight the size of a starship lifted off her shoulders at the thought, and an unconscious sigh exited her mouth. She powered on her HDC and swiped to the commlink. She'd start with Wrench and see if he could help her bypass the false narrative she and Sleuth had filled the crew's minds with—that the engines were damaged.

She'd need Wrench to do some magic on his HDC and get the holocomps to recognize that the engines operated just fine. The problem was that Sleuth had hacked into the system, and she didn't know if anyone could un-hack what he'd done.

There was a rap at the door and Diana's lips downturned. She pulled up the outside holocams. She tilted her head, her lips frowning more. Wrench stood outside, his greasy hands on his hips.

"Unlock and open," she said.

The door opened, and she waved Wrench inside. The door closed behind him. She cupped her hands on her desk. "I didn't call you to my quarters."

Wrench slapped his hand on the back of his neck and looked down. "My apologies, Ma'am. Ya' obviously wasn't expectin' me. I was told to come here by Sleuth himself. He said captain's orders or somethin' 'er other, so I complied."

She stood in a hurry. "Do you have a weapon on you?"

Wrench stood back, his hands up, his eyebrows high. "N-no Ma'am. I wouldn't pull a gun on ya'."

"No, we need—"

Her door whooshed open, and there stood Sleuth, two *Sirona* Guards by his side, a rifle in their hands. Sleuth held a gun as well, and a holopad in his other hand.

Wrench moved toward the captain and Diana crossed her arms, her jaw set. "What's the meaning of this?"

Sleuth and the Guards stepped inside, their rifles pointed at her. Sleuth holstered his gun and tapped a few buttons on his holopad. The door closed behind them. "Lock and unlock only on my command," he said. He glanced up and pulled his sidearm out, aiming it at Wrench. "Hi, you two. Glad you could join the party." He gave Wrench a wink and set the holopad on Diana's desk. He shoved his hand in his pocket and pulled out a small beam drive—a round holocomp instrument designed for encrypting or decoding HDC data, vids, and schematics. He handed it to Wrench. "Put it in Diana's HDC."

Wrench didn't take it. "What are ya' givin' me?"

Sleuth shoved it in Wrench's hands.

Diana took a step forward. "Wrench should not be involved in this crap you started." The Guards took a step forward, targeting Diana. She put her hands up and eased away from Sleuth.

Sleuth rolled his eyes. "I didn't start this crap on my own. You had a major hand in it. The only way I can lock my commands on the *Sirona* servers is if you're both here. That's how I designed my hack, never thinking I would have to actually do this." He scowled at Diana.

"Now, Wrench," continued Sleuth, "Put this in Diana's HDC, type in your password, and open the vids under loop, and look at the days and times."

Wrench stroked his gray beard, then shook his head and leaned close to Sleuth. "Shouldn't ya' be eatin' lunch?"

Diana could tell Wrench was trying to delay things for her sake, but of all people, she didn't want him dying under her watch.

"Those bit furry people have gotten in yo' mind, huh? They stir the calm. Ya' hear them, don't ya'?" asked Wrench.

Sleuth crinkled his brow.

Diana put her hand up. "Wrench, he's got a gun, and I'm sure he's coward enough to use it."

Wrench turned to Diana. "If I do what Sleuth here says, will it harm tha' ship and ya' crew, Ma'am?"

She dipped her head. "Yes."

"Aye, captain." Wrench faced Sleuth and crossed his arms, the beam drive in his hand. "My answer is no."

Sleuth lifted the gun and pointed the muzzle at Wrench's forehead. "Diana, grab the beam drive from Wrench, or I put one in his brain."

Wrench dropped the beam drive on the floor and lifted his foot to crush it.

A *phtah* cracked in the room, and Wrench tumbled to the floor, his hand on his shoulder, blood oozing between his fingers and down his arm. Smoke rose from Sleuth's gun's muzzle.

Diana rushed to Wrench's side. "Are you okay?"

Wrench winced in pain. "I've been better, Ma'am."

Sleuth grabbed the holopad, pressed a few buttons, and shoved it in Wrench's face. A beep sounded, and Sleuth pulled back, a wry grin on his face. "Thanks for your iris scan. It'll bypass the codes I needed from you."

"What are you doing, Sleuth?" asked Diana.

Sleuth went around her desk, motioning for the Guards to move closer to Wrench and Diana. They complied.

"You're all traitors," said Diana. "None of you will get away with this."

"You're lecturing us on being a traitor?" Sleuth snorted. "That's a good one." He held the holopad up to Diana's HDC holodisplay, and another beep sounded. "Confirmation and I'm in."

Sleuth began typing, talking under his breath, something that always annoyed Diana. "Bypass all ports, hatches, launch bay door, anything that lets anyone come in and out of this big sucker of a ship."

Wrench lay on the ground, his eyes blinking. "This smarts. Never been shot before, and I don't think I wanna' do it again." He gave a sideways smile, the pain notching his smile down a moment later.

"Bypass them to do what?" asked Diana, her breathing shallow. She imagined bull-rushing the guards and taking their weapons, then sending several bullets in each one of them, Sleuth first, but that'd just get her killed, along with Wrench.

Sleuth continued to type. "To not open...at all. They'll be locked. I'll be the only one who can unlock them from this point forward. Enlil's orders." He eyed the beam drive on the floor. "Sergeant Jaffey, toss me the beam drive."

The guard bent over and picked up the drive. He walked over and dropped the drive in Sleuth's hand.

Sleuth eyed Diana. "Me and a few others are rendezvousing with Enlil. We'll be safe. Remember that weapon Eden warned you about?" He giggled like a spoiled brat. "Well, it'll practice its power on this ship pretty damn soon."

Diana went to her feet. "You son of a—"

"Don't take another step," said a guard, his weapon a few inches from her nose.

Sleuth pushed the beam drive into the HDC insert port. He placed his elbow on the desk, resting his chin on his palm, and tapped his fingers on the desk's surface. He typed in commands, then leaned back in the chair, his hands behind his neck. "Diana, you changed your password on me."

She'd done it after Sleuth threatened her like any half-brained nitwit would. She kept her lips tight. She was on her knees, pressing her hand just above Wrench's wound, hoping to slow the blood flow. He cringed in pain. "I'm sorry, Wrench."

He patted her forearm. "Not yo' fault, Ma'am."

"Guards," said Sleuth. "Put another bullet in Wrench. Let him die a slow, painful death."

Diana put her hand up and leaned over Wrench's body. "You'll do no such thing."

"Then what's your password, Diana?" demanded Sleuth.

Wrench shook his head back and forth. "All onboard the ship will die, Diana. Don't give 'em the password."

Sleuth leaned forward in the chair. "One in the leg."

"No, don't shoot." Diana squeezed her eyes shut. She had the Space Templars on the ship, and maybe she could get them to undo what Sleuth had done after she gave him the password.

The guards glanced at Sleuth. He put his hand up, halting them. "What's the password, Diana?"

"Sirona777Sirona."

"Excellent." Sleuth pecked away at the holokeypad, doing Guild knows what. "Lock all perimeter exits." He pushed the chair back, and it rolled toward the wall, his body still plopped down in it. He stretched his arms high. "Confirmed." He held a wide smile.

Wrench glared at Sleuth. "Why ya' grinnin'? This ain't funny, man."

"I have a sick sense of humor." Sleuth stood, stretching. "Now, it's time for us to get off this boat." He gave a nod to the Guards, his lower lip trembling slightly. "Gentlemen?"

They raised their weapons, and Diana covered Wrench more. "You piece of ebb, Sleuth. You piece of—"

The guards opened fire, and bullets ripped through her skin, sinking into her arms, legs, and back. She rolled off of Wrench and the weapon fire ceased. She spit out blood and turned her head toward

Wrench. Blood covered his body, some oozing out of his mouth. He blinked at her and extended his hand, somehow finding her fingers.

She squeezed his hand. "I'm...sorry."

He shook his head. "It's...okay, ma'am. It's...okay." He closed his eyes, and his fingers relaxed.

Her breathing came fast and labored as her body turned cold. She shivered. Her eyes shut, and all sound faded around her. I deserve this, she told herself. Keep my crew safe, Sirona. Keep them safe. Her body went limp, and her heart slowed. She opened her eyes one last time. Out of her periphery, she saw Sleuth and the Guards leaving the room.

She turned her head to a Robert Rose painting on the wall that depicted a Space Templar with a helmet on and wearing a white jumpsuit. The Templar was a woman, and she had her hand raised in victory. She was standing over a giant, a gleaming sword in her hand. Several Templars were running toward her, their hands up in victory as well, a building behind them in ruins.

Diana closed her eyes and let the forever sleep take hold.

31

EDEN

Starship Sirona, Eos

Nyx held up a dagger, looking mesmerized by the gleam shining off of it from the corridor lights. "I'd be happy to be the one." She winked at Eden.

Skye placed his hand on Nyx's dagger, pushing it down and away from Nyx. Nyx relaxed and sheathed the weapon in her belt.

"Thank you, Nyx, but we'll all be the one," Skye said.

Nyx sighed. "Oh, all right." Her head swiveled from side to side as she tried to keep a frown from showing.

Eden stood in the corridor, her arms crossed. Earlier, she'd explained the discoveries she, Hank, and William made. With the Anunnaki leader's coordinates in hand and Diana and Sleuth exposed, Skye ordered every Space Templar on the ship to the place they stood now—near Diana's quarters.

Time to throw the traitors in the brig thought Eden. *Swift's* brig.

"I'm ready when you are, Skye," said Nyx. The side of her lip quivered as if she couldn't wait for the hunt.

"Let's go. I lead," he replied, Jantu and Nyx beside him, a long line of human and Sirian Space Templars behind him. The light in the

221

hallway dimmed, then flickered. The sound of gunshots reverberated off the walls. Skye paused and glanced around. "That's not normal."

Eden's heart sank. Deep down, sadness rose, perhaps sensed by her new Sight abilities. Every cell in her body screamed at her that someone close, someone important, hadn't survived those bullets. She touched her gut, holding in the want to cry, to mourn, but for who?

They rounded a corner toward where the gunshots sounded. Skye slowed and placed his finger to his lips, telling them to be quiet. He paused and peeked around another corner. He held his hand up in a fist, his other hand clutching a gun. He opened his fist, letting them know the coast was clear.

Eden crept behind Nyx, Jantu on her rear, his long rifle pointing forward. His tall frame gave him a higher vantage point and a clear shot. They headed around the corner, Skye still in the lead. He picked up his pace, and so did the rest of the Space Templars. They wound through another set of passageways.

"Thunderstrokes, this is annoying," said Nyx, clearly impatient.

Skye stopped at a doorway, taking a peek. "Weapons at the ready. We have a problem." He and the rest of the Templars cautiously moved forward.

Eden lowered her weapon, her mouth agape. She gasped. "Wrench?"

Diana's quarter's door was open. Wrench and Diana lay in a pool of blood, their hands touching, though motionless. Commotion and footsteps pounded down the hallway.

"They're coming," said Jantu, turning around, his rifle extended.

A half a dozen *Sirona* Guard came around the corner, halting the moment they saw more than a dozen Space Templars with weapons drawn. It didn't look good.

"Use your wrist band shield things," said Eden.

Nyx snorted. "There's no fun in that."

"We are *Sirona* Marines. All of you," said a soldier, "drop your weapons."

Eden slowly shook her head. "This isn't necessary. We heard the weapon's discharge and came to investigate."

"For all I know, you pulled the triggers," said a guard. "Now, drop your weapons." He looked around the Space Templar and into Diana's quarters. "I see blood. Is that the captain?"

Eden nodded. "Yes. Her and Wrench."

A Marine narrowed his eyes, his breath shallow. It didn't take the Sight to see anger boiling in him. He spoke into his shoulder com. "Alert all *Sirona* Guards. We have a code eleven at the Captain's Quarters. I repeat, a code eleven." He kept his eyes on Eden. "I'll ask you one more time. Drop. Your. Weapons."

"No, sirs, you drop your weapons," hissed Nyx. She tilted her head, sizing up the men in front of them. "That's if you don't want to end up like your precious captain."

Heavy footsteps echoed down the corridor, and a dozen more *Sirona* Guards came on the scene. The lead guard motioned with the flick of his head toward the Space Templars. "Take them into custody."

"Stand down," called Skye. "I understand your fear, and I understand the situation doesn't look pleasing to you or your fellow Guards, but we are the Space Templars. We don't surrender, and we don't stand down unless I give that order." He paused. "I won't be giving that order."

A rumbling sound came from outside, and the ship began vibrating. Everyone looked around.

"And that is?" said Nyx.

Skye closed his eyes, concentrating. "The weapon is nearing us."

The lead guard brought his lips closer to his shoulder com. "This is Sergeant Wilcox. Lift outside armor plating from corridor wing nine, and now." The rumbling grew louder.

"I'm sorry, Sergeant. I can't comply with that order unless the captain gives us the order directly," came a reply.

"Captain Diana Johnson is dead." Wilcox's voice raised. "We have a situation outside the ship that needs immediate eyes." The armor over the windows didn't move. Wilcox leaned closer to his com. "Do not make me come down there."

"Sir," came the response. "The armor is locked. I can't bypass it on the holocomps, and I don't know why."

Wilcox lifted his gaze to Eden. "What are you guys trying to pull here?"

Before Eden could reply, a voice carried from down the corridor and behind the Marines. "Excuse me. Official business. Let us through."

Eden craned her neck, looking past the *Sirona* Guards. "Hank?"

"I've tracked a new set of codes coming from the Captain's Quarters. It's seized the ship, locking it down. I need to get through. Move it, move it." Hank held his ID Card in hand, William in tow, also holding up his card.

"I'm a doctor, let me through," barked William.

The Marines parted, keeping their eyes and rifles on the Space Templars.

"Move, move." Hank's big body squeezed past the guards. He halted when he saw Wrench and Diana on the ground, his face going pale. "Oh, my Guild. Wrench?"

William rushed past Hank and went to one knee beside the two dead bodies, feeling for pulses.

Hank put his hand to his mouth, his voice hushed. "Did you—"

"No," said Eden. "We'd never do such a thing."

"Sleuth," muttered Hank, moving forward and into the quarters. He sat at Diana's desk and cracked his knuckles. His mouth downturned, he cursed under his breath, muttering Sleuth's name several times.

Nyx turned and smirked at the *Sirona* Guards. "Looks like we have an old standoff here, ladies and gentlemen. Who will pull the trigger first?"

"Nyx," said Skye. "Don't provoke them."

Nyx frowned. "Oh, but it's so fun. These poor guards don't have a chance."

Hank held up his hand, his voice booming into the corridor. "Listen up. Don't interrupt the HDC guru while I'm figuring shit out. Sleuth hacked the crap out of *Sirona*'s system, and the maestro—me—needs quiet time to work."

Eden nodded at the soldier in front of her. "Don't talk, everyone. He'll lift the window armor soon."

The ship shuddered.

"That's odd," Hank said softly, "even the captain's HDC has been locked out of all functions on this ship." He moved his fingers quickly on the holokeypad as if conducting an orchestra. "That's easy to fix. You just need some Hank love and then whamo." He pressed several more buttons on the keypad and nodded to himself. "Yep, you just hack into Sleuth's HDC, change the code, just like that." He continued muttering and typing at the same time. "And now you have all the systems unlocked and bam." He frowned. "Well, all except engines. That will take me a while."

The armor moved upward, lifting from the windows. Sunset glowed across the sky, and shadows stretched on the ebb rock outside. The sound from outside grew louder, as an even bigger shadow coming into view. The Space Templars and the *Sirona* Guard, forgetting their standoff, peered through the windows.

"It's the weapon," said Skye. "It's here."

Wilcox's eyes hardened. "Tell me everything you know."

Skye dipped his head, his voice calm. "A weapon of mass destruction, and it'll be here soon. It's no doubt geared to destroy the ship and all inhabitants. This is not a joke. Get your men and women off this ship, and now."

"Off this ship?" countered Wilcox. "We leave this ship, we die. We can't breathe out there."

Skye stood straight, his eyes set on the guards in front of him. "Space Templars, suck up your egos. It's time to use our shields." Skye and the rest of the Space Templars raised their arms. Shields materialized from their wrist bands. The soldiers stiffened, their weapons pointed on the Templars. Skye glanced over his shoulder. "Jantu."

Jantu nodded and turned to face the windows. He pressed his rifle's trigger several times, sending blasts of plasma bolts into the handful of windows and shattering them. A few bullets cracked from the Matrona Guard's own rifles and were absorbed into the shields.

"Stand down," yelled Wilcox.

A breeze came in, and the weapon outside was now louder. The guards shuffled on their feet, a few covering their mouths and holding their breath. Another guard took a shot at the Templars. The bullet sizzled as it slammed into a Templar's shield.

"Space Templars," shouted Skye. "Do not return fire."

"Cease fire," yelled Wilcox, his weapon lowered, his body facing the broken windows. He sniffed, taking in a breath. "What the hell?"

"Guys," interrupted Hank. "A woman named S is typing on my screen, telling me we need to evacuate immediately. The weapon is almost in position, and we won't survive."

Skye and Nyx stiffened. Nyx turned her head. "Did you say S? Sabra?"

"Just S. I don't know a Sabra," said Hank.

"How much time did she say we have?" asked Skye.

"She didn't give a time. She's off the screen now." Hank stood and pulled William away from the captain. "Let's get out of here."

"Hank," said Skye, "can you let everyone on the starship know they need to evacuate the ship immediately?"

Wilcox moved away from the window. "Everyone, sound the alarm, and get as many people off this ship as you can." The guards turned and rushed down the hall, disappearing around a corridor corner.

Hank sat at Diana's desk again, bringing up the holodisplay. "Commlink on. Patch me to all speakers on the starship." He looked at Skye. "What do you want me to say?"

Skye nodded at Nyx. She turned and rushed into Diana's room and stopped at Hank's side. "Move."

Hank stood quickly, his hands up. "All right, all right."

Nyx sat. She pressed her lips against the com, and in a perfect impression and with the same pitch as Diana's voice, she spoke. "Attention, this is Captain Diana Johnson. This is not a drill. A weapon of mass destruction is at our doorstep. We are evacuating the ship. I repeat we are evacuating the ship." She put her hand on the com, her tone hushed. "Is *Swift* on her way, Eden."

Eden closed her eyes and took a deep breath. Her hands warmed, and the Sight activated. A sensation, like a pull, tugged at her heart. An image popped in her head, one of *Swift* flying through the clouds, heading their way. Eden opened her eyes. "Yes, *Swift* will be here soon."

Nyx's expression lightened. "Good job, Eden." She pressed her lips into the mic again. "You are to board another starship which will be landing beside us soon. It has been a lie that Eos doesn't have a breathable atmosphere. You can breathe Eos's air. Question nothing until we are all safe. You question and you hold up the entire evacuation process. This is not a drill. Begin evacuation now."

Hank pursed his lips. "I've always wanted to do this." He pressed a button on the HDC. Alarms blared throughout the ship. "Time to evacuate."

3 2

ALI

Dirn Garum, Eos

Ali smiled, thinking of her father. She remembered a time as a kid, chasing grasshoppers with him. Shae had winked at her. "You catch five and I'll buy you a lollipop. If you don't catch five, then you owe me a lollipop, okay?"

Ali wrinkled her nose, laughing. "I don't have money to buy you a lollipop." The one time she lost, and she hadn't grabbed the allotted number of grasshoppers her dad assigned, she cried. She didn't want to disappoint her father for failing her mission.

He sat with her, holding her in his arms. "You know this isn't working."

Ali leaned away from him, eyeing his brown eyes. "What daddy? What's not working?" She sniffed.

He touched the tip of her nose. "You know, this crying."

She wiped a tear. "But—"

He snickered, grinning widely. "You still owe me a lollipop. This crying won't get you out of it. Now, how are you going to get the money to buy it?"

They sat on their farmhouse porch. She sniffed again and wiped more tears. She looked around, and her eyes landed on rows and rows of cabbage. "I'll pull the weeds around the cabbage for fifty cents."

He held up his index finger. "Twenty cents for one hour."

She stood and held out her hand, something she'd seen her father do with other farmers and businessmen on countless occasions.

He shook her hand. "Deal?"

Ali shook his hand harder. "Deal."

Like that day, Ali would have to do the work to get herself out of here. Crying wouldn't get her anywhere.

"Ali," came Daf's voice. "Snap out of it."

Ali came to her senses and heard chains clank down the long, rocky corridor. She held her arms against her chest, her butt on the stone-cold ground, her back against the cell wall.

Daf stood, shooting a glance at Ali. "Get ready. It might be our rescue."

Footsteps traveled down the long corridor. Shadows came into view, then small men followed. They held torches, illuminating a dozen faces.

"Stand," came a booming voice.

Ali moved to her feet, touching the hilt of her sword.

The voice spoke again, "Rest your hand elsewhere."

Ali dropped her arm by her side. "Who are you?"

The chains clambered against the bars. Ali narrowed her eyes, realizing the chains weren't chains at all. They were keys, dozens of them connected to a large ring.

"Silence," said the man, sliding a key into the keyhole and twisting. A click sounded.

The cell door sprang open.

A small hooded man entered, holding a pickaxe in one hand and a sword in the other. He looked at Ali. "You're to be executed at once."

He held the sword out to Daf, who backed away. Ali went to protest, but the next words out of his mouth nearly paralyzed her.

"Daf will execute you."

"What's he saying?" asked Daf.

Rage boiled under Ali's skin, her response low and sharp. "He wants you to kill me."

Daf covered her mouth and shook her head. "Hell, no."

Ali brandished her sword. "Over my dead body."

The small man jumped back and out of the cell. Laughter erupted from the group. Some bent over and held their bellies. Others leaned against the rocky wall, having a good time of it.

Ali sheathed her sword. "Are you all drunk?"

The man who backed out of the cell pushed his hood off his head.

"King Bilrak?" Daf shouted.

"Yes, it's me." He dropped his pickaxe, banging it against the floor. He thumbed over his shoulder at the rest of the group. "They wanted a good laugh. I'm sorry."

Ali gave Bilrak a cold stare, then rolled her eyes.

Bilrak pulled a gun from his belt. He held it out to Daf. "Take it."

Daf slapped her palm against her chest. "If you're asking me to take that, my answer is no. I'm not killing Ali."

"This weapon," spoke Bilrak, stifling a chuckle, "is for you." He stepped closer. "Take it. You'll need it. It's a plasma pistol, and we have many stored in wooden crates, awaiting the day for battle."

Daf tilted her head, exhaling an annoyed breath. "Now what's he saying?"

Ali pointed to the weapon. "It's a plasma gun. He wants you to have it."

Daf glared at the gun. "What for?"

Ali shifted her eyes to Bilrak. "What exactly will she need it for?"

"I apologize for my son, Harak." He jabbed a man standing beside him in the side. To Ali's surprise, it was Harak. The jerk looked at the floor, grumbling something Ali couldn't understand.

Ali crossed her arms. "Tell him to leave. The piece of Guild threw me in this cell."

Harak grunted. "You can't tell me what to do, sun-dweller."

"You're a pain in my ass, and if you want me to comply and help your Bawn race, then don't show your face around me again."

Harak grunted. "Oh, I'll put a pain in your ass."

"Try it." She took out her sword, tightening her grip, a fire spreading around Sol's edges. "You don't know how much I'd love to rid you from my life." Her cheeks flushed red, and the power coming from Sol rushed through her, giving her strength and a clear mind.

Harak folded his arms, his chest out. "Hand to hand, coward."

Ali sheathed her sword. "Gladly."

Bilrak threw his hands up. "Enough." He pushed Harak into a Bawn, and the Bawn pushed Harak away until he vanished into the shadows.

Ali placed her hands on her hips. "Tell your son I'm ready any time."

"I'm sure he heard you." Bilrak's expression was tight. "It's almost sundown, and soon we're entering the mouth of the eastern tunnel that leads to our enemy's doorstep. It's a half-day journey and Daf will be with our army. You'll pilot Starship *Tranquil*. When we sound the battle horns, our workers at their stations below us will notify you that it's time to fly *Tranquil* out of Mount Gabriel and bring fire down upon our enemies."

"What?" asked Daf. "I'm tired of not understanding them."

Ali explained to Daf what Bilrak instructed.

Daf shrugged. "And if I refuse?"

Ali faced Bilrak. "And if we refuse?"

Bilrak's face gnarled, his voice rising. "Thun told me you'd accept." He rubbed his face as if stressed. "If you refuse, then we fight anyway. It'd be unfortunate, though. We dug the tunnel because you had the sword, and the prophecy foretold our victory, the Chosen One leading the way."

Ali tapped her scabbard. "Will Harak be near me?"

Bilrak bowed his head at the sword. "Yes. He'll be part of your crew. I apologize, but these are my terms, and I won't stray from them. Both of my sons are in the *Bawn Seer*, both of them will sit inside Starship *Tranquil's* bridge as the prophecies state. I understand you're the bloodline that unlocks Sol from its long slumber. You are the only one of us who can communicate with Starship *Tranquil*, but we'll leave *Tranquil* altogether if you do not help us. We will continue to search for our own way back to our true home without you."

"Earth?" asked Ali, her heart abruptly yearning for her father. An image popped into her head of her and her dad reuniting with Helen, her mother. Their hugs, their tears, and her mother's relief filled Ali's heart. She brightened at the thought. She couldn't wait to end this entire conflict and get back home.

Bilrak grumbled and stroked his long beard. "Yes, Earth." He slapped Ali's arm and gave a friendly squeeze. "We are like brothers and sisters, your race and mine. Take us back to our home, my lady, and we'll walk side by side on Gaia once again."

Ali looked at Daf. Her friend bit her cheek, probably wondering what they said. Ali grasped Bilrak's shoulder, squeezing as he had done with her. "You help us end this conflict, then you have mine and Daf's loyalty."

"Then we fight." Bilrak cheered, hoisting his pickaxe into the air. Everyone roared and several Bawns entered the cell, escorting Daf out. Daf pushed out her bottom lip. "I guess I'll see you later, Ali?"

"We're helping them, so yes, you'll see me later."

Daf disappeared past the shadows the torches cast, and out of Ali's view. Bilrak remained in the cell.

"Bilrak, you'll keep Daf safe?"

He slapped his hands together, rubbing them like he had soap in his hands. "I can tell she's not a warrior, so skinny and fragile, unlike you, but my answer is yes. She'll be on our rear, and away from battle. It won't be a long, drawn-out fight. We'll have the Anunnaki utterly surprised."

"Good," said Ali.

"Chan-Ru," shouted Bilrak.

Chan came out of the shadows, Thun by his side, and walked toward Ali's cell. "Why is she still inside?" He motioned for her to exit the cell, the giant towering over the small Bawn.

"Yes, yes. You are free." Bilrak gestured for Ali to step out of the cell. "Again." He looked off in Harak's direction with a scowl. "I apologize for my son. I'll knock some sense into him one of these days, but not today. He rides with you, according to the prophecies. Don't fear, your crew has your back, and their eyes are on Harak, per my orders."

Ali didn't like the idea but figured her continued objections wouldn't get her far. "He tries something, he's dead."

"I told him as much."

"Good."

"We have a small crew for you," said Chan.

Thun extended his arm outward at a group of Bawn waiting in the corridor. "Meet Algona, Bavila, Ramira, Magil, Dilgor, and Thodion." After each name, they stepped forward bowing.

Ali bowed back, her stomach tightening, wanting to push these men and women away. If she could pilot *Tranquil* by herself like she had during her first test run, she didn't need this crew.

"And," continued Thun, "you have me, Chan, and Harak."

She shoved her fists onto her hips, standing strong and erect. She eyed Harak. "Do nothing stupid."

Harak grunted and stepped forward. "Don't order me around. This is my crew, just as it's yours."

"The hell it is."

"Ramira," interrupted Bilrak, "is my daughter. She's noble and wise."

Ramira bowed. She had long, brown, curly hair with penetrating green eyes, an eye color Ali didn't notice on Bawns before. "I'll be your best crew member."

Several Bawns grumbled their objections at Ramira's words.

Bilrak raised his fist. "Stop." He pointed to an older woman, who had hair like snow in the biosphere, and wrinkles lining her yellowing face. "This is Algona. She's wise and one of our best medicine women. She healed Daf's leg. Algona can heal anything under the earth and sun."

Ali looked toward Magil, Dilgor, and Thodion. They wobbled from too much drink. Caped and hooded, their beards hung low and past their bellies. One had his beard tucked under his belt.

"What are their specialties?" asked Ali.

"Magil," said Bilrak, "is the strongest of us by far. He carries the heaviest swords, eats the most meals, and can drink a wicked amount of mead." He walked to Magil and gave the man a hearty hug. They matched laughter and as Bilrak turned, he wiped spit off of his jovial lips. He eyed Ali, his happy expression falling. "I've disturbed you?"

She couldn't care less about their strength or who could drink the most. "That's not what I asked. What can he do for us on the ship?"

"You can figure it out." Bilrak hurried past Ali, calling over his shoulder. "I'm late for the tunnel. If I don't catch up to them now, they'll leave their king no fighting scraps."

Harak slapped his hands together, his pickaxe leaning against his thigh. "Let's go," he ordered, snaking himself around everyone and to the head of the line. He pointed down the corridor in the opposite direction of his father. "To *Tranquil*."

Ali stood her ground, her arms folded at her chest. "Do not order my crew...on or off my ship."

Harak pinched his lips shut, his body stiffening. He marched to Ali, his nose to her belly, and glared up at her. "These are my people. When my father is not in the presence of my people, I am king by birthright. You cannot tell me what to do, lassie."

Ali flicked her head to the side, motioning toward Thun. "From what I hear, your brother, Thun, is first in line as king. Regardless, the ship does not move unless I move it. I have full authority over everyone, or we don't fly." Ali wanted to kick the man as hard as she could, just to drive home her point.

Harak brandished a sword from behind his long cape. Ali's hand quickly moved to Sol, almost as if Sol pulled her to it. Harak took a swing, and Ali caught his sword upon hers. Steel against steel reverberated off the walls. Ali pressed against his sword, and Harak fell to one knee, cringing, his muscles shaking against her power and Sol's strong force.

"That's enough, Harak." Thun kicked his brother in the side and Harak tumbled to the floor.

Ali sheathed her sword into her baldric. She did her best to maintain calm, though her insides wanted to rip Harak limb from limb. "He won't stop trying to kill me."

Thun shrugged. "No, Ali. He wouldn't kill you. Not anymore. Father would skin him alive."

"Then what do you call that?"

"Just a little banter, you know, a little play."

Ali glared at Harak. "Play or not, you try that again, and this sword gets rammed down your throat."

Harak kicked the dirt. "Don't talk to me like that." He smirked at Ali. "Let's move. *Tranquil* awaits."

"We have a half a day to wait," replied Ali.

Harak walked onward, ignoring her. Thun patted Ali's elbow, standing with the other crew members. "He'll lighten up."

Chan shuffled forward. "You're the captain, Ali. Lead by example. Lead with your heart. Sometimes people like Harak need examples to change their minds, and I believe he'll change his mind."

Ali almost chuckled at the idea. The guy couldn't light a torch without growling at the torch for not lighting itself. "Yeah, I hope so." She took a step in the city's direction, where they'd jump in the elevator and to the starship. "Everyone, let's go."

A cheer rose in the corridor, and they clanged their weapons against the rocky walls and ground, following their captain to the starship.

A ship that would take them to their first battle.

A battle Ali couldn't afford to lose.

33

SHAE

Starhawk Transport, Unknown

Shae stared out the cockpit window. Y'taul's giant ship loomed over the Starhawk, its belly opening like a monster about to devour its prey. "I'll kill anyone who thinks they can buy me and Devon. That's a fact."

"I know Y'taul's game," said Kalista. "Don't say anything while we're inside his ship and whatever you do, no aggression." The transport shook, the Starhawk passing through the bottom of the ship. Thick metal planks extended downward on either side of the belly's opening. Blue lights lined the plating, wildly flashing, nearly blinding Shae.

Kalista took an uneasy breath. "Here we go."

"Give me a gun," demanded Shae.

"No." Kalista held her hand over her holstered weapon nearest Shae. "You'll get another bullet in you if I hand you a gun. Do what I say and what I do. Trust me, gentlemen."

The Starhawk entered the docking bay, the blue light changing to a hazy red. The Starhawk turned and touched down gently on the docking bay floor, vibrating gently. The underbelly closed, and the bay's lights switched to soft, white light.

"Welcome," said Kalista, sarcastically. "You being here may be a good distraction."

"Distraction for what?" asked Devon.

She opened the pilot-side door and walked out, ignoring Devon's question. A conversation from outside carried into the cockpit too muffled to understand. Shae stood, walking into the Starhawk's cabin and paced. "If anything goes awry, stick as close to me as you can so we don't get separated. We see a weapon, we grab it, all right?"

Devon eyed him, biting his bottom lip. "Understood, Admiral."

"Do your best to maintain composure, no matter what. Can you do that?"

Devon nodded, rubbing his hands up and down his pant legs, clearly nervous. "I think so."

Shae stopped pacing. "Know so. Tell your entire body to remain calm and collected."

"Yes, sir."

Shae paused, peering into Devon's eyes. "Close your eyes and focus on every part of you, calming yourself down and telling yourself you'll know what to do when an opportunity shows itself. Athletes do it, and I do it. It's a golden ticket to better decision making."

Devon closed his eyes, his body relaxing. The muffles outside became louder. He opened his eyes. "I did it...I think."

"Good." Shae faced the side cabin door. The door clicked and slid open. A cool breeze swirled inside. Kalista stood before Shae, and beside her smiled Y'taul, along with three tall humanoids.

Y'taul motioned for Shae and Devon to come forward. "Here...to us, humans." He bowed diplomatically.

Devon looked at Shae. Shae nodded and stepped forward, walking out of the transport.

"We Plearians," stated Y'taul. "You humans. Kali is Anunnaki." He shook his head and pointed to his chest. "Plearians worth no money. Anunnaki fight if we try to take Anunnaki. Very strong. Kill many Plearians. Humans worth a lot of money on market. Not strong. Not kill other races as easily as Anunnaki. Do you see?"

Shae didn't see. Once the brainwashing wore off on his race, they fought tooth and nail against the strong Anunnaki. Taking Shae's race for granted was fool's gold.

Y'taul turned and walked to an open door leading out of the bay and nodded, gesturing for everyone to follow. The door led into a stark corridor, lit by glowing blue cyan walls. A soft textile made up the floor, and every step squished slightly downward, along with a translucent purple that shimmered with every footfall.

Y'taul led them into a room full of artistic designs—paintings that morphed into a beautiful flower, then to waterfalls, then to mountain landscapes, and on and on. Chairs and a small table sat in the middle of the room. Y'taul motioned for them to sit. "My people are taking the five-hundred troy ounce now, Kali."

Kalista bared her teeth. "King Anu will have your heads."

Y'taul glared. "First, you say Enlil will have my head and now you say King Anu. How many heads do I have?"

Kalista sat down, seething. "What are you going to do with the white powder gold?"

"Consume it. Like you and your race do." He held up his hand as if holding a glass of mead. "We toast, as you say." He glanced at Shae and Devon, as if proud that he knew human customs. "We toast to longevity."

Kalista didn't move. "We use the white powder gold for our atmosphere. Nothing more."

Y'taul held in a laugh. "Oh? I see. That is also consumed through breathing, no? I imagine that if it touches food or soil, it also consumed one way or another?" He winked at her. "Don't think me as dumb as humans."

Kalista straightened her lips and fell back into the chair, breathing shallowly.

Y'taul faced Shae. "Do you know what white powder gold does?" He didn't wait for a reply. "What you humans have slaved for years, years beyond..." he put his hand to his chin, concentrating. "You mine on planet Eos. Your Eos give ebb. Ebb is full of gold...other stuffs, too." He wiggled his fingers, flashing a few rings with shiny crystals. "You slave for Anunnaki's longevity." He pointed at Kalista. "Her longevity.

You slave for DNA repair. This white powder gold recharges, re-balances, and heals DNA. You no need to die...for a long, long time."

Kalista crossed her arms, raising her chin. "You share our secrets? Let me share yours."

Y'taul put his hand up. "You tell our secrets, I show King Anu vids. Yes, vids that show you sell gold. I show Enlil, as well. He likes to kill."

Devon slowly raised his hand, moving his head hesitantly from Y'taul to Kalista, then back to Y'taul.

"You need something?" asked Y'taul.

"If what you say is true, then our DNA has holes in it?" Devon shook his head as if dismissing his own words. "I mean, over time, our DNA falls apart?"

Y'taul interlaced his fingers, resting them in his lap. "Yes. You have Suficell Pods, am I correct?" Again, he continued without waiting for an answer. "Those pods can repair your DNA through the DNA healing frequency, which falsely be labeled Immune Support. You quietly be told to use to extend your life, but that frequency is frequency for monoatomic gold or, its other name, white powder gold. It keeps you alive longer than your current lifespan if you wish. And—"

Devon interrupted. "Say that again? We can stay alive much longer?"

Y'taul chuckled as if he were talking to a child. "If you do not die from other circumstances, such as crash ship, then yes. You have ability with white powder gold to live for an abundant long amount of years. Ingest this gold on a continual basis...body regenerates, fixes DNA, and opens other DNA channels. The disease of aging goes away, mostly." Y'taul eyed Kalista. "This can be done with the Suficell Pods? I'm correct, no?"

Kalista looked away. "Your guess is as good as mine. That's Space Templar technology, something I know nothing about. Orion's hell, talk to a gene expert about this crap, Y'taul, not a cargo pilot."

Devon's eyes widened. "You're saying Suficell Pods can make me live for a thousand years, perhaps longer?"

"Yes, but I don't think as easy to do with pods, unlike taking monoatomic gold," said Y'taul. "But maybe same thing." He pointed to his heart. "I'm friend. Kali and her race enemy to your people. They liars. We—"

Kalista snorted. "Friends? Friendly? You've killed just about as many humans as we have."

Y'taul shot Kalista a look full of daggers. "You walk thin line." He made a cutting motion over his throat. "I can be unfriendly fast-like. Okay?"

"You would enslave them, just like we Anunnaki enslaved them."

"Kalista, you went over my patience." Y'taul pressed a button on his chair. A side door opened, and four tall, thin men entered. Two men walked toward Kalista and grabbed her by the arms, pulling her out of her seat. Two others hurried toward Shae and Devon.

There was a loud grunt, and the two men heading in Shae's and Devon's direction glanced at Kalista, then rushed her way. The other two lay on the ground near her feet, one out cold, the other rubbing his chin. The two other men approached her quickly.

Kalista grabbed one by his shirt and threw him head over heels. He bounced against a wall, smacking into the floor a moment later. She sent the fourth on his back next.

Shae furrowed his brow. This Kalista didn't just fly cargo, she exhibited military training.

Y'taul stood, a gun in his hand, and moved quickly toward Kalista. Shae reacted, lunging for Y'taul, swiping the gun out of his hand and tackling the tall guy to the floor. Kalista snagged the gun and kicked Y'taul in the side. She stepped hard on his chest, aiming the weapon at his forehead. "Hi, Y'taul." She gave him a wink.

Shae grabbed a gun on the floor, dropped from a Plearian. He noticed a man getting up and going for a weapon strapped to his side. Shae sent a hard kick to the guy's chin, sending him onto his stomach. The Plearian's weapon bounced on the floor. Shae snatched the gun and slid it to Devon. Devon slipped his finger through the trigger guard, targeting Y'taul. Shae did the same.

"Those are different weapons than you're used to," said Kalista. "Be careful." She held the gun closer to Y'taul's face, her eyes on Shae.

"They only use them to stun. They thought they had us easy, but no one has it easy against me." She glared at Y'taul. "Next time, be smart. Have your gun's ready when threatening an Anunnaki. Make us work for it. I don't like this easy crap."

A whirring sound filled the room, and a ray extended from Devon's gun like an energetic ripple and slammed into Y'taul's lower back. Y'taul jerked a few times, his arms and hands shaking violently. An instant later, he went still.

Kalista stepped back. "Wait until I'm not right next to him before you do something like that, dummy."

Devon put his hands up, dropping the weapon. "I'm sorry. It was an accident."

"Who cares." Kalista hurried toward Devon, grabbing his hand. "You only stunned him, idiot. Unfortunately, Y'taul will be fine in two minutes." Kalista tugged him along, heading for a door at the far side of the room. "Until then, we're getting our butts out of here."

Shae ran beside her, dwarfed by her massive frame. They exited and sirens shrieked, and red lights illuminated the corridor. Footsteps echoed in the distance. No doubt more Plearians headed their way, and Shae figured they'd have their weapons drawn this time, kill function activated.

"Over here," said Kalista, letting go of Devon's arm.

They turned down another corridor and through a doorway into a small, darkened room, highlighted by a dim red light. The door to the room shut behind them. Opposite the door stood a large window the size of a wall, and on the other side of the window hung rows of red lights.

"The docking bay?" said Shae.

"Yep, right past that window." Kalista hurried to a panel beside the closed door, smashing it with her elbow. The panel sparked, smoke twirling into the air. "That may slow them down." She pointed her gun at the window. "Stand back." She pulled the trigger. Nothing happened. She shook the gun, then aimed a second time.

Nothing.

She reared back and threw the pistol at the glass. It ricocheted off the glass and slid across the floor, spinning. "The gun is a dud." She flicked a look at Shae. "Change the dial on your gun. You'll see it on the barrel just above the trigger guard. It'll change the gun from stun to kill."

Shae clicked the dial forward and targeted the long, wide glass. Pulling the trigger, he heard a click, then another click. He studied the weapon. "Mine's a dud too."

Kalista punched the air, her face flushing red. "Blasted shades of Orion's crack," she cursed. "All right, here goes." She made her way to the long, wide window and leaned against it, pushing. It slightly bowed. "I think we can break this." She tipped her head to the side, motioning at something beyond the glass. "And there's our Starhawk down there."

A loud bang jostled the door behind them, then another. Shae turned, expecting the door to burst from its seams by a blast any second, exposing them.

Kalista stepped away and grunted loudly as she rushed forward. She rammed her shoulder into the window. It didn't budge.

A whining sound of metal against metal reverberated off the walls. The door to the room crept open, lifting a quarter of a meter off the ground. A metallic pry bar appeared through the small opening, sharp and thin at the end, nudging the door open a few millimeters more.

"We all run through this window together," said Kalista.

Devon's eyes widened. "Really?"

Shae glanced down at the bay below. "It's the only way. Like she said, our Starhawk is right there."

"On my count," Kalista called out. "One...two...go."

Shae dug his boots into the floor and ran as fast as he could, jumping into the window, Devon and Kalista doing the same. The window bowed outward, then pushed back, throwing them onto the floor. More metal against metal sounded in the room. The door opened another quarter of a meter, and a gun pointed through the opening.

34

SHAE

Y'taul's Ship, Unknown

"Move, move," yelled Shae, pushing Kalista and Devon across the room. He shoved them beside several circular chairs, and Devon toppled over.

A light flashed from the gun thrust through the small opening between the floor and the door. A spark clanged off the floor.

"The bar," said Shae. He looked Kalista up and down. He thought her strength topped five Plearians put together. "Grab the gun and the bar."

"The bar easy, the gun...no. The barrel is wicked hot and would melt my skin off." She stood. "Step back, boys." She ran toward the door, slid and kicked the gun out of the Plearian's hand. Simultaneously, she yanked the crowbar loose and pulled it into her chest. Nothing held up the door now, and it shut.

Without a second thought, Kalista dashed wildly at the window, screaming. She slid her grip down the shaft of the bar, leaned on her back foot, and took a giant swing. The bar connected, and the window shattered, sending thousands of pieces of glass to the bay below. She jumped a few levels to the docking bay floor and landed athletically. She gathered herself and looked up at Devon and Shae. "Let's go. I'll

245

catch you. One at a time." Kalista held her arms out, the red lights in the bay streaking across her body.

"The last time I jumped from this high, I about broke my legs," said Devon, his voice shaky.

"We've got to go now." Shae nudged Devon forward.

Devon took another step and jumped, his arms flailing about. Kalista caught him and set him on his feet. Shae took a step and let himself fall, the air rushing up against him. Kalista caught him as well, like a baby falling to its mother.

"They'll be here any second," she said.

"Let's move." Shae ran as fast as he could to the Starhawk and opened the co-pilot door, jumping in. He rolled off the seat and moved to the cabin. Devon did the same.

"What's she doing?" He rushed to the cockpit, Devon in tow.

"And where is she going?" asked Devon.

Kalista raced toward another, smaller ship.

Shae slumped, his heart jumping to his throat. "I think she's leaving us behind. We're her distraction." He sat in the pilot's seat, the chair's wide frame making it feel like he was a child in an adult's lounge chair. He scooted to the edge of the seat, held the control stick, and pressed on the holomonitor. His heart picked up a beat when he noticed the icons and flight commands didn't match the Star Guild ships he piloted. "Ignition, where are you?" He swiped through application windows and stopped on something that looked like an engine icon. "That might be it."

He pressed on the holographic display, his fingers turning several colors as the pixels beamed on his finger. The engines purred, and the lights in the cockpit and cabin dimmed. He looked over his shoulder at Devon. "Hold on. We're getting out of here, with or without her." Shae jerked back when the wall in front of him disappeared like a hologram, revealing expansive space lit by a million stars.

"How did...?" Devon pointed at the now-vanished wall.

"No idea, but we can question that later."

A hazy gravity field stretched from the top and bottom of the opening, a technology similar to some Star Guild's vessels. It kept the vacuum of space out yet allowed ships to freely leave and return without issue. The co-pilot door lurched open, and a hand appeared out of the corner of Shae's periphery. He ducked out of the way, though a moment too late. Strong fingers gripped his arm and pulled him out of the pilot's chair, tossing him like a stuffed doll into the cabin. He slid on his back, stopping near Devon's feet.

"Get out of my seat," yelled Kalista. She slammed the co-pilot door and jumped into the pilot seat. "You boys trying to leave without me?"

Shae rubbed his lower back, gasping for breath. Devon pulled Shae to the bench seat and strapped him in just as the Starhawk shuddered and lifted. The ship jerked back as boosters activated, then pushed forward, rocketing past the gravity field and into space. "This is how you guys treat me? Just leave me?" She eyed the radar and slapped her hand down. "Nibiru's blasphemy. We have bandits." She banked hard right as a beam of some sort zoomed by the Starhawk.

Shae rubbed the back of his neck, trying to ease an ache taking hold. "We didn't leave you. You were leaving us."

"I was what?" she said. "You idiots. I had to—" She pulled the Starhawk up and to the left, again avoiding another weapon's fire. "I had to open the docking bay doors through—" She pressed her control stick forward, avoiding another potential hit. "Through one of Y'taul's ships. This Starhawk isn't linked into Y'tauls pirating vessel and—" Kalista maneuvered away from more enemy fire.

"Can't you just hyperjump to the next system?" asked Shae.

Devon nodded. "Isn't this ship equipped with NMJ drives?"

Kalista made a fist and shook it. "I can't put the coordinates in. I'm too busy trying to keep us alive."

Not too busy to shake your damn fist, thought Shae. Shae unbuckled and stood, then toppled to the side, bracing his hand against the top of Devon's shoulder to steady himself. He took a step forward and lost his balance as Kalista dodged another strange beam. The weapons the Plearians had were unique, to say the least. "I'm coming to help."

"Sit down," ordered Kalista.

A blast hit the ship's stern, tossing Shae to the floor. His eyes widened as a rush of adrenaline took over, and in a flash, he found himself back on his feet, leaping for the co-pilot chair. He grasped the chair's arm and pulled himself into the seat.

"Y'taul's ship is equipped with long-range phase wave cannons, and he seems happy to use them. We're pulling away from him, but—" The ship shook as another beam hit its mark. The flight console brought up a display with a red flashing light under the belly of their Starhawk, indicating damage.

"Give me a break," groaned Kalista. She swiped her hand across the display, turning it off. "It's just one of our landing sleds." She pulled back on her control stick, then immediately pushed forward.

The flight console brought up another display and beeped several times, showing their current location, along with Y'taul's, and several other smaller crafts in pursuit. Kalista pressed a holographic button and turned off the beeping sound. "Shut up." She hammered her fist into the pilot seat's armrest. "How did I get myself into this mess?"

Shae extended his hand toward the nav dial. "We have to get out of here. We're ill-equipped for a fight. I'm typing in Matrona's coordinates."

Kalista pushed his hand away. "Don't. Get your hand away from the course module drive."

Shae attempted to reach again, and she batted his hand away a second time. She quickly pressed several numbers on the course module and activated NMJ drivers.

A loud pop and a sensation took over, catapulting Shae and the rest of them a thousand times faster in a blink of an eye. Space before him filled with stars streaking like lines across the window, changing from white, to yellow, to purple, and back to white again. Silence filled the cockpit as if he floated on black clouds full of stars.

As quickly as it began, it stopped. Shae inhaled a deep breath, sensation coming back to him. He rubbed his eyes, stunned at what he saw in front of him. "Starbase Matrona?" Hope grabbed at Shae as the beautiful starbase stared back at him.

Kalista pointed ahead. "Does that planet look like the same green planet Matrona was orbiting?"

Shae tilted his head. The starbase orbited a gorgeous blue planet, with patches of green here and there, its aura stretching outward.

She sighed. "That's Starbase Ceres, you bonehead. How am I going to explain this to my boss? In my damn hurry, I put in the wrong coordinates."

Shae eyed the starbase in front of him. "What the hell is Starbase Ceres?"

Kalista groaned. "How am I going to explain this? I can't just jump out of here. NMJ drives need to recharge."

"That planet is gorgeous," Devon whispered loudly. "It's as blue as any blue I have ever seen."

For a moment, Shae thought of Earth, and as the thought came, another memory jumped to the surface. He held Helen's hand, watching Ali read the first lines of a book. She couldn't have been more than five years old. Ali glanced up and grinned. "I did it." She threw her hands in the air. "I read. I really can read."

Helen squeezed Shae's hand and kissed Shae's cheek. "She's smart as a whip."

Shae rubbed his nose against Helen's. "She gets her smarts from you, and her looks."

Kalista palmed her forehead, the slapping sound taking Shae out of his thoughts.

"We're in Cygnus Alpha quadrant of the Milky Way Galaxy," said Kalista. "It's a water planet named Opus. I don't want to be here."

"Starbase Matrona isn't the only starbase in the galaxy?" asked Shae.

"Nope," said Kalista. "I'm afraid not."

Shae sunk in his chair. "Are there humans on that starbase?"

Kalista nodded. "Yep. You're not the only human slaves Enlil has in the galaxy."

"Mining gold?" Devon chimed in.

"Yes," replied Kalista. "You're catching on, aren't you?"

"Starhawk," came a voice over the commlink. "Please identify yourself. Your Starhawk signature is not on our flight plan today. I have you as Starhawk signature one-three-five, is that correct?" A short pause, then, "Kalista?"

"Hey, Al, and yes, this is Kalista. I was en route to assist mining operations on Otto's moon. My NMJ drives aren't working correctly and I found myself in a small asteroid belt. An asteroid broke one of my landing gears."

"Kalista," replied Al chuckling. "First off, you Starhawk pilots don't assist in the mining operations. You all sit in your ships on your butt while we load the rocks in your cargo bay. Second, we still haven't met a single Starhawk pilot. Any chance we can finally meet you?"

"We can't show ourselves because of classified reasons, Al. Plus, you couldn't handle me." She grinned as if she enjoyed playing this game with Al.

"Yeah, yeah. Head to Opus, Underpost Nine. I'll tell them about your landing gear. We can have you patched up in no time."

"Thank you, Al."

"You're welcome, Kalista. Maybe we can meet someday."

"Out." Kalista clicked off her commlink.

Devon pointed to the blue planet. "We're heading planetside?"

Shae knew the answer before Kalista responded. He shook his head, trying to figure out how he could get back to Ali or Matrona, and eventually home to Earth. For the first time that he could remember, he missed Helen more than anything and wanted nothing more than to be with her. He somehow felt her strong, sweet presence all around him.

"Yep, we're heading planetside." Kalista pushed the throttle forward. "Hang on, boys. This planet and this landing will be a bit...different."

ENLIL

Eos Two

Enlil sat at his desk, listening intently to the audio and video playing on his holocomp display. He paused it, growling under his breath.

He glanced at his assistant and rose from his seat, all eleven feet of him. "I've got to get some sleep," he said, rubbing his eyes. He pointed at his holodisplay, raising his brow at his assistant. "What do you think?"

"Captain Diana Johnson was a traitor and deserved to die. That's what I think." His assistant, about the same height and girth as Enlil, looked up with trepidation, hoping he'd said nothing wrong.

"Correct," replied Enlil. "We can thank Sleuth for the vids and information. Too bad he'll die soon and never receive our gratitude."

The assistant lifted a brow. "So, the weapon is almost there?"

Enlil grinned. "I think my sister had a hand in destabilizing the core reactors, nearly turning that thing into a firework's display before it ever reached Starship *Sirona*, but we have it fully under our control now."

"When does it reach *Sirona*?"

Enlil sat down, his elbows on his desk. He leaned forward and scratched his chin. "It's about there now."

"Yes, sir." The assistant looked at his chronometer on his wrist. "I'm worried about the weapon's instability. The problem—"

Enlil put his hand up. "The only problem is that we have not tested it. I've heard it a million times. This will be the test. Get it as close to the starship as possible. Sleuth will keep all holocams offline with a loop feed in place. The crew on the ship won't know what hit them."

The assistant bowed and turned to walk out of the room.

Enlil wrung his hands together. "Along with killing *Sirona* and the humans who live onboard, we're also hitting another group of humans where they least expect it. We'll take a mass horde of them."

The assistant stopped at the doorway. "Excuse me, sir?"

"Earth. We're attacking Earth, sending them back to their cave-man-like ways to create a massive breeding and slave program there… again." He gave a wry grin, looking off. "I have several races helping us."

The assistant raised his brows. "Yes, yes."

"And," added Enlil, "prepare the explosives. The Bawns are on their way."

Enlil waved his hand over a glowing red orb on his desk as his assistant walked out. "Produce paper. Address message to King Bilrak in Bawn writing."

He cleared his throat. "Write message now." He shifted in his seat, getting comfortable. "Dearest Bilrak," he said with a smirk. "I have this message linked via a control chip to a detonation device. I connected the detonation device to explosives strategically placed in this palace, from floor to ceiling. If you lift this paper, which I suspect you will since you're a curious lot, you'll have ten seconds to leave the palace. The problem is it takes longer than ten seconds to leave. Enjoy your death."

Enlil liked to play games, and this would be a good game if the Bawn took the bait, and they would. He liked the Bawn. An ambitious lot, courageous and bullheaded. They never bothered him and his people, so he'd left them alone inside the mountain, not wanting to deal with another issue on his already long list. Now they scurried in a tunnel like rats to his palace, and he knew exactly where their tunnel ended.

At the palace study.

The upper right portion of his desk opened, and a paper with Anunnaki writing, other than King Bilrak's name, emerged. "Dammit." He frowned, forgetting to translate the entire message into Bawn. He knew Chan-Ru had escaped to the city inside the mountain, so maybe he'd by chance join them on their warring escapade and read the note.

His grin grew wider. An even more fun game. The Bawn's survival now depended on Chan. The idiot would see the Anunnaki writing and read it. Maybe. "Nah, definitely. Bawn are a damn curious breed. They'll pick it up if Chan doesn't." He stood, paper in hand, and headed to his palace study. He'd leave the paper on a desk and link up the detonator chip.

The game would go well...for Enlil.

36

SHAE

Starhawk Transport, Planet Opus

Kalista steered the Starhawk on approach to the blue planet. "Entering upper atmosphere."

Shae craned his neck, taking a glance at Devon in the cabin. "You okay, kid?"

Devon gave Shae a thumbs up. "I think so."

Shae didn't believe him. "Yeah, I'm not either."

Kalista rubbed her stomach. "Are you guys hungry?"

"Starving," said Devon.

Kalista tapped the commlink. "Al, this is Kalista."

"Yes?"

"I'm starving. Can I have three plates of your finest meal when I get down to Underpost Nine?"

"Wow. How many people you got on that transport, Kalista?"

"Just me. Why?"

"I'm just flicking you Crustacean spray. I don't know how you can fit all that in one stomach, but I'll have it delivered to you in the holding bay."

"Thank you." She flipped the commlink off. "Are you all strapped in?"

Shae tugged on his restraints. "I'm all good."

"I'm buckled in," came Devon.

"Good, we're going down into Opus waters."

She tilted the craft, bringing the grand blue planet into view. Unlike Eos or Tanza, this planet shimmered turquoise. She pushed the throttle forward. "Entry shield." An instant later, she shot Shae a look. "I said, entry shield."

Shae straightened. "Right." He leaned forward, pressing a holographic button in the middle console between them. Unlike the rest of the craft, activating entry shields on a Starhawk mirrored other Star Guild ships. "Got it. Entry shield activated."

"OMS activated," she said, tilting the craft at a forty-degree angle. "Aft thrusters stable." The craft entered planet Opus's upper atmosphere, the entry friction illuminating the shield and yellow-red flames grabbed at the ship's nose.

Shae squeezed his armrests, pressing his feet hard against the floorboard. Gravity intensified, and his body felt heavy. He flexed his muscles as the Starhawk vibrated back and forth, a growling sound booming into the cockpit. A moment later the fire died down, extinguishing in the lower atmosphere, and the sound vanished to nothing.

Kalista glided the craft and leveled out. "Boys, take a good look. It's a beautiful thing." Thousands of meters below sparkled water, elegantly dazzling from the rays of a sun.

Shae mouthed a wow, and deep down wished Helen could see this. "You seeing that, Devon?"

"Oh, yes." Devon peered out the window. "Breathtaking." Blue water went on for as far as the eye could see. Devon unbuckled himself. "I have to get a better look."

Kalista put her hand up. "Stay seated. We're heading to Underpost Nine. Strap back in."

"All right."

The Starhawk dipped forward, nosing straight toward the water. Shae held on, his boots digging into the floor as the rush of weight slammed into him. "Pull up, pull up."

Kalista kept the ship on its trajectory, ignoring Shae. About to hit the water, Kalista pulled back on the control stick and hovered the Starhawk in place about five feet above the water's surface.

"What the Guild are you doing?" Shae flexed his fingers, making a fist. "Trying to impress us with your flying skills or something?" If so, she did a terrible job.

"Going down," she said.

The craft lowered into the water, then sank below the surface. When the bubbles cleared, Shae instinctively jerked away from the side window. A creature bobbed up and down with its snout pressed against the glass. It looked into Shae's eyes, its mouth slightly upturned as if smiling. "A dolphin?" If memory served him right, he'd seen plenty of dolphins as an admiral in the United States Navy. He paused, his eyes widening. The United States? He shook his head. Perhaps it had to do with Earth. The creature knocked its nose on the co-pilot's door a few times, then swam away.

"What are those?" said Devon, as another dolphin swam to take a peek.

"It's a Crustacean species known as dolphins," said Kalista. "They like playing with our crafts when we submerge. They chase us. It's a game to them."

Devon unstrapped and made his way to Shae, leaning against the co-pilot seat. "They seem intelligent. Look how they watch us. They're curious."

"They have larger brains than you and use more of their brain than humans. So, in essence, they're smarter than your species." Kalista flicked a lever and Shae whipped forward, the restraining belt pulling him back into his seat. Devon tumbled backward, slamming against the bulkhead.

"I told you to sit down and stay strapped, bumblehead," said Kalista. The ship sped under the water, bubbles cascading off the windows. The dolphins kept up, swimming beside the craft. "If they could speak our language, I don't think they'd allow us on their planet. At least, I wouldn't." Colorful fish came into view, parting as the ship sped forward.

"You don't agree with your race being here?" asked Shae.

Kalista shifted in her seat. "I'm in conflict, yes. I don't think they should enslave anyone."

A large coral reef appeared to the right like spires reaching toward the surface. Fish and other sea creatures busied themselves around the white reef, roaming, hunting, and hiding.

"Then why do you take part?" questioned Shae.

"I do what I have to do to survive and help keep my race from dying out. But things are changing. I can feel it. Some of my race are doing their best to find another way to keep our race alive."

"Why are they dying out?"

"I didn't say we were dying out, but we would if people like me didn't do their job. We have a failing atmosphere because of past strenuous civil wars. White powder gold helps repair it, though it takes a long, long time it seems." She clicked on her commlink. "Underpost Nine, this is Kalista. I'm heading in for repairs."

"Hey, Kalista," came Al. "Steer to the inline and we'll pull you in."

Kalista slightly moved her control stick and slowed the vessel. A clank sounded, momentarily pushing the Starhawk backward. Light from a massive dome in the distance beamed through the water, highlighting a metallic line attached to the Starhawk's bow. The line tugged, lurching Shae forward, pulling them along at an incredible speed.

Kalista took her hands off the controls. "They have a magnetic suction that connects to docking Starhawks. We'll get some food while they repair our ship."

"Then what?" asked Devon, rubbing his lower back, walking toward the bench seat.

"Once they fix everything, we get back up top and to Nibiru."

Shae's insides contracted at her words.

Up ahead, a large, disk-like structure loomed. Round lights surrounded its top and pulsed a bright white light, sending beams outward and around the Starhawk. "We'll head in there. Whatever you do, don't exit the craft. They're under the same protocols as your starbase. They're not to see the occupants of a Starhawk," instructed

Kalista. "The only difference is that they communicate with us. Your society never has."

"Is my race really that dumb not to question such a strange code of conduct?" questioned Shae. "It just seems so preposterous."

Kalista chuckled. "Don't ask me how unintelligent your race is. You went along with it, right?" She rolled her eyes. "You're all stupid if you ask me. The chemicals we put in your water don't help you any."

Devon sat and strapped himself in. "Yeah, we read about those. If you didn't spread them through our water and lace them in our food, we'd be a lot smarter than you could ever imagine."

"I doubt that."

"I suppose the inhabitants of this base are stupid too?" asked Shae. Being stupid took a lot of brainwashing.

"Yes, they're unintelligent. Here we are," Kalista announced.

They entered through a large opening in the disk-like structure, bringing them to a small, one ship-sized docking bay big enough for a Starhawk. The bay door closed, and the water level lowered, eventually draining completely. The tow winch attached to the craft's bow unmagnetized, spooling into a frame attached to the middle of the docking bay wall in front of them. The wall slid up and light flooded in.

A man wearing clothes similar to Star Guild military attire waved them onward, and Kalista flipped a few switches on the ceiling above her. The Starhawk shifted and moved forward on a yellow track and into a large holding bay that housed countless other craft—Starhawks, Starjumpers, and several foreign-looking crafts Shae eyed for the first time. Their craft came to a stop.

Kalista wagged her finger at a large, saucer-shaped craft. "Those are Seabirds, used for sea excursion. These people mine all over Opus, drilling into underwater caverns and volcanoes. It's dangerous, but these nitwits have mastered underwater mining, so only a few accidents occur a year." She cleared her throat. "The year cycle here differs from what you're used to. Your year amounts to three here."

A man with a scruffy beard, tan, and a smile showing white teeth, tapped on the window. He held a metal box, motioning toward the back of the Starhawk.

"Our food awaits." She unstrapped. She walked to the cargo bay door, pressing on a control panel. "We have these handy package delivery systems. They place the food, or whatever else I'm asking for, through a little panel in the back of the Starhawk, and…" As if on cue, a ping sounded, announcing a delivery. "Most importantly, they don't see me." She grabbed the package and returned to her seat. She sniffed the package, lifting her nose in delight. "These people know how to cook."

The aroma wafted to Shae's nose. His mouth instantly watered. He couldn't remember the last time he ate.

Kalista opened the box. It held three tiers of shelving, each with a plate of food. She reached behind her, plate in hand. "Devon, here." Devon took it, and she placed a plate on Shae's lap. "Eat up."

Shae picked up a fork, mesmerized by the beautiful presentation of food before him. Something akin to mashed potatoes and gravy steamed upward, the smell like heaven. Green and yellow vegetables he couldn't identify, garnished with a sauce, also screamed for Shae to hurry and shove a fork full in his mouth. Shae took a bite, savoring the flavor, wanting to moan with enjoyment.

"What exactly is in our water back on Matrona?" asked Devon, his mouth full.

"Chemicals…stuff. I'm not a scientist. All I know is that they put chemicals in your water to dumb you down, to narrow your frame of thinking, and to keep you controlled. We do that with your food as you probably already know."

Shae dropped his fork on his plate, his meal not so appealing anymore. "It's in this stuff too, isn't it?"

Kalista shook her head. "Orion's slimy belt, no. They make Starhawk meals from a different supply." A fist banged on the window and the mechanic gave a thumbs up. Kalista cracked her knuckles and rolled her neck around. "Let's go." She put the plate down, tucking it inside the metallic box. "Come on. You two put your plates in. I don't have an eternity."

Shae took another bite, slid the plate on the middle box shelf and handed the box to Devon.

Kalista activated the engines. "The guy who pounded on our window wore a hybrid outfit. Did you see that? Kinda odd."

Shae eyed the man. He wore gray and green fatigues, different from the blue and red the rest of the crew in the docking bay wore. "A hybrid outfit?"

"Yeah." She buckled her restraining belt. "Get your restraints on. We're leaving."

The Starhawk quivered, and a long cable tractored them out into the smaller docking bay. The wall shut in front of them, and the bay began filling with water. Kalista swiped across her holodisplay, pressing a button, and the Starhawk unhooked from the cable. The bay door behind them opened and the vast ocean reached around them, sucking them into the sea. She turned the ship around and sped forward.

Kalista slapped the back of her neck and rubbed. "Who was that guy?" She puffed out her cheeks in thought. She spoke, though softly to herself. "Payson is a hybrid, trained in special ops. Most hybrids live undercover until called, and—" she gasped. "No, no. That guy better not have done what I think he did."

Shae straightened, not liking the nervous tone in her voice. "What did the guy do?"

Kalista threw her hands in the air. "I don't know who... perhaps Y'taul...but we've been ratted on." She pressed several keys on the HDC, bringing up a schematic of the ship. "I'm looking for changes on our Starhawk." She scanned the blueprint, her finger moving back and forth, searching for something peculiar. "Tell me if you see any heat changes that—" She punched her fist onto her thigh. "Nibiru's curse. They put extras on the bottom of my Starhawk."

Shae wrinkled his nose. "Extras?"

She let out a gush of air. "Probably a bomb." She pulled back on the throttle, slowing, and eventually stopping the Starhawk. It bobbed in the water, hovering up and down as the thrusters constantly rebalanced the craft, keeping it submerged.

She grimaced. "I'm guessing we only have a few minutes." She stood and hurried toward Devon, pushing him off the bench seat, knocking him to the floor. "You're constantly in the way." She pulled out the toolbox, opening it, and grabbed a thick wedge. "Who'll volunteer to knock the device off the Starhawk?"

Devon fidgeted. "How do you know it's a bomb?"

"I know bombs. I know the heat signature they give off. I'm certain it's a bomb." She handed the tool to Devon. "Here. I'm scared sick of water. You do this now or we die."

EDEN

Starship Sirona, Eos

Eden dashed through the corridor, William and Hank on her tail.

From what Eden could gather, the *Sirona* Guard was doing a hell of a job getting these people off the ship, but it was still too slow.

Sirona's *inhabitants are boarding me,* came *Swift.*

Eden almost halted, her hand coming to her heart. "You're here?"

I am. Hurry. The weapon is charging. It will fire soon.

Can you engage the weapon while people board you? asked Eden.

Negative. And after initial scans, the weapon is carrying unstable elements. We open fire upon it, and our impacts won't only destroy the weapon, but everything around it in a two-kilometer radius.

"Crap. Well, scrap that idea."

Consider it scrapped.

Eden continued to run. The rest of the Space Templars, including Nyx, ran ahead of them, Hank struggling to keep up.

"What did you say, Eden?" asked William, his breathing hastened.

"Nothing. Keep going." She sensed Hank behind her, and an image came to mind of his heart pumping blood through clogged arteries. She shook her head, pushing it out of her mind, wondering where that could have possibly come from, and why. She stopped and turned. Best not ignore the Sight. Hank had fallen far behind, his cheeks flush red and white blotches dotted his face. She grabbed William's wrist. "He's close to having a heart attack."

"Who?" William almost slipped from her sudden grasp and clutched Eden's arm to hold himself upright.

She pointed. "Hank." The alarms were blaring, and men and women hurried past them, heading toward one of the launch bays. She and William waded through the near stampede, making their way to Hank. The big guy threw his hands on his knees and bent over, wheezing. "I'm sorry. I can't keep up. I'll walk. Just go on without me."

William rubbed his back. "Take in a slow, deep breath and let it out. Keep doing so until your heartbeat slows down." His voice was soft and mellow.

Hank shook his head, sweat dripping from his nose. "Keep going. You have a ship to board, and by Guild, I'm not letting you miss it." He looked up, his face wet from perspiration. "Go."

Eden went to a knee and looked into Hank's eyes. "Trust me, okay? We'll be beside you the entire time, but you can't run. We'll walk with you, all right?"

He jerked his head upward. "What? No. You don't have time."

Eden closed her eyes. Swift, *how long do we have?*

From what my scanners view, seven minutes, maybe eight at most. Are you able to get to me, Eden?

I'll try.

"Walk, don't run," demanded Eden, helping Hank straighten his back. "Let's go."

"Leave me be. I don't care." He pushed her hand away. "Just, you two, get the hell off the damn ship. Forget about me."

Eden set her hands on her hips. "I ain't moving until you move. Now walk."

Hank looked at Eden like she was crazy. "What? We'll all be killed."

"Well, if we keep waiting around, then yes. We die," said William.

"Fine." Hank walked forward, and Eden and William took slow strides down the corridor.

People bumped into them, moving past them in a panic. Eden

moved around a corner, her hand rubbing Hank's back, doing her best to calm his heart rate. They closed in on the launch bay. There they would make their way down a ramp to the outside, and finally to one of *Swift*'s bays.

Five minutes, Eden, said *Swift*.

Eden's heartbeat picked up. Dammit. *Okay, I'm coming.* They moved through another corridor. "Up ahead. We're almost there." They entered the launch bay filled with unmanned starfighters, tools strewn about, and abandoned work vehicles littering the area. Hank picked up speed when they saw the launch bay door open.

Two minutes. I repeat, two minutes, said *Swift*.

Men and women in the hundreds, maybe thousands, rushed toward the ramp, some falling, others shouting. Eden helped a woman up, then slapped her rear. "Go, go." William and Hank made it to the top edge of the ramp, Eden just behind them. They went down and toward the orb-like ship shimmering across the way, several of its launch bay ramps down. People ran up the ramps, entering the behemoth craft.

"I can't believe I'm breathing actual air," said Hank, sniffing in as much oxygen as he could.

"It's pure, too," mentioned William.

"Almost there." Eden motioned toward *Swift*.

Hank stopped, wide-eyed and taking it all in, standing in between the two starships, his mouth open.

"What are you doing?" William grabbed him, almost tripping him to the ground.

Hank stumbled but kept his balance. He nodded, his eyes wide. "Yes, yes. Go, go."

A blast shook the earth, and a bright light filled the sky. Eden was lifted off her feet, and wind threw her to the ground. She hit hard, yelping, and tumbled to her side. She slid to a stop. Metal tore against metal and screeching sounds filled the air. She glanced up and saw *Sirona* warp, twist, and whine, the sounds almost deafening.

"No." Eden reached forward.

Not all the crew had made it off of the ship. As if a vacuum sucked from inside *Sirona*, men and women heading down the ramps were lifted off their feet and flew backward into the ship. Their arms and legs flailed, and their screams pierced Eden's eardrums. She pushed up and rushed toward Hank and William, who lay nearly paralyzed on the ground, staring at their old ship falling apart before them.

Eden squinted, following a stream of light focused on Starship *Sirona*'s midsection. She shifted her gaze to a wide cannon barrel in the distance. The cannon sat atop and attached to a platform; the platform held up by a couple dozen hefty thrusters hovering it in place.

A screeching sound and Eden faced *Sirona*. The ship buckled, folding in on itself. Eden grabbed William and Hank by their shirts, pulling on them with all her strengths. "Get up." They stood and twisted around, running toward *Swift*.

"*Swift*," screamed Eden. "Blow the damn weapon to hell and back."

I'm sorry. Like I said, I can't. Sensors show it would end all life in the area, including myself.

A blast growled inside *Sirona*, and the ship groaned heavily, shooting silvery orange and yellow sparks outward. It pushed Eden off her feet as she reached *Swift*'s ramp, landing sideways against the ramp's grated metal. William and Hank landed beside her, the ramp shaking as people tumbled onto it. A loud boom and Eden twisted to her back.

Sirona turned into what appeared to be a bright star, much like a supernova Eden had seen on holomovies and holodocumentaries. The ship sucked inward, almost as if it scrunched together into a ball, metal crunching, glass shattering. Eden gasped when it disappeared into itself as if sucked into a wormhole and then was completely gone. Her mouth remained open, and all went silent. She froze in place, unable to move or even blink.

Eden, get in my bay, said *Swift*. *The weapon is already recharging. We're next.*

Eden shook her head like a wet puppy, and all sound returned; the screams, the boots pounding up the ramp, Hank grunting as he went to stand.

Eden nodded. "Yes, go, go." She ran up the ramp, looking over her shoulder at Hank and William. "The weapon will fire at us soon. Get your asses up here." She reached the top and entered the launch bay. Men and women lay on the bay floor, some hurt, others out of breath. Several Space Templars assisted them, communicating, pointing here and there, sending people quickly down corridors.

She reached her arms out to Hank and William, noticing the skin on her arms and hands were now streaked with cuts and bleeding. "We're the last ones to board. Get inside." They reached out to Eden, and she grasped their wrists, leaning back. They flopped forward, falling to the floor, and sliding into the bay.

Closing all launch bay doors, said *Swift*. The ramp sucked inward, and the door slid downward, clanging loudly.

Eden lay on the ground, her breath heaving in and out. She turned her head to the side, staring at an orb starfighter parked next to her. It was shimmering like diamonds and fading in and out as if it were half in this dimension and half in the next.

"An Aven," she said to herself. If she remembered correctly, Skye mentioned *Swift* had hundreds of them in her launch bays. At the moment, she took his word for it, not wanting to stand up and count.

A woman bent down beside her, crouching. "How you doing, sailor?"

Eden glanced up, her lips forming a smile at the gorgeous woman staring back at her. "Are we safe?"

Nyx shook her head. "We're not out of this yet." She tapped on the floor. "*Swift*, any time now."

I've not detected anyone else alive outside. So, yes, it's time to leave, replied *Swift*. *The weapon has no way to target us when we reach a thousand meters or more. We're almost in the clear. Swift* lifted off the ground, the launch bay vibrating.

"Where are we headed," said William, sitting up.

Eden touched her heart, her fingers splayed, her back still on the ground. "*Swift*, where are we headed?"

To Eos Two, Starship Tranquil.

"Starship *Tranquil*?" Eden shouted. "Another starship?"

Yes.

Hank breathed heavily, trying to catch his breath. "Who are you talking to?"

"The ship and don't ask. I don't want to explain how we communicate."

William stood, rubbing his arm. "Okay, well...where did it say we're going?"

"Eos Two."

William and Hank looked at each other. "Eos Two?"

"The other side of Eos," she said.

Hank gave her a blank expression. "You realize the other side of Eos is the radiation zone."

Eden pushed off the ground and wiped her palms back and forth. "Another lie. You'll get used to it."

38

ALI

Dirn Garum, Eos

Ali slouched in Starship *Tranquil's* captain's chair, looking at the vidscreen surrounding the entire bridge. She glanced at Harak, who sat next to her with his arms folded, his expression emotionless. "Harak, that's Thun's chair. He's my second in command."

He squeezed his arms tighter, not saying a word.

Ali shook her head at the stubborn prick. Fighting about it wouldn't get her anywhere because Harak would actually fight to keep the damn chair. She rubbed her eyes and yawned. She waited for the all go from one of the Bawn working at the rock-like stations just outside Starship *Tranquil*.

"We have orders from my father, King Bilrak, not to leave until they are at the end of the tunnel." Harak raised his hand in a fist. "That's when we strike."

Way to show your leadership, thought Ali, sarcastically.

Chan, standing next to her, spoke softly in her ear. "Problems?"

Ali eyed the vidscreen, seeing nothing but the mountainous rock wall. "Harak. Give me time. I'll break him."

Harak wiggled his beard, keeping his eyes forward, though obviously hearing her.

Chan leaned closer. "Breaking will only get you a broken Harak. We want him full, at his best, and defending you because he respects you beyond all else. Gain his respect, and you'll gain a powerful warrior."

"Impossible."

"Ali, remember that to gain respect from a Bawn warrior is to beat him at his best game—fighting," Chan said in a hushed tone. "Or, better yet, help them win this fight and do well in battle, and he will respect you for the rest of his life."

Ali nodded, her lips close to Chan's ear. "With Sol, I can take him easily."

"When the time comes, best him." Chan stood to full height and stepped back, watching the room and the Bawns.

Harak jumped off his seat and stood. "What are you whispering? Are you such a coward you have to keep your voice low, scared I might hear?" He cocked his head to the side, the whiskers around his lips twitching. He threw a dismissive hand. "I have better things to worry about." He paced around the bridge, his eyes wide with an intense stare. "The fight for our very souls will start soon. Everyone be prepared."

Ali held in a laugh. The guy looked psychotic.

"Ali, I've noticed you have trepidation about this fight about this coming battle." Thun approached, sitting where Harak had been moments ago. "Fear not. We Bawns can beat five men on our own, and two giants if need be."

"Your brother won't like it you took his seat."

"I don't fear my brother. He's a pisser, but I love him the same. Like you said, this is my seat. He wants it? He can try to take it."

Ali shifted her eyes to Harak, who took slow steps from station to station, muttering something to the Bawn crewmembers. "You're the next in line to be king, Thun. Your brother is a disgrace. Stay safe, because I fear for your race if something were to happen to you and your father."

Thun didn't respond. He looked at the axe lying in his lap. He contemplated for a moment, nodding. A horn went off, and everyone jerked to attention.

They've reached the end of the tunnel, Ali, announced *Tranquil.*

"It's time to go," yelled Harak. He took a step toward the seat he'd occupied, then paused, his breath immediately shallowing, his lips flat. He turned and sat at an empty station.

Ali eyed Chan and then Thun. "You two ready?"

Thun raised a fist. "Ready."

Chan dipped his head.

Ali, I know you want to head to Sirona, *came* Tranquil. *Swift, however, is on her way. They'll evacuate* Sirona *soon. I advise we head to the end of the tunnel the Bawn created.*

Ali sat up, not liking the idea. "Are you sure?"

I am.

She sighed heavily and leaned forward. She stared intently at the screen. "I trust you." Her heart ached at the words that exited her mouth. "All Bawn, strap in. It's time to fly. *Tranquil,* lift us out of the cavern and fly us to the end of the Bawn's tunnel."

As you command. Tranquil rose as the inside of the mountain opened. The fading sun's light filtered in, brightening the area. *Tranquil* turned, her boosters engaging and blasted through the opening. Ali's back pressed against the backrest. Several Bawns gasped. It was their first time in flight. It probably scared the tar out of them.

We'll be there shortly. The ship charged forward like a bolt of lightning, zipping toward the clouds. Out of the corner of her eyes, Ali could see Thun's fingers squeezing the armrests, his knuckles turning pale. She let out a soft giggle. Below them, the terrain blurred until *Tranquil* slowed.

We're arriving.

They entered Eos Two, the vast city Ali saw on her first trip onboard *Tranquil.* The city spread out before her with buildings of fine architecture reaching for the sky. Lights blinked on tall towers and platforms, and a large statue of a man holding a spear dazzled in the middle of the city.

Ali touched her sword's hilt, her confidence abruptly soaring. The sword sent vibrations of energy surging through her. "It's time to land."

As you wish. I'll find a place to land.

Tranquil descended, and Thun pointed at the holovid displaying a large palace coming into view. "That has to be the palace. From under there, my people will sneak inside and cut off the head of the dragon."

Ali thought of Enlil. The head of the dragon. Her heart fumed. He used to haunt her dreams, and then her life. She thought she killed him a week or so ago, hitting him with several gunshots before she entered the mountain, but he hadn't bled out and most likely survived. She and Sol wouldn't give him a second chance.

Ali, said *Tranquil. I'm receiving a message from Starship Swift. She's alerting me that the massive weapon is in range of Starship Sirona.*

Ali cleared her throat, pushing down nerves that wanted to crawl out of her pores. *Sirona* and her people needed help. To her, that should come first, not this silly battle.

"Hold, *Tranquil.*" The ship stopped and hovered. She looked at the Bawns, who stared at her, awaiting orders. "Can Starship *Swift* handle this weapon alone, or shall we attack it now?"

I'm scanning it. One moment, please.

Harak stood, clutching his axe. "Why are we stopped?"

Ali held up her middle finger, a strange Earth custom she hardly remembered. The little she recalled, the gesture didn't mean pleasant things. She raised her voice. "*Tranquil* is speaking. Shut your mouth and let me communicate."

The weapon is unmanned, guided by remote. Destroying it would destroy everything around it, including Sirona. The technology is unstable and highly reactive.

Harak grumbled and Thun put up his hand, stopping his brother from complaining further.

Swift *has landed beside* Sirona. *They're evacuating.*

Ali bit her lip. "If they don't evacuate in time?"

From what my sensors show, if they don't escape before the weapon fires upon them, they'll die. Have faith, Ali.

Ali leaned back, her gut flexing. "With two starships, *Sirona* could evacuate much more quickly." Every ounce of her wished she'd stuck with her original plan.

Our arrival would stir confusion, and with confusion comes caution. Things would slow down. I advise staying here.

Harak stomped his foot. "What are you talking to *Tranquil* about?" He pointed his finger at the floor. "My father and my people are down there. We go knock on the palace with our hammers, now." He stepped toward Ali.

Thun stood his axe in hand and faced Harak. "Don't come any closer, brother."

Harak hit the butt of his axe on the floor. "She's deciding the fate of us all. The fate of our people. We'll easily win this fight. She's taking our upper hand and throwing it away like garbage."

Thun lifted his chest, his chin high. "She leads, and we don't question."

"Not on my life." Harak continued forward and lifted his axe.

Thun reared back, axe in hand, and let his axe loose, connecting against his brother's axe handle, flinging it out of his hands and across the bridge. It thumped and bounced on the floor, slamming against a wall.

Harak looked behind him, his eyes on his axe. "You—"

Before he could finish his sentence, Thun rushed, tackling him. He curled Harak's arm between his legs and arched his back, placing his brother in a submission hold. "Hold fast your tongue," yelled Thun. "Our time for revenge comes today. The enemy leader will be ours soon enough. Have patience."

Ali turned her attention back to the vidscreen after seeing that Thun had control of the situation. She squinted, watching the city. There weren't any Anunnaki walking around, or any starfighters or ships deployed to ward *Tranquil* away. Nothing stirred inside the city. It was a ghost town.

Ali huffed. "*Tranquil*, scan the city for life forms. Every single nook and cranny."

It will take me a few moments.

Ali fidgeted with her sleeve, taking a gander at Harak and Thun rolling on the floor, Harak doing his best to get out of Thun's hold. The other Bawns seemed pleased with the wrestling.

I see no signs of life, other than the Bawn waiting beneath the palace, responded *Tranquil.*

"All right, take us down. We'll have every Bawn board. We'll then hurry our asses to *Sirona* and off this planet."

"What's going on?" spat Harak, spit coming from his lips, his face red.

"There's no sign of life anywhere in the city. It's abandoned. I'm having the Bawns board the ship, and then we're heading to help another ship. Do you understand?"

Thun let go of his brother, kicking him in the stomach. "He understands."

Harak curled, holding his stomach, doing his best to catch his breath.

Thun sat in the chair beside Ali, his face calm, his breathing easy as if nothing important had occurred.

I see a place to land big enough for my size, said *Tranquil. It's close to the palace.*

The starship rotated and flew onward, slowing and descending in a long, wide field with thick patches of grass and ebb. It looked big enough for five starships, if not more. *Tranquil* shook, absorbing a small shock from the landing sleds touching down.

"Let's exit and get the Bawn inside the ship," ordered Ali, heading for the bridge's exit at the ship's bow.

The platform they stood upon shuddered, then lowered. Fresh air washed over Ali's body, and she took a deep breath. A hum filled the sky.

Ali stepped off the platform, moving away from *Tranquil.* A ship came into view, heading for her position. Ali swallowed hard. "Get back inside and in the ship. The Anunnaki are coming."

SHAE

Unknown

Devon's face turned as white as a ghost. "I'm sorry, but I'm not going out there."

Kalista tightened her fingers into a fist and shook it in front of his face. "Wrong answer. You're going, or we're dead."

Devon looked at Kalista's fist, then at her cold, stern expression. He narrowed his eyes and let out a huff, holding his hand out. "Give me the water clothes, or whatever you call them."

"It's a wetsuit." She reached under the bench and pulled out another large box. She opened it and reached in. "Here." She held up a gigantic suit, twice the size of Devon.

Shae shook his head. "That's made for an Anunnaki." He wanted to force the suit on her and shove her in the water. "Get that on and stop being so damn scared."

She turned, gritting her teeth. "Water scares the living stardust out of me, plus, I don't know how to swim."

Shae walked to the side door window and stared into the beautiful turquoise water. "Is the water was warm enough for us to go out there without a wet suit?"

"Sure. Probably." Kalista pulled a metallic tool out of the toolbox.

"Here." She shoved the tool in Shae's hands. "You do it. Use this to dislodge the bomb."

Shae studied the tool. A crowbar. Apparently, these things were universal. "I need goggles."

"Goggles?" She shrugged. "I don't know what those are. We don't have time. Go. Now." Kalista motioned toward the stern. "I'll open the cargo bay door. Once you're inside, we'll shut it. Hold on to the side railings, because I'm going to open the outside door slowly to let the water trickle in until it is full enough that you're submerged." She paused, then bent down and dug through the toolbox, pulling out a mask. "You need this in order to breathe. This has about thirty minutes of air."

"Again, that's too big," said Shae. "Just get me out there."

"Too big or not, there's a hose inside. You can breathe through your mouth."

"I can do that."

She handed Shae the mask and hurried to her seat. She pressed a few buttons on her HDC.

The interior door at the back of the ship opened, and behind it were the secured white powder gold containers. Y'taul hadn't taken much, leaving a hefty amount crowding the cargo hold.

"Get in there," said Kalista, making her way to the cargo bay.

Shae rushed to the cargo bay, his heartbeat picking up. According to Kalista, they didn't have much time until the bomb blew.

Kalista pointed to a comm panel in the bay. "You'll be able to talk to me through the commlink. Once you have the mask on, communicate through the commlink installed in the mask. Understand?"

Shae shook his head. "This is too big for me. I can breathe through this tube in the masks' mouth but talking just ain't happening unless I want a mouth full of water."

Kalista nodded. "Dammit." She held up her finger. "Wait, my children."

Shae cocked his head to the side. "Say what?"

"I'm acting like you brainless humans. You're rubbing off on me, and that's not good."

She dashed to the toolbox, nearly pushing Devon over. She fished out a small mask and tossed it to Shae. "My kids accompany me sometimes on the job, you know, to see what humans look like and how you interact and all that crap. I have these suits for emergencies. Never did I think I'd actually use one of them." She pointed a shaky finger at Shae. "I'm shutting the bay door." She moved to her pilot's seat and pressed a holographic button.

The door shut. Shae dropped the crowbar and put on the small mask. "Fits good, though a little tight," he said to himself. He picked up the crowbar.

"You hear me?" asked Kalista, her voice hollow and filled with static.

"I hear you."

"You ready for me to open up the exterior cargo bay door?"

Shae wanted to say no, but dipped his head anyway, giving the door in front of him a thumbs up.

"Okay, I'm going to open the exterior cargo door slowly, so you don't wash out too quickly and lose your sense of direction." A red light flashed overhead, and the exterior door slowly rose, liters of water rushing in, and in under thirty-seconds, completely submerging him.

The water warm, Shae floated toward the ceiling and pushed off the wall with his legs, guiding himself under the door and into the open water. His eyes widened, and his legs kicked. His stomach momentarily balled up in a fit of nerves. For an instant, he was paralyzed. He'd been in a biosphere river, but never in water this expansive.

Kalista's voice boomed through his com, jostling him out of his short paralysis. "Get going."

He surveyed the vast ocean before him, thousands of fish swimming by, their beautiful colors practically glowing. Shae swam toward the ship's belly. "I'm heading to the underbelly." He grasped a handle on the back of the craft and reached for another one. "I see something." A disc the size of a dish plate was attached to the middle of the underbelly. "It's the bomb." He shoved off the handle and swam toward the disc.

"Good. Now, pry it off," said Kalista.

Shae kicked his legs and propelled forward. He lifted the crowbar toward the bomb, now only meters from it. A digital timer displayed eleven seconds. His eyes widened. "Holy Guild."

"What?" replied Kalista.

"Listen up. Fire aft engines and pull back on the control stick, now."

"Now? Why?" said Kalista, her voice rising.

Eight seconds.

Shae dug the tool between the bomb and the craft. "Don't question. Do it."

Six seconds.

He jiggled the bomb loose, and it fell slowly toward the ocean floor. The craft shuddered and Shae swam to grab a handle near the Starhawk's front landing sled. The ship sped upward through the water, and Shae held on for dear life, the water pushing against him, trying to kick him off the ship. The Starhawk shot out of the water like a missile. Water streamed off the craft's stern as it shed itself from the sea. Shae grimaced, dropping the crowbar and using his free hand to grab another handhold. He clung tightly, his arms shaking as the ship skyrocketed upward.

Kalista screamed in his ear, but he couldn't make out what she said. The ship vibrated violently, numbing his fingers. One finger slipped, then another. His stomach wrenched. "Not good." One more finger let loose and his body went with it. The wind rushed around him, and he swung his arms like a windmill, trying to grasp at something, anything. He descended fast, and everything went quiet.

Figuring he had a long way down Shae straightened like a stick, his only hope to survive the impact with the water. A concussion blast of sea and fish skin, blood, and guts erupted against his feet and up his chest, pieces landing all over his mask.

The bomb had exploded.

He closed his eyes and arrowed his feet and hands toward the oncoming ocean and braced. His feet sliced the water, splaying his right leg to the side. The water's suction and the push of speed buckled his femur, cracking it on impact. The rest of his body immersed into the sea, pain blasting into his hip and side.

He yelped in pain, and saltwater filled his throat. Somewhere on impact, his masked yanked off. Oxygen bubbles rose to the surface, and he suddenly slowed his steep dive. Blood streamed past his now stinging, open eyes. He glanced down at the searing pain in his leg and jerked his head back. Oh, no.

At about mid-leg, his femur bone had torn through his lateral quadricep muscles. It poked through his skin and pants. He swam toward the surface, moving his arms as fast and best he could while keeping his leg immobile before numbness took over. Reaching the surface, he grunted loudly. He coughed, spitting out water.

A loud boom filled the sky, and he looked up at the Starhawk turning in his direction. Somehow, Kalista's voice mumbled from somewhere nearby. "Shae, where exactly are you?"

"The mask," muttered Shae, peering over the gentle waves, not needing to look far. He reached out and grasped the mask. He pulled it over his head, doing his best to stay above the surface by kicking his good leg. "Head directly to the explosion site." He cringed. "I broke my leg, so the faster, the better."

"On my way," said Kalista.

The water rippled wide and far as the Starhawk lowered into a hover several meters above him, then positioned to the right, and lowered into the water. The exterior cargo bay door opened.

"Can you swim to us?" asked Kalista.

"Maybe." He reached one arm out and pulled it across his body, repeating the stroke with the other arm. "One of you pull me into the cargo bay."

"Devon's on it," Kalista told him.

Shae continued to pull himself forward. He reached out for the stern of the ship and grabbed hold. He attempted to lift himself, but his muscles shook, and each attempt sent a sharp pain up his leg and through his lower back.

"I'm here, Admiral."

Devon stretched his arms, reaching for him. Grasping Shae's hands, he leaned back and pulled Shae into the bay. Yelping when his bad leg hit the edge, Shae rolled to the side, grimacing.

Kalista's footsteps pounded toward Shae. "We need to get him in the cabin quickly. We don't know if we'll be attacked soon, or what. We've got to get out of here." She shoved Devon to the side and grabbed Shae's arms by the wrist. She dragged Shae across the ship's floor. Kalista halted at the bench seat next to the toolkit.

Shae glanced at his leg and wished he hadn't when he saw blood oozing. Kalista grabbed a syringe out of a side compartment on the toolbox. He began shaking, his body going into shock. His heart raced, and his breaths were quick and shallow. He couldn't feel his leg, but damn, his whole body didn't want to cooperate no matter what.

Devon rushed to Shae's side and grasped his hand. "You'll be fine. I promise." He gave Kalista a questioning look, wondering if he spoke the truth or not. "Stay calm. I'm here. All right, man?" He stroked Shae's hair, not knowing what else to do.

Shae gently pushed Devon's hand off his head. "Devon, I'm not a dog."

Kalista dug into the compartment and came up with a vial with a clear solution inside. She sucked the liquid out of the vial with the syringe, then held the syringe to her eyes, looking at it like a predator barreling down on its prey. "You ready?"

Without waiting for a response, she stabbed Shae's leg. With Shae's leg numb, he didn't feel a thing. She emptied the syringe's contents. She pulled it out and reared back, throwing it past the cargo bay and into the water.

Shae's breathing slowed, a calming sensation taking hold. "That feels better."

"We'll wrap your leg up and get out of here. You need a healer," said Kalista, rummaging through the large tool kit. She handed Devon the bandage wrap. "Here, do something useful."

Devon began wrapping Shae's leg. "The bleeding has stopped already." He tightened the wrap. "Is that from the injection?"

Kalista smirked. "Yes."

Shae's head spun, though his body felt good and alive. "I know plenty of doctors at the starbase. Get me there."

Kalista shook her head. "Your doctors are limited and don't know what they're doing. My race did that on purpose." She shrugged. "We only taught them the basics that even our young Anunnaki know. If it weren't for the Space Templars, you wouldn't have even had the Suficell Pods. So, no, we're not going to your precious starbase. We're going to Nibiru."

Shae gave her a fixed stare. "You said it wouldn't be a good idea for Devon and me to go to Nibiru or be seen there. We're going to the starbase. I can get patched up, they can set my leg, and I can get into the Suficell Pods."

"Orion's buckle," spat Kalista, as if remembering something. "After our run in with Y'taul, I guarantee that monster outed me to the Nibiru authorities. My king and the council will know I've been selling white powdered gold to that worthless Plearian. They'll arrest me on the spot if I land on Nibiru."

"Then it's settled," said Shae. "Take me to Starbase Matrona."

"You're a lucky bastard, Admiral." She helped Shae up and set him on the bench. "Devon, strap him in. We're heading back to your ugly starbase." She walked to the pilot seat. "Closing cargo bay door and taking off."

Devon strapped Shae in and headed to the co-pilot chair. Shae squeezed his eyes shut, giving silent gratitude for surviving amid the pain and chaos he'd just gone through.

The cargo door shut, and the Starhawk lifted into the air. Kalista punched the throttle forward and pulled back on the control stick, speeding the Starhawk to the upper atmosphere. It carved a path into the exosphere and into the black cosmos. A burst of stars, millions and more, sparkled across the infinite.

"Hold on tight, 'cause here we go," said Kalista. "Initiating NMJ drive."

The universe filled with streaking stars. All went quiet, and the craft halted, its nose pointed at Starbase Matrona. Shae exhaled, staring out the cockpit window from the bench seat, happy to see his home. "We made it." He tilted his head, and his brows wrinkling sharply. "No." He reached out as if to snag the starbase before it could go any further.

The starbase brightened and a yellow halo shot outward from its core, ebbing in and out like a throbbing energy ripple, spreading into the black vastness around them. A moment later the starbase vanished.

"They activated NMJ drives?" Shae brought his hand to his side, his eyes like saucers. "Why?"

40

SHAE

Unknown

Quiet filled the ship until Kalista put her hands behind her neck. "We can't go to Nibiru, and your starbase jumped somewhere. Where do we go next?"

Shae wanted to get up and hail the starbase, but wherever it had gone, it was far out of range of the commlink.

"Who would order a jump?" Shae shot Devon a look, rubbing his hurt leg. "Payson?"

Devon shook his head. "Naveya doesn't lie. She said he died, along with his team."

Shae crossed his arms. "I'll believe it when I see it." He looked away and touched the pendant behind his jumpsuit, feeling its metal against his chest. Naveya shared a similar Space Templar pendant. It meant she ranked somewhere in the Templar knighthood, and Templars performed magic, according to the fairy tales. Maybe Devon told the truth, maybe the young man could hear her in his mind.

"Devon, can you talk to that Naveya woman right now? Can she tell us where they jumped?" Shae massaged his temple, not believing those words came out of his mouth. He sounded like a little kid, hoping magic existed.

"Let me see." He closed his eyes, then shook his head. "I don't have a connection. She's too far away."

Kalista gave Devon a look. "What are you two talking about?"

Shae threw a dismissive hand. "Nothing. Don't worry about it."

Kalista shifted in her seat. "Good, because I have enough to worry about."

Devon glanced over his shoulder. "How's your leg?"

"I can't feel a thing. I'm no medical genius, but I suspect that to save my leg, I need a doctor and a Suficell Pod soon."

Kalista sat up straighter. "All right, geniuses. Enough chatter. How do we find out where Matrona went? It could be my only safe haven at the moment."

Devon rested his hands on the flight console, looking around. "There has to be a way to track them."

Kalista leaned back, thinking. She nodded. "Like I said before, hanging around you guys makes me dumb. It sounds mean, but it's true." She held up her index finger. "A starbase is tagged, or in other words, numbered." She leaned forward, swiping across the holodisplay and typing on the holokeypad.

"What are you doing?" asked Shae.

"I'm getting us to Starbase Matrona." She swiped an application, pulling it up. "This will show her location." After a brief pause, Kalista nodded. "Yep, there she is. Now, I press on the location. The coordinates should show up on the course module drive."

Devon eyed the drive. "New coordinates showing."

"Here goes." She interlaced her fingers, stretching them out and cracking her knuckles. She put her hand on the NMJ drive button. "Hold on to your britches. We'll be at the starbase in no time." She dropped her hand to her side and slumped in her chair, closing her eyes. "Never mind."

"What are you doing?" asked Devon.

Shae leaned back. "Get some shuteye, Devon. The NMJ drives need to recharge. It'll be a while."

41

ALI

Eos

Tranquil's elevator touched down. Ali pulled out her sword. *"Tranquil*, get us back up. We have incoming."

That's a friendly. It's Starship Swift.

Swift's low hum grew louder the closer she approached, it's glowing, iridescent armor almost too mesmerizing to look at.

Thun gripped his axe and the rest of the Bawn took defensive positions. "It's the Anunnaki here to fight."

Chan shook his head, gesturing with his hands for the Bawn to calm. "It's an ally." He eyed Ali. "I believe your friends have arrived."

"I don't know them, but *Tranquil* said they're friendly, so I'm going with that."

Chan escorted her off the platform. "It's a ghost town here. There won't be a fight. It's usually busy on Eos Two, at least during my short visit here." Chan rubbed his chin. "Very odd."

Thun stepped between them. "Let's check for Anunnaki scum, anyway."

Swift positioned itself near *Tranquil* and began descending into a landing.

Harak rested his axe on his shoulder. "I'm not waiting around. I'm heading to the palace to see my people and congratulate them for scaring the Anunnaki out of the city." He ran down a cobblestone street followed by his brother and the rest of the Bawn crew. They disappeared around a tall, spired building, it's reach nearly a hundred stories.

"It's best we're with the Bawn. We calm them down," said Chan. "They may rampage the palace before we can search it over to find any clue where the Anunnaki disappeared to."

"Good idea."

They raced after the Bawn, their footsteps clacking on the cobblestone. They rounded the tall, white spire-like structure. Coming around, Ali noticed the palace and other buildings around a public square with a large statue of an Anunnaki. The statue held a tipped bowl which poured water into a pool at the statue's feet, where green plant reeds poked through the water. They reached the palace, and Ali leaped from giant step to giant step.

Entering through the main doorway, Chan and Ali walked into the main lobby. The ceilings were high and arched from one wall to the next. The lobby led to hallways and doors opening to large rooms with marble-like desks, all with HDC's, all neat and tidy as if the Anunnaki had a cleaning service come through right after leaving the building.

A loud bang stopped Ali in her tracks. "What's that?"

"This way," said Chan.

Ali hurried after him as he rounded a hallway and entered a room big enough for a large gathering. Inside, rows of holocomps and holomonitors lined the walls, and furniture sat around in an organized manner. A place for royalty, no doubt. Harak stood in the middle of the room, slamming a giant hammer on the marble floor.

"This is probably Enlil's study," said Chan. "We passed his office back there."

Another Bawn swung a pickaxe beside Harak. Chunks of marble flooring crumbled beneath their hefty blows, kicking pieces up as they continued to whack away.

Ali pursed her lips, a rage grabbing at her. "I think Enlil is still alive."

"Why would you think otherwise?" asked Chan, the pounding of tools against marble echoing in the room.

"I shot him so many times, a human would have been dead by now."

"Your bullets are small compared to our bigger bodies. He probably recovered, no doubt his medical staff fixing him up quickly."

Ali huffed. "That's what I feared."

Another clang and the sound of falling rock tumbling into a newly created cavernous hole echoed in the room. They had opened up the floor to the tunnel below. Thun rushed to his brother and extended his hands into the floor's new opening.

"Father, grab hold," said Thun.

Hands grabbed both Thun's wrists. He pulled, and King Bilrak emerged. Thun and Harak helped him up.

"Let's get blood," shouted Bilrak, axe in hand, moving past Ali and out of the office. He glanced behind him, observing more Bawn coming out of the opening. "Get your butts up here and fight."

"The Anunnaki aren't here," said Ali.

Bilrak seethed, murder in his eyes. "You better not be lying to me."

"Nope. The Anunnaki left. You want to take up residence?" she asked sarcastically.

"Oh, they're gone, you say? Wrong. Because here they come." Bilrak moved into a defensive stance, axe held over his shoulder as if he were about to slash someone.

Around a corner came a throng of humans. The one in front, a woman as distinct as any warrior Ali had ever seen, stopped and stood her ground. She held a bow in one hand and a clip of arrows in the other. Ali squeezed her fingers around Sol, its edges lighting up in a plasma flame.

"Nyx," said a male voice. "Stand down."

Nyx's face went slack, her eyebrows creasing. "Are you sure? Because this would be fun."

Ali took a gander over her shoulder. A couple dozen Brawn were behind her, their weapons drawn, and more still pouring out from the hole.

A man waved his hand in front of Nyx. "Don't create an issue where there's none." The man wore a robe, had a pleasant face, and exuded a strange calmness. He faced Ali and slipped his hands inside his sleeves. "I'm Skye Vortek, Grand Master of the Space Templars. We're here to help you." He shifted his eyes to Sol, his eyebrows lifting. He walked toward Ali. "You're of the bloodline, and so is Eden." He pointed to a brunette woman about Ali's height and build.

Ali narrowed her eyes. She relaxed her fingers on Sol's hilt, the plasma dying down. "You're the Space Templars?"

"Yes, we're here to assist. Many of the *Sirona* crew are with us."

Her mouth opened slightly. "They evacuated safely?"

"Yes."

Ali's body tensed, thinking of the effort she went through to keep the inhabitants of *Sirona* alive. She let out a big breath and closed her eyes, her lips curling upward. "Thank, Guild."

A Bawn gasped, and commotion ensued. Ali glanced around, doing her best to find the sudden problem. She spotted a creature, covered in blue fur, tall as an Anunnaki, making his way to Skye. He nodded to the creature, silently understanding what the big thing had to say. "My fellow Templar has just informed me we need to leave the building as fast as we can."

Bilrak squeezed the grip of his axe handle, his knuckles whitening. "Not until I find some Anunnaki to slay."

"Jantu's Sight, or intuition, is rarely wrong. I'd suggest we follow his advice," said Skye.

"Father," yelled Harak. "Come here. A note with your name on it, but I don't know what the rest of it says."

Bilrak pushed his way through Enlil's study. He grabbed the note. "They wrote the rest in a different language."

Chan hurried to him, swiping the note from Bilrak's hand. "It's in my language." He read and his face went ashen. He raised his head, letting the note fall from his fingertips. "Everyone out of the palace this instant. This place is set to blow."

A rumble shook the building, and the ground trembled wildly, buckling upward, huge slabs of marble breaking. Skye, Jantu, and Nyx rushed into the study.

"No," yelled Ali, moving away from the room. "Get out of there."

Bawns dashed toward the doorway. Eden grabbed Ali and pulled her to the floor. "Hold on."

Ali went to get up. "What are you doing?" Another Space Templar crouched by her side, holding up his wrist. Ali paused, seeing Nyx leap over the hole in the study and crouch next to it. She raised her aim toward the ceiling. Skye and more Space Templars did the same, moving around the office, holding up their fists.

Ali went to stand, but Eden and the man held her down.

"We need to evacuate. Let me go," screamed Ali.

"No time," said Eden.

A concussion blast lifted the ground. Rock, marble, and ebb spurted upward. The ceiling cracked open, and the walls folded inward, toppling and crashing down on everyone below.

42

SHAE

Shae had his arms around Helen, the sun gleaming off the Lake Michigan waves. He sat in the sand, his legs wrapped around hers. He moved his hand over her hard and firm pregnant belly. Helen reached up behind her, lovingly tapping his cheek with two fingers. "I dreamt her name."

Shae pushed out his lips. "Her?"

"I dreamt she was a girl, and her name was Alison."

Shae smiled. "A good name." He leaned back, propping himself up with both hands behind him.

Helen leaned back against him. "You'll be a good dad, too."

"Did you dream that, too, Love?"

Love. Yes, that was the nickname he had called her shortly after they met and courted.

Shae rubbed the back of his head and blinked the blur out of his eyes, coming back to the present. After waiting for a few hours for the NMJ drives to recharge, they had finally jumped. Traveling across space and time always screwed with him, yet this time wasn't so bad, especially since a memory of his wife came to the surface.

"We're here," said Kalista, her tone monotone, as if she couldn't care less.

Shae, keeping his bad leg straight, scooted forward to the edge of the bench seat. There, through the window and out in the deep void of space, floated Starbase Matrona, a bright light shining off its apex.

Devon turned in his seat, a smile on his face. "We made it." His upturning lips then dropped into a straight line. "Where are we exactly?"

Behind Matrona hovered a glowing orange, green, and blue planet. Two moons, one large and yellow with silver rings and the other plain and red in color, orbited the planet.

Kalista cleared her throat as if to get their attention away from the gorgeous scene in front of them. "We're at the worst planet in the history of the galaxy."

"The worst planet?" To Shae, this seemed like the most gorgeous. "Give me a little hint as to why."

Kalista palmed her forehead, sighing loudly. "I can't believe I'm here. I'm actually at this piece of Orion's butt—"

"What is it?" interrupted Shae.

"Planet Aurora." She grunted. "Home of the Space Templars."

Devon leaned his head against his chair's headrest. "The home of the Space Templars can't be a bad place."

"To you, yes. It's a great place." She bit her bottom lip, her cheeks flushing. "To me, no. Enki is a Templar leader, and although he's an Anunnaki, he'll want to kill me as soon as he sees me." She grabbed the control stick. "I don't want to be here."

Shae attempted to lift off the bench to stop her from moving the ship, then fell back in pain. "Don't leave."

"Try and stop me," she growled.

"You piece of ebb," yelled Shae. "You coward beyond—"

"Shut it." Kalista sliced her arm across the air. "They'll likely do worse than kill me."

Devon tilted his head, shooting her an odd look. "What?"

"They'll want me to join their stupid cult, their alliance to save the galaxy of scum like my race and Y'taul's."

Shae crossed his arms, pulling in a deep breath. "I promise you I'll make sure you'll leave safely after you drop us off. If they don't, you have permission to shoot me on the spot."

"I should shoot you now and just leave."

"But you have no home," said Devon. "Won't Y'taul show that you sold white powder gold to—"

"We don't know that for sure. It's just speculation," said Kalista. She dropped her hands to her lap and let out an exasperated breath. "But you're right, and I hate to say that. If I go back to Nibiru, and Y'taul contacts them, they'll throw me in prison for the rest of my life, or they'll execute me." She threw her hands up. "What about my family?"

Shae sat up. "Maybe that Enki fellow could send word to your family and get them here?"

She didn't respond and pushed the throttle forward, steering away from Matrona.

"Where are you going?" shouted Devon, standing.

"Sit down, if you know what's good for you." She flicked her head toward planet Aurora. "I'm heading planet-side."

Shae shook his head, pointing at his leg. "I need to get to Matrona. A doctor has to set my leg and then get me into a Suficell Pod."

Kalista snorted. "You brainless twerp. The Space Templars could heal you much faster, and with more skill. We're heading down there, not to your damn precious Matrona."

Shae's gut contracted, not liking the idea. He wanted to see his friends, his nephew, and maybe get word to his daughter. How were Manning and Louise faring after the fight with Payson? He wanted intel.

"What do they look like?" asked Devon, his tone serious, his expression like stone. "Do they have multiple legs?"

"You're kidding me, right?" replied Kalista, moving the ship past Matrona and closer to Aurora. "Most sentient beings walk on two legs." She shrugged. "The Templars are mostly human with some Anunnaki, Sirian, Arcturian, and even a few Plearian members."

A beep sounded, and an orb-like spacecraft materialized on the holodisplay. It headed toward them, then took a sharp turn, moving closer to Starbase Matrona.

"That's a Space Templar frigate, probably picking up humans and dropping them off planetside," explained Kalista. "Maybe they're evacuating the starbase and getting people on a planet where they belong. Maybe your race has a new home." The holodisplay zoomed out and shifted its focus to Aurora again. A dozen more ships, similar class, flew toward Matrona.

Devon shook his head. "I think things have drastically changed. I saw none of this in my visions, nor did Naveya. Maybe my visions and paintings were warnings instead of prophecies? Maybe if we didn't change our ways or if we lost the battle, my paintings would've been correct."

Both Kalista and Shae shot Devon a look.

Devon leaned away. "Forget I said anything."

"Gladly," muttered Kalista.

The Starhawk flew onward and entered the planet's exosphere. The commlink crackled online. "Fleet Admiral Shae Lutz, this is Sabra of the Space Templars."

Shae cocked his head to the side. "How would she know I'm on this ship?"

"It's the Space Templars. They seem to know…things," said Kalista.

Devon pressed the com. "Yes, we're here."

"Welcome to Aurora," greeted Sabra. "We're shuttling everyone off the starbase and to my planet. You have free passage to your new home. You'll find it more pleasing than the starbase. On planet-side, we'll set you on your next mission."

"Next mission? Please explain your meaning," responded Shae, hoping Sabra could hear him from the cabin.

The comm went silent.

Devon leaned closer to the com. "Sabra, do you read? Sabra?"

No response.

Devon clicked off the commlink and leaned back, shrugging. "I don't know."

Shae furrowed his brow. "What the Guild is she talking about?"

Kalista giggled. "You poor saps. Don't worry, you're a perfect match for them. Love at first sight. Like birds twitting and—"

"A perfect match?" said Shae.

"You both have a desire to help humanity, and ultimately, every Being that exists in the galaxy." She snorted. "You know, the hero complex."

"So, everything is fine on Matrona?" questioned Devon.

"Yes, and like I said, you're dealing with the Space Templars. They wouldn't harm your starbase or anyone on it."

Devon looked off, fidgeting with the side of the flight console. "Then what exactly is this mission?"

"Yeah, that's odd. I'd think they'd let your race rest before they sent you on another mission. Something must be up." She pushed on the throttle, speeding up the Starhawk.

Devon scooted forward in his chair. "Maybe my sister, mom, and dad are down there."

Kalista faked a happy clap. "Maybe my mommy and daddy and sissy are there, too." She shook her head. "Oh, please. You humans are far too emotional." She slapped Devon's forearm. "Sit back. We're heading into the upper atmosphere soon."

Devon sat against the backrest, adjusting the shoulder and waist restraints. "Naveya said humans are unique compared to any other Being in the galaxy because of our emotions. We can go from love to hate and back to love in a matter of seconds. I don't know why, but she said when humans are in a positive state of wellbeing, we can change the balance of the galaxy and send a wave of energy that can shift the very nature of an imbalanced society."

"Huh?" responded Kalista. "Okay, whoever this Naveya is, I imagine she's smoking some drugs. You humans whine and cower in fear too much for my taste."

"But when we aren't, we're powerful," said Shae. "I'd think you'd change your stance after you witnessed my race band together and stand up to yours."

Kalista adjusted the ship's trajectory, heading into the planet's upper atmosphere. "You have a point, Fleet Admiral." She pressed several holographic buttons. "Now, hang on. We'll be planet side soon."

ALI

Eos

Debris and dust filled the hallway and Enlil's study. The morning sunlight saturated the room through the torn apart ceiling.

"No roof," Ali said to herself, waving her hand about, pushing away the hazy dust cloud. She coughed several times. "And no walls." A deep gash separated the study, exposing the Bawns' tunnel system below. Pieces of ebb and marble littered the ground and covered dozens of unconscious and lifeless Bawn.

As the dust settled, Ali's eyes widened. The light in the room wasn't sunlight cascading through the soot and grime like she originally thought. It came from inside the room and pierced the haze like a sharp knife through cloth.

Nyx knelt on the floor, her fist in the air. Light from her wrist band expanded and connected like a grid to other light sources, looking much like an umbrella. Ali followed the light sources to dozens of Space Templars, all mimicking Nyx, their arms toward the sky.

Eden stood next to Ali. "I think we saved most."

"How?" asked Ali.

Eden gestured with her head toward the nearest Space Templar. "Energy shields."

Rocks crumbled and fell a short distance to the floor. Coughing penetrated the room. Thun pushed debris off of him and stood, dusting himself off. The lights blinked off and the Space Templars' arms, almost in unison, dropped to their sides. The morning dawn held a glint of light from the rising sun, but nothing like the light from the shields.

"Ali?"

Ali knew that voice. "Daf?"

Daf coughed. "Over here." She crouched next to a Bawn. He lay face down, his arms lifeless and wrapped around someone. Dust covered his face, his eyes closed. Daf waved Ali over. "It's King Bilrak."

Ali sidestepped and walked over several unconscious Bawn. She stopped and crouched by Daf's side, touching her back. "I'm glad you made it safely." She eyed Bilrak and saw that he breathed lightly.

Daf dipped her head. "I don't know about safely, but I'm alive."

"You know what I mean."

Daf winked. "Love you too." She put her hand on Bilrak's shoulder and shook. "Yo, buddy. You want to wake up for us anytime soon?"

Thun came to Ali's side, his stare empty. "My father?" His face went pale, and he took his father's arm, moving it away from someone's face. Thun stepped back. "My brother?"

Harak lay underneath Bilrak and spit out dust. As if suddenly realizing the situation, he furiously wiggled out from under his father, shoving more rock and ceiling debris out of the way.

"Help me, brother," said Thun, bending down to move slabs of rock off Bilrak. They cleaned their father from debris and moved him on his side. Thun held on to his father. "Harak, find mother."

Harak stood immediately, looking wildly about. "Mother?"

Bawn moved about the room, helping their fellow kinsmen while Harak rushed around like a chicken with his head cut off.

"How many do you think are dead?" Daf said in a soft hush.

Ali glanced around the room. Many lay on the ground, not

moving. She didn't know if they'd died or were unconscious. Some began to stir, pushing pieces of ceiling off of them.

Harak hurried back to Thun, tears welling in his eyes. "I can't find mother."

"Wipe the piss out of your eyes, son." Bilrak struggled to a sitting position. He hacked several coughs, spitting on the floor. "Death is nothing to cry over. Being covered in this white crud, that's another story." He stared blankly at his hands and clapped them together, puffing out a small white cloud in front of him.

"Let's get out of here," said Ali. "We don't know if another—"

A loud cry filled the room. "Mother," yelled Harak, peering into a large hole in the floor. He raised his eyes to the heavens, arms wide, tears dripping from his beard.

A blue furred giant, Jantu, rushed past Ali, his arm brushing against hers. He hopped down into the opening and pushed rubble off Harak's mother. He felt for her pulse and then shook his head, his chin falling to his chest. "Her life force has left her body. She dwells with her ancestors now." He shifted his gaze to Harak. "She has a message for you..."

Ali wiggled her ears back and forth with her finger. How did he talk without moving his lips?

Harak and several more Bawn, including Thun and Bilrak came closer to the blue creature. Thun's lower lip was quivering. Bilrak went to his knees at the edge of the opening, his hands together, his shoulders lowered.

"I don't know how," said Bilrak, "But I hear you, blue furred... friend." He bowed, touching his hands to his forehead. "I would like to hear what my wife has to say."

Harak threw a fist in the air. "I told you, father. That heathen, Ali, her presence killed our mother. The prophecy was right." He pulled at his hair, spinning around. "My poor mother." He raised his voice. "I curse you, Anunnaki. I will give you all a slow, painful death." He turned and glared at Ali. "I'll give you a slow death as well."

Jantu stood. "This message isn't for the King. It's for her son, whom she calls Harak."

Harak paused and faced Jantu, wiping the tears off his face, grimacing like a mad man. "Then speak."

Jantu bowed deeply. "As you wish. She tells me she won't return to life but will remain on the other side where your ancestors' dwell." He paused as if hearing more. "It's beautiful there, so beautiful. But the beauty doesn't dwell in you, Harak. You push it away, you cut it in half like it's an enemy, when in fact, it's your guide."

Harak rushed to the edge, his fist raised. "You speak lies."

Jantu held up his hand. "Don't interrupt. You do again, I'll hold you down in front of every man and woman in here, and you'll hear all that she has to say."

Harak looked around, huffing. He grabbed an axe off the floor and lay it on his shoulder. "Try it, blue freak."

Bilrak ran at his son and tackled him. "I'll hold him down for you…in front of the men and women here." Harak struggled as Bilrak held him down, clearly stronger than his son.

"Thank you." Jantu nodded. "She wants Harak to be kind to his brother. He may never love…Thun…more than his mother and father, but he needs to get along. If he doesn't and continues to disobey, he'll surely die and enter the realm his mother has." He bowed again. "That's all."

Bilrak slowly stood and released his grip on Harak, who grunted and scowled, pushing to a standing position. He gripped his axe tightly, roaring loudly.

"No," yelled Bilrak.

Thun reached out, diving for his brother a moment too late. Harak heaved the weapon at Jantu, the axe flipping end over end.

Jantu stood his ground and caught the axe. He crouched and jumped, landing near Harak. "Your axe." He handed him his weapon and walked toward Skye.

Harak lifted his axe again, ready to throw. Ali thrust her sword in front of her, purple flames dazzling off the edges. "Harak, that's enough."

Harak pursed his lips, eyeing her sword, and dropped the axe.

Thun grabbed her arm, his eyes wet and dull. "Let him cool."

"Fine." She sheathed her sword and swiped her hands together. Thun was probably right. She could teach Harak a lesson another time. "We need to get out of here."

"Yes," said Nyx. She looked Ali up and down. "I like your style, woman." She held up her bow. "We return to our starships immediately and get off the planet. Follow us."

Ali followed Nyx and Eden, along with the rest of the Templars, as they made their way down the hallway and into the palace lobby. They exited the building and moved quickly down the steps toward their ships parked on the field.

Thun pointed ahead, grunting. "Chan."

Chan stood at one of *Tranquil*'s launch bay ramps, pointing and guiding Bawn into the ship.

Ali headed toward the platform on the ground at the ship's bow. "Where's the rest of the crew?"

Thun threw a thumb over his shoulder. "Harak is behind us, but the rest of the crew...I don't know." He looked down. "I couldn't find them. Maybe they're dead."

"We ain't," said a gruff voice. Magil, supposedly the strongest Bawn, rushed to Thun's side. "Thodion, Algona, and yours and Harak's sister, Ramira, are already on the big flying thing."

Thun's eyebrows rose, his lips curling upward. "And our Chief Medicine Woman, Bavila?"

Magil slapped Thun on the back, laughing. "Stop your worrying. Bawns don't whimper, you sun-lover." He guffawed loudly. "Bavila is a little banged up, but okay."

A hum filled the air and a strong wind picked up. The ground rumbled and the other starship hovered off the ground, moving to the side as if waiting for the rest of Ali's crew and Bawn to board *Tranquil*.

"We're following them, right?" said Daf.

"That's the plan," said Ali.

Daf turned and walked backward in front of Ali, saluting her. "I'm at your service, Captain Alison Johnson." She dropped her hand. "Oh, Guild, I'll have to get used to that."

"She ain't our captain," huffed Harak.

"Sol says she is, and so do the prophecies," said Bilrak. "So, shut your mouth son and do what your mother asked, be kind and obey."

"She asked that I be kind to my brother, not anyone else."

They reached the platform and Ali and the rest stepped on. The elevator rose. Thun looked around. "We're missing someone."

Thodion nodded. "Dilgor. He's on the bridge already. We'll see him in a moment. He has eyes for Ramira." Thodion elbowed Thun and laughed again.

Thun punched him in the shoulder. "That's my sister."

The elevator reached the bridge, clicking in place. Daf's mouth slackened. "Whoa. Never been on a bridge before. It's pretty intense."

"Take a seat somewhere, Daf," ordered Ali, making her way to the command chair. "Where's Chan? Still helping the Bawn up the ramp?"

"I'm on board, but in *Tranquil*'s engine room," came Chan's voice over the intercom. "All are aboard. You can give the order to take *Tranquil* skyward when ready."

Are you ready, Ali? asked *Tranquil.*

"We're ready. Follow Starship *Swift.*"

Aye, my friend.

The starship lifted off the ground. The vidscreen surrounding the bridge came to life, zooming in on *Swift,* who climbed high toward the Eos clouds.

Tranquil? asked Ali. *Where are we following them to?*

On another mission.

Ali slouched in her chair. "Another mission? Please tell me you're kidding." She wanted to get back to Starbase Matrona and to her father, then back to Eos to get to the sarcophagus. Simple.

"Who are you talking to?" asked Daf from across the bridge.

"To the starship."

"Oh, right." Daf sat back. "I guess, carry on?"

Thun, in the seat next to Ali, leaned over. "We're going on a mission?"

"Yes." She closed her eyes, taking in a deep breath. Tranquil, *where does our mission take us?*

Earth.

EDEN

Eos

Eden looked incredulously at Skye, her shoulders rolling forward. "We have *Sirona*'s people. Yet, we're going on another mission?" She wanted to get them back home on the starbase where they belonged.

Skye nodded. "We received a distress signal from a Space Temple outlier. A massive armada is on their way to Earth's system, hyper hopping from system to system until they reach Earth. They'll be there sooner rather than later."

Other than the short details Skye had given Eden about Earth, she didn't know much about it, other than it was beautiful and where her race had originated. She didn't have an emotional tie, but she did have an emotional tie for her people in Star Guild, and here they were, on Starship *Swift*, being taken to another potential fight.

Eden's nostrils flared. "We need to head back to Starbase Matrona and drop these people off before we jump into Earth's system." She eyed the vidscreen. Planet Eos displayed on the screen via the rear cams, shrinking smaller as they flew farther from it.

Nyx held a glass of water in her hand. "Drink up, Eden."

Eden pushed it away, shaking her head. "I'm not thirsty."

Nyx moved the glass in front of Eden's nose. "I said, drink up."

Eden released a breath and took the glass of water. "Fine."

Skye raised his hands to his chest, his voice lightening. "I'm sorry, but this isn't up for a vote." He put his palm out, face up, jabbing his index finger in the middle of his palm. "That's Earth's Solar System." He tapped his palm again in the same place. "Enlil and his allies, some of whom are the Graxic and Reptilians—half-human, half-lizard hybrids—are jumping into this location soon." He tapped on his forearm. "We're somewhere over here and if we don't get to my palm, the humans on Earth won't be able to defend themselves with any success. They'll put up a good fight, but the armada will wipe the humans off the face of the planet."

Eden took a swig of water and swished it around in her mouth before gulping it down. "And when we get there, we fight. Do we stand a chance? We don't have a fleet other than our two ships."

A smile grew on Skye's face. "Our own armada is on the way. We'll defend Earth, and we'll defend her well. Trust me."

She took another drink of water. "Good, because it wasn't adding up. So—" A surge of energy rushed through her. She glanced at the half-full glass, wondering what the heck Nyx spiked it with. She shook her head, taking a seat at the station where she had stood, and watched the Space Templars monitoring the holoscreens at their stations.

Nyx slapped her hands together, rubbing them back and forth. "I can't wait to persuade those evil pricks to leave."

"Is it that easy? A simple persuasion?" asked Eden. Maybe all Beings feared the Space Templars' fleet. Perhaps just showing up would cause the enemy to retreat. One could hope.

"No," replied Nyx. "What would be the fun in that?"

Eden tilted her head back. "So, we definitely fight." She wanted her people to live, to have a break from battle. It didn't look like that would be happening.

Skye crossed his arms. "We fight." He held his hand out for Eden. She grasped his hand like a handshake, and Nyx wrapped her fingers around their locked hands. "This will be one for the history books," said Skye.

Eden locked eyes with Nyx. She couldn't get out of the coming battle, and the *Sirona* crew on the ship couldn't get out of it either. Best not to fight it, but deep down, she held back a grin. She couldn't wait to knock the Anunnaki and their allies around. "All right, let's kick some Anunnaki tail."

"Now you're talking, Eden." Nyx's lips twitched. "Your aura... changed." She stared above Eden's head and shoulders, her eyes scanning. "You're ready. I can't believe my own ears when I say this, but dammit girl, you're ready." She twisted to the side, her hand extended to the captain's chair. "Do your thing."

Eden splayed her fingers on her chest. "My thing?"

Skye cocked his head to the side. "Are you sure, Nyx?"

"I didn't want it in the first place, but yes, she's ready."

Skye extended his hand toward the middle of the bridge, mimicking Nyx. "Eden, you're the captain now."

Eden wrinkled her brow. "You're serious?"

"Don't make us change our minds," came Skye.

She lifted her chest and set her jaw. She wouldn't mess this up twice. She strode to the captain's chair and sat. "*Swift*, set coordinates to our first hyper hop."

Coordinates set.

Eden pulled up the com, opening all channels. "Man all quarter stations. Secure all loose gear about the decks and bays. Stand by for a Negative Matter Jump. Find restraints and secure yourselves." She eyed the time on the holodisplay at the front of the bridge. "Stand by for time check. On signal, the time will be four hundred hours, thirty-six minutes. Stand by. Mark."

We're ready, Eden, came *Swift*.

Eden dipped her head. "Stand by to jump."

The NMJ drives activated, and Eden bit her lip to hold down a smile. She didn't know if her commands met Space Templars' protocol, but they felt damn good coming out of her mouth.

45

SHAE

Aurora

Shae sat on a bench. Green frond trees stood behind him in a semi-circle, shading him. He rested his elbows on his knees. Throughout his life, Shae had glimpses of large, wide-open skies, wispy white clouds, and the sun beaming down on a large field of yellow grass called wheat. He never understood why these scenes would explode like a movie in his mind, but now that he realized the Anunnaki had wiped his memory and placed new memories in him, the glimpses made more sense.

"That was Earth," he told himself.

He glanced up at Aurora's big sky, though not entirely blue, but large like Earth's. The sky here held a purple hue, perhaps from the ringed moon that orbited the planet. He shook his head, wishing Ali were here, not knowing exactly where she was or if she was safe. His gut twisted, worry for his daughter slamming into him worse than he imagined. It consumed him like a nightmare. The worst scenarios he could bring up dangled themselves at the forefront of his brain. He squeezed his eyes shut. "I have to get used to this father stuff."

He stared at his old home—Starbase Matrona. It floated like a silver gem in front of Aurora's moons. Word had it that the Templars were decommissioning it and tearing it apart. All living organisms on the starbase, including plants and animals, would be transported planet-side.

He turned away, shifting his focus to the orange-colored hills that rolled across the countryside, lush with foliage and leafy green trees. "This is what freedom is." Yet he still felt like he needed to monitor ebb transports reports, ebb mining, and fleet training like he had before the Anunnaki attacked.

He used to work fifteen hours a day, and when he slept, his dreams threw paperwork at him, and upon waking, mornings threw meetings, paperwork, and more paperwork at him. The rest of the day mimicked the mornings. Now, he didn't have a damn thing to do, other than heal.

When Kalista touched the Starhawk down on this planet, the Space Templar healers transported him away. He barely had time enough to wave to the piss-ant, Kalista, and the nice kid, Devon. The healers set his bone, sent him to something similar to a Suficell Pod, but with twice the healing power, and hours later, here he sat...free.

"Hi, Admiral."

Shae lifted his head. "Devon." He smiled. "If this is your new home, I'm jealous."

"My home? It's your home, too."

Shae didn't have the heart to tell the kid he wouldn't be living here long. Instead, he winked. "Yeah, what you said."

Devon turned, gesturing toward a translucent domed building. A path led from their spot to the domed building's door a quarter of a kilometer away. Kalista sat on a grassy knoll beside the pathway, picking blades of grass and tossing them aside like a bored child. Devon chuckled. "I don't think she's the grump she pretends to be."

A soft rumble of engines filled the sky. Dozens of vessels appeared on the horizon, heading their direction. Shae lifted his chin as a loud boom in the heavens took his attention away from the coming ships. Several more craft entered Aurora, coming in fast, then slowed and leveled. "Looks like the Space Templars are gearing up for something.

Unless this is normal." Shae doubted there was any "normal" to the arriving ships, especially in such growing numbers.

Thunder shook the earth, and Shae turned, glancing behind him. A ship, almost out of nowhere, headed in for a landing on a pad in the fields of blue and green grass off to his right. Wind picked up, and blew Shae's hair as the vessel hovered. Landing sleds extended from underneath, and the ship touched down on the pad, its almond-like appearance making Shae gape. "Wow."

Cannons jutting from the edges and in the front rotated and slid inward, hugging against the ship's exterior. Shae stood, keeping more weight on his good leg, something he wasn't used to. Although his leg felt all right, he took a hobbling step forward. "What a beauty."

The ship had a sleek design. There was a tinted cockpit window set in the front that widened around the sides. He could tell the thing was fast, not in space, but planetside. It'd be a worthy opponent.

A hiss and a ramp opened from the underbelly, extending to the pad. Boots came into view on the ramp, and then pants, and finally, a woman.

She turned and faced Shae, giving him a gentle nod. She strolled toward him, her long strides athletic, almost sexy, her face perfectly sculpted. Devon inched beside Shae.

She bowed, her hands folded at her chest, her palms touching. "The light in me bows to the light in you."

Shae shot Devon a look, then eyed the tall woman, bowing. "Thank you."

"That's the Space Templars' greeting to all Beings." She smiled. "My name is Sabra and we have a mission for you two."

"I heard that on the com, but ma'am, we just got here," said Devon. He glanced past her at the ship. "Did Naveya come down with you, or my parents and sister?"

"Naveya is managing the evacuation of your old home, and I'm sorry, but I don't know who your sister and parents are. If they aren't here, I assure you if they survived the main attack, they're alive. They may be part of the last evacuation wave." Sabra looked upon Shae.

"Fleet Admiral Shae Lutz," she shifted her gaze, "and Robert Rose, follow me."

"Robert Rose?" asked Shae.

"Yes," said Sabra.

Devon shook his head. "It's a long story. Don't ask."

"Well, I'm going to ask sometime," Shae replied.

Another ship hummed overhead, coming in for a landing on a nearby landing pad. Shae, Devon, and Sabra made their way toward a forest at the base of the nearest hill. Pushing aside massive ferns that grew at the forest's edge, and ducking under the wide palm leaves, Shae's boots sunk into the soft, forest soil at every step.

He stepped over exposed roots and past hanging vines that held leaves as colorful as the flowers attached to them. A large insect with multiple legs walked in front of him, white and bulbous. They continued on in silence, jumping over a thin stream. Finally, Sabra pushed through thick shrubbery, practically disappearing inside it. Shae and Devon stopped at the hedge. She poked through the shrubs, her hand extended, waving them to follow. "C'mon."

Shae pushed through the thick leaves, some thin branches cracking as he did so. He quickly emerged on the other side, Devon in tow.

Sabra raised her hand. "We're here." A small clearing surrounded them, thick and tall green brush encircling the area.

Shae scratched his chin. "Where is here, exactly?"

She clasped her hands together. "I have something for you. It's been waiting for the right person for centuries, probably longer." She pointed to the dirt-laden ground. Patches of moss and grass peppered the area. "It's been charging." She bent down, pressing on a small clump. A small box lifted upward as soil cascaded away from it. She lifted the box and held it out to Shae. "Open it. But understand, we have added more elements to it, more life."

Shae took the box and opened it. He stared at an oval blue crystal with what looked like a small dab of ash spotting the inside. "What is this?"

Sabra cupped her hands behind her back. "Please understand that you, your daughter, and another, have a mix of Anunnaki DNA inside of you. Very few in your race have such a…" she paused, thinking for a moment, "…a blessing in their lives, if one may look at it in a positive perspective. The Space Templars of old encoded three such crystals, placing one in the hilt of a sword, with similar mixed DNA. Those who have the DNA may activate one of three starships. This mix is few and far between, but when one of your kind is discovered, a Space Templar will choose whoever we consider the best of the Chosen Ones and grant you these crystals."

Shae pursed his lips, cocking his head to the side. "What are you saying?"

"You have one more mission, Fleet Admiral." She held up her index finger. "One more mission to save your people."

"I understand about one last mission, but what I don't understand is what does that have to do with me and this crystal?"

Sabra gave Shae an understanding nod. "We'll give you a starship. You'll use this starship and our vast Space Templar fleet to defend your home."

He glanced up at the sky, eyeing the starbase. "I thought my home was being evacuated as we speak?"

"I'm speaking of your old home, Earth. Enlil and his Navy, along with several of his allies, are en route to Earth. They plan on breaking an intergalactic treaty that leaves Earth alone, to leave them to their own evolutionary gains. Enlil and his allies are planning on killing and enslaving humans…on their home planet."

Helen immediately came to mind, and an invisible gut-punch slammed into his belly. He took in a deep breath, his chin set. "I accept, and I'll lead."

"As I'd expect." Sabra touched Shae's chest. "Take out your Space Templar pendant."

Shae did.

"Now, touch the crystal and the pendant together."

Shae pressed the crystal on his pendant and felt a melding, a twisting and turning. He glanced down and his eyes widened. In seconds, the crystal surrounded the pendant, like blue glass molding and cooling around a coin.

"You may tuck it under your shirt now," she said.

Shae complied. The moment the pendant touched his chest, sorrow vibrated through him. He lost strength and fell to his knees.

Devon rushed to his side. "Admiral, are you okay?"

Shae went on all fours, swallowing tears and forcing down a rage that burned through him. He shook his head, doing his best to shake the emotions, the strange sensations begging to burst out of him. "What's...happening?" he demanded, blinking rapidly.

Sabra bent down, rubbing his back like Devon. "Listen, Fleet Admiral. This will hit you hard, but understand, they saved the entire starbase."

Shae pushed up, pressing his hands over his eyes. "No." He knew before the words came out of her mouth because somehow, he had felt them, their presence, their souls.

"We found your friends and nephew floating outside Matrona. We gathered them and gave them a remembrance of life." She cleared her throat as if she were choking up. "Thousands came, Admiral. Thousands. We sprinkled a piece of them, their ashes, in your crystal. The rest of their ashes float in the cosmos."

"Koda?" Shae fell, unable to grasp that his nephew, the closest family he'd ever known until he reunited with Ali, had died. "Louise? Manning?"

Devon backed away. "Koda? Dead? I can't... I can't believe it."

"All three saved the starbase, Shae," said Sabra. "They gave their lives to open the airlock and rid the starbase of the toxin. In the process, they rid the starbase of Payson and his men. It took your friend's lives, but they'll be remembered as heroes, always."

Shae sat on his rear and let out a deep breath. "They were heroes in my life. I...I'm..." He bit his lips. Now wasn't the time to mourn, it was a time to make them proud, to continue their journey, and save the rest of humanity.

"When do we start the mission?" Shae stood, choking down his tears. He pulled Devon in, his arm around Devon's shoulders. "I'm sorry. We'll make this right."

Devon's shoulders jostled up and down, doing his best to keep his crying at bay, though not successfully.

"As a Chosen One, Shae, you must understand you serve the galaxy, humanity, and all Beings. It's the Space Templar way."

Shae nodded and stood proud. "Yes."

"Okay," said Sabra, turning and heading for the shrubbery. "To your new ship and your crew, then to Earth."

46

EDEN

Starship Swift

A chill stung Eden's skin. She stood barefoot in the snow, and the white cold blanketed the ground all around her. Where am I?

She'd left Starship *Swift*'s bridge more than an hour ago after they jumped into another star system, hopping closer and closer to the mythical Earth-place her people had originated from.

After each Negative Matter Jump, the accumulators that powered *Swift*'s drives needed re-energizing. Systems would need to cool as power regenerated from the reactors, allowing the accumulators to build enough steam for another jump. It took hours, sometimes half a day. The perfect time to eat and sleep. The last thing Eden remembered was flopping on a comfortable bed in her sleeping quarters, and closing her eyes as she hit the mattress.

She took a step, the cold crunch of snow sounding underneath her boots. She outstretched her hand to touch the cold, ice-packed bark on a frozen tree. She inhaled sharply and stepped back as a fog abruptly formed and swirled before her. The fog thinned, and there stood a man in a billowy robe, his back to her.

"Eden, you beckoned me?" He turned, lowering his hood. He blinked his eyes as if adjusting to the newness around him.

"Skye?"

He tilted his head, his eyes narrowed. "You wish to train? Now?"

She puffed out her bottom lip, shrugging. "I just want to know where the hell we are." Snow sprinkled from a gray, clouded sky. Barren trees surrounded the area, and nothing more.

"You're getting better at the Sight, whether you know it or not." Skye looked around, nodding as if impressed. "Nyx and my mentors can bring me into their dreams, but I've not even met a Sirian or anyone else that can do so. You're more advanced than I thought."

"I didn't beckon you."

"I'm sorry for butting heads with your belief, but you did. You've wanted more training." He put his palms up. "I guess I'm here to deliver."

A sensation touched the side of Eden's head, something she'd felt whenever her mom was about to throw something at her when Eden wasn't looking. It came in handy, especially the time Eden ducked before a vase shattered against the wall above her head.

Skye put his hands up. "Keep your heart central. We with the Sight seek the middle path, the one less traveled, the one less believed. With a calm heart, you can work wonders. With rage, you can create chaos."

Eden threw her fist upward and to the side, quickly moving out of the way as the center of an icicle broke apart against the back of her hand. She froze her eyes like saucers. "How did I do that?"

Skye laughed. "One, it's your dream. You can do anything you please. Two, it's the Sight. From your memory, you've felt it before. Your dream is teaching you how to use it."

Out of the ether, a bow dropped at her feet, denting the snow. She blinked and jerked back, the shaft of an arrow now in her teeth. She spat it out. "What the Guild?"

Skye snorted. "It ain't my dream." He lifted a brow, as if to say, bring it on. He went into a defensive stance, turning slightly, his knees bent and his arms by his side. "Hit me."

"What?"

"You heard me." He pointed at the bow and arrow. "Pick up your weapon, aim, and shoot. It might surprise you at the intuition you have with a natural instrument in your hand instead of a gun."

"You're serious?" She bent down, picking up the bow and arrow and shaking the snow off. "You want me to shoot at you?"

Skye shook his head. "Never shoot at. Shoot through." He bounced up and down in his stance, getting ready to move out of the way, or do something Templar-like, which usually included breaking the laws of physics. "I'm not the target, Eden. A meter behind me, through my forehead, is the target. Remember that when using a bow."

"You're serious? You want me to shoot you?"

"Again, through me. Now, go."

She aimed, surprised she innately knew how to notch the arrow upward against the center serving nock point on the string. Nock point? Center serving? She didn't know how those words entered her mind, but they did. She tightened her grasp on the wooden grip, aiming past Skye's forehead, knowing if she shot true, it would stick in his third eye. This is just a dream, she told herself. Energy picked up in her, soaring up her spine and straightening her posture as she eyed her target. "Are you sure, Skye?"

He gave a wide grin. "I'm sure."

She took a deep breath and pulled the string, the bow curling. Emotions boiled inside her; the time she pulled a hard side spin maneuver to win the Star Guild Academy Games while piloting her Thunderbird—elation. The time she stood up to the school bully when she was a young teen, getting bloodied and bruised in the process—fury.

She blew her emotions outward, her breath touching the arrow as she let go. A scream followed from somewhere deep within her, sending an electric-blue force that only in her dreams she could see. The force spun around the arrow as it flew.

Skye lifted his arm, catching the arrow before it split his skull, the tip millimeters from his forehead.

"The Sight, the scream, the energy from within, is the secret with archery," instructed Skye. "Nyx is a master, preferring the bow and arrow over any other weapon. The natural instrument is under your control, you choose its speed, even its direction." He paused, studying the arrow, electricity passing through it and around it, circling his knuckles and fingers. "If I had been anyone else, even Nyx or Jantu, I wouldn't have been able to catch this."

Eden rubbed her temple. "I felt that electric-blue energy come out of me. But it's just a dream."

"Dream, reality. With the Sight training, it's all the same." He threw the arrow back at her as if he'd used a bow himself. She caught it. "Again, and again, until we get this right. Then hand to hand combat. In a dream, Sight training can last for days, weeks, or months, even though you're only asleep for hours."

Eden notched the arrow and shot, the emotions more intense, the scream focused like the point of the arrow. Repeatedly, the arrow moved faster, and over and over again, Skye caught it. Until he didn't. The arrow passed through his forehead like an illusion, and he faded, then illuminated, coming back to his original, non-translucent form.

"Tell yourself you'll remember this," said Skye, the snow beginning to fall harder, big white flakes topping his hair.

Eden flicked a flake off her nose. "I'll remember."

"Louder."

She glared at the dark, gray clouds moving in, yelling at the top of her lungs. "I will remember." The earth shook, the sky growled, and lightning struck a tree, singeing off a branch, sending smoke into the air.

"Good, now you'll remember."

She wiped the sweat off her brow. "How long has it been?"

"What do you mean?"

"You said in a dream a few hours of sleep can actually be days, weeks, or months."

He thought for a moment, nodding when the answer came. "Months."

It felt long, but not that long. "Months of shooting an arrow, over and over?"

"In dream time, yes." He kicked snow to the side. "You're good with the bow now, so let's put that down and dance, shall we?"

Eden dropped the bow and arrow, both vanishing before they hit the ground. "Dance?"

"The Sight can be much like a dance." He swiped his hand in front of him, and Eden's feet lifted off the ground. She landed on her back on the soft snow.

She pushed up, smiling, cocking a brow. "This ought to be fun."

"It will take a lot longer than a month, trust me. I hope you have a lot of sleep in you tonight."

Energy shifted inside her, her arms tingling and her lungs expanding. She threw both arms out, asking the energy around Skye to partner with her and instantly getting the confirmation. She pulled her arms back like she was pulling a sheet out from under his feet. He lost balance for a moment, then steadied himself. "Kinda weak, but good."

He dug his boot in the snow and charged. "We'll add some hand to hand combat, too."

47

ALI

Starship Tranquil

Ali couldn't sleep. At a time like this, how could anyone? She looked around *Tranquil's* bridge at the Bawn, and Daf, all conked out in their reclining chairs, slumbering, snoring, and slobbering.

She never figured out what ship-related skills the crew had. In Star Guild, that was a necessity. Here on Starship *Tranquil* where the ship practically flew itself, there wasn't a need. The crew could more or less call themselves passengers.

They followed *Swift* into a new system, and like *Swift* and apparently Ali's crew, *Tranquil* needed rest and recharge. Heck, Ali needed rest and recharge. She wanted nothing more than to sleep, and of course, she couldn't.

She viewed Eden's vessel on the holovid, mesmerized by *Swift's* incredible design, noting *Tranquil* donned the same design. The starship's orbed front, long midsection carrying giant boosters on the sides that extended back to the orbed stern, made the simple design somehow look complicated, high-tech, and badass.

Earlier, over the vidscreen, Nyx had briefed Ali. She gave Ali the rundown on the Anunnaki and their allies heading like a hot comet toward Earth, and it burned her soul. If Ali could go back in time, she'd make sure she'd put enough bullets in Enlil he'd never get up.

"Screw with my fellow Earthlings, pal?" She shook her head. "Not on my watch." She'd focus on Enlil's ship first, if possible, and blast the bastard out of the cosmos and into the stars. Since she couldn't fight Enlil at the moment or sleep, she needed to do something, or she'd die of boredom.

She walked to the bridge's exit and the door opened with a whoosh. Her thick boots squeaked on the floor as she made her way down corridor after corridor, and finally into the midsection where landings upon landings attached to the walls like shelves. On the landings sat domes, thousands upon thousands of them.

She bit her cheek. "Where are my quarters?" Maybe the captain had a special dome, one twice the size of the others, with a pool, maid-bots, chef-bots, and massage-bots.

One could dream.

She walked up a few stairs to the first balcony, passing an empty dome. Maybe this was it? No pool. No maids. No name engraved on the door. She moved onward, thinking maybe someone labeled her quarters. She passed a dome, making sure not to stare through the open door at a large man lying on a bed.

"Hey," came a male voice.

She stopped and turned. She stiffened, then let down her guard, sighing. "Hank, I can break your nose again." What the hell was he doing on this ship? Did he switch ships? The answer stared her in the face. He did.

He touched his belly as he sat up. "I'm losing some weight." He dropped his chin to his chest as if he didn't want to say that. "You know, I'm trying to change a little." He looked down, stubbing the front of his shoe on the floor at the foot of his bed. "We worried about you and Daf after you left *Sirona*. From what that Chan guy said, you may be the one who saved all of us from a grizzly death."

"Did Chan let you on this ship?"

Hank bobbed his head up and down. "Yeah, he said they needed me here. What I'm needed for, I don't know." He looked around, tilting his head back and peering through the clear roof and at the landing above him. "This ship is amazing. Have you checked it out at all? It's nothing like *Sirona* or any vessel in our fleet. I mean, the synapses fire—"

Ali held up her hand. "What do you want? Just to chat?"

Hank patted his bed for her to sit next to him.

Ali's shoulder's drooped before standing erect again like a true captain. The guy didn't change. "Hank, I'm this ship's captain. Do you understand? I have the authority to throw you in the brig. Hell, I have the authority to throw you off this ship."

"No, please. It wasn't a pass at you. I just need to talk."

Ali looked him up and down, pursing her lips. Something in his look and tone told her he spoke the truth. "All right. But any funny stuff, and I'm not kidding, I get a Bawn to throw your ass in the brig."

He crinkled his brow. "Bawn?"

She made her way to his entrance and leaned against the crystal-like door frame. "Yes, the little guys. They're all over this ship if you hadn't noticed. They're stronger than a bear and—"

"Bear?"

Ali threw a dismissive hand. "Never mind." Bears lived on Earth and were an animal Hank knew nothing about. "So, Hank, what is it?"

He put up his index finger. "One, and I'm sincere when I say this, I'm glad you're alive." He put up two fingers. "Two, I'm scared out of my mind."

Finally, something she could relate to. "I am too. And thank you. Strangely enough, it's actually nice to see you…sort of."

"Please sit." He gestured to a chair in the room.

"Good choice." She walked in and sat down, rubbing her blurry eyes and yawning. "I can't sleep."

"I haven't slept in weeks." He moaned, yawning as well. "Well, a little here and there, but I've spent most of my hours since the attack wondering if I'll die tonight or tomorrow."

"What's the change?"

"What do you mean?"

"You were Mister Cocky-pants on *Sirona*. Now you're acting vulnerable."

He shrugged. "Other than being scared shitless? Maybe I'm growing up."

"You almost died, didn't you?" That would grow someone up in a hurry.

He lowered his chin, his eyes going to his lap. "Yes, and I saw... heard..." He let out a hefty breath. "I witnessed deaths I can't ever erase out of my mind."

Ali dipped her head. The last month, maybe longer, had filled her mind full of horrors she'd never wish on anyone.

"Ali?" asked Hank. "Where exactly are we going?"

"Earth."

"Earth?" He gave a pinched expression. "We're heading into battle, aren't we?"

"Yes."

He squeezed his eyes shut, then opened them wide. "I was afraid of that. We need to find someone then."

"Find someone?"

"Sleuth."

"Why?"

"He's not working for our side. He's working for the Anunnaki."

"How do you know this?"

"If you don't believe me, ask Eden. She knows. She dealt with him."

"You said we needed to find Sleuth. Again, why?"

Hank leaned forward. "I don't know what ship he's on, but I saw him on Starship *Swift*'s launch bay when we evacuated."

Ali put her hands out. "What can he do? Hide?"

"I think..." Hank lowered his voice. "I think he's got more than just an in with the enemy. I'm confident he's directing some of their moves, letting them know where we were at. He's their inside guy. Listen, the guy is a wizard on the holocomps. He can figure out any system. Now, I know little about these starships, but if anyone can figure these ships out, it'd be him. We need to throw him in prison or kill the piece of ebb. He can't remain unattended on one of these ships for long. He's a virus. He'll infect everything."

"Then it's settled," said Ali. She stood.

"Where are you going?"

"I'm alerting the entire crew on both ships. We'll find him and throw him in the brig."

"That won't do."

"It'll have to do."

Hank gathered himself, his face flush. "Listen, he isn't just some nerd that's good with holonets and holochannels. He practically orchestrated the entire attack...or helped...I don't know for sure. I've been piecing the puzzle together these last few days. He'll figure out how to destroy these ships from the inside out."

An alarm sounded. "Captain Ali Johnson," came Daf's voice. "You're needed on the bridge."

Hank threw his hands up. "Let me come. Whatever it is, it's probably Sleuth. I can un-hack what he's hacking."

The ship shuddered, and Ali went to a knee, holding onto the edge of the doorway. She looked up, her eyes narrowed. "Then let's go."

48

ENLIL

Unknown

Enlil stood, his body restrained by straps connected to the command console surrounding him in a half-moon orientation. He looked at the rest of the crew on the bridge. They sat at stations, pressing buttons and monitoring data and holomaps.

Enlil eyed the holoscreen. They'd just hyper hopped into another system, and there was an asteroid field in front of them.

"Where are we?" Spit came out of his mouth, his body adjusting to the space warp that a Negative Matter Jump created.

A female Anunnaki turned, her hair in a bun, wearing the make-shift Enlil Monarch black and gold jumpsuit he created for his own fleet—a fleet his father, King Anu, would never approve.

"Elipsus system. Next jump, Earth's Solar System," she said.

A flash of light erupted on the holoscreen and blinked out a moment later. A Graxic ship had jumped in, its signature dragon-head bow, and long, bat-like wings flaring outward on the dreadnaught. Four boosters pushed the ship forward, two each on the port and starboard, extending past the stern. Pulse cannons littered the dreadnaught's exterior.

More flashes entered the system. Hundreds of Graxic and

Reptilian ships jumped in, accompanying Enlil's own vessels, creating an armada Earth couldn't fend off even in their dreams.

Enlil shifted his gaze to the holographic display on his console. "Any word from Sleuth?" Enlil couldn't believe the guy had survived the weapon he'd sent to end *Sirona*. He reminded Enlil of a Nibiru-roach, practically unkillable. He not only lived, the little bastard remained Team Enlil. He'd also somehow snuck onto a Space Templar ship and sent messages via his holopad to Enlil's, the way they communicated before the weapon of mass destruction pulverized Starship *Sirona*.

"Messages arrived, sir," said the woman. "They will come up on your monitor soon."

"Excellent."

A hologram lifted off the console, the words floating in front of him. He rubbed his cheek and read.

Message Code 114, Sleuth Entry: *There are too many people in this ship's control room. I can't get anything done, nor can I do so in private. They seem suspicious of me, so I'll communicate to you once I locate more private quarters.*

"A message as worthless as your race." Enlil swiped his finger on the hologram, bringing up the next message.

Message Code 115, Sleuth Entry: *I have accessed this ship's CIC, and heading to CC now to figure out how to stop these Space Templar starships. They're heading your way. Please reply, and with a monetary number of what I'll be rewarded for my loyalty.*

Enlil laughed. "Rewarded?" he said under his breath. "The only reward is that I might let you live."

Message Code 116, Sleuth Entry: *I'm able to access both ships through one of the ship's holonet. It connects these starships like none I've seen. It's almost like they communicate together. I'm hacking now, trying to disrupt engine cores.*

Message 117, Sleuth Entry: *I will need a pick-up. I have a location, so let me know when you get this message. Both ships are experiencing severe issues. You're welcome. And please, let me know the amount of my reward.*

Message 118, Sleuth Entry: *Where are you? I need a pick-up. I'll patch location to you but get here soon.*

Enlil frowned. "The poor man thinks I'll pick him up?" He shook his head. "Console four, dictate, please." He moved closer to the console's mic. "Your reward will be handsome, I assure you. A ship is en route. Continue interrupting the ships. You're our hero over here. The Anunnaki and I, Enlil, owe you our lives." He ended the message, his shoulders moving up and down in a low chuckle, trying to keep his tone hushed.

He loved lying and playing games with humans. "They're so naïve. So, so naïve." He lifted his head. "How long until we can jump into Earth's system?"

"Twelve hours, sir."

"Excellent. I can't wait to see all of humanity's faces when I show up and take the planet as my own."

49

EDEN

Starship Swift

Eden awoke with a bang, the dome shaking violently. Her bed jostled back and forth. She bolted to a sitting position.

She'd just mastered the bow, got whipped in hand to hand combat against Skye, and played with the Sight, manipulating energy. It had seemed like months, maybe years. She didn't know, but right now, the ship was under attack or being pummeled by asteroids.

She closed her eyes. Swift, *what's going on?*

I've identified the problem, and I'm working on it, though I sense holo-comp bugs crawling inside me.

Eden scrunched up her nose. *Bugs?*

A holonet virus, inert cells seeking my core like a missile. It's powerful.

What do I do?

Find the source, Eden. It's coming from this ship. It's affecting Tranquil *as well.*

The source?

Eden knew nothing about holocomps, holochannels, or holonets. She understood piloting, leading, training, and now some new Space Templar tricks.

Eden, said *Swift. The source is human.*

5 0

SHAE

Starship Ascension

Shae leaned forward in his chair with an alert gaze, his chin set high. "We punch in now." He'd only had a few jumps to get used to his new starship, *Ascension*. It spoke to him every so often, but he put a stop to that strange sensation. The odd words flowing through his mind interrupted his own thoughts.

Sabra sat at the helm. "Ten more minutes and *Ascension* will be ready."

"NMJ drives still charging?"

Sabra smiled. "Yes."

Shae crossed his arms. "What I hear in my head is real? The ship speaks to me?"

"Yes, and you can speak to it, either verbally or with your thoughts," said Sabra.

Devon adjusted in his seat as if uncomfortable at a station to Shae's right. "What am I supposed to be doing?"

"You're our white hat. Any attack on *Swift*'s holocomps and internal bio-computer core, you make sure it doesn't last long," said Shae.

Devon pressed several buttons, bringing up his holodisplay. "Got it." He paused, glancing down at his keypad. "Where is Naveya?"

Sabra chuckled. "Of all people, Naveya needed a vacation. She spent years helping uplift humanity, doing her best to seed information while being on the front line, while acting homeless, while getting stomped on by uncompassionate souls in a hurry to get to work or home." Sabra put her hands together at her chest. "That's why she's still on Aurora, hopefully with her butt plopped in the sand at one of Aurora's beaches."

Shae eyed the time. "Five minutes."

Sabra dipped her head. "Stay in the moment, Shae."

"We have coordinates set for the specific entry point?" Shae figured the armada he led could jump three light seconds from Enlil's and his allies' flotillas. Once Shae's fleet popped in, they'd target and send every weapon they had at the enemy. At three light seconds, Enlil and his group of assholes would have three seconds to react. It'd take them three seconds to realize what just dropped in on them. Shae hoped his Templar fleet's first wave would devastate the invaders, ultimately crippling them.

"Yes, Shae. We're good to go," said Sabra.

Shae stared at the holovid's clock in the upper left corner. He scanned the Space Templar fleet before him as well: mostly orbed ships, some large, some small, hundreds of them dotting the surrounding blackness; cruisers, destroyers, dreadnaughts, battleships, and more with names he'd never heard before. Starlancers, which held a long, sword-like bow, most likely for ramming. Starassaults, a cross between the size of a starfighter and a Starhawk transport, they looked fast and scary, two lances on either side that extended past the bow.

Sabra spoke into her chair's com. "White powder gold vials, please." She leaned back, resting her hands in her lap.

Shae gave her a blank look. "Did you just order something?"

She played off this soon-to-be-in-combat thing really well as if jumping into the next system where they'd face the Anunnaki fleet would be a cakewalk.

"Yes," she said.

He rubbed the wrinkles on his forehead. "Okay, what're the vials about?"

"Glad you asked." She cleared her throat. "White powered gold is the secret to our long lives. It also raises energy levels and steadies the mind, enhancing brainpower. You'll make better decisions. You'll be sharper."

"CJ at your service," said a Space Templar, walking onto the bridge, the door shutting in a hiss behind him. He held several vials full of a white substance.

"Thank you, CJ." Sabra stood and met him across the bridge, grabbing the vials. "Love your promptness."

"Like I said, at your service, ma'am." He spun on his heels and left the bridge.

Sabra sat at the helm, reaching back and handing Shae a vial. "This much should last you a month. Take a dab daily."

"Then what?" asked Shae.

"You'll see."

Shae looked at the men and women in their Space Templar garb, all at stations around the bridge.

"All right," said Shae. He sat taller. He wanted to get this show on the road. He didn't want anyone to harm his home planet, especially Helen. He glanced at the clock. It was nearly time to punch in.

Shae leaned into the intercom. "Man all flight quarters stations. Stand by to start all engines." He paused, waiting for a Templar on the bridge to indicate the pilots were in their Aven starfighters, and ready to go. A Templar turned in her station, dipping her head.

Shae nodded. "Start engines." He glanced at the vidscreen, switching to an open channel across the entire fleet. "Prepare for jump."

Again, he waited for another nod to confirm all ships in the fleet called at ready. It came and Shae continued, "Time check, ten seconds. Set countdown. Prepare to jump." He watched the clock on the vid, his lips moving at each passing second. Seat restraints automatically flipped over his shoulders and down his body, like an octopus sneaking up on its prey. Several clicks told him he had strapped in.

Shae wiggled in his chair, the restraints moving effortlessly with him. What he'd thought would make him feel confined and trapped, proved the opposite. Shae dabbed white powder gold into his palm. He licked it, his eyes on the time. A wave of concentration took over, his mind becoming clear, and his energy rising.

"Three, two..." whispered Shae, and a streak of light cut across the vidscreen. The colors of the rainbow leaped toward him, swirling in a long line, then opening into a tunnel.

In seconds, he'd be in front of an armada, bringing an armada of his own, and turning the enemy into fiery hell.

EDEN

Starship Swift

Eden hustled onto the bridge, the ship moving back and forth as if falling apart. She eyed the holodisplay, seeing a split screen. One side displayed several planets, colorful and distant, with stars twinkling around them. On the other side stood Ali, doing her best to stand upright. Her ship jostled like Eden's.

Nyx motioned toward Ali. "As you can see, Captain Ali Johnson is on the com."

Eden dipped her head, taking a seat. "Thank you, Nyx."

"Hank over there..." Ali thrust a thumb over her shoulder, "... patched into our ship's mainframe, pulled up an encryption, and bypassed the codes. He's actively looking for the source of the irritation now."

"Do you have any ideas, Ali?" asked Eden, sitting down.

She nodded. "Do you know a man by the name of Sleuth?"

Eden leaned back, the name striking her like a lightning bolt in the chest. She'd rather forget that snake's name for the rest of her life. "I met him a few times, yes."

"Sleuth was my first thought," said Skye.

Eden craned her neck. Skye sat at a station, giving her a nod, a gleam in his eye. He held a knowing grin, almost as if telling her she did a good job during their dream training. A voice mumbled in the background on Ali's bridge. Eden turned, facing the vidscreen.

Ali slapped her hands together. "Hank found that Sleuth's definitely the culprit. He's messing with our main power core. He's on your ship, not ours."

Eden grasped her gun from her holster, almost wishing it were a bow and arrow, her newfound love. "Send the location to *Swift*, and *Swift*, let me know when you have the location."

"On it," said Ali. Her screen blinked off, and the holovid extended into one long view, showing Starship *Tranquil* just off the port side.

"Nyx," said Eden. "Man the bridge." She flicked her head toward Jantu, who sat at a station, monitoring data streaming off a screen. "Jantu, get your rifle ready. You're coming with me."

Eden, I scanned the decks. There appears to be an unknown on the Computer Control deck, room 4E. It's a short man, balding with glasses.

"That's Sleuth." *Thank you,* Swift. Eden hurried out of the bridge, moving quickly down a corridor. Jantu walked behind her. *Sirona's* techs were most likely manning the CC room and probably doing nothing as usual. To get Computer Control techs to do anything, donuts usually worked.

She turned down another corridor, her finger pressing against her gun's trigger guard. "You with me, Jantu?"

"As always, Captain."

Her lips were slightly upturned as Jantu's voice calmly penetrated her mind. She enjoyed being called captain and liked it even more than the tall, burly Sirian had her six.

They hurried to an elevator and went down several decks. Opening the door, CC 1E quarters stood in front of her, its door closed. Eden moved around the elevator doorway and into the corridor, passing 2E. She slowed, her gun outstretched. She glanced over her shoulder. Jantu raised his rifle above her head and slightly away. They walked by 3E, stepping away from the wall and to the side of 4E's closed door. "*Swift*," she said. "Is the subject still in the room?"

Yes. He's unaware of your presence.

Can you just zap him?

I don't have weapons pointing inside.

Eden shrugged. *I tried.*

Noted, replied *Swift. Are you ready?*

Eden faced Jantu. He dipped his head. She nodded back. *Ready.*

Opening door now.

The door whooshed open, sliding upward and sucking into the wall. Eden stood clear of the wall, sweeping her gun up and down the empty doorway.

He's unarmed, Eden, came *Swift.*

"Good, that makes things a hell of a lot easier." She walked inside a rectangular room, a dim, blue light glowed from the ceiling. Holographic console displays lined the walls, and some sat on tables in the middle of the room.

A chair moved, squeaking. Someone stood. Eden and Jantu rounded an HDC island, filled with holocomps and monitors, blocking anyone from view sitting or standing on the other side. Eden paused, her finger against the trigger. "What are you doing, Sleuth?"

Sleuth lifted his hands above his head, the hair on the side of his nearly bald head standing on end. His skin appeared pale, and from the looks of things, he lost some weight from the last time she laid eyes on him, making his clothes seem baggy.

He moved his hands down slowly.

Eden jutted her gun in his direction. "Don't move."

He shook his head, continuing to move his arms. "I don't care." His voice sounded weak, and his eyes twitched like a madman, as perspiration dotted his skin.

"I'll shoot if you do anything sudden," she yelled.

He touched his glasses, moving them up the ridge of his nose. "I don't care." He sat, flopping in a chair next to a holocomp that blinked several strange scripts and codes on the monitor. He sighed, sliding lower. "They aren't coming for me. I did everything." He slapped his face, then did it again, and again, hard, as if punishing himself. He was losing his mind. "I did everything for Enlil. He said I'd be rewarded.

He said he'd come for me. It's…it's all a lie." He faced Eden. "He wants me dead."

"Undo what you did, Sleuth," ordered Eden, moving a step closer. "Clean what you messed up in the systems."

"I can and might." He turned, slouching, and held up his index finger. The ship shuttered. "But…"

"But what?" Eden moved to the side, sensing a change in his energy field.

"I'll do something better if you don't jail me."

She could tell he had this idea forming for a while, ready to use it if he needed to.

Jantu lowered his rifle and leaned on his right leg, placing his hand on his hip.

"Okay, what is it you can do better?" said Eden.

"I have access to Enlil's ship, and," his voice rose, his anger seething, "I can mess with his fleet's activenet. You know where he's going, right?"

Eden nodded.

"He'll be there soon," continued Sleuth. "If I scramble his systems, screw with his targeting array…the list goes on as to what I can do to him. How much easier would it be for you to defeat him?" He smiled.

"What's in it for you?"

He moved his middle and index finger over his thumb, rubbing back and forth. "Money. So much that refusing would be akin to blowing my brains out. An amount I'd be an idiot to turn down."

Eden rolled her eyes, taking a glimpse at Jantu. "Should I just shoot him now?"

"Shoot me?" Sleuth laughed, hovering his hand over a holokeypad. "I can destroy this ship so quickly you'd never know what hit you."

He can do no such a thing, Eden, said *Swift.*

Eden's lips curled upward, and she took a step closer.

"Why are you smiling?" Sleuth lowered his hand. "I have your life literally at the tip of my finger."

"Do it." She gestured toward the keypad. "Pressing it now would be nice. Come on, hurry."

Sleuth pushed away from the holocomp and steepled his hands as if he had all the leverage in the world. "I help you, and you help me."

"Up now. You're going to the brig." Eden eyed her Sirian friend. "Jantu, help me get him to lockup."

"Wait, wait," said Sleuth, clutching his chair's armrest. "I can disrupt Enlil's entire force. I mean, not his allies, but his own fleet, and you could tear them apart easily."

"Turn off the hack first, and I'll let you do what you want to Enlil."

Sleuth turned and typed, his lips moving as he worked. He tapped one more holobutton and lifted his finger. "There." The ship calmed, and the shaking ceased.

Eden looked the jerk up and down, as if scanning his energy, a new ability that turned on and off whenever it wanted. She could tell he spoke the truth, and he'd do what he said, though his heart wasn't in it. He wanted money and piles of it. Eden gripped Sleuth's arm by his bicep and tugged him out of the chair.

"Where are you taking me?"

"To the bridge. When we enter Earth's system, you hack away at the Anunnaki fleet, or I send a plasma bolt through your brain."

ALI

Starship Tranquil

"Great job, Hank." Ali straightened her lips, refusing to smile at the guy, though pleased he did such a good job finding Sleuth.

Hank looked up from his holomonitor, a Bawn standing next to him, waiting impatiently for his station back. "Did they find the bald prick?"

"Eden said they found Sleuth, and they have him in custody and are apparently watching him closely." She straightened in her posture. "*Tranquil*, notify everyone that we're jumping into Earth space, and to hold on. We don't know exactly what we're jumping into."

Yes, Captain.

Hank stood, leaving the bridge. "Sorry, I'll piss my pants if I see something I don't want to see on the other end of this jump." He waved and exited.

Ali let out a sigh. "Wimp." She sat back, gripping her armrests. She didn't know what would be on the other end of this jump. Whatever faced them, *Tranquil* would get them back to the Space Templar fleet. "Patch me to Eden first."

Eden appeared on the screen, swiping her black hair out of her face. "Yes, Captain?"

Captain? Ali wanted to roll her eyes. She'd never get used to her new title. "We're ready to jump."

Eden dipped her head, slightly closing her eyelids and then opening them as if sensing something. "Good. My ship and crew are ready as well." She turned to her bridge. "Everyone, we jump on my mark. Open all comm channels."

The vidscreen changed from Eden to the stars in front of Ali. She gulped down any hesitation or fear of the battle to come. Eden's voice boomed over the speakers, counting down from ten and finally to one.

Swift blinked out of existence. A wake of rainbow colors drifted apart like a dissipating fog. *Tranquil* vibrated for a moment, then Ali's consciousness faded, blinking out. Light filled her vision, then more rainbow colors danced on the vidscreen.

An instant later, all beauty ceased, and hell awoke on the other side.

53

EDEN

Starship Swift

Eden's eyes widened when she saw Earth. Her beauty and her blue highlights tugged at Eden's heart, nearly making her gasp. If this was her race's birthplace, then holy hell, she'd make this her home in a flash.

"Welcome to our real home, Eden," said Skye from his station.

She wanted to take *Swift* low into the atmosphere and land on one of the green and brown masses below. She could explore this wondrous world, dip her toes in the water, breathe precious air, and bury her hands in the sand.

Nyx patted Eden's forearm. "Yes, she's spectacular and all that adorable stuff. She's my planet too, and I plan on defending her, not swooning over her."

"The armada isn't here yet," said Skye. "How long, Jantu?"

Jantu swiped across his station's holomonitor. "I detect high frequency and low wavelength thermal emissions nearing us. They're coming, Captain, and they'll be here soon."

"When will they enter the system?" Eden asked.

"Twenty-eight seconds, give or take a second or two," responded Jantu.

Swift began to turn. Eden rubbed her heart and narrowed her eyes. "We'll open fire the moment they blink in, all right?"

Skye dipped his head. "Yes."

"*Swift*, search for Starship *Tranquil*."

Swift turned to face a black canvas with dotted lights, Earth behind her. *She'll jump in any second now.*

"Let's hope it's before the armada arrives." Eden opened all channels inside her ship. "If we have any Thunderbird pilots on board, go to launch bays, and get inside Avens. They're Space Templar starfighters. When you're ready, launch. Attack the enemy at first sight." Eden turned off the open com. "*Swift*, open the launch bay doors when the pilots are ready. I'm not familiar with Avens, so give them instruction in the meantime."

Each Aven will give instructions to each pilot.

"All right, even better." Eden raised her brows at the vidscreen as the blackness of space lit up in an array of colors. "Here they come." She turned and faced the weasel sitting at his station. "Sleuth, are you ready to hack their systems?"

Sweat dripped from his face, his lips pale, his face ashen. "Y-yes. Ready." His hands shook, no doubt freaked out that life wasn't under his control. "This craft is amazing, but no match for the Anunnaki fleet. We're doomed, Eden. I don't know what you all are thinking, trying to defend this world. Let them burn. Let us live."

"Oh, cry me a river. Now, do your job, or I'll end you quick-like," said Nyx.

One after another, ship upon large ship jumped into existence.

"They're 22.8 thousand kilometers away," said Jantu. "I count a hundred and seven ships, and more arriving."

Eden squeezed her hands in fists, her heartbeat picking up steam. "We need more than just *Tranquil*. Where is the Space Templar fleet?"

Both the fleet and Tranquil *are on their way, I assure you,* responded *Swift*.

Nyx let out an unexpected laugh. "They're hailing us, those stupid bastards. I'm bringing them online as per your authorization, Eden."

Eden nodded and faced the screen.

A male with a lizard-like face, light-green scaly skin, and thick neck muscles, wearing a black shirt and a green pendant, materialized on the screen. Eden clutched her crystal pendant hidden underneath her shirt and swallowed hard. She hadn't expected to see such a menacing creature.

"Welcome, Space Templars." The lizard's voice was serene and charismatic. "I'm Korrell of the Graxic Alliance. I'm their noble ruler, leading this expedition. Enlil's Anunnaki and Leader Boll's Reptilian's fleet accompany my own." He smirked. "It's rare I show myself to others, let alone to anyone I consider an enemy. But alas, the planet you attempt to protect doesn't need your protection anymore. Earth is in alignment with our alliance. Their governments have given us amnesty to do what we will in exchange for technology and information. You have no dominion here. If you don't leave, you will die." He made an X with his arms over his chest and bowed his head. "Very simple."

Eden stood and walked toward the vidscreen. "Korrell, I'm Captain Eden Gaines of the Space Templars. A heavily armed Space Templar armada is on its way. Turn your ships around. You're invading human space. From experience, we of the Space Templars understand governments rarely abide by the will of the people, so no, you won't take this planet."

She continued, doing her best to take up as much time as she could until *Tranquil* and the Space Templars showed. "As a human myself, I and billions of other humans, don't give you permission to stay here, or to kill, maim, or induce fear on anyone on this planet. Do you understand?"

Korrel laughed. "I abide by a higher law, one of power. So, Captain Eden Gaines, I have one question. Who will shoot first?"

"Will you leave this system?" said Eden.

Korrel shook his head and licked his reptile lips with his thick tongue, like a greedy monster waiting for its food. "I hope you taste good, tender and succulent."

"Leave. You don't understand what's about to hit you." Eden eyed the vidscreen, scanning all around. Where the hell was *Tranquil* and our armada?

Korrel glared into the screen. "What's your answer?"

"To what question?" She knew the question, but taking time would work to her advantage.

"Who'll shoot first, little Earthling?"

The enemy ships flew toward Earth, coming ever so closer to their position. Eden and her crew were the only barrier between the armada and the planet. Eden took a deep, long breath. "*Swift*, fire at will."

My pleasure.

"I always love a good fight," said Nyx.

Eden jumped into the captain's chair, straps automatically belting her in. Korrel blipped off the screen, and his dragon ship came into view.

"They're 20.2 thousand kilometers from us," said Jantu.

The bridge heated and the lights dimmed as plasma bolts blasted from *Swift*'s bow cannons. The bolts spread out long and wide, moving across in a zigzag pattern. In space, at this distance, erratic plasma fire had more chance of hitting moving targets than a single stream on a specific target. "*Swift*, we need some laser-guided missiles."

Aye, Captain. Dozens of missiles launched from *Swift*, bluish-white fire flaming out the back of them, pushing them at a breakneck pace. *I've targeted Korrel's ship. The missiles will continue to pulse laser sensors at the target until it gets a steady lock. Until they lock on, they'll fly in a predictive trajectory.*

Does that mean they might miss?

Yes, a few will miss. Most will hit.

Eden raised her chin, taking in a gush of air. "*Swift*, send another wave of missiles." In Star Guild, missiles were labeled depending on their types, sizes, and types within types; space-to-space, space or air-to-surface, surface-to-surface, surface-to-space or air, assault, short-range, medium-range, long-range, and the list went on and on. Eden didn't have time to get to know every type at this moment. That'd come later if she survived. Right now, generic weapon orders would have to do.

Swift vibrated as she launched more missiles toward the armada. *Swift* then reversed at a forty-five-degree angle. She tilted to the side, and pushed her throttle forward, moving forward and diving at a thirty-degree angle.

"*Swift*, zoom in on our first wave missiles." The vidscreen zoomed past the second wave, landing on the first wave, just in time.

Korrel's ship, its bow that of a dragon's head, arms tucked into the sides of the dreadnaught, came into view. It drifted, dipping at a twenty-degree angle. The missiles sank in, ripping into shields. The impact caused a shimmer in the invisible energy surrounding the giant ship. One by one, the missiles seemingly evaporated against the shields.

The second wave dove into the same location, evaporating as well, until some managed to poke through, perhaps that portion of the shields deactivated from the focused pounding. The missiles rammed into the port side, and metal, debris, and broken cannons chipped away from the ship.

Avens released, Eden.

"Inbound missiles," said Jantu.

Nyx's lips tightened at the bright lights on the vidscreen. Thousands of missiles headed their way, the rocket boosters propelling the projectiles forward.

"Impact in eight seconds," said Jantu.

Activating anti-missiles. I don't know if I'll get all of them, but I'm a crack shot.

Eden pursed her lips. "*Swift*, order the Avens to target the missiles locking onto us."

Already ordered.

Avens in the hundreds steered toward the projectiles, and lasers flashed from the starfighter's aft. *Swift*'s antimissile system did the same, flashing lasers. Eden watched as enemy missiles turned into small fireballs, turning into hundreds of explosions in space. Yet, some missiles barreled through.

"All power to starboard and bow graviton shields," yelled Eden.

Already done.

Do you even need a crew? It was a question Eden said and thought many times.

More than you know. Explosions sunk into the shields, the ship shuttering from the energetic impact. Out of the corner of the vidscreen, Avens screamed toward the enemy, creating a heavy response of enemy return fire.

"Avens closing distance on the armada. Two seconds until they're in weapons range," came Jantu.

Missiles and beam weapons new to Eden blasted toward the Avens. The Space Templar fighters ducked and dodged, clearly steered by their own AI systems, doing things and reacting in ways humans wouldn't be able to. Eden sucked in wind when an Aven tore apart, a beam hitting its center, and then another beam shattering an Aven into hundreds of pieces. She bit her bottom lip, her eyes narrowed. "Send more firepower the bastard's way, *Swift.*"

Plasma bolts expelled from *Swift*, again the vessel vibrating, and again the bolts erratic, spreading out wide. *With any luck, a few will hit targets and with more luck, a few will down targets.*

Skye stood. "The Avens will bring a bit of chaos." He walked toward the bridge's exit. "Now it's my turn. I'll have some fun out there. See you soon." He marched out of the bridge, nearly taking half of Eden's confidence with him.

She pulled back into her seat and gathered herself. She eyed dozens of ships breaking off formation and heading toward Earth. "*Swift* cut them off."

Swift activated port and aft boosters, quickly turning. She barreled toward them, her speed faster than any behemoth ship Eden had ever seen. *Swift* targeted a cruise-size vessel, her starboard shaking as several vrooms sounded across the bridge. Large plasma torpedoes exited torp-tubes. Plasma cannons fired a moment later.

The cruiser, now under ten thousand kilometers, buckled when the torpedo hit, the torpedo angling through an either failed or flawed shield. Internal fire blew out the cruiser's seams and tore the ship in half. *Swift's* cannon fire met with several smaller ships accompanying the cruiser, hitting a few, turning their lights out and splitting them apart, armor and pieces of engine twirling in space.

"We need a few Avens for assistance here," shouted Eden, her finger pointed at three other large ships not turning from their trajectory toward Earth.

"On it," came Skye's voice through the intercom. "I'm in the launch tubes and will have them in range soon."

"Continue to fire, *Swift,*" ordered Eden.

Swift did and more cannon bolts sliced through another craft, fire erupting out of its stern, the ship exploding like a fireworks display.

Skye's Aven shot out of *Swift,* and he quickly gained on the two remaining vessels. He made short work of them and turned a hundred-and-eighty degree to head toward a battle of red and orange eruptions in the middle of the enemy fleet.

The bridge shuddered, and *Swift* jerked, turning away from more enemy impacts.

"Did any of those hits penetrate through the shields?" Eden scanned the vidscreen, not seeing any warnings.

One, but I'm repairing now.

Nyx pointed ahead. "More ships scrambling to Earth."

The armada was relentless. "*Swift,* those ships are getting a little too close to Earth for my comfort," said Eden.

On it.

Swift moved fast, the graviton shields absorbing more waves of direct hits. She veered away from the armada, and toward the ships nearing Earth. *Swift* opened fire. Two smaller ships exploded in a blaze, extinguishing moments later. Three more starfighter-like ships, triangular in form, spun around to face *Swift.*

Too late. *Swift* sent plasma torpedoes down their throats, piercing the cockpits, and blasting fire outward. Sparks fizzed out a moment later.

Swift took a cannon blast, the bridge jostling from the hefty slam into its gravitons. Eden pushed hard into the side of her armrest. "Nyx, how is the crew doing?"

Nyx threw her arm out wide. "How are you all doing back there?"

Eden rolled her eyes. She could have done that.

They gave thumbs up as if everything they'd experienced so far was just a walk in the park and an entire armada looming over them wasn't a big deal. Regardless, where the hell did *Tranquil* go, and when would the Space Templar armada show?

Eden craned her neck. "Sleuth, you screwing with their systems yet?"

Sleuth scowled as his fingers typed rapidly on a holokeypad. "Don't bother me. I'm attempting to patch into their weapons system. It took me forever to get there, so don't screw me up now."

"More ships heading toward Earth," Nyx called out.

Eden wanted to pull her hair out. "All right, *Swift*, head them off."

Yes, Ma'am.

Swift shifted, spinning around, and upped her throttle. Enemy starfighters curled in less than a thousand kilometers starboard side, sending energy beams *Swift*'s way.

Swift didn't budge, taking the brunt of the hits, the graviton shields holding well against the starfighter's small weaponry. *Swift* then sent a barrage of bolts, tagging several bandits, breaking them apart easily. Others dodged, avoiding the fast plasma. *Swift* flew onward, closing in fast on a medium-sized battleship leading a small squadron of starfighters and what could only be a dozen large transports, most likely full of enemy troops.

I'm almost in range for shots they can't avoid.

Eden tightened her jaw. "When you're in range, end them. Don't miss." They were getting far too close to Earth.

Dozens of missiles and torpedoes launched from *Swift*, streaking forward and plummeting into the battleship's shields. As more hit, the shields failed and torpedoes and missiles punctured the vessel's armor, cracking it open. It spat out fire, and turned, no doubt attempting to volley with *Swift*, but a few more direct hits from *Swift* and the ship went dark.

Swift targeted another ship, this one much smaller than the battleship. It continued its flight pattern toward Earth. Missiles flew from

Swift, sizzling against the ship's shields, turning the missiles into ash and debris. *Swift* sent forth more weapon fire. The shields deactivated, failing, and missiles blasted against its exterior. The vessel tipped to its side, then corrected itself, buckling several seconds later as a plasma blast from *Swift* hit true, causing a secondary burst within the enemy ship. It split apart, breaking like glass dropping from a five-story building.

Swift targeted the rest of the squadron. They separated, giving up on their approach on Earth.

"Excellent," said Eden. "We—"

Swift jerked and veered to the left. She turned, violently vibrating as she did so.

"We're hit, and it broke through graviton shields," said Nyx.

Tell her it's nothing I can't heal from, said *Swift*.

"We're fine. Damage is being fixed now," informed Eden.

Eden, listen, time is of the essence, and we've already stayed alive longer than I statistically calculated without the Space Templar fleet arriving. We—

A bright light flashed in front of them, blinking brightly between *Swift* and the armada. Eden inhaled sharply. "*Tranquil* is here." They jumped into the wrong place at the wrong time. "We need to help them."

Swift jostled back and forth from a hefty hit and Eden knocked back against her seat, whiplashing her head. She blinked several times, gathering her bearings, and rubbed the back of her neck. She eyed the viewscreen. "Are we slowly spinning?"

Yes. We've just experienced a substantial hit.

54

ALI

Starship Tranquil

An armada vast and deep filled Ali's screen. Ships with long, bat-like wings, dragon heads as bows, and spikes crossing the length of the ships were in front of her. Large Anunnaki pyramid-like ships, along with their rectangular cruisers and battleships, hovered along-side the dragon vessels. The bigger problem: from bow to bow, *Tranquil* couldn't be more than a thousand kilometers from them and closing.

Amid it all, Avens flew like a swarm of bees, blasting the armada. An Aven and then another turned into a flower of flames, though it appeared they had chipped away at the defenses and lit up more enemy starfighters than they lost.

"Holy Guild," said Ali, her tone soft.

"Let's kick some Anunnaki ass," yelled Thun, his fist in the air.

Two against...hundreds thought Ali. The odds were more than stacked against her and Eden.

Ali, directly behind you is your home. Earth. Defend it with all you have, said *Tranquil. We'll fight and take as many bruises as we can. Soon, the Space Templar fleet will arrive.*

Ali bit her fingernail. *They better.*

Do I have permission to fire, Ali?

Yes!

Tranquil moved into position, taking an energy weapon straight in the bow, the graviton shields rippling from the hit. *Tranquil* returned fire, letting loose bolts from plasma cannons. It sliced through an enemy craft's shields, dissipating the gravitons, and ravaged the craft's long spiked nose, and then plastered the ship's whale-like body with missiles.

What the hell was a whale? An image came to her, and she quickly shook it off. Now—especially now—wasn't the time for memory lane.

Tranquil dipped underneath the whale-ship, rattling the large underbelly with direct hits, peeling metal off like dandruff from a Bawn's head. A flash of light brightened the screen. Ali instinctively put her forearm over her eyes, her heart beating fast from the sudden light. "What was the flash?"

Swift came to help us, said *Tranquil,* pulling away from the whale-ship, its bow now completely gone. *Swift engaged the craft with a photon torpedo. The enemy ship is permanently out of commission.*

Ali's eyes widened as she watched the ship's occupants sucked out of the craft, past wires that curled around the craft's broken edges, and twirled lifeless in space. The ship spun, cracking against a nearby pyramid-ship, and sending out a ball of fire where it hit, then bouncing away, doing little damage.

Chan put his hands together and began humming monotone words she didn't recognize.

What's he doing? thought Ali as *Tranquil* pitched, taking several projectiles in the shields, starboard side.

He's praying, replied *Tranquil.*

Praying? Why? She could think of thousands of things he could do to help, and praying didn't make the cut.

He's praying because it's two against hundreds. Statistically, we don't have a chance.

Ali's heart ran to her throat, wanting to exit the ship with or without her. "Where exactly are the Space Templars?"

On the way.
When will they get here?
We don't know.

55

SHAE

Starship Ascension

The tunnel dissipated and Shae stared at the back end of an enormous armada, a laser show of lights and explosions in the distance in front of him. "Let it fly."

They jumped in three light seconds from the enemy, nearly thirty thousand kilometers. Graxic, Reptilian, and Enlil's fleet's sensors wouldn't pick up Shae's large flotilla for three seconds. By then, they'd have five seconds at most to react.

Space Templar cruisers, destroyers, dreadnaughts, battleships, assault ships, and lancers sent photon torpedoes, then missiles, and lit up space with plasma bolts. In under ten seconds, explosions filled the viewscreen as Shae exposed Enlil's armada's rear. They sat as easy targets, most of their gravitons directed to power the front and sides of their shields to protect them from the fight in front of them, making them vulnerable from behind.

"Sabra, I don't know the groups in the fleet, but we need this fast and simple. Split the fleet into three, name a lead for two of them. We each attack based on location. And *Ascension*, bring up coordinates on the screen." A grid appeared along with numbers at each crossing line. "Sabra, group one engages the armada at coordinates eleven-zero-seven. Group two engages the enemy at coordinates thirty-six-nine-teen. We take a large squadron onward, straight ahead, and hit them in the middle."

Sabra dipped her head. "Open all fleet comm channels." She cleared her throat. "Squadrons Dees, Meen, Es, Limmu, Ia, and Imin, break formation and attack at will, coordinates sent to you. Captain Senna Lightwell, you're group captain."

Senna's affirmative bounced back, and a group of Space Templar ships to the left of *Ascension's* screen split off from the fleet, heading toward the coordinates Sabra gave, their boosters beaming blue after-burner. Sabra continued barking orders and calling for another group captain to lead. A portion of the fleet broke off, heading to the next specified coordinates.

"Full steam ahead," yelled Shae, watching small crafts dodge, spin, and weave in and out of enemy weapon's fire in front of the glowing blue gem—Earth. Shae couldn't help but smile, happy to see his old home, and glad he remembered what it looked like. "Open ship inter-com," said Shae. "Flight deck prepare for Avens to take off. *Ascension,* open launch bay doors."

Yes, Admiral. Launch bay doors opening.

"Avens, start engines. Launch when ready. Engage the enemy. Don't let up."

Avens launching now, Admiral.

"Thank you." Shae wiggled his ear and shook his head. "Hearing this ship speak will take a lot of getting used to."

Avens shot off in a cluster toward the enemy, slowly turning into small lights the farther away they flew. Starship *Ascension* flew onward, heading for the meat of the battle.

Shae glanced at Devon rooted to his chair, typing away as script flowed quickly down his holomonitor.

Sabra unstrapped and stood. "May I join the Aven squadron?"

Shae cocked his head to the side. "You want to fight in a starfighter?"

"I'm better suited there than in here...if you want to down more ships, that is."

Shae dipped his head, his nerves rising slightly. He didn't know this ship well and thought Sabra would be of help. Apparently, she wanted to be of more help out there. All the better. Shae motioned toward the bridge's exit. "Be my guest."

She bowed. "Thank you, Admiral. I'll make you proud."

"Good."

Shae eyed the vidscreen. "Zoom in." *Ascension* zoomed in on the center of the conflict. His Avens had entered engagement, lighting up ships with plasma bolts, a technology new to him, though a weapon system not that difficult to understand. He winced when several Avens erupted in an array of colors. An enormous ship, with long wings and a dragon head on the bow, came into view, taking several Avens out of existence.

"Target that ship," said Shae. "Hit him hard."

Ascension shook, and the bridge vibrated. Two large, purple orbs flew outward, heading at incredible speed toward the vessel. *"Ascension, get word to all Aven pilots in that ship's vicinity to move away from their targets. Torpedoes are on their way."*

Affirmative, Admiral.

The Avens zoomed away, engaging ships far from the dragon craft. A torpedo hit, slicing through the dragon ship's shields, a ripple dipping inward and flowing outward. Electricity spun around the ship, like a snake squeezing its prey. A second torpedo slammed into its back boosters unabated, sending a large explosive blast that winked out an instant later. The stern broke apart. Internal explosions lit up space, and pieces split off the ship in chunks.

One dragon boat down, a handful more to go.

The bridge's door opened, hissing loudly. Shae spun in his seat, hesitating for a moment. "Kalista? What the Guild are you doing here?"

"That Sabra lady called me in here. Apparently, there's a seat open, and you need someone you know by your side." She shook her head. "Humans and your needs."

Shae didn't need her. He had Devon, but maybe she could help. "Okay, sit. Sabra's seat is there."

She gave him a lazy salute. "Will do, Cap'n."

"Admiral," he corrected.

"Right, Admiral."

He faced the vidscreen as they closed in on the enemy fleet. "Drop low. We attack from beneath," ordered Shae.

The ship and the group he led— a dozen cruisers, a handful of battleships and destroyers, and several lancers and assault ships— moved lower in its trajectory, heading for the enemy's underbelly. Shae leaned forward. "We have an Anunnaki pyramid twenty-one klicks port forward. *Ascension*, target ship, and let loose." Plasma blasts expelled, and in seconds impacted the pyramid ship's shields. "Keep going." *Ascension* threw more weapon fire, successfully tearing through a portion of the shields. Fire blew from the pyramid's exterior, though doing minimal damage.

Avens pounded the pyramid as well, more explosions pocking the exterior. The pyramid's return fire came back erratically as if their weapon's systems had become faulty. Several cruisers took the brunt of the hits, their shields holding strong. They returned fire, jabbing the pyramid.

"Sir," said Devon. "I'm sensing a malfunction within the Anunnaki holonet. They're being hacked." He jerked back in surprise. "Whoa, they just lost all defenses."

Shae pointed at the screen. "That pyramid ship?"

"No, the entire Anunnaki fleet. I don't see it with the Reptilians or the Graxic, but the Anunnaki are essentially defenseless."

Shae sat straighter. "Open all channels now."

Open, Admiral.

"All ships focus on the Anunnaki fleet. They are defenseless. I repeat, they are defenseless. Send the message to the entire armada and cripple these Anunnaki assholes."

Kalista unstrapped and stood, her hand in a fist. "Hey, do not say those words about my race."

"Negative. They are assholes of the worst kind. You want to be tormented and enslaved your entire life?"

She looked at him blankly.

He shook his head. "Yeah, I didn't think so. So, yes, your race is full of pricks. Now sit down."

Kalista, acting as if Shae had overreacted, sat down and strapped back in. Shae shifted his focus to the screen as the Space Templar fleet shifted, like bees connected to their queen, doing what Shae needed at a moment's notice. An assault ship split in half on his port, and a battleship took massive hits, its shields down.

A throng of Avens circled an Anunnaki destroyer, dodging the destroyer's blasts. The Avens gradually stripped its armor with well-targeted shots until the ship went dark, all systems going offline. A few more hits and the Anunnaki vessel cracked in two, sparks flying out the new opening.

Shae raised his arm at a large pyramid-ship, wanting to end the damn thing. He made a throwing motion, emotion pushing up from his belly. "Fire torpedoes."

Avens pulled away as *Ascension*, assault ships, lancers, cruisers, and destroyers in his group sent forth torpedoes. The pyramid erupted in a last burst of hellfire, sending debris like shrapnel that pounded an enemy cruiser kilometers away.

Ascension dipped forward and turned, the constant pounding of enemy fire dwindling the gravitons on the port side. A missile slipped through a malfunctioning graviton, and *Ascension* rocked. Shae lurched forward, the restraints pulling him gently back into the seat. The vidscreen split, bringing up a display of *Ascension's* blueprint, showing effects to her stern, followed by internal explosions.

Ascension rounded a ship with a dragon's face, clearly the biggest vessel in the fleet, and pelted it with plasma bursts. The dragon ship took the hits on the chin, the shields absorbing each blow.

"We might not want to mess with that one. I know those Graxic ships, and they're kill-proof," said Kalista.

Graxic ships are not impenetrable.

"Continue to fire," shouted Shae, watching the rest of the Templar ships in his group fire upon the behemoth. A ripple of energy emitted from the Graxic ship and a haze-like fog surrounded *Ascension*.

Ascension froze. *They have us locked in a tractor beam.*

Shae flared his nostrils, his insides tightening. "Another tractor beam," he said under his breath. It was a repeat of when Y'taul captured him.

Kalista's arms fell to her sides, defeated. "Smooth move, Admiral." Shae could tell she had an excellent idea of what would happen next. She gave him a farewell nod. "We had a fun ride while it lasted...I guess."

The bow of the Graxic ship—the dragon's mouth—lit up in red, revving up a weapon. A second later, it fired a wide energy beam. Shae grabbed hold of his chair. "Brace yourselves."

ALI

Starship Tranquil

Tranquil dodged cannon pulse beams, or whatever they were because Ali had no clue. The beams seemed to come from every direction. Graviton shields held well.

The Space Templar fleet has jumped into the system and has entered the battle.

Ali pressed her hand against her forehead. "Thank Guild."

Tranquil dipped, an enemy shot hitting high on *Tranquil*'s bow shields.

The comm channel opened, and a familiar voice rang over the com. "All ships focus on the Anunnaki fleet. They are defenseless. I repeat, they are defenseless. Send the message to the entire armada and cripple these Anunnaki pricks."

"Dad?" said Ali, more to herself than to anyone else. Daf gave Ali a look, nodding as if confirming Ali was right.

"You heard him," said Ali. "*Tranquil*, shift targets, we head right for the Anunnaki."

Thun grinned, his eye squinting as if evil thoughts raced through his head. "Any way we can board these evil ships and take the crew out, one by one?"

Ali shook her head, focusing on the screen. *Tranquil* headed for the pyramid-like ships up ahead, their colossal bodies growing bigger by the instant.

Bilrak let out a yell, perhaps a Bawn war cry. "I second Thun, and I'm sure Harak agrees." He held up a sword. "Let's board a ship and whack some Anunnaki sun-worshipers."

Ali wrinkled the skin around her eyes. "No." The ship lurched from missile impact.

Harak grunted. "She's scared. I know it. Our warrior, our Chosen One, is frightened beyond—"

Ali pulled her boot off and flung it at Harak, hitting him square in the face. She had nothing else to throw. He jerked back, swiping his hand in front of him, his reaction too late. Thun laughed, and a few Bawns followed suit. Harak went to stand, and Ali pulled out her gun. "Sit, or you get a slug in your chest."

Harak gave his father a quick glance.

Bilrak crossed his arms over his chest. "I'd listen to the lady."

Harak grunted.

Chan dipped his head Ali's way. "Concentrate."

Tranquil slipped by an enemy battleship, heading for the flying pyramids. Ali pointed. "Dead ahead."

Swift is in dire need. We must act fast, said *Tranquil*.

Chan pointed to the right side of the vidscreen. "*Swift* is at coordinates six-zero-nine."

"Then that's where we go," said Ali. "Patch through to Eden."

Nothing on that ship is operational, responded *Tranquil*.

Nerves tingled up Ali's feet and to her stomach. "Get us there as fast as you can."

Swift will heal herself, but we need to protect her as best we can. I'm adjusting our course to her coordinates now.

Tranquil pitched right, and the screen changed, the view now on a significant dot in the middle of a vast array of small ships blasting *Swift* with everything they had. "*Tranquil*, get as many Avens in the area as possible. When in range, we'll fire every Guild'n thing we have."

ENLIL

Earth's Solar System

Enlil pounded the command console, his fist making a dent. His pyramid ship bucked back, and sparks flew from the ceiling and skipped across the bridge.

"Get my fleet operational," he yelled, his teeth clenched.

"Sir," said a man, twisting around at his station. "Our targeting array is offline."

Enlil's jaw tightened. "Get it online." Another blast jostled the ship.

"Yes, sir. We're attempting. We don't know why none of our ships can target the Space Templars."

Space Templars echoed in Enlil's mind. It was a word, a title, a group he hated more than life itself. He eyed the screen, viewing the battle happening all around him. "Where's Ali?"

"We don't know, sir."

Enlil watched a cruiser in his fleet blow apart by insignificant Space Templar starfighters. "Her chip. Locate her chip. Her chip went offline a week ago."

The man dipped his head. "We'll continue to try to locate her."

Enlil seethed. "Try?" He unholstered his gun and pointed at the man's head. He pulled the trigger several times. The man lurched forward at his station, his head falling against his HDC desk. Blood dripped from the station's desk to the floor.

Korrel, the Graxic leader, appeared on Enlil's screen. "We didn't come here to fight while your entire fleet sat back and watched. You got us into this mess, now help us or by Graxicca, I will kill you."

Enlil threw his hands up. "If you're so incompetent not to see our entire fleet's system is corrupted, then you're as blind as you are brain dead."

Scales flared from the sides of Korrel's neck. "We're outmatched only because you sit idly by. A few more attempts to reach Earth and if they fail, and by Graxicca they better not, we'll jump out of this system." He held up a fist, his nostrils wide. "Your refusal to fight won't sit well with the alliance council. We'll sever off that head of yours."

"Then you'd have my father's fleet to deal with, Korrel." Enlil lifted his chin. "Do you want that?"

Korrel blipped off the screen.

Enlil grimaced and squeezed his fists, wanting to wrap his fingers around the lizard-head's thick neck. He turned to the man he'd just shot, about to ask him a question. He shook his head and assumed he would have answered with an affirmative.

He opened the commlink. "Everyone listen up. Let our entire fleet know we're punching out. We'll leave on my mark and let these Reptilians and Graxic fend for themselves. We can do nothing here but watch our people die."

On the viewscreen, a battleship in Enlil's fleet broke apart, fire spewed and then fluttered out.

"Ready...on my mark..."

EDEN

Starship Swift

Eden slammed into her backrest, the restraints tightening around her. She clenched the armrests with both hands, her knuckles going white, sweat dripping down her cheek. Swift, *are you there?* The craft jostled, the lights on the bridge flickering. She stared at the vidscreen, the ship spinning, and Earth passing in front of them and then out of view.

Nyx's brows drew low, as if she wanted to end the Anunnaki from existence here and now.

"Nyx," yelled Eden. "Any ideas?" The vidscreen blinked out, displaying black.

"We wait," replied Nyx, closing her eyes, as if going into meditation.

"Wait?" replied Eden. "Isn't there anything we can do to steer the ship on our own without *Swift*? These Graxic and Reptilian ships are tearing us apart."

Nyx's eyes remained closed as she shook her head. "No. All systems have failed." The ship rocked back and forth from another hit and spun faster.

"Eden," Jantu's voice came to Eden's mind. "Seek faith and speak those faithful words out loud. The Master knows the power of the word." A hum vibrated across the bridge, loud and almost deafening.

Eden ignored it, turning her captain's chair toward Jantu's station. "Seek faith? And—" She paused, her lips downturned. Jantu and the rest of Sirians and humans chanted, their heads bowed, eyes shut. She side glanced at Nyx, who now muttered words she couldn't understand.

"What are you all—"

I'm coming online, Eden, said *Swift. We need better teamwork, you and I.*

Eden jolted to the side as another weapon met its mark on *Swift's* starboard. The chanting ceased, and everyone went back to business as the vidscreen blipped on.

"*Swift,* where are our shields at?" asked Nyx.

The screen split, displaying *Swift's* blueprint. Port and bow shields blinked in the red, displaying nine percent. The rest of the craft highlighted in yellow with percentages all over the board. Nine percent jumped to eleven percent.

I'm healing, said *Swift.*

"Straighten out," Eden ordered.

Straightening out.

Swift's spin slowed and Eden's eyes widened. "Bandit, twelve o'clock." A ship with a silver sheen sparkled at Eden, barreling down on *Swift.* A hoard of smaller craft tailed it, moving in fast.

Nyx lurched forward. "Evade, evade. The bastard is coming in for..." She calmed. "Never mind." A smile crept on her face.

The ship sent plasma bursts slinging past *Swift,* the tailing ships doing the same. "*Tranquil?*" Eden blurted.

"And a mess of Avens," said Nyx, her chin high.

A cheer engulfed the bridge as Starship *Tranquil* flew by, followed by dozens of fast-moving Avens, their weapons' fire sweeping across the darkness and hitting their targets.

Jantu gave Eden a nod, getting back to business as the starship revved up and healed more. She turned to see how Sleuth had faired, only to see him passed out at his station. Or dead from fright. Eden didn't know and had no time to find out.

Eden, the Space Templar armada has arrived and is decimating the Anunnaki fleet.

Eden pursed her lips. "Let's continue to turn the tide. Get as many Avens with us as possible, and let's push the Graxic and Reptilians out of this system."

Swift spun, following *Tranquil* and the Aven, a path of destroyed ships speckling the space before them. A hoard of Graxic ships propelled forward in the distance, heading for Earth.

"Any report on those ships?" said Eden.

All are fully functioning, barely a scratch on them. We'll be in range soon.

"Do we have anything that can reach them now?"

"Plasma torpedoes, though only four on the ship left," said Nyx.

The enemy closed in on Earth.

Eden pointed ahead. "Target the four largest, most heavily armed ships, *Swift*. Anticipate their trajectory. Let's hope one hits. Fire, now." The bridge turned into a sauna for a moment. It vibrated wildly, nearly too uncomfortable for Eden. Large, purple fiery orbs expelled, screaming toward the Graxic's backsides. Eden clenched her jaw, waiting.

A blaze lit up the screen, explosions and bursts dotted two Graxic ships an instant later, then blinked out.

In range, firing missiles. Projectiles blasted toward the remaining ships. The ship's sizzled from missile impact, but *Swift* continued to land shots. The shields failed, and the crafts erupted into fiery blasts.

Eden's pulse rose. "What do you got for me, *Swift*?"

All ships are either dead from direct hits or offline from collateral damage. They aren't a threat anymore. Swift switched direction, heading away from Earth. *We have an emergency. Admiral Shae Lutz is in trouble.*

Eden about fell out of her chair. "What do you mean, Admiral Shae Lutz? Star Guild is here?"

No. Shae leads a crew much like this one, and on a similar ship named Ascension.

"What? How?" It didn't matter, and she threw her arm forward, her index finger extended. "Go, go."

The last person she wanted dead was her mentor, Shae Lutz, the only person she could call a father, her biological father had left long before she was two years of age. How had they gotten Shae in a ship like hers, and how long had he been with the Space Templars?

Ali's face appeared on the lower corner of the vidscreen, her eye's twitching as if something was wrong, her brows high. "Starship *Ascension* is caught in a tractor beam. They need help now. You're closer. Get there as soon as you can." She blinked off the screen.

Eden nodded. "Gladly."

Swift changed direction and headed for a Space Templar starship much like *Swift*. That must be Shae, and he's headed for a Graxic ship as if he's out of his own control.

The Graxic ship's dragon's head lit up in red, ready to fire. Eden's stomach contracted, anger rising. "*Swift*, fire everything you've got."

59

SHAE

Starship Ascension

Starship *Ascension* trembled. Kalista yelled words in a language Shae couldn't understand. He looked down at his arms, jostling violently as if the entire craft were about to pull apart.

Shae, listen to me, said Ascension. *I'm attempting to disengage the tractor beam, though I don't think I'll have enough time before the beam completes its job. Devon's hacks are working, though. Tell him to keep it up. One of his viruses might be strong enough to navigate through their systems and take them offline.*

"What is this wide beam?"

It's draining our shields quickly. I give us precisely two minutes, eleven seconds. It'll then send a kill blast once shields have drained completely. It's blocking all inbound and outbound communication to our fleet.

Perfect, thought Shae. He thought of Helen. His heart filled with wanting to see her again, but it was most likely a fleeting desire. If he didn't make it, the rest of the Space Templar fleet and Ali would keep Helen and his human family on Earth safe and alive. He knew it.

He grimaced, wanting to stay alive and be with Ali and Helen again, but death was part of war, and he'd accept whatever came his way as long as he fought with honor and courage. Until death arrived, he'd do everything in his power to keep his crew alive.

Shae craned his neck. "Devon, you got a hit on the tractor beam?"

Devon kept his eyes on the holomonitor, typing diligently. "It's an unfamiliar comp language altogether, so it's a mess. I'm throwing viruses at it left and right, but do they stick?" He shrugged. "I don't know, because I don't understand what I'm looking at."

Shae nodded sympathetically and told Devon it was okay, and the kid was doing well.

Kalista's voice boomed. "Get the damn viruses sticking then."

Devon went back to work, and Shae gave her a thumb's up. "He'll get it done."

A Space Templar at a station lifted a fist. "We have incoming friendlies."

Shae eyed the vidscreen and watched bursts of fire erupting from the dragon ship's nose. A plasma blast struck the heavy armor just under the dragon's chin. Starship *Ascension* stopped shaking and the surrounding beam disappeared.

We're loose. Falling back now, said Ascension.

"Who shot those plasma bolts?" asked Shae.

Swift.

Ascension reversed thrusters, sliding away from the Graxic ship as Starship *Swift* came into view, then *Tranquil* and dozens of Avens a moment later.

"I think a virus stuck," said Devon, a grin growing on his lips.

The Graxic ship took hit after hit, though it didn't return fire, either unable because of the virus or because it had spent most of its energy using the weapon beam. Shae bet on the former.

Exterior armor blew away from the Graxic vessel, and it broke in half, spitting fire, its lights dimming and going out.

It's offline and done, said *Ascension.*

Ascension angled off behind *Tranquil* and *Swift*, engaging boosters and moving toward several enemy craft making another run at Earth.

"Zoom out, *Ascension*," said Shae.

A wide shot of space filled the screen. At *Ascension's* bow floated Earth, though still some distance away.

"Rear cams." Shae held down a smile. Behind him, the Space Templars' fleet decimated the enemy armada, the tide changing for the better.

"Normal view," called Shae, and bow view appeared on the screen.

"I detect all enemy craft defenses are offline," said Devon. "A virus worked."

Ahead of them, *Swift* and *Tranquil*, along with several Avens, sent forth blast after blast, downing the ships heading toward his birthplace. It was a miserable, failed attempt by the Graxic.

The enemy is leaving, Admiral.

"Rear cams again," he ordered.

A handful of enemy ships lit up in rainbow colors and blinked out of existence. Shae raised his chest, his posture straight. "They're retreating." He looked around the bridge, seeing everyone relax, even Kalista. "*Ascension*, bring us around." *Ascension's* starboard thrusters initiated while the rear boosters continued to fire, and the giant turned a hundred and eighty degrees.

Shae took in a deep breath, his heart lightening and the weight on his shoulder's lessening. One by one, enemy ship after enemy ship blipped off the screen, jumping out of Earth's system. The myriad of remaining ships in the Space Templar fleet floated, their shots ceasing. Shae threw his hands to his face, rubbing back and forth.

Avens approaching landing bay. Opening landing bay doors.

Shae nodded. The corner of the vidscreen had a shot of Earth. He stared at his old planet, massaging the back of his neck, thoughts invading his mind.

I'd suggest strongly against it at this moment. We need to recoup and head to Aurora. Several Earth governments picked up on our activity, and entering Earth's atmosphere may escalate a conflict we don't want.

"When can I see her again?" said Shae.

I don't know.

Shae dipped his head, a knot forming in his throat. "I understand." He'd just been through a major conflict. Seeing his wife wasn't his reward, saving her life was. Shae unstrapped and stood, stretching. He eyed the crew. "After we get our legs under us, we'll head home." He cleared his throat. "*Ascension*, open coms to all ships in the fleet."

You're on the comm now. Go ahead.

"Attention Space Templar fleet. This is Admiral Shae Lutz, and I'm grateful for your help defending our original home, Earth. You outperformed what I could ever imagine. We've sent the armada away, with the Space Templars burned in their minds, hopefully never to return. Remember our own that fell today. Hold them close to your heart." He paced. "We leave a third of the fleet here, designated by Sabra. We do this to keep Earth safe for the time being. Until then, get your space legs moving. We'll be jumping back to Aurora soon."

60

ALI

Aurora

Ali sniffed the Aurora air. Fresh flowers from the edge of a forest nearby wafted to her nostrils. The sky had a silvery-purple hue as the sun settled across the horizon. She sat on a soft, warm patch of grass, her legs crossed. She gazed at her lap, thinking.

They had taken several jumps back to Aurora, leaving a third of the fleet behind to monitor and fend off any more intruders wanting to screw over her people on Earth. Sleuth walked off the ship, proud of his heroics, and Ali couldn't have been more impressed with his work messing with the Anunnaki fleet. It impressed the Space Templars as well, though they carted him off in handcuffs. He had other crimes, which had nearly wiped Star Guild and Starbase Matrona clear off the galactic map.

She didn't want to live on this planet, Aurora. It was beautiful, and the air was as pure as anything she'd ever breathed. Yet, she'd wanted to stay behind with the third of the fleet. She wanted to take a trip to see her mother, to be with her, to hug her.

"You know," her mother once said, "your dad loved you very much. He did everything with you, taught you as much as he could, watched you play, and I can't tell you how many times he brought you up in conversations with family and friends. You were the apple of his eye."

At the time, Ali sat at her mom's table. The next day would be her first day teaching at the University of Michigan. Ali nodded to her mom, biting her bottom lip. "If it wasn't for your pictures, I think I'd forget what he looked like. I can never forget his love, because like you said, it was always there, and no matter what I did, he was kind to me."

"It's rare, dear. You were lucky to have it in your life for a time, though short, but be grateful."

A cool breeze ruffled her hair, bringing her back to planet Aurora. "I miss you, Mom."

Footsteps crunched on the ground, heading in her direction. "Are you ready, kiddo?" Shae extended his hand, helping her up.

"When will we see Mom?" asked Ali.

Shae brought her into a hug, his hands warm against her back. "I'm working on it."

"Good."

In front of them stood a cobblestone path leading to an enormous crystalline dome. Two large red doors, tall and wide, stood out like a sore thumb. Hours ago, and in passing, a Space Templar mentioned it was an assembly hall.

"We head there?" asked Ali.

"Yes."

As they walked, Shae pointed at a massive shipyard. There sat three starships—*Ascension*, *Swift*, and *Tranquil*. "I can't get enough of those beauties." Ali couldn't get enough of them either. It seemed as if those ships came from a different dimension, built by advanced beings, and then handed to the Templars.

She absently rubbed her arm. "You know, I enjoyed my time on *Tranquil*...well, when we weren't nearly dying in combat, but it will be a long time before someone gets me in one of those things again."

"For me, never." Shae shook his head. "Like I said, I'm working on getting us back home. All we need is a Starjumper, and we can get there, and surprise the living daylights out of Helen."

"As long as we don't give her a heart attack."

Shae laughed. "True." He motioned toward the dome. "Let's see why Sabra asked us to meet her in the assembly hall." They continued down the cobble path.

"Are they going to bolster the forces around Earth?" asked Ali.

Shae nodded. "They're building a base on the far side of Earth's moon. There they can monitor and keep supplies ready for an entire fleet if needed. If the Anunnaki have an itch up their ass and attack Earth again, the Space Templars will be ready and waiting."

Ali lifted her shoulders and took in a big breath. "Good." She lifted her hand to push open the door. She stopped as memories abruptly flooded her mind. She shook her head and shoved away the image of near death when she first encountered Enlil in her mining mech, and he in his starfighter. She'd miraculously survived because S scrambled the starfighter's targeting systems.

She rubbed her temples and squinted as more memories surfaced, seeming to run through her mind like a slide show. The battle above Earth, the Bawn, the attempt to take *Tranquil* to get Starship *Sirona's* people off their ship and onto Ali's, the tunnel inside Mount Gabriel. On and on, Hendrick's death, kidnapped from Earth, and her father missing from her life.

Her shoulders fell, and she turned, embracing her father, his arms pulling her in tight. She rested her head against his chest, sobbing.

He patted her back and kissed the top of her head. "I won't let you go this time. Never again. All right?"

She nodded, pulling away, and wiping tears from her eyes, chuckling. "Look at me. I'm a damn mess."

He helped wipe a tear. "You ready?"

She shrugged. "I don't know what we're supposed to be ready for, but yes." She habitually touched her sword's hilt—Sol—almost forgetting it was there. It reminded her of Chan and Thun, and the prick, Harak, since he created the baldric for her. She let her fingers fall off the hilt and pushed open the door. Light flooded in, and her father stepped through the doorway by her side. The doors shut, clicking loudly, echoing off the tall ceiling and walls.

All eyes turned toward Ali, and she slowed in her walk, stunned. In front of her stood her friends; Thun, Chan-Ru, Daf, Hank, and William. By their side stood the Space Templar Grand Master, Skye Vortek, and then Nyx, and the blue-furred creature named Jantu. Thun gave her a wink, his whiskers lifting in a smile.

She halted. "What's going on?"

Several sets of boots clicked and clacked, reverberating across the giant room. Through an archway near the rear of the assembly hall in walked two large individuals, Anunnaki, a man and a woman with red hair. They stopped in front of Shae and Ali and bowed.

"My name is Enki, and to my right is my sister, Sabra. We are leaders in the Space Templar alliance."

Ali bowed back. "I'm Ali."

Shae followed suit. "I'm Fleet Admiral Shae Lutz of Star Guild. Hello again, Sabra."

"Nice to see you in one piece, Admiral," she said.

He patted his chest. "Nice to be in one piece."

Enki placed his palms together and interlaced his fingers. "I know you don't like my kind, and if I was in your position, I'd feel the same. Although I hope Chan-Ru showed you a side of our race that is good."

Ali unconsciously touched her heart. "Chan did just that." Chan bowed a thank you.

Enki continued. "Enlil is mine and Sabra's brother. We're aligned against everything he stands for. That's why we joined the Space Templars and are here standing before you today."

Sabra nodded, eyeing Ali's sword. "You, your father, and Captain Eden Gaines are of the bloodline. Without you three and all the wonderful souls who helped, the people of Star Guild and of Starbase Matrona would not be here today."

Shae slightly jerked his head back. Sabra had mentioned Eden in present tense. "Yes, Eden. Though she wasn't a captain, she deserved to be. She was of the bloodline, like Ali and I?"

Sabra went to talk, her mouth opening, but Ali couldn't help but feel something familiar with this woman. Ali slightly tilted her head. "Wait, what's your name again?"

"Sabra, sister to Enki, and daughter of King Anu." She grinned. "You stepped up when I asked you to find your way to Mount Gabriel. You have more courage than most I've met."

Ali cocked her head more to the side, her brows squishing together. "S?" She threw her hands to her mouth. "You saved me and Daf so many times. I owe you...I don't know what I owe you, but Guild, you are the reason I survived."

Sabra interlaced her fingers together. "I helped as best I could under the circumstances."

"You sacrificed yourself to save me and Daf."

Shae interrupted. "Why is everyone here?"

"We're here for a last farewell," said Sabra. "A goodbye."

"A goodbye?" asked Shae.

"We're sending you to your home, Earth," replied Enki. "It's been long overdue that you see your wife."

Ali's eyes widened, and her heart about leaped out of her chest. "Are you serious?" She pointed to the floor. "Now?"

Sabra gestured toward the two enormous doors. "We have a ship ready and waiting for you."

Shae put his hands on his chest. "Thank you."

"You both deserve it," said Sabra.

Ali stared into her father's eyes. "We'll see Mom."

His lips upturned. "Well, your mom, my wife, but yes."

She turned to her friends and spotted Daf. Her friend held a frown, her eyes misty.

"Fleet Admiral Shae Lutz." A woman walked through the arched doors in the room's rear, the same doors Enki and Sabra came through. Eden hurried into the assembly hall, her eyes beaming. "I'll miss you."

Shae did a double-take, his eyes about bursting out of his sockets. "Eden?" He hurried toward her. "What in the..." He hugged her and stood back, grasping her shoulders, looking her up and down like she'd just come back from the dead. "You're alive?"

Eden let out a laugh. "Yes, thanks to Skye and the rest of the Space

Templars. I'm a captain now. I commanded Starship *Tranquil* during the battle."

Shae's eyes welled up. "You saved Matrona and us when you risked your life in your Thunderbird. I can't believe you're alive."

Eden gestured toward Skye. "Blame it on Space Templar technology." Eden reached out, touching her palm against Shae's chest, her expression turning serious. "I'll never forget you. You're the only father I ever had." She shifted her eyes to Ali. "For a long time, without your knowledge, you lent him to me. I'm forever grateful. I'm glad, albeit sad you're getting him back."

Ali gave her a nod. "You'll always be family."

Eden dipped her head. "Thank you."

Ali made her way to her friends, letting Eden and Shae say their goodbyes. She gave a farewell to Thun, Chan, Hank, and William. She stopped in front of Daf and held the girl's hands. "You're the reason I kept going, even if I didn't know it. You pushed me, though you pissed me off more than I'd have liked, but you're the best friend that I've ever had."

Daf shook her head, a tear dripping from her eye. Her voice cracking, she said, "Any chance you can stay?"

"Any chance I can take you with me?"

Daf laughed. "Never." She pointed to the ground. "I have a new home and my screwed-up parents and brother to take care of."

"I understand." Ali stepped back and unsheathed her sword and eyed it. She set it down on the ground and unstrapped her baldric, setting it alongside Sol. She dipped her head at Skye, and then at Sabra and Enki.

Shae slipped his Space Templar pendant off, stared it at while walking toward Ali, then set it on the floor. "We're ready to go." He looked around. "But where is Devon? I'd like to say goodbye to that young man."

Sabra pressed her lips together. "He is at an Aurora beach, spending time with his mentor, Naveya."

Enki extended his arm, pointing toward the main doors. "Your ship awaits."

Ali looked at her dad, who nodded back at her. "I guess admirals go first."

"Not today." Shae grinned. "We go together."

They walked past their friends and toward the door, heading toward the ship ready to take them home.

EDEN

Planet Aurora

Eden sat on her bed inside her new home, a crystalline dome that glimmered all around her. She patted the bedspread and ran her hand up and down it, the soft texture practically massaging her palm. She let out a sigh. She'd miss Shae, her mentor, her non-biological father. He had more confidence in her than anyone alive. He'd left in his ship an hour ago to the dismay of everyone, though he needed to get back to his wife and his own home.

A knock on her door jostled her out of her thoughts. She lifted her head. "Yes?"

"May I come in?" asked Skye.

Eden stood, cupping her hands behind her back, sensing Skye doing the same. "Go ahead."

The door opened and Skye walked in, his hands behind his back. He grinned. "I see you're getting better at the Sight."

"I think I am. It gradually grows in me every day."

"Good." He walked to where several chairs sat and tapped the wall next to them. A beautiful wood table extended from the wall, its gorgeously crafted legs unfolding and setting gently on the floor.

"Well, I guess you learn something new every day."

"Indeed." Skye sat, placing his hands on the table. "Please sit." He motioned to a chair on the other side of the table across from him. A sense of gloom surrounded him with a bit of excitement swirling underneath.

Eden couldn't make sense out of his current emotions. She walked over and sat. "What's going on?"

"I'll come out and say it. I have a mission in the Nibiru system, and I don't know how long I'll be gone. Maybe months, maybe years. It's a lengthy trip, but it's for my training."

Eden put her hand up. "You need more training?" How the hell could someone with Skye's abilities need more training?

"I do, and believe it or not, I have a lot to learn." He winked at her. "Unlike you, I don't learn the Sight at the drop of a hat."

"What does any of this have to do with me?"

"You'll be training too."

Eden's brows nearly lifted to her hairline, and she did her best not to drum her feet underneath the table. "You said it's a lone trip for you."

"My training is more difficult, so I'll be heading to a much more unique system than you. You, my friend, will go to Earth."

She nearly fell out of her seat. "Excuse me?" Earth had simple technology. How much could she learn on that planet?

"Yes, you'll be learning in a jungle, in a place no one but the Masters dwell. Do you understand?"

"Do I understand? Not in the slightest. Who are the Masters?"

"The Masters taught me the Sight, and they live on Earth. They're excited to teach you."

"Who exactly are the Masters?"

"Monks, but dedicated to the cause, more advanced in tech and ability than anyone on Earth. They're in a remote area, there for Space Templar training."

"When do I leave?"

Skye stood. "I have a flight scheduled. You'll be leaving soon."

Eden stood. "Today?"

"Today."

"You're joking, right?"

He smiled calmly. "No, Eden. I'm not. I'm here to help you the best way I can, so you can one day fulfill your destiny."

Eden wanted to roll her eyes. The destiny thing again. It seemed to flow through Space Templar talk often. "What exactly is my destiny?"

"You'll take over my position as Grand Master. When you're ready, you'll lead us, just like you led Starship *Swift*'s crew."

Eden blinked several times and sat still so she didn't fall from the sudden weakness in her knees. She put a hand up. "Okay, you're saying I'll be the Grand Master of the Space Templars?" This was all too much. "What will happen to you once you step down as Grand Master?"

"I'll be a monk, helping more Beings in the galaxy learn the Sight. It's what we do. We bring up a new Grand Master and move on. You're in the wings, and I don't want to wait around any longer to find another person worthy enough to be a Grand Master, so please make me proud."

Eden rubbed her eyes. "Oh, my Guild." She shook her head. "I can't believe it." She took a deep breath and lifted her chest. "Well, son of a Guild. I guess my next question is, what time do I leave?"

"In an hour."

SHAE

Lowell, Michigan—Earth, 1945

On the corner of Parnell Avenue and Bennett Street, and at twenty-one hundred hours as the sun set into twilight on a summer's eve, Shae and Ali stood at the edge of a short gravel road lined with shrubbery. Not far down the road and within view was a yellow farmhouse with white trim. A soft light glowed above the small, wooden porch.

Shae rubbed his chest, closing his eyes. He'd been in military conflicts, had seen death in ways most humans wouldn't dare imagine, and had pulled the trigger on a man he once admired, killing him at point-blank range. Yet tonight had him choking on a fear he'd never experienced before, meeting his wife, a woman he hadn't seen in over twenty years.

Would she have a heart attack when she saw him? Would she turn him away, call him names for leaving? Hell, would she believe where he went?

"Do you think she remarried?" asked Shae.

Ali shook her head. "That's not Mom. Before I left four years ago, she hadn't gone on a date, let alone talked about another man since the moment you went missing."

Shae straightened his jumpsuit, then let his hands fall to his sides. "I'm not dressed for the occasion."

Ali grabbed his hand and pulled him down the gravel drive. "I'll be right here next to you, Dad."

"Should you go in first? She might not recognize me." He was a man knocking on a woman's door at this late hour, he thought. It wouldn't look good. He knew Helen and remembered she kept a rifle inside by the door. Did she still keep that weapon there?

"We'll meet her together," Ali said.

Gravel crunched under boots as they made their way to the porch. The wooden stairs creaked as they stepped up to the front door, the hand railing a bit loose for Shae's liking. He'd fix it tomorrow. Shae made a fist and went to rap his knuckles on the wooden door, a slight difference from an automatic vertically sliding door on the ships and the starbase.

He dropped his hand and closed his eyes, his insides tossing and turning. He exhaled loudly. "Let's do this tomorrow. We can think of a plan that will help get her ready for a reunion with us." He nodded. "Yes, we'll start with a note, place it in her mailbox, and maybe a picture of us the next day, and then—"

Ali grabbed his wrist as he went to walk off the porch and begin his new strategy, Operation Helen. Ali knocked on the door.

Shae gasped. "What are you doing?"

"I'm seeing Mom." She tipped her head to the side, her hands on her hips. He'd seen Helen in that stance many times. "And you're seeing her too."

"Coming," came Helen's muffled voice.

Shae froze. "Ali, are you sure? I don't want her hurting herself if she faints," he whispered.

Helen's footsteps shuffled across the floor, the way Shae remembered her walking when she'd wear slippers in the house. She still wore slippers. His heart lightened. The footsteps stopped at the door, and her sweet voice carried through it. "Who is it?"

"Mom? It's Ali."

Silence. Shae stiffened, his feet rooted to the porch. Even if he wanted to turn and run, he couldn't now.

Ali placed her hand on the door, her fingers splayed against the wood. "Mom, it's really me. A lot of things happened, and, well...I'm back. I...I want you to see who I brought with me."

A longer pause, and Helen finally spoke. "Ali?"

Ali nodded, her voice cracking. A tear left her eye and raced down her cheek, followed by more. "Yes, Mom. It's me. Please, open the door."

The doorknob twisted slowly, and the door creaked open. Helen stood before them in a robe and slippers, glasses on, her graying hair up in a bun. Shae's heart melted, like the first time they met. She aged, but beauty aged even better with her as if she'd grown more gorgeous as the years went on.

Helen threw her hand to her mouth, stepping back. "Ali?" She shifted her gaze, letting out a yelp when her eyes locked onto Shae's. "My...Shae?" She walked backward as if seeing ghosts. "Please tell me you're real. Please, please be real."

Ali stepped forward through the doorway and onto the wooden floor. "Mom." Helen's eyes widened more when Ali wrapped her arms around her. Helen's chin quivered, and she went into a sob, her arms limp by her side as if unable to lift them.

"I love you, Mom." Ali turned her head to Shae, her eyes and cheeks dripping wet. "I found Dad of all things."

"It's me, love," said Shae, taking several steps forward. He held out his hands, not knowing what to do, his heart racing faster than a holocar speeding down a starbase road. "It's me..." he gulped down the knot forming in his throat, "...Shae."

"Shae?" She shook her head as if she were dreaming. "It can't be."

Ali extended her arm, bringing Shae into a hug with them. He held them tightly, allowing his tears to fall.

"I don't know if I'm dreaming, but I missed you two so, so much," cried Helen, her voice soft. "I need to sit." She led them to the couch in the living room and sat, Ali and Shae finding a spot on either side of her.

"I missed you too, Helen," said Shae.

"Where…where did you two…where were you?" Helen sniffed and grabbed a tissue off the coffee table.

Ali took in a deep breath. "It's a long story. A story we can tell another day."

Shae nodded. "Yes, right now, let's just hold each other."

Helen wiped her nose and patted Shae's leg. "I'd like that." She leaned back, holding Ali's hand, her other hand resting on Shae's thigh. She laid her head on Shae's shoulder. "I'd like that a lot."

EPILOGUE

Ali awoke with a start, hearing the crickets outside her window, a night breeze flowing in her room. It had been a few months since living in the house she grew up in. Her mom and dad were like newly-weds, unable to keep their hands off each other. She rolled her eyes, giggling to herself. "Those horny bastards."

They both deserved each other, back together in love, and that's all that mattered. Friends and family had made a spectacle about the missing people coming back into Helen's life—her and her father. That had since died down, and life continued as normal for everyone except Ali and Shae. They had to adjust, and that adjusting took time.

It was hard for her mother to follow the story; how the Anunnaki took Shae and Ali and brought them to an unfamiliar world, and the flying ships and the battles went way over her head, along with the slave-race thing. Whether her mom believed them or not, being back at home, on a world she grew up on, and with a mom and dad that loved her, couldn't be better.

She rubbed her eyes, wiping the sleep out of them. She looked at the clock on the nightstand by her bed and turned on the lamp. "Three in the morning?" She grunted and flopped down in bed. "Why am I awake?"

Maybe because she needed to find a job. She didn't want to go back to teaching at the university. It was hell getting that job in the first place, being a woman and all. Though her archaeology mind recently took over and the lust to go on another dig had surrounded her like a blanket. She couldn't wait to find artifacts thousands of years old and to write about her discoveries.

She shook her head. "Go to sleep." Tomorrow would be a long day searching for work. Perhaps she could find some shifts at the local restaurant. With her good looks, she'd be an easy hire at food joints. She curled her fingers in a fist. "It's not about the looks, stupid." Serving food would never be her first choice, anyway. She could help her dad on the farm. The farm threw a handful of problems at him daily, and he probably wanted help.

She crinkled her brow, pushing herself up and staring out of the window. "Why is the window open?" She'd shut it last night. As summer faded and fall rushed in, the cool air found its way back into her small town in Michigan, and she didn't like it.

"Because I opened it."

Ali jumped back, startled, and knocked her head on the bed's head-board. A man walked out from the shadows in the room's corner, his arms tucked into a Space Templar robe, his hood covering his head and face. He pushed the hood back, letting it fall against his shoulders, his blue eyes shining at her. "I'm Skye Vor—"

She shoved the covers off of her and pushed out of bed. "No, no, no. You go back to Aurora or wherever it is you came from." She pushed him toward the open window, wanting to get him as far away from her and her family as possible. "I'm not going on any missions. I'm not fighting any evil guys. I'm staying here." Throwing him out the window wouldn't hurt too much. It was only a two-meter drop if that. Maybe more, but who cared. No way would she let Skye recruit her again, and by Guild, she wouldn't let Skye get to her dad. Shae's need to help every damn Being in the galaxy would guide him quickly back into the Space Templar ranks, even if it tore him from his two greatest loves—Helen and her.

Skye stopped moving as if cemented to the floor, some Space

Templar trick. "Ali, I'm not moving, no matter how hard you push me." He held a smile, his face as gentle as a teddy bear.

Ali sighed and walked back to her bed, sitting like a teenager that didn't get her way. "No, Skye. I'm not going back. It's been two months, and I..." She nodded... "Okay, yes, I miss my friends there, and some people on my mining team, especially Daf. I miss her a lot, but my mom and my dad and—"

He put his hand up. "I'm not asking you to leave Earth. I'm here to ask you to help Earth and her people."

Ali cocked her head. "What do you mean?" Did he want to send her on a humanitarian trip?

He walked closer, frowning. "A lot has transpired in a short period of time since you and your father came home." He bit his lower lip, as if not wanting to tell more. "Someone murdered King Anu. Enlil was the next in line and has taken over the throne on planet Nibiru. Against Sabra's and Enki's wishes, he plans to bring Anu's entire fleet and the Graxic allies to Earth."

Ali sat straighter. "And create another slave planet, another slave race?" Her nostrils flared. "That piece of ebb."

"This planet is where humanity originated, and it's where the Anunnaki created their first slave race. Yes, they plan on doing it again, believing they own you. To do so, they must decimate the population to an easily controlled, more manageable number."

Ali's heart burned, and her veins boiled. She stood. "Enlil...that son of a pig swine." She wanted to growl, to throw something, to take a knife and stab it into Enlil's chest. She paced. "What do you need?"

"They'll come soon, but how soon? I don't know. We're monitoring Nibiru and their fleet's movements. So far, they haven't left their sector. But they will, and when they do, they'll strike hard."

"Again, what do you need from me and my father?"

"We need you to command *Tranquil* and *Ascension*."

Of course. "Where's *Swift*?"

"Here, on Earth, with Eden."

"Eden is here?"

Skye dipped his head. "She's been here as long as you have, studying the art of the Sight."

"The art of the..." she didn't want to ask. "Where are *Tranquil* and *Ascension?*"

"We tugged them to your Solar System. They're at our base on Earth's moon, waiting for you and your father." He reached behind his back, pulling a sword from its sheath and lifting it over his shoulder. "Sol awaits your touch." He set the sword on her bed. He reached into his robe's pocket and pulled out a necklace. He placed it on her bed. "Your father's Space Templar crystal and pendant, if he shall take it."

Ali eyed the items, pushing off her bed and stepping away. She let out a gush of air. "I didn't sign up for any of this."

He dipped his head. "Neither did I, but here we are—"

"Ready to take on the galaxy, to serve all of its creatures and Beings, and all that mumbo jumbo." She nodded, her eyes fixed on Sol. "Is that what you were going to say?"

"Something like that." The floorboards creaked as he walked toward the window. "It's not much of a choice when they are coming to your planet. I await your decision, nonetheless."

Ali shot him a look. He was gone as if vanished, the window now closed. She grimaced, her heart flaring with an anger she couldn't quench quick enough before she lurched for the sword and picked it up. She held it up and squeezed its hilt. Purple flames crept outward from the edges. She let out a grunt, tightening her grip. She gasped when a plasma bolt shot from the sword's tip.

White dust and cracked wood fell on her as she loosened her fingers around the hilt, a hole now in her mom's ceiling and roof. She wiped off her hair and face with her free hand and opened the window. She slipped through the opening and landed on her feet in the backyard.

As she walked, her heart screamed and her gut twisted, wanting to end Enlil more than ever. She pushed through the back hedge that separated the yard from the wheat field. She made her way to the middle of the field and raised her sword, curling her fingers around the hilt.

The sword blazed, plasma fire flaming from its edges. She tilted her head toward the stars. "Skye Vortek of the Space Templars," she yelled. "I accept." She breathed heavily, thrusting the sword higher toward the night. "I'll end Enlil," she said under her breath. "I'll end him."

Thunder cracked across the sky in the distance, followed by a flash of lightning. She loosened her grasp on Sol, and the plasma flames extinguished. She let the sword drop to the ground. She fell on her rear and eyed the moon. "I should have known the war wasn't over." She shook her head. "I should have known, but this time, I'll end it." She grabbed a fistful of dirt and blades of wheat and threw them. "I'll end it once and for all."

The End

AUTHOR NOTES - BRANDON ELLIS

MAY 22, 2020

Thank you so much for reading another Star Guild novel. I hope you enjoyed it as much as I enjoyed writing it.

Right now, I'm in Bali, isolated in a gorgeous house twenty meters from the ocean. My front yard is black sand, and a giant volcano sits to my left. The sunset is beyond amazing.

Not all of us are this lucky in the world during these trying times. We have a political divide, a pandemic, and a divide amongst the pandemic as well, not to mention the dying and diseased.

I want to give a heart-felt love and light (Bali-style) to all the essential workers. We love you dearly and thank you. With all that's occurring, there are always people helping, giving, and smiling. If you can keep that in mind, then please do.

Humanity is filled with kind souls. I believe you are one and I believe I am too. So when this all ends, let's find a way to tell those we love, that we do indeed love them.

From my heart to yours, I thank you and send you wildly happy thoughts.

Much love,
Brandon

CONNECT WITH BRANDON

Enjoy the book? Then take a gander at Brandon's Facebook Group where you can help him and the rest of his rag-tag team of readers decide on pertinent information in the next books in this series or any other series he's writing... https://www.facebook.com/groups/EllisIsland/

His Facebook crew are fun, engaged readers, and can think of an alien race name for his books in a minute flat. There, you can read early chapter drafts for books Brandon is working on, join his ARC Team and read finished books before they are released, and much more. Again, here is the link: https://www.facebook.com/groups/EllisIsland/

And, join Brandon's Sci-Fi rebellion as well by subscribing to his newsletter. Brandon's a sucker for ancient alien information (is it real, or fake?), writing about ancient archeological sites that will blow your mind, and mixing in SciFi as well in just about every email he sends to you. Grab his free bestselling book, Starfighter: Freedom Star Book 1 (https://dl.bookfunnel.com/utmbp42qyd), to hop on his list. He doesn't spam, so sit back and enjoy the entertaining ride.

BOOKS BY BRANDON ELLIS

You can find a complete list of Brandon's books on his website here:

https://brandonelliswrites.com/books/
Or at Amazon here:

https://www.amazon.com/kindle-dbs/entity/author/B00BLVIYNW

OTHER LMBPN PUBLISHING BOOKS

To be notified of new releases and special promotions from LMBPN publishing, please join our email list:

http://lmbpn.com/email/

For a complete list of books published by LMBPN please visit the following pages:

https://lmbpn.com/books-by-lmbpn-publishing/

All LMBPN Audiobooks are Available at Audible.com and iTunes. For a complete list of audiobooks visit:

www.lmbpn.com/audible

www.ingramcontent.com/pod-product-compliance
Lightning Source LLC
Chambersburg PA
CBHW032001120726
47898CB00005BA/1416